'LA, ... ches
the n ... oked
in a ... itish
crim ... tain
toda ...

... wski

'Birn ... oky
tales ... rose
and ... iant
colle ... nd.'
... rby

'Co ... he
mea ... t a
tim ... sed
wit ... m,
it's ... is
ofte ... till
hur ... ey
bec ...

... ffy

'Dreams, as one of the contributors observes, are dangerous things – and danger lurks within these pages in an impressive kaleidoscope of settings. These are stories of betrayal, of communication breakdown and obsession. Some show the human cost of losing our ethics, while others reveal how madness can lurk in the supposed safety of a shopping mall or cathedral. But there is humour here too, and an awareness that we can make our lives better. Simon Avery's perfectly observed narrative about moving on from a broken marriage is worth the cover price alone. Birmingham's criminal underworld and sex industry are laid bare in these entertaining, saddening and shocking pages. Lock up your daughters, sons and the family cat until you've learned from these stories of crime in the city.'

Carol Anne Davis

Birmingham Noir

edited by

Joel Lane and Steve Bishop

TINDAL STREET PRESS

First published in 2002 by
Tindal Street Press Ltd
217 The Custard Factory, Gibb Street, Birmingham, B9 4AA
www.tindalstreet.org.uk

Copy Editor: Emma Hargrave
Typesetting: Tindal Street Press Ltd

A CIP catalogue reference for this book is available from the British Library.

ISBN 0 9535895 9 5

Printed and bound in Great Britain by
Biddles Ltd, Woodbridge Park Estate, Guildford.

In memory of
Robert Bloch
and Bill Hicks . . .
still laughing at the darkness.

Acknowledgements

The editors would like to thank: Emma Hargrave, Jackie Gay, Alan Mahar and Penny Rendall for their help and support; the contributors for their inspiring work; Bharat Patel for his superb cover design; Stella Duffy, Joolz Denby, Maxim Jakubowski and Carol Anne Davis for their encouraging words; Murder One Bookshop for keeping the flame; and Rog Peyton for introducing us to the twilight world of Cornell Woolrich.

Contents

Introduction: City of Night

The Midlands is, like, a weird place. Nobody really knows where it is or what happens there.

Terry Hall

What is noir fiction? What happens in it? The expression 'noir fiction' is derived from a classic French series of American crime novels in translation, *Série Noire*. But a better-known connection is with the genre of 1940s and 1950s movies known as 'film noir'. Filmed in black and white and conceived in shades of grey, these movies portrayed a world of uncertain morality and unpredictable violence. *Rear Window*, *Night of the Hunter*, *Cape Fear*, *The Maltese Falcon* – these were literate, socially aware films that used mystery and suspense to explore serious themes.

Film noir drew heavily on the American crime fiction of its era: the dark-toned urban thrillers of Raymond Chandler, Dashiell Hammett, Cornell Woolrich, James M. Cain and others. This was a new kind of crime fiction. It combined graphic realism with emotional depth, and its key theme was the corruption of society. In this, it was fiercely opposed to the English tradition of detective fiction, in which eccentric patricians used logic to solve bizarre crimes. In his famous essay 'The Simple Art of Murder', Chandler observed that the characters in such tales were stereotypes because real people could never do the absurd things required of them by the plot. He went on to say: 'Hammett gave murder back to the kind of people who commit it for reasons, not just to provide a corpse; and with the means at hand, not with handwrought duelling pistols, curare, and tropical fish.'

The novels of Chandler and Hammett became known as 'hard-boiled' crime fiction. They pitted tough-minded heroes against the corruption of organized crime and of the establishment. The fight for justice and fairness engaged them in real life as well. Hammett went to prison for refusing to name names before a McCarthyite committee – and according to his partner Lillian Hellman, he didn't even have the information they demanded.

Noir fiction was politicized too. It dealt with social deprivation and the corrupting power of wealth, with police brutality and press hypocrisy. But its perspective was bleaker than that of the 'hard-boiled' school. It struck a match in the hidden places of the soul, and then let it burn out. The great noir writers – Cornell Woolrich, James M. Cain, David Goodis, Jim Thompson – wrote about the lonely, the hopeless, the lost. Their novels had titles like *Street of No Return* and *Rendezvous in Black*. Most of these writers enjoyed the occasional drink or two.

The tradition of noir fiction has continued to the present day. Robert Bloch's novels explored the psychology of serial killers in a way that was both disturbing and compassionate. In Britain, Derek Raymond's 'Factory' novels examined the conditions that make murder possible: bigotry, racism, greed and isolation. The work of James Ellroy, Thomas Harris and others has shown the black and crimson threads of noir fiction being woven deep into the fabric of contemporary literature.

The landscape of British crime fiction has long been dominated by London. The capital bears a certain resemblance to New York: the river, the finance, the criminal fraternities. But in recent years, other British cities have become known as scenes of fictional crime: Edinburgh, Liverpool, Nottingham, Glasgow – and Birmingham.

In some ways, modern-day Birmingham resembles the Los Angeles of Chandler and Ellroy. It's a huge conurbation dominated by roads and cars, with no easily defined centre. Its ethnic diversity comes from well-established communities. Its working life is a mixture of trade, industry and commerce. Pragmatism and creative improvisation are familiar themes in West Midlands culture. Everything is put to use. In the traditional slang of industry, a 'Brummagem screwdriver' is a hammer.

Mystery and fear play a part in the industrial folklore of the region: the canals and railways bred their own early 'urban myths'. Something of that darkness has bled into the rock music of the Black Country: the heavy metal of Black Sabbath, Led Zeppelin and Napalm Death echoes the thump of forges and thunder of train wheels across points. A sense of urban threat gave the blue beat of Coventry band The Specials its urgency and meaning. The pop culture of the Midlands is moody, but not theatrical: its sound is honest and direct.

At only 200 years old, Birmingham is one of Britain's newest major cities. Unlike London, Bristol and Liverpool, it does not have a history rooted in the slave trade and colonial interests. As a multicultural city, it has been able to make a relatively clean start – despite Enoch Powell's vicious and manipulative speech at the Midland Hotel in 1968. The classic Brummie outlook is sceptical, wary and sardonic, quicker to say 'I don't believe' than 'I believe'. The lack of a strong self-image may lead to inhibition, but it also encourages a willingness to suspend judgement. Demagogues find little response here.

In *City* (1968), the poet Roy Fisher wrote of Birmingham: 'These lost streets are decaying only very slowly.' These days, they're changing fast. Regeneration has brought a stark newness to the old Black Country towns. The flash hotels and restaurants of Broad Street contrast with the poverty of the inner city. Money is pouring into new developments, but the gap between rich and poor is widening. Our worst housing estates are being demolished, but so are our hospitals. Ten years ago, the opening of a jazz club was seen as a sign of the city's cultural vitality. Now it's a lap-dancing club. Street prostitution is fading out, but pay-per-view flesh is a conspicuous new industry.

With the ambiguous renewal of the West Midlands has come a new generation of crime fiction. Judith Cutler's novels play out their suspenseful narratives in Birmingham's inner city and suburbs. Patrick Thompson's *Seeing the Wires* uncovers strange rituals in the industrial hinterland of the Black Country. John Dalton's *The City Trap* (Tindal Street Press, 2002) walks through a shadowy West Midlands landscape of the corrupt, the crooked and the confused.

When we started to collect stories from Midlands writers of crime fiction, the noir tradition was an important framework. We were looking for tales that explored the tensions and dangers of urban life with passion and insight, not crude exploitation or conservative moralizing. We wanted to challenge the conventional view that kick-ass narrative and literary depth are incompatible. We wanted the darkness of pain, the brightness of anger, the hard music of a society in transition.

We got all of that. And more. We're proud to offer you a book of stories that will appeal to enthusiasts of crime fiction and of contemporary realism. And those who just want a great read.

*

The contributors to *Birmingham Noir* range from renowned authors of crime and suspense fiction to newcomers whose raw talent is frankly scary. There's John Harvey, author of the highly acclaimed Resnick novels. Judith Cutler, the creator of two tough heroines of Midlands crime fiction: Sophie Rivers and Kate Power. Nicholas Royle, whose unique novels combine mystery, suspense and dark psychology. Paul Finch, whose scripts have injected claustrophobia into ITV's *The Bill*. And such rising talents as Wayne Dean-Richards, Rubina Din and Simon Avery.

Like any popular genre, crime fiction has its share of stereotypes. We took care to avoid hard-drinking heroes, scheming disfigured villains, hapless female victims and whores with hearts of gold. There's only one detective in this book, and we allowed him in because the focus of his story is moral corruption, not logic: the mentality, not the little grey cells. Gangsters, prostitutes and killers inhabit these stories, but they are real people living in a recognizable world.

Five themes recur among these stories: murder, organized crime, prostitution, money and madness. The tales that focus on murder are perhaps the most disturbing. In Judith Cutler's hard-edged 'Doctor's Orders', an abused wife looks within herself for the means of survival. Pauline Gould's narrator is trapped in a cycle of need and obsession, while the black humour of Kay Fletcher's 'Pest Control' masks a bleak image of loneliness. The tragedy of the family in Elizabeth Mulrey's 'Passing Over' is more quietly evoked. By contrast, Rubina Din's 'Games Without Rules' plays out its violent drama in the harsh glow of mania. And Nicholas Royle links murder to art and Birmingham to Venice in an icy portrayal of a serial killer.

Birmingham Noir's gangsters are victims of their own

myths. Mick Scully explores a 1980s underworld of failing villains, in which a killer has a poignant encounter with a desperate European migrant. The narrator of Rachel Taylor's 'Dyed Blonde' is trying to escape her criminal past, but it stays with her like the scars on her face. Don Nixon links the commercialized sentiment of Christmas with a still more ruthless greed. In Paul Finch's 'Trashman', the trail of a vigilante leads a police investigator into a twilight realm. And in Simon Avery's powerful tale of betrayal and redemption, the narrator learns that crime is like love: you can walk away from it, but you always leave part of yourself behind.

Several of our writers use prostitution as a symbol of corrupted intimacy. The sex industry represents capitalism at its most raw: slavery may have been abolished two hundred years ago, but it remains a problem in your neighbourhood. In John Harvey's gently pessimistic 'Smile', the legality of stripping covers the manipulating hands of a gangster. Simon Avery portrays a more naked brutality – and the victim's will to survive is correspondingly more stark. Mike Chinn's account of old villainy in the 'new Birmingham' juxtaposes lap-dancing with images of loneliness and loss. And in Claire Thomas's 'Means to an End', a teenage runaway is given an unforgettable lesson in the realities of city life.

The corrupting power of money is a classic noir theme, powerfully expressed in Horace McCoy's *They Shoot Horses, Don't They?* Greed is the keynote of the criminal lives depicted by Mick Scully, Don Nixon and Mike Chinn: not the need of the dispossessed, but the cold ambition of the Thatcherite entrepreneur. John Dalton's 'The Mentality' identifies capitalism as an attitude: the calculating eye that judges human beings as mere commodities. And in Rob Smith's 'The Kiss', the lure of money and fame causes a photographer to betray the ideals he claims for his work.

Madness underlies most of these stories: the rational madness that leads people to kill or exploit for personal gain. But a few stories approach the territory of horror fiction, where madness has its own bleak logic. Rubina Din and Pauline Gould portray killers trapped in their own never-ending film reels. Wayne Dean-Richards' 'The End of Something' is a snapshot of love warped in the heat of adolescence. 'His Own Skeleton' by Andrew Newsham uses manic humour to depict a man trapped by a phobia of deformity – not a crime tale, but certainly a noir one. And Pauline E. Dungate takes us deep into the soul's midnight with her story of a homeless mother and baby circling around a city centre whose doors will never open.

The most dangerous madness is that of society. John Mulcreevy's story of the persecution of a disturbed loner has the vigilantist mentality of the tabloids firmly in its sights. And in the downward-spiralling narrative of Zulfiqar Ali's 'Vendetta', we hear a grim echo of political conflicts that have escalated to the point of no return.

It's no surprise to encounter murder or prostitution in the criminal world. But noir fiction looks beyond these themes to wider human issues: the stages of life and the cost of survival. A number of the authors in *Birmingham Noir* describe rites of passage in which the young try to prove that they belong in the adult world, or to escape from a damaged life into a new realm of freedom. The criminal underworld offers means by which outsiders can gain status and dignity. But even down there, real choices and responsibilities don't go away. Some of the most tainted figures in these stories are heroic in their refusal to compromise, to let go of what is left of their innocence.

The loneliness of the criminal, the terror of the victim and the unease of the witness are variations on a common theme: the fear of losing identity. Part of this fear stems from the conditions of modern life, the controlling grip of money and power. But part of it is the same fear embodied in the traditional symbol of a skull with a winged hourglass beneath it. In the noir tradition, the sense of mortality triggers violence and greed – but it can also provoke a need to make peace.

The world of *Birmingham Noir* is a dark place. Blood is spilt, breath is stifled, lessons are learned. These characters not only live in fear, they have the street map of it. But the spirit of redemption is never far from these pages. At the heart of noir fiction is the hope for a better world: the hope of the villain in the Richard Thompson song who'd trade 'all the wicked things I've been' for a glimpse of true happiness.

Welcome to the Midlands. The noir train is about to depart.

Joel Lane and Steve Bishop
July 2002

The Kiss

Rob Smith

It was just before eleven, just before coffee on a Friday, when Ray saw her face for the first time.

'She's probably a witch in the flesh. All ready to lead you on before spitting you out,' said Billy, as if to counteract her spell.

But Ray didn't comment.

'Most likely she's a prostitute. Probably a junkie too. Disowned by her family. You know what they're like, these Asians.' Ray watched Billy brood for a second, then: 'There's definitely something about those eyes. A bit skinny but still, I wouldn't turn her out of my bed on a cold night.' Billy wasn't fishing for sympathy. It was just that, six months on from his split with Sameena, everything still came down to that: his empty bed.

Billy wiped his eyes and held the contact strip under the viewer again. 'That's not a bad shot. Very harem.'

Ray spoke: 'Who's the customer?'

'I know him vaguely. From the Prince. He's expecting to have an exhibition and has asked to come in to oversee some developing. His stuff's not bad, but as for exhibiting, I can't see it. I've seen quite a few of her before. Must have some money because we ain't cheap when it comes to small orders like this one.'

'Want me to package them up?'

'If you like. Whatever. I'm nipping out for a quick ciggie and a breath of air. Then I'll be off.'

Ray pulled the line of contact prints back under the light and scrutinized it frame by frame. Then, moving quickly, he slipped the entire order into a return envelope and carried it across to his own desk, pushing it to the bottom of his intray. He picked up a stray order from the day before and, sealing it, carried it through to Deirdre. 'Needs to go today,' he told her, like he cared.

Billy reappeared a moment later. 'Right. Looks like I'm out of here.'

'Yeah. So what is it this weekend? Blues are playing at home, aren't they?'

'Sunday, yeah. No, tomorrow there's a jump down at Bidford.'

'Hope the weather stays clear for you.'

'Cheers, Ray.' With that, Billy, his case and jacket under his arm, said a few words round the edge of Peter's door and left.

As soon as the door swung shut, Ray was back in the dark room. It didn't take him long to identify the best shots. He had a good eye. There were three that showed her face, caught with that indefinable expression. The long, still quietness that had held his attention the moment he saw it. Absorbed in his work, and with a physical sensation that was close to pain, he watched that crisp moment bounce out of the negative and onto the paper. He'd just hung up the last of the enlargements when there was a tap at the door.

It was Peter. 'It's coming up to seven, you ought to be finishing up.' His eyes wandered.

Ray spoke quickly. 'Peter, I'm worried about Billy. He left early again. We're carrying him. When's he going to start pulling his weight? Sameena's leaving is starting to wear a bit thin as an excuse. You *said* you were going to talk to him.'

Peter sighed. 'I know. But it takes time. What that cow did to Billy after more than five years together, stinks. Talk about biting the hand. The woman's a bitch.'

Ray nodded compliantly. 'I'm not saying I don't sympathize. It's just that you're his elder brother. As managing director, you should be . . .'

Without irony, Peter interrupted with the old line he'd used when Ray first joined Union Processing Ltd. 'Yes, and this just isn't the kind of business that can carry a passenger.' But then filial loyalty reasserted itself: 'It's just he's had a real blow to his self-esteem. We've got to give him *some* latitude.'

Ray often wondered about working in the Robinson family business. Billy and Peter had brought him in straight after uni when their father – a retired antiques dealer – had put up the capital. Old Mr Robinson was a freemason and head of his local Orange Lodge. He had the business acumen of a hyena, much of which had rubbed off on his eldest son, Peter. Ray knew, as an outsider, that he was never likely to be granted the 'latitude' of a partnership.

Billy occupied Ray's thoughts as he drove home. Billy and graceful, doe-eyed Sameena. Billy had taken her in. Rescued her from a hostel when she fell out with her parents after an 'arranged' marriage. But then she'd got tired of him. Tired of his possessiveness, the assumption that he owned her. Ray remembered the long telephone conversations he'd had with her. And the trouble was he could see her point of view. She was sick of always having to be grateful to Billy. And when their rows started getting violent she moved out, secretly staying at Ray's while she looked for another place. It took two weeks. Then, within a month she had a new boyfriend, an Asian; a new job in the boyfriend's firm *and* a new Beamer.

No surprise then that Billy was embittered. After a week

or so of calling her to see if she'd come back, he switched instead to cursing her for all the sacrifices he claimed to have made for her over the last five years. It was as though he was having an early midlife crisis, except it wasn't remotely funny. He became a rabid Bluenose, never missing a match. Then he started going out clubbing and binge drinking. He'd drag himself in on a Monday morning, looking like shit and being about as much use. He evidently made Charlie a regular feature of his weekends as well, judging from his foul mood swings. And, predictably, there'd been a string of girlfriends. Each one seemed to be younger, more naive and pathetic than the last. He'd ferry them around in his silver Alfa for a week or so, then, scarcely concealing his pleasure, he'd give them the boot.

II

Three weeks later and there she was again. This time she was wearing nothing, not even the flimsy robe-type costume of the last set. And she wasn't alone. She was wrapped, grotesquely, in the arms of a muscly, square-jawed male model. Her head was thrown back, glued to his. This time the mood of the shots was different. She was mute and hideously dwarfed by her partner. Ray processed the order and found himself breathlessly running off a set of contact prints even as he told himself how ugly the pictures were.

'*He* looks like a faggot,' was Billy's comment. Ray agreed. 'Are you making any deliveries tomorrow?'

Ray sensed a favour looming. 'You know I am. I've got to drop off those Mackadown test strips. Then Peter's asked me to take a finished order to Optix in Shepherd's Bush. So that's my Saturday done.'

'So there's no chance you could drop me off somewhere mid-morning?'

As part of his determination to relive his adolescence, Billy had taken up a succession of dangerous sports: skydiving and hang-gliding among them. Ray contemplated a drive out to the Clee Hills. 'What's wrong with the Alfa?'

'Nothing. It's in for a service.'

'Where you going?'

'Only Walsall.' And in response to Ray's raised eyebrow: 'Away game. Local derby.'

Billy knew that Ray didn't have the slightest interest in football and he was expecting disapproval. Ray frowned. 'And what's wrong with the bus?' He glanced up slyly. 'Just kidding. Yeah, OK. I'll pick you up about ten thirty. As long as you don't expect me to come and carry the bits home after you're done.'

Billy shrugged off the comment. 'No, no. That was a one-off. Believe me.'

Ray regarded him with mock suspicion. 'Are you sure?'

'Yeah, yeah. Christ, you're beginning to sound like Peter.'

It'd been Peter who'd driven down to the police station to vouch for his brother after a match two Saturdays before. Billy had been arrested following 'a violent incident between fans' – as the *Mail* had put it. Peter had openly rowed with him. But beneath the criticism, Ray thought he could detect in Peter a vicarious pleasure in what his little brother had been up to.

Billy was shame-faced in front of Peter but once he was alone with Ray, far from being embarrassed about the episode, he kept enthusing about it.

'You weren't there. It was like nothing you've ever . . . Look, I've been skydiving, I've bungee jumped. I've done all that. This was something else. Not just adrenaline. You get lost in there with the others. There was something *tribal* about it.'

'Oh sure. Until you're on the receiving end. Can't wait to hear you telling me that from a hospital bed.'

'But no one gets really hurt. At least not often. And then it's between consenting adults. You're there and they're there. So that's the chance you take. Anyway, I'm not going to get hurt.'

'What are you talking about? How do you work that one out?'

'I stick close to Barfire. He's an old hand at it. No one touches Barfire.'

'Oh great, it's getting better and better.' Ray had met Barfire on the one occasion he'd reluctantly gone to a game with Billy. At the pre-match drink, Billy was hailed by a group of hard cases over in the corner of the bar. One in particular had RANGERS tattooed on his neck, a Union Jack T-shirt and eyes crushed and remote behind slab-like lenses. They called him Barfire. He'd lived in Birmingham for a while and exile from Scotland had crystallized him into a stereotype of the Glaswegian hardman. After the game, following a few phone calls, the group slipped away, shifty-eyed. 'You coming?' Billy asked him as looks were exchanged with Barfire.

Ray said, 'No, you're all right.' And he'd gone home alone, vowing to steer well clear of any further involvement in Billy's social calendar. The following Monday he had asked Billy, 'Why do they call him Barfire? Did he set fire to a pub or something?'

'No,' came the explanation. 'His parents are from Belfast and he was in the Glasgow chapter of the UFF. A barfire was his favourite instrument of torture.'

III

Driving home that night, Ray thought about the order. Not just about the girl but about the eye behind the lens. He imagined the package arriving, then he stretched his imagination further to visualize the photographer. Whose viewpoint did he share when he looked at her? With prints he admired, Ray often speculated as to the character of the photographer, telling himself he could somehow read it, piece it together like a ghostly identikit. On one level he certainly could. He could easily tell the difference between a seasoned lensman and a novice. These shots spoke of a practised eye. The angles, the fleshtones were all perfect. In the first set, the girl's dignity had been preserved. There was nothing lewd in the images. The evenness of her gaze straight into the lens – almost a look of concern – disconcerted him. Convinced she trusted the photographer completely, he created an image of a man in his fifties, with white stubble and brushed, almost shoulder-length hair, a benevolent eagle-eyed old man with a dispassionate appreciation of the beauty before him.

But that night – as he studied again her eyes, her posture, the thick, hanging black hair and her submission in the newer photographs – he marked a hardness, a relentless, almost heartless insistence behind the camera. The male model was oblivious, complicit, while she submitted to that insistence. Ray compared. No, it wasn't there in the earlier shots. In those, she had some pride in the hold of her head, some fierceness in the set of her lips. Now, totally vulnerable, her stillness offered only the slightest petal-like resistance to his gaze. He was overwhelmed.

IV

After three solid months of cloud and rain – the first sun of a New Year; a bright Saturday morning like the ones where God suddenly announces his existence by blessing the weekend with a hundred miles of solid azure sky.

Ray was behind the wheel of his Discovery and, having dropped Billy off near Walsall, was driving back down into the city. The sun was hammering gold along the top of the central crash barrier and he felt like singing. Peter had decided he wanted to do the Shepherd's Bush run after all. It was an important contract and he thought he might be able to pick up some extra work. So Ray's Saturday was free.

He drove into the city centre and then back out towards the Balti Belt. He knew the road where the Photographer lived, and wanted to look at the house. But then Birmingham pulled one of its surprises on him. He'd expected the house to stand in a fashionable part of the city, to be one of the huge Victorian houses divided up into half a dozen flatlets, or to be a gentrified mansion set back behind a thick holly hedge. That's what best fitted the white-haired old man he'd envisaged. But he was wrong. The road where he stopped was Bloomfield, not Birchfield – which meant that he was lost.

Half an hour later, an *A–Z* to hand, he wound down the hill, away from sprucely kept detached houses to rows of terraces. He soon registered that his face was the only white one on the street. The old man's white hair began to yellow with nicotine now, his skin silvered and scaled around his mouth in a fishy smile. The eyes behind the viewfinder became taunting, cruel.

Ray found a bench in the untidy park from which to watch a doorway in the terrace opposite that opened straight onto the main road. During the hour and a half of his wait, he avoided and discouraged a man in sunglasses and leather trilby who offered him 'draw'; he glanced warily at the old man in the dirty anorak who loitered on the corner by the traffic lights making comments as women passed by; and he glared at grimy children chasing round his bench and back onto the gibbeted tyres that wriggled on their iron gallows.

V

Monday morning once more. And thankfully Ray had an

office full of problems to keep his mind off his wasted weekend. Peter and Billy were out. Peter had left a note saying he was sorting things out in London. But when Ray tried to call Billy he got no response.

On Tuesday, Peter explained: 'Billy's down in London. I've asked him to scout around a little. There are a lot of opportunities down there. And,' he held up Billy's mobile, '*that's* why you can't reach him. The battery's flat. He left it by the kettle.'

It sounded odd to Ray. 'London? Are you looking to expand? Things must be picking up. Can I expect a raise soon?'

Peter laughed nervously. 'Early days yet. We'll have to see.'

VI

Ray had made up his mind to see her. So, a fortnight after his first expedition, he braved the park bench again, nodded to the man in the trilby and watched the children torturing their captive car tyres. This time, he hadn't long to wait. A student type in a black leather jacket stepped from the doorway and walked quickly up the street. Ray sprinted to draw level with him, and emerged through the park gateway at a casual saunter. He was daunted. There was no question in his mind that this was him, the Photographer. His dream of staging a dramatic rescue fizzled as the ogre he had cast refused his part. Instead, an indefinable air of sophistication cloaked his rival. He was stylishly dressed. His hair, at first glance dishevelled, on closer inspection revealed a moussed exactitude.

Ray shadowed him into town, only once having to pause, slap his pockets and consult his watch when the Photographer turned in his direction. Any doubts about what he was doing, that he was carrying this thing too far, that he'd allowed himself to become obsessed by this woman, evaporated as he watched the Photographer choose a wimple of carnations at a flowerseller's. They had to be for *her*.

They boarded another bus. This time, heading south out of the city. From behind his paper, Ray watched the Photographer disembark at the top of the steep hill that swept down towards Bournville. He was off at the next stop and had to sprint for the second time that day to regain the crest. He watched his quarry approach a pelican crossing, then dodge between cars to cross the road. He reached the top of the hill and with relief saw the Photographer halfway down an avenue of stumpy-knuckled lindens. At any moment he expected him to turn into a driveway, disappear behind a door. But the figure continued its walk. Finally, where the road forked, it entered the gateway of what looked like a large park. Ray increased his speed. He was still imagining his first glimpse of her when he reached the gateway and read the dusty signboard: LODGE HILL CEMETERY.

The search was over. All the energy that had driven him to follow this person he knew nothing about, all his desire, drained away. The ugliness, the childishness of what he was doing stung him. How could he continue with it now?

VII

Work was swallowing Ray whole. With Billy still down in London, he had more on than he could manage. He was getting in before eight each morning and leaving at nine each night. Every day brought a new pile of orders and new clients to deal with. Every night he went home to a microwave supper then swift, unbroken sleep. He'd never worked so hard. But the thought that she was dead, that he would never see her, made him glad of it.

Then, one Friday, when Ray was taking a New Deal trainee through some basic procedures in the processing room, he heard an unfamiliar voice coming from Peter's office. He'd barely put his foot outside the processing room door before he was back, pulse racing. It was the Photographer. Had he been spotted and tailed back to Union Processing? Sweating, he imagined being confronted and humiliated. He did a few rows of test prints with Gary, the new trainee, waiting for Peter to call him into the office. Instead, after ten minutes, he heard the murmur of goodbyes and the sound of Peter's door closing.

When he went in later on some suitable pretext, Peter was bent over a strip of negatives. 'Who was that?' Ray asked.

'Name's Will Rodman.' Peter straightened. 'That photographer who's preparing an exhibition. He's made an appointment to come in for a darkroom session. I've told him I'll take care of it personally. He's paying big bucks.' Peter spoke absently and slid the negatives back into their sleeve.

It was unusual. Peter hadn't been in the darkroom for six months. But Ray didn't care. He was jubilant. He'd been wrong. She wasn't dead. 'Want me to put the negs in the safe?'

'No, it's OK, I'll deal with them.' Peter placed them next to the open case on his desk.

Ray sat down and flicked through the wad of orders in his hand. 'Have you heard how Billy's getting on?'

Peter seemed distracted and unwilling to talk. He picked up a sheaf of folders and thrust them into his case. 'Yes. Fine. Look, I've got an appointment at eleven thirty. Can you hold the fort till after lunch?'

'No problem. But you need to sign a couple of cheques before you go.' He waved an order form. 'For the iMac upgrade.'

'OK, I'll do that now.' Peter left the room and Ray got up to follow him.

VIII

That evening at ten, Peter called him at home. 'Have you been in my case?'

'What?'

'I said, have you been in my case?'

'What are you talking about? Of course I haven't.'

Peter was in a real state. 'Look, there's something missing from my case. You were there when . . .'

Suitably restrained, Ray butted in, 'For Christ's sake, what's the matter? What have you lost?'

'Look, it's something really important, all right? I swear I put it in my case. Now it's not there.'

'But what is it?' Then he pushed again, 'Is it something to do with that special order?' Peter didn't say anything. 'You haven't gone and lost the negs, have you? But why were you taking them home? I thought you were going to put them in the safe.' Total silence from Peter. 'Peter? What's going on?' Still no answer. 'Peter, are you there?'

'Yeah yeah, I'm here.'

'Look, we're both under a lot of pressure. You're overtired. Whatever it is, it'll turn up on Monday morning.'

Peter sounded grateful. 'You're right, you're right. I'm sorry. I'm sorry to accuse you like that. Forget it, OK?'

Ray put down the phone. His curiosity as to what was on the negatives sharpened. He'd planned to retrieve them, then develop them on the sly, first thing on Monday morning. It had only taken a few seconds to remove them from under the pile of folders in Peter's case and slide them out of sight under the edge of the filing cabinet.

IX

The next evening, Ray took a taxi straight to a likely Moseley pub. He propped himself against the bar, eyeing the clientele.

'Yes, sir?' Kevin the barman had his bear-like hand

wrapped round a pump, ready to throttle it. Moments later, a flat and chestnut-brown pint in his hand, Ray swung round looking for a corner. The Photographer was at his elbow. Quickly, Ray wiped the expression of horror off his face. He'd expected to have to tour round several pubs. Thankfully, the Photographer's eyes stayed fixed on Kevin. He also ordered a pint of Flowers, and the coast was clear for Ray to take a seat and plan his next move.

The corner he headed for – oddly, the seat he'd often occupied on summery Saturday afternoons before now – had a leather jacket draped over it. He sat next to it, put down his pint, fumbled in his pocket for cigarettes and lit up before the Photographer joined him.

In those few seconds, he tried to think of an opening line, a story he could tell to steer the conversation in the right direction. A missing lover? An unhappy affair? But it was the Photographer who broke the ice, some remark about the strength of the ale. His mood was celebratory, not a smudge of wistfulness. This wasn't a man in mourning. Anticipation suffused Ray's entire body.

There was smug assurance on the Photographer's face as he told of his good fortune: 'Things are taking a turn for the better.'

'Oh?' Ray waited for the elaboration that was a little slow in coming. 'What? Financially?' And then recklessly, 'Or is it a woman?'

'Money, yes.'

'You won the pools.' It was an idiotic, over-familiar query such as should reassure the Photographer that he posed no threat. *Go on*, he prompted silently, *patronize me. I'm Joe Bloggs, you can tell me the whole thing*. Then relished the uptake of his offer.

For the Photographer was prepared to allow humble Ray into his world and there was a degree of pride in the way he conducted the tour. He was all set to open up, precious and vain as a flower. Ray sat mouth agape for the next few minutes, observing his rival.

'Well no, it's not just money. It's recognition. My work has been recognized. I've got my first exhibition.' By way of explanation: 'You see, I'm an Artist.'

'Artist? You mean, like, *painter* . . . ?' Ray tailed off, allowing his inflexion to suggest he had omitted to add the words 'and decorator' as though the only type of paint he knew anything about was the Dulux variety. He was rewarded by a fleeting, disdainful grimace.

'No, I take photographs, actually.'

Ray took a deep drag on his cigarette, enjoying the power he had over this little hourglass. How much more would he know by the time it was finished? He had another drag to draw that moment closer and monitored his specimen. The challenge now was to draw out the information he wanted, to find out about her. 'What of?'

'What of?' The Photographer's eyes half closed in a chuckle. He warmed to this explanation of the finer points of his craft. 'Things that interest me. Issues. I'm interested in class. In race.' He paused, consciously unmincing, as the words dragged Ray in, 'In beauty. Form.'

'Oh, like still life? That sort of stuff?'

'No. I'm more interested in documentary subjects. Although I don't always take my inspiration,' he slowed as though becoming aware of what he was saying, 'from life . . .' and stopped.

Ray felt a clawing in his chest. Sudden doubts emerged from his sea of joy like jagged, foundering rocks. 'Not always from life?' he stammered. 'You mean you sometimes photograph dead things?' It was the most flippant remark he could manage. Because he needed to know that those carnations were not for *her* grave.

The Photographer let the question hang unanswered for a few seconds. He'd jolted onto the back of his chair at the word 'dead' and his mouth was opening and closing slightly in a goldfish splutter. 'Don't be stupid.'

Ray squirmed and sought refuge in a mouthful of Flowers. He no longer felt in control. 'How about tastefully done nudes?' he blurted.

The Photographer surveyed him thoughtfully, then nodded. 'Yes, I've done nudes.' He corrected himself: 'I *used* to do nudes.' With deliberation, 'I say "used to" because the model, my girlfriend, she's dead.'

Ray slumped rubberily in his seat. Desperately feigning an apology, he offered a cigarette and lit himself another. 'I'm sorry. I didn't know that. You said things were taking a turn for the better.'

'They are. They are.' The Photographer, satisfied with Ray's contrition, compressed his lips in a smile. 'I don't want to bore you with a tale of woe. In spite of what happened to Niki, things really *are* on the up.'

Niki.

He said the name so easily. Ray felt a dry rage stoking up inside. Niki.

'Have a look at this.' The Photographer drew out a black wallet, all fat and sleek, and pulled out a folded cutting from the arts review pages of a recent Sunday newspaper. It was a full half-page. Ray skimmed through it. Unreserved in its praise. He had the sudden urge to lash out against this man who had known her, touched her, and lost her. 'Who wrote this? Your uncle?'

The Photographer took it as a joke. 'No. Photography is the one thing I'm good at. I just do it, or it does me.'

Now everything he said sounded glib and poisonously smug.

'I mean, I freely admit it, I'm not much good at anything else, some people would say that includes personal relationships.' He took up the cutting that Ray had neatly folded and placed in a puddle of beer.

'Oh, sorry.'

'That's OK.' He wiped it on his jeans and made to slide it back into his wallet. A corner of shiny photographic paper slipped out past his clutching fingers and onto the floor next to Ray's right foot. He bent to retrieve it. It was her. His her. A shot from the first set. Ray had a series of this frame – the best of the batch – six ten-by-sevens running from one-second exposure to ten, those eyes emerging from snow and retreating into darkness, mounted above his bed. He held it carefully, allowing his nicotine-stained fingers to make contact only with the edges. Niki's eyes curled their tendrils of longing out again into his. 'Is this her? Your girlfriend?'

'That's Niki. She was never *really* my girlfriend. I mean, it was never serious on my side. She latched onto me. The camera loved her. But I was never going to get involved with her. Like that. I mean, do you know what these Asian families are like? She's got five brothers, for God's sake. Sikhs've got these big curved swords, forged in the Punjab. They'd all be out for my blood. I'm still scared they might decide to track me down.'

'What happened? To her, I mean?'

The Photographer didn't answer immediately but studied him as if making up his mind about something. 'I don't want to talk about it here. But I can show you. I want you to see.' Ray looked at him questioningly. 'Finish your drink. I want you to come round to my place. I want you to see my work. That'll answer your question.'

X

In the street overlooked by the litter-strewn park and the gibbeted car tyres, they got out of a taxi. The Photographer's front door opened straight into the sitting room. Ray's eyes ranged hungrily round the room, taking in every detail. The walls had photographs and pictures from newspapers and magazines stuck on every available inch of wall space.

'Do you want a whisky?' The Photographer gestured for him to sit down. He seemed weary, and had lost his air of self-assurance.

Ray, lodging himself in an overstuffed armchair, rolled his eyes across the collage. 'OK.' He listened to the sounds of the tap running, the clink of glasses, the *scree-scree* of a cap being unscrewed. He picked up a postcard from the floor, a postcard that had been used as a coaster many times over. It was D'Oisneau's *The Kiss*. A young couple in a clinch on a Parisian pavement. There was another A3 Athena print of it pinned to the wall over the fire. The Photographer, returning with the drinks, followed his gaze.

'It's a very popular print.' Dismissive. 'It provided the inspiration for my latest project. What I regard as my best work. What I brought you here to see. So it's hung in a place of honour.' He was restless. 'Come into the back.'

Ray followed him into a back room that was empty of furniture and lit by five or six strong wall lights, each illuminating a print. The Photographer beckoned. Ray shivered as he joined him. From all sides she wrapped him round. Blindly he studied the photos he already knew so well. 'She's beautiful, beautiful.' He kept his face turned away. 'So how did she die?'

'I'm going to show you.' There was something feverish in the way the Photographer spoke as he bent down and unzipped a large portfolio that was leaning against the wall. He sorted through a set of prints, talking as he did so. 'That D'Oisneau in there. I wanted to update the idea. Put it in the context of Britain today. I thought of using a mixed-race couple but it wasn't enough. Then I spotted a Socialist Worker poster for a demonstration in Bloxwich. There was a BNP candidate standing in the local elections and I wanted to get a shot of *The Kiss – The (New Multi-*

Ethnic) Kiss if you like – in front of a line of BNP skinheads. D'you get it? It was a political statement. I didn't think. It never occurred to me what might happen.'

'Jesus Christ!' The angry flame in his chest choked off Ray's voice.

He had killed her.

'She was stabbed. It didn't happen . . . I mean we'd barely begun the shoot when these big Special Branch officers moved in and arrested us for causing a breach of the peace. It was as though they were fascist sympathizers. We were taken off in a van. Suddenly she started screaming. I suppose she must have been in shock. There was blood everywhere. Then she fainted so they diverted to the hospital and dropped her off. They detained me for two hours, took all my equipment as soon as we reached the station and confiscated my films. By the time I got back to the hospital she was dead. I couldn't believe it. Now they're trying to cover it up. They said there was no evidence that it happened in front of the demonstration. That's crazy, because the only other place was in the van. And they're saying they can't round up the people from the demo without firm evidence.' He grinned, but without pleasure. 'And that's where they're making a mistake. You see, I saved the film. I took it out while they were panicking about Niki's injury. In fact, at first I thought she was providing me with cover.'

He started handing the precious prints to Ray one at a time. A line of men holding placards and Union Jacks. Shielding them, in front of the camera, a thin blue line of police. Then there was Niki and next to her the scared-looking, square-jawed Adonis, dressed in a belted raincoat. The next shot was composed. In the foreground, the couple stood woodenly with the fascists directly behind them. The male model had opened his overcoat and was throwing a wary glance over one shoulder at three or four men in full skinhead regalia: green swastika'd flak jackets and calf-length Doc Martens. Ray took the last, already guessing what it would show.

And there it was. *The Kiss.* Ray breathed heavily. They were in a clasp identical to those posed clinches taken in the studio. A simulacrum of love. The camera angle was low, the black hair hung from her head, thrown back to receive his mouth. The still embrace, like a boulder in a stream, centred the eye before sending it out into the detail beyond.

The kiss had obviously caused outrage among the BNP supporters. The police line had been breached as they surged forward, a mass of tilted flag-masts and placard poles, a mess of waving arms and hands. No face was turned their way except one: a howling hate-filled mask, visible over Niki's shoulder, was bearing down on them. Ray blinked.

'I think that's him, the one who stabbed her.'

It was Billy. To his left was the unmistakable pebble-lensed face of Barfire.

'I wanted someone else to see it. It probably sounds stupid, but just in case something happens to me. This last week or so, I've had this feeling of being followed.' The Photographer mistook Ray's guilty silence for incredulity. 'I know it sounds paranoid. But this photo is *evidence*.' He plucked it from Ray's fingers. 'And it's not *just* evidence. It's got to be an award-winner. It *has* to be. You see, if you attach it to the story, it's newsworthy. You know, *The Kiss of Death* blah blah. It could make the front pages. I've already got a London PR firm interested. I'm meeting them tomorrow.'

Ray struggled with a sense that he was falling. 'Where did you take it? When?'

The Photographer looked curiously at him. 'I told you. Bloxwich. Little town near Walsall. Three weeks ago.'

He thought back to that beautiful morning. Dropping Billy off. 'Local derby.' As if. Since which time Billy had been in hiding. Now he understood Peter's concern about the negatives. And that he, Ray, shouldn't see them. Peter was looking out for his younger brother.

He had killed her.

From the corner of the room, the telephone abruptly rung out. The Photographer's answerphone was on, and after his brief message a voice addressed them. A Scottish voice. Barfire's. It said, 'We know you're home, you little shite. We're on our way round so put the kettle on, there's a good laddie.'

Ray looked at the Photographer. His face had taken on the colour of candle wax. A hammering started at the front door. The Photographer was looking wildly round. 'Quick. You've got to get out of here.' He ran through the kitchen and opened the back door. '*I* can't leave. All my work's here. If they get in, who knows what they'll do.' But Ray didn't move. The Photographer urged him frantically, 'Quick. Go. What are you doing?'

The hammering was replaced now by heavier dull thuds.

He shoved the set of prints into Ray's hands, his voice rising. 'Look after these for me. Go. *Now*.'

But Ray stood stupidly looking at him as though paralysed.

The thumping started up again. But his ears were deaf to everything, even to the noise of the doorframe as it splintered with a sound like the smack of hungry lips.

He had killed her.

Dyed Blonde

Rachel Taylor

Once Dunc had gone, things went a little crazy.

I thought I was invincible and that because Dunc had been sent down, no one would care what I did. I'd been his girl and I thought I'd be protected.

I was wrong.

It's New Year's Eve and I'm waiting for Jimbo in the cathedral. We decided to meet here because of the unsuspecting type the place attracts – those who only want to look for the good in people. Also, it's quiet. All around, in the bars and in Centenary Square, people are partying in spite of rain-soaked banners dripping on their heads and the slushy pavements underfoot. The cathedral is a calm eye in the revelling storm. And there's no police in here. Outside, they're everywhere. Even if we'd met in a dark alley, we might have been seen and my face is famous now. The service has finished and I sit down in one of the back rows and wait. A few stragglers are milling around in quiet desperation. I wonder about some of them, what it is that they're looking for. One or two sit down and pray fervently, determined, as if God is listening out especially hard on New Year's Eve. One man kneels at the front and rests his elbows on the wooden bar before the altar. He talks out loud and even shouts sometimes. He raises his hands up in a pleading gesture. I guess he's having a bad time. Good luck to him I say, and the rest of them. I hope it works. I'm not willing to chance pressing my palms together and giving up a confession. With all this rain, God doesn't need much of an excuse to summon a thunderbolt from his pinkie to do a nice fry-up job on me.

One of the stragglers catches my eye. A man with tobacco-stained skin and greasy hair. Homeless person, tramp, down-and-out, or what you will. Seeking out warmth like a dog pawing round a fire. I watch him and wait for the flicker of a change in his expression as he checks me out. It takes the briefest second for someone to see it. The milky, mashed up sightlessness of my left eye, in contrast to the clear topaz stare of the right. A young woman – disfigured. A waterfall of fine red scars trailing down my cheek completes the image of pity. And I wonder what story he's writing for me. Car crash? The random violence of a maniac boyfriend? Rape? Mugging? It doesn't matter. Without exception, people assume I was the victim. If Dunc'd got hurt that night instead of me, they'd know straight away. He deserved it, he's a wide boy, a thug, they'd say. But no, Mr Down-and-Out has already performed a little sorrowful shake of his head. 'Poor girl,' it says. 'Who could have done such a thing to her?'

Then he looks down, carries on walking and rewraps himself in his own self-pity.

I keep on with my thinking about Marilyn Monroe. Last night I watched a documentary about how she died, whether she was murdered or not. It's been reeling around on a loop behind my eyes all day. Even someone like me shouldn't watch creepy programmes in a hotel room on my own. I hate all that unknown history that lurks in hotel rooms, as if they've seen the worst deeds of the baddest kinds of people. Me and mine can hide in these anonymous places and change who we are or finish a job, while the supposedly good people can book in for a night or two and act out their secret perversions. All this happens behind bland rows of doors along stale corridors. No one will know. And as long as you keep it in the room and settle your bill, no one will care. If the walls in my room could talk, what would they say about last night? What would they make of the woman dyeing her hair blond and looking into the grainy blue of Marilyn's pool on TV? It certainly made *me* uneasy. But it's just a disguise. I kept staring into the mirror, trying to get used to it. I suppose Marilyn *was* killed. She was too powerful. At least, they thought she was, which might've been enough.

I wish Jimbo would come.

Now I'm thinking about Dunc again. Poor Dunc. *Poor Dunc.* I practise the thought in my head. Wanting to mean it. Wanting to believe that I mean it. Poor Dunc. But do I? I feel like I've killed him and I don't know whether to care. Should I even admit to myself that I'm confused? I'm still in trouble. I still need to be alert, to be strong.

The stained-glass windows in here have too much red in them – red robes, red skies, red banners. In the one at the front, Jesus ascends to heaven. People crowd below him, looking up and praying. He reaches down to them with his right hand and points up with his left. He shows them the way. It doesn't move me. And I hate the red, so red it's more like crimson. I'm not a spiritual person. The window's trying too hard to make a dramatic statement. Dunc made the same mistake.

I run my finger along the bumpy edge of the scars just under my hairline. Maybe I should wear an eye patch. It might be more fitting. Then I'd have the look of a pirate.

But Dunc was cruel and, in many ways, stupid. He killed a man in his own back yard. We both paid for it. The dead guy was one of Artie's men and not just a dealer, a real heavy, a somebody. So I shopped Dunc to save myself. But I didn't quite manage it. Artie's blokes weren't happy with Dunc being banged up; they wanted a piece of me as well. And they got it.

It's getting quieter now. Even the stragglers are leaving and no one else is coming in. I wish Jimbo'd come. Jimbo never lets me down. It'll be all right. He'll bring the money. Then I can get away before Dunc finds out what I did.

How could I do it to him?

I can picture him asking me that. I can still see his face and the long dark wool coat he wore when we met. He could've been a businessman, but there was something in the way he looked at you that made you realise that this guy was no accountant. One of the girls upstairs told me about the big bloke with the *och-aye* accent who'd just moved in. I looked out for him, had a feeling he'd be useful. And he was. But he used to scare me. Because I knew he was weak, and a screwed up psycho with it. He'd have nightmares and then wake up screaming for his big soft Scottish mother. He never knew his father, had to be more of a man than any other man to make up for it. But it was a great set-up we had, most of the time.

We had people working for us. Wide-boy losers and ageing wasters who'd come up to the flat and hand over dirty, fat envelopes of cash. They'd say to me, 'Is he lookin after you, darlin?' and I'd wink; flirt and tell them that I'd be knocking on their door the minute he let me down. The truth was, I wanted to puke just looking at them.

And now, thanks to Artie's gang and their acid makeover, my face is cracked. People like looking at me for different reasons now. They won't admit it but when they think I can't see them, they stare. As soon as I look back, their eyes dart away and they fiddle with their hair or go back to reading the paper as if this might convince me that they were far too busy to stare at me in the first place. Morbid curiosity. I suppose I can understand it. We're all so freaked out that bad things might happen to us that we love to make the most of it when we can see someone else has suffered. Fine – let them look. I don't care any more. I just want to get away and get away safe.

I need that money. But Jimbo's still not here; I'm on my own now. The balconies on either side creak above me. A draught blows through the organ pipes and they let out asthmatic moans. I'm nervous and half-blind but I should be getting used to feeling vulnerable these days. I'm different in other ways too: a blonde, a Marilyn. I look at the windows again. It's starting to get to me now. Perhaps I'm like the rest of them, the ones in here before, hoping for comfort, reassurance or even a revelation.

I remember that Dunc used to wear a gold crucifix on a heavy chain. It suited him because it shouldn't have. It was a more powerful symbol around Dunc's neck than it is in here, hanging high on the wall. Up there, it's just a piece of furniture, made of wood and nailed on. On him, it'd be warm to the touch from his skin; it'd float in front of my eyes when he was on top of me, glinting like a talisman. He told me that he'd stolen it when he was thirteen and had worn it ever since. But I think his mother gave it to him. I spoke to her a few times on the phone, not very often, but when I did she always seemed a godly sort of a woman, always just back from church or from collecting for Christian Aid. When she dies she'll be floating up, like the ones in that window. She'll be shown the way. But once I'm done for, I'm worm-meat. So I look away from the windows. They don't apply to me.

I turn around to see a vicar in crimson robes coming through the door at the back. He walks down the central aisle slowly; every footstep a deliberate beat on the stone flags. He goes to a small table where people have lit candles and takes a long flaky spill and lights another.

Smiles to himself, then bends his head in prayer. There are grooves visible in his hair from where he's combed it.

I lower my eyes and pretend to pray too. I wonder what he'd say if he knew what I'd done and suddenly I feel suffocated. The organ pipes moan more loudly; frosted lights hang above me on grey rattling chains. Then, clumsy footsteps (two sets?) clatter on the balcony overhead. Jimbo? I look up but can't see anyone. Afraid and desperate, I try to pray for real but don't know how to begin. And when I try to summon a good spirit all I can see is Marilyn's face, scarred to match mine. So I pray to her.

There's a bang – unmistakably gunshot. I know the sound too well. But for some reason I tell myself it's a firework going off. I glance to the windows at the front and still I imagine that the colours of the stained glass are chemicals burning prettily in the sky outside. It brings me round again when Jimbo lands in front of me. The chairs tumble and break under the weight of him. He's fallen awkwardly, but not awkwardly enough. I stand up but I don't move. I'm cruel and heartless even now, with a friend dying painfully right by me. I turn my blind side to him. He is grotesque and twisted. But I hear him speak, his last word forced through a half-strangled throat.

'Dunc.'

What did I expect?

The vicar walks towards me. Then I recognize him. It's one of Dunc's guys from way back. Perry. A slimy little shit who got a real kick from doing the dirty stuff. I never liked him and he knows it. He's going to enjoy this.

As he pulls a gun from under his robes I can hear the other guy, the one who shot Jimbo, coming down the stairs. Why isn't anyone here? How have they done this?

Perry presses the end of the gun under my chin and I notice the dirty thumbprint he's made on the plasticky white surface of his dog collar. The other guy grabs me from behind. Perry speaks.

'Hello, Blondie. Changed your image, eh? Shame you didn't get your face fixed while you were at it.'

I'm saying nothing. All the answers have gone. In fact, I never had a smart mouth. Instinctively, I know there's nothing I can do. But my mind betrays me for just a second and I look for a way out. There isn't one and they're leading me away; I have to try and think about something else.

Drums and music outside. More bangs. Only this time they really are fireworks. How can they be celebrating? They've no right to be happy, not in this world. But, just for tonight, they think they can change it all. Images come back to me from earlier. When I was walking here I saw them: full of deceptive vigour and borrowed power. Families wearing anoraks, scarves and woolly hats. Teenagers smoking and drinking from litre bottles of cider, getting drunk for the first time. Queues of women wearing too much lipstick and men shivering in shirtsleeves on Broad Street. All of them believing that a New Year is about to start. That's with a capital N, capital Y. The best night out of the year and then we'll do it all again. But we'll do it so much better and we'll be so much richer, thinner and happier. We'll go to the gym three times a week. We won't shout at the kids and we'll read to them every night instead of letting them watch cartoons in their bedrooms. And tomorrow everyone will be virtuous. Everyone will be good.

Fuck it. I wouldn't fit in anyway.

The heavies lead me up a dark staircase at the back of the cathedral. A round, cold, metal circle prods at the bare skin in the small of my back. They speak and they threaten. I will die frightened and abused because that's how Dunc wants it. I don't hear their words; only feel the aggressive spray of saliva on the back of my neck.

I think about the better world of tomorrow. And the lies that'll be told to make everyone believe in it. If I had time, I could tell a story. Let them be inspired when they hear about the woman who almost died but survived and became a saint with the marks of her ugly past on her face.

Could it be true?

Or would I rather be a legend? I have to think of my descendants, those of my kind. Dead and dubious legends are more use to them. They wouldn't be interested in how mundane it could be and how all the big talk was so empty.

They take me into a small room with a shuttered window at the far end. One of the men opens it. The flame of a firework rises in the sky. Phosphorus white, then a fountain trail of diamonds through the black.

Marilyn's face is at the window. She curls a finger and beckons me.

Smile

John Harvey

Soho, Manchester, Birmingham – why was it that Chinatown and the gay quarter were in such close proximity? Cantonese restaurants, pubs and bars, Ocean Travel, the Chung Ying Garden, City Tattooing, Clone Zone, the Amsterdam Experience Adults Only Shop and Cinema. Kiley turned down an alley alongside a shop front hung liberally with wind-dried chickens and within moments he was lost among an uneven criss-cross of streets which seemed to lead nowhere except back into themselves. When he'd stepped off the London train less than thirty minutes earlier and set off on the short walk down from New Street Station, it had all seemed so simple. Instead of the dog-eared copy of *Farewell, My Lovely* he'd brought to read on the journey, a Birmingham *A–Z* would've been more useful.

Finding his way back onto Hurst Street, Kiley ducked into the first bar he found. He ordered a bottle of Kronenbourg 1664 with a glass from an Australian with cropped red hair and carried his drink over to a seat near the window, where, taking his time over his beer, he could think again about what he was doing and watch the couples strolling by outside, holding hands.

When he went back to the bar, the barman greeted him

like they were old friends. 'Ready for another? Kronenbourg, right?'

Kiley shook his head. 'You know a place called Kicks?'

'Kicks? No, I don't think so. What kind of a place is it?'

'It's a club.'

'No, sorry.' The barman shook his head and two gold rings danced in the lobe of his left ear. 'Wait up, though, I'll ask.'

'Thanks.'

Inside a few minutes, he was back. 'You're in luck. Tina says it's off the underpass near the library. Paradise Circus. Some name, huh? Just take a right out of here and follow your nose.'

'OK,' Kiley said. 'Thanks again.'

'Drop back later. I'll keep one cold for you.'

Kiley nodded and turned away, the limp in his right leg barely noticeable as he crossed towards the door.

The steps led down below several lanes of fast-moving traffic, the subway itself tiled and surprisingly clean, the muted stink of urine cut through with disinfectant and the smoky-sweet drift of petrol fumes. Discarded newspapers and fast-food wrapping clotted here and there in corners, but not so much.

He followed round the slow curve of the arcade; a faint, accented clip from his heels. Several small restaurants were open and, as yet, largely empty; shop fronts were barred and shuttered across. Forty, fifty yards more and there it was facing him, the name in green neon over the top of a bright pink door. More fuchsia than mere pink. The door itself was closed, windows either side discreet with frosted glass. Posters gave some idea of what to expect inside, a smiling mostly naked woman spilling out of her leopardskin bra, Mel B twinned with Lara Croft. Alongside the licensing details above the door was a sign:

PLEASE NOTE THIS IS A GENTLEMEN'S ONLY CLUB.

Kiley was surprised there wasn't a doorman outside, muscles threatening the seams of his rented suit. No bell to ring, he pushed at the centre of the door and it swung slowly back, inviting him into a pool of tinted violet light. A sharp-faced blonde greeted him from inside a kiosk to his right and treated him to a smile that would have had no trouble cutting glass.

'Good evening, sir. Are you a member?' And when Kiley shook his head: 'Membership fee is fifty pounds. That includes your first night's admission. We take Visa,' she added helpfully. 'American Express.'

Heavy velvet curtains shielded the interior of the club itself. The sounds of music, muffled, seventies disco but with a different beat.

'Suppose I just want to pay for tonight?'

'I'm afraid that's not possible.'

'Look, the thing is . . .' Kiley moved closer, trying on the charm. As well try to charm an anaconda. ' . . . There's a girl, I think she works here. Anna.'

'We have no Anna.'

'I just wanted to check, you know. As long as she's working then . . .'

'We have no Anna.'

'I knew her, in London.'

But now she was looking past his shoulder, maybe she'd pressed some warning buzzer, Kiley didn't know, but when he turned there was his doorman, two of them in fact, the Lennox Lewis twins.

'Is there a problem here?'

'No, no problem.'

'Cause if there's a problem we can talk about it outside.' One spoke, the other didn't, his voice a soft mix of Caribbean and Brummie.

'He was asking about one of the girls,' said the blonde.

They moved towards him; Kiley stood his ground. 'Sir, please, why don't we just step outside?' Polite. Threateningly polite.

'Look,' Kiley said. 'Suppose I pay the membership fee and –?'

'I'm sorry, sir, I'm afraid membership closed. Now if we can step outside.'

Kiley shrugged. The two men exchanged glances; the silent one pulled the door open and the talker escorted Kiley through.

Wind rattled an empty food tray along one side of the underpass. The man was taller than Kiley by three or four inches, heavier by some forty pounds.

'You not from round here.'

Kiley shook his head.

'In town for business?'

'Something like that.'

The man held out his hand. 'No hard feelings, huh? Why not try somewhere else?' His grip was swift and strong.

'Look,' Kiley said, stepping back. 'I wonder if you'd take a look at this?'

He had scarcely reached inside the lapel of his coat when a fist caught him low, beneath the heart. Before he could touch the ground with his knees, two hands seized him and swung him round. The brickwork alongside the club door closed on him fast. As he buckled and started to slide, another blow struck him in the kidneys and finally a punch to the side of the head. A pool of darkness opened at his feet and he dived into it – as Chandler might have said.

Kiley worked out of two rooms above a bookshop in Belsize Park, a chancy business with a good address. A little over a year now since Kate had rescued him from the lower depths of Upper Holloway and invited him, lock, stock and baggage, to her flat in Highbury Fields, thus enabling him, most weeks, to pay the quite exorbitant office rent.

'You do realize,' he'd said, the first or second evening after supper in her three-storey late-Victorian house, 'keeping that place going's not going to leave me much to contribute here.'

'Contribute?'

'You know, towards the electricity, gas, the council tax.'

'We'll think of something.' Kate had laughed, and poured the last of the white Burgundy into her glass.

In the outer office were a filing cabinet, a computer with printer attached, a Rolodex, a telephone with answering machine and fax. Two mornings a week, Irena, a young Romanian, crossed the street from Café Pasta where she worked, and did his secretarial work, updated his accounts. In Bucharest, she had been a high school teacher with a good degree; here she fetched and carried through six long shifts, Linguine con Capesante, Penne con Salsiccia – black pepper, sir? Parmesan? – bottles of house red.

It had been earlier that month that Irena had mentioned her friend, Anna, for the first time.

'She wants to meet you.' Irena blushed. 'She thinks you are my lover.'

'I'm flattered.'

Irena was slender as a boy, slim-hipped and small-breasted, with deep brown eyes just a fraction too large and a mouth that was generous and wide. Her hair was cut short, close-cropped, severe enough in strong light for her scalp to show through.

'I tell her,' Irena said, 'of course, it is not true.'

'Of course.'

'You are making fun of me.'

'No, not at all. Well, yes, maybe a little.'

Irena returned his smile. 'This afternoon, when I finish my shift. She comes then.'

'OK.'

What, Kiley wondered, was the Romanian for chalk and cheese? Anna was taller than Irena and more voluptuously built, raven hair falling past her shoulders to her middle back, lips a rich purply-red, eye-shadow a striking blue. She wore a slinky top, one size too small, tight jeans, high heels.

'Irena has told me much about you.'

'I'll bet.'

Irena blushed again.

It was warm enough for them to be sitting at one of the pavement tables outside the café where Irena worked.

'So,' Kiley said. 'You and Irena, you're from the same part of Romania?'

Anna tossed her head. 'No, not really. I am from Constanza. It is on the Black Sea coast. Irena came for one year to teach in our school.'

'She taught you? Irena?'

'Yes.' Anna laughed. 'She is much older than me. Did you not know?'

'Not so much,' Irena protested.

For a moment, Anna touched Kiley's arm with her own. 'I am only nineteen, what do you think?'

Kiley thought he would change the subject. He signalled to one of Irena's colleagues and ordered coffee for himself, mineral water for Irena, for Anna Coke with ice and lemon.

'So what are you doing in London?' Kiley asked, once Anna had offered them both a cigarette and lit her own.

'I am dancer.'

'A dancer?'

'Yes. Perhaps you do not believe?'

Kiley believed her, though he doubted it was Ballet Rambert. 'Where do you dance?'

'Club Moroc. It is on Finchley Road.'

'I have seen her,' Irena said. 'Pole dance. It is remarkable.'

'I'll bet.'

'I study for three weeks,' Anna said seriously.

'Pole dancing?'

'Of course. Table dancing also. I have diploma.'

Irena leaned forward, glass in both hands. 'Anna thinks I should take lessons, go and work with her.'

'Instead of this, of course. With me you can earn two hundred, two hundred fifty pounds one night. Here you are slave.'

'At least,' Irena said, 'I keep on my clothes.'

Anna poked out her tongue.

Kiley saw her again two weeks later, unannounced in his outer office, her hair tied back in a ponytail and her makeup smeared.

'Anna, what is it?'

She looked at him helplessly, suddenly awash with tears.

'Come through here; come and sit down.' Helping her first to the couch, he hurried to the bathroom he shared with the financial consultant upstairs. 'Here. Drink this.'

She sipped from the glass of water, then set it aside. Dabbed at her eyes.

'All right, now tell me; tell me what's wrong.' It was enough to set her off again, and Kiley pressed several clean tissues into her hands, sat back in the chair opposite and waited for her to become calm.

After several moments, she blew her nose and reached inside her bag for a cigarette; while she fumbled with her lighter, Kiley fetched the saucer that served as an ashtray and placed it near her feet. An ambulance siren, sudden and shrill, broke through the steady churn of traffic passing outside.

'Coming to this country,' she began falteringly, 'it was

not easy for me. I pay, I have to pay much money. A lot of money.'

'How much?'

'Five thousand pounds.'

'You had that much?'

'No, of course not. I pay it back now. That is why . . . why I work as I do. I pay, each week, as much as I can. And last night . . . last night the man who arrange for me to come here, he tell me I must give him more. Five thousand more. The same again. Or he will report me and I will be sent home.' Ash spilled from the end of her cigarette and she brushed it across her jeans. 'Since Ceausescu, there has been much change in my country. My parents say, yes, this is better, we can do, say what we like. Travel if we want. But what I see, there is no work. No money. Not for me. For Irena, maybe, she has qualifications, degree. She can work there if she wish. But me . . . you think I can dance in Bucharest, earn money, wear nice clothes, you think this?'

Kiley didn't know what he thought. He got to his feet and didn't know where to go. The light through the window was muted and pale, the sky a mottled grey.

'What if you refuse to pay?'

Anna laughed: there was no pleasure in the sound. 'One of the other girls did this. He cut her face. Oh, not himself. He told someone. Someone else.' Lightly, she touched one hand against her cheek. 'Either that or he will have me sent back home.' She stubbed out her cigarette. 'You know what will happen to me if I go back home? Where I will be? Standing beside the road from Bucharest to Sofia, waiting for some lorry driver to pull over and fuck me in his cab for the price of a meal and a pack of cigarettes.'

The room was suddenly airless and Kiley opened the window a crack and the sound of voices rolled in; early afternoon and people, some of them, were heading back to work after lunch. Others would be waiting for the first performance at the cinema up the street, going into the bookshop downstairs to browse and buy.

'This man, the one who says you owe him money, does he have a name?'

'Aldo. Aldo Fusco.'

'Do you want me to talk to him?'

'Oh, yes. Yes, please, if you will.'

'When are you meant to see him again?'

'I don't know. For certain, I mean. Sometimes he comes to the club, sometimes he sends message for me to meet him. Usually it is Soho, Berwick Street.' She placed the emphasis on the first syllable, sounded the middle letter. 'He has office above shop that sells jewellery.'

'You meet him there, his office?'

Anna shook her head. 'Coffee bar across the street.'

'If he contacts you, phone me,' Kiley said, giving her one of his cards. 'Let me know. Meantime, I'll do what I can.'

'Thank you. Thank you.' She caught his arm and kissed him hard, leaving what remained of her lipstick like a purple bruise beside his mouth.

There was little he could do but wait. Walking in and confronting Fusco direct, always assuming he could find him, would likely cause more trouble than it was worth. For Anna as well as for himself. So Kiley waited for the phone to ring, attended to other things. One morning, after meeting Kate for coffee in Maison Bertaux, he strolled up through Soho and located the shop in Berwick Street, costume jewellery in the window, the door leading to the upper floors firmly closed, several bells with no name attached. In a café a little way up the street, half a dozen men, leather-jacketed, dark-haired, sat around a table playing cards. When one of them chanced to look up and see Kiley through the glass, he held his stare till Kiley turned and walked away.

Two more days, three, then four. Irena came across from Café Pasta, concern clouding her eyes. 'I went to the club looking for Anna and they told me she didn't work there any more. That is all they would tell me. Her flat, the place she shared with two of the other girls, most of her clothes have gone too.'

'The girls, did they have any idea where she went?'

'No. All they knew, that man came to the club, the one she owed money to. The next thing she was packing her things into a bag, there was a car waiting downstairs.'

Irena sighed and closed her eyes and Kiley placed one hand on her shoulder and she lowered her head until it rested on his chest. 'It'll be OK,' he said quietly. 'Don't worry.' When he kissed the top of her head, he was amazed at the softness of her hair.

'Aldo fucking Fusco. Claims he's Italian. Sicilian even. It's all so much horseshit. His real name's Sali, Sali Mejdani. He's Albanian. From Tirana.'

Kiley had called his friend Maggie, a barrister who dealt with a lot of cases involving refugees, applications for asylum – 'Was there anybody in Immigration who might talk to him, off the record?' Which was why he and Barker were walking between Westminster Bridge and Vauxhall, tour boats slowly passing both ways along the river. Two fortyish men in topcoats, talking over old times.

'This girl,' Barker said. 'Anna? You think she'd give evidence? In court?'

Kiley shook his head.

Barker broke his stride to light another cigarette. 'They never do. Even if they say they will, when it comes down to it, they won't. Too frightened about what might happen. Getting deported back to whatever shithole it is they come from. So these people go on squeezing money out of them. The lucky ones, like your Anna, they work the clubs. For others, it's massage parlours, brothels. Twelve, fourteen hours a day; hundred, hundred and fifty cocks a week.'

'You haven't got enough,' Kiley said, 'without her, to have him arrested?'

'Sure. Every once in a while we do.' Barker released a plume of smoke out into the air. 'He can afford a better solicitor, better barrister. We can never hold him. So we keep a watch, as much as we can, wait for him to slip up. A container ship stuffed full of asphyxiated bodies we can trace back to him direct. That would do the trick.'

'And he knows?'

'Fusco? That we're watching him? Oh, yes. And he loves it, makes him feel big. Important. A made guy.'

'If I want to talk to him, you've no quarrel?'

Barker shook his head. 'I'll come along. Ride shotgun. Maggie might not forgive me if I let you get hurt.'

They were playing blackjack, five of them. Fusco had just bought another card on eighteen and gone over the top. 'Fuck!' he said.

'Nice,' Barker said from the doorway, 'that you know your name.'

Three of the men round the table started to rise, but Fusco waved them back down. A couple by the wall drank their last mouthfuls of cappuccino and headed for the door. Barker and Kiley stood aside to let them past.

'Hey,' Fusco said, looking at Barker. 'You never give up.'

'You know a girl called Anna?' Kiley said. 'The Club Maroc.'

Fusco eased back into his chair, tilting it onto its rear legs. 'Sure, what of it?'

'According to you, she owes you money.'

'Not any more.'

Kiley moved closer. Behind him, someone came breezily through the café door, caught the eye of the woman behind the counter and stepped back out. 'You mean she paid you? What?'

Amusement played in Fusco's eyes. 'No, she didn't pay me. I sold her, that's what.'

'Sold her? What d'you mean, you fucking sold her? Where do you think you are?'

The man nearest to Kiley was half out of his chair and Kiley levered him back down, hand tight against his neck. Across the room Barker was thinking a little more backup might've been nice.

'You're right,' Fusco said, 'she owed me money. She didn't want to pay. I sold the debt.'

'You sold the debt?'

'Hey.' Fusco laughed. 'You hear pretty good.'

Kiley went for him then, fists raised, and there were two men quick to block his path, holding his arms till he shook them off.

'Jack,' Barker said, clear but not loud. 'Let's not.'

Slowly, Fusco lowered his chair back onto all four legs. He was still grinning his broad grin and Kiley wanted to tear it from his face.

'Jack,' Barker said again.

Kiley eased back.

'I tell you this because of your friend,' Fusco said, indicating Barker with a nod of the head. 'The one who took over the debt, he is called O'Hagan. He has a club in Birmingham. Kicks. You best hope she is working there. If not, get someone to drive you up and down the Hagley Road.' Scooping up the cards, he proceeded to shuffle and deal.

'The Hagley Road,' Barker said when they were back on the street. 'It's . . .'

'I know what it is.'

They set off south towards the tube. 'You'll go? Brum?'

Kiley nodded. 'Yes.'

'Tread carefully.'

'You know this O'Hagan?'

'Not personally. But I could give you the name of someone who might.' On the corner of Old Compton Street, Barker stopped and wrote a name inside the top of a cigarette pack, tore it off and pushed it into Kiley's hand. 'West Midlands Crime Squad. You can use my name.'

'Thanks.'

At the station they went their separate ways.

The last thing Kiley wanted, the last thing he wanted there and then, following the altercation outside Kicks, was several hours spent in A&E. Hailing a cab, he got the driver to take him to the nearest late-night chemist where he stocked up on plasters, bandages and antiseptic cream. When he asked for suggestions for a hotel, the cabby took him to his sister-in-law's B&B on the Pershore Road, near Pebble Mill. Clean sheets, a pot of tea and a glass of scotch, full breakfast in the morning and change from fifty pounds.

'You look like warmed-over shit,' Mackay said next day, drinking an early lunch in the anonymity of an All Bar One. Mackay, detective sergeant in the West Midlands Crime Squad, Birmingham by way of Aberdeen. Suit from Top Man, shirt and tie from Next.

Kiley thought they could skip the small talk and asked about O'Hagan instead.

Mackay laughed. A cheery sound. 'Casinos, that's his thing. Any kind of gambling. That club you got yourself thrown out of, as much for show as anything. Entertaining. When one of our lot had his retirement bash six months back, that's where it was. O'Hagan's treat. Sign of respect.' He laughed again. 'Not an official donor to the Police Benevolent Fund, you understand, but here and there he does his bit.'

'Widows and orphans.'

'That type of thing.'

'How about nineteen year olds from Romania?'

'He has his share.' Mackay drained his whisky glass and pushed it across a foot or so of polished pine. Kiley sought a refill at the bar, another coffee for himself.

'You're not drinking?' Mackay asked, eyebrow raised.

'How does he treat his girls?' Kiley asked.

'O'Hagan? Well enough. So long as they stay in line.'

'And if not?'

Mackay tasted his scotch, lit a cigarette. 'A wee bit of trouble with his enforcers once or twice. But that was gambling, debts not paid. The local lads sorted it as I recall.'

'These enforcers – a couple of big guys, black, look as if they could box.'

Mackay laughed again. 'Cyril and Claude. Brothers. Twins. And, aye, box is right. But they're straight enough, not the kind of enforcers I meant at all. Those bastards are still in the open razor stage. Cyril and Claude, much more smooth.' He chuckled into his glass. 'Which one was it, I wonder, rearranged your face?'

'The talkative one.'

'That'd be Claude. He works out in a gym not far from here. You know, he's really not so bad a guy.' Finishing his drink, Mackay got to his feet. 'If you bump into him again, make sure you give him my best.'

Kiley watched Claude spar three rounds with a big-boned Yugoslav, work out on the heavy bag, and waited while he towelled down. They sat on a bench off to one side of the main room, high on the scent of sweat and wintergreen, the small thunder of feet and fists about their ears.

'Sorry about last night,' Claude offered.

Kiley shook his head.

'Like, when I saw you reach inside your coat, I thought . . . See, not so long back, me and Cyril we're escorting this high-roller out of the club and he's offerin money, all sorts, to let him stay. We get him outside an I think he's reachin for his wallet an suddenly he's wavin this gun . . .' Claude grinned, almost sheepishly. 'I wasn't goin to make that mistake again.'

Kiley nodded to show he understood.

'This girl you looking for . . .'

'Anna.'

'Anna, yes, she there. Nice lookin, too. You and she . . .?'

'No.'

'Just lookin out for her, somethin like that.'

'Something like that.'

'Mr O'Hagan, he heard you was there, askin for her.' Claude frowned. 'I don't know. I think he had words with her. Somethin about stickin by the rules. He don't like no boyfriends, no one like that comin round.'

'She's OK?'

'I reckon so.'

'I'd like to see her. Just, you know, to make sure. Make sure she's all right. She has a friend in London, works for me. Worried about her. I promised I'd check. If I could.'

Claude tapped his fists together lightly as he thought. 'Come by the club later, you can do that? But not so late, you know? Around nine. Mr O'Hagan, no way he's there then. Cyril or me, we meet you out front, take you in another door. What d'you say?'

Kiley said thank you very much.

The dressing room was low-ceilinged and small, a brightly lit mirror the length of one wall, makeup littered along the shelf below. Clothes hung here and there from wire hangers, were draped over the backs of chairs. The other girls were working, the sound of Gloria Gaynor distinct enough through the closed door. Anna sat on a folding chair, cardigan across her shoulders, spangles on her micro-skirt and skimpy top. Carefully applied foundation and blusher didn't hide the bruise discolouring her cheek.

Gently, Kiley turned her face towards the light. Fear stalked her eyes.

'I slip,' she said hastily. 'Climbing down from the stage.'

'Nothing to do with O'Hagan, then,' Kiley said. She flinched at the sound of his name. Kiley leaned towards her, held her hand. 'Anna, look, I think if you came with me now, walked out of here, with me, it would be all right.'

'No, no, I . . .'

'Come back down to London, maybe you could stay with Irena for a bit. She might even be able to wangle you a job. Or some kind of course, college. Then you could apply for a visa. A student visa.'

'No, it is not possible.' She pulled herself free from his hand and turned aside. 'I must . . . I must stay here. Pay what I owe.'

'But you don't –'

'Yes. Yes, I do. You don't understand.'

'Anna, listen, please . . .'

Slowly, she turned back to face him. 'I can earn much money here, I think. In a year maybe, debt will be no more. What I have to do: remember the rules, be respectful. Remember what I learn for my diploma. Which moves. And my hands, always look after my hands. This is important. A manicure. When you dance at table, be a good listener. Smile. Always smile. Make eye contact with the guests. Look them in the eyes. Look at the bridge of the nose, right between the eyes. And smile.'

Tears were tracing slowly down her cheeks and around the edges of her chin, running down her neck, falling onto bare thighs.

'Please,' she said. 'Please, you must go now. Please.'

'I Will Survive' had long finished, to be replaced by something Kiley failed to recognize. He took one of his cards from his wallet and set it down. 'Call,' he said. 'Either Irena or myself. Call.'

Anna smiled and reached for some tissues to wipe her face. Another fifteen minutes and she was due on stage. The Basic Spin. The Lick and Flick. The Nipple Squeeze. The Bump and Grind. And smile. Always smile.

In the following months, Anna phoned Irena twice; both calls were fragmentary and short, she seemed to be speaking on someone else's mobile phone. Sure, everything was OK, fine. Lots of love. Then, when Kiley arrived one morning at his office, there was a message from Claude on his answerphone. Anna had quit the club, something to do with complaints from a customer, Claude wasn't sure; he had no idea where she'd gone.

Nothing for another three months, then a card to Irena, posted in Bucharest. 'Dear Irena, I hope you remember me. As you can see, I am back in our country now, but hope soon to return to UK. Pray for me. Love, Anna. PS A kiss for Jack.'

It is cold and trade on the autoroute north towards Budapest is slow. Anna pulls her fake fur jacket tighter across her chest and lights another cigarette. The seam of her denim shorts sticks uncomfortably into the crack of her behind, but at least her boots cover her legs above the knee. Her forearms and thighs are shadowed with the marks of bruises, old and new. An articulated lorry, hauling aggregate towards Oradea, slows out of the road's curve and approaches the makeshift lay-by where she has stationed herself. The driver, bearded, tattoos on his arms, leans down from his cab to give her the once-over, and Anna steps towards him. Smile, she tells herself, smile.

The End of Something

Wayne Dean-Richards

'Manny's gonna shag your sister tomorrow night!'

'I bet Charlie goes red. You go red, don't you, Charlie?'

I look at Richy, then at Mango. They're both grinning – the same grin they wear when they light a banger and chuck it into someone's garden, at a cat, or a passing car. Mean, the pair of them. They could be brothers, but they're not, just lads drawn together by their interest in causing trouble, which is what they're trying to do now.

I balance an empty lager bottle on the wall beside the gym and walk away from it, knowing Richy and Mango are watching me closely. The sun's going down – everything's orange. It's been so hot I have a headache, but it doesn't impede me. Suddenly, I spin on my left foot, whipping my right arm round fast. I release the stone – half the size of my fist – and it hits the lager bottle and smashes it, the glass showering the steps outside the boys' changing room. Ordinarily I'd worry about that – about the caretaker, fat fuck that he is, having to clear it up. But now my mind's on what Richy and Mango have just told me.

'Gavin the gunfighter,' Richy says. The skinny little sod is grinning. He likes my stone-throwing routine because it's beyond him. Usually, I like it too: it makes me feel good. But not tonight.

'Who told you that shit about my sister?' I ask, trying to sound bored, knowing that if they think they can wind me up they will.

'Dale,' Richy answers, having bought it.

'Dale's full of shit!' I say.

'Sometimes,' Mango agrees. 'But when he said Maxine Givens was pregnant, it wasn't shit.'

Richy nods sagely at this. You pair of bastards! I think, but I follow them across the school field, dry and hard, my mind spinning, burning.

At the edge of the field we sit with our backs against the wall that separates the field from the churchyard. Richy's smile flags a bit, which means he's trying to think. I feel like screaming. Like smashing my head against the wall. I wonder what my blood would look like in this orange light.

'Manny reckons he's shagged every girl in 10C,' Richy says.

'He's a bullshitter!' I say, angry that the words slipped out.

'Sarah Toomy says he's got a nine-inch dick,' Mango offers, sensing my unease, probing for it.

This time, though, I check my words and we sit and watch the orange light turn black.

The thought of Gemma with Manny makes me want to puke. That night I lie on top of the bed, wearing only my boxers, sweating. Gemma is small and has bright blue eyes. She had pneumonia when she was little; Mom says that's what made her eyes so blue. To go with her eyes she has blond, spiky hair. She's fifteen, a year older than me. We used to look alike. Used to help each other out. Me and Gemma. Gemma and me. Then everything changed. I don't know why, or even exactly when, I just know things changed between us. For the worse.

Someone's turned the bass on my headache way up. I want things to be the way they used to be between me and Gemma, and I know if Manny shags her that can't ever be. Manny Cooper . . . I fucking hate him. What's worse is: Gemma knows it. How could she even think about letting him shag her? Is it because he really has got a nine-inch dick? Is that all that counts now? I can't remember ever being this angry, this hot, having a headache that hurt this much. When I started Bret Cross, Manny Cooper put my head down the bog and flushed. He was a year older than me and a lot bigger. He thought it was really funny and I had to fight back the tears. I hate him for what he did and because he's everything I'm not. Manny's got the gift of the gab, is what they say. Even the teachers like him, though he's thick as shit. He wears a leather jacket instead of his school blazer and gets away with it. The bottom line is: I hate him and I won't let him shag my sister.

The next day I start following her.

Over breakfast I watch her closely. Mom's at work. The house is a pigsty, the sink full of unwashed plates, and Gemma's spooning in Shreddies. Any doubts I had are quickly dispelled. In her face I can see she's going to let Manny shag her. I've buttered myself a slice of toast but I can't eat it. The smell of margarine sickens me. I want to tell her what I'm feeling, but I know it'd be a waste of time. Talking rarely works. You have to do. Leaving my toast, I fiddle with the radio till she leaves, then trail after her, walking on the opposite side of the street, my hands in my pockets.

The day blurs past. When I get home I skip through my schoolbooks. I see the date and recognize my handwriting, but I don't remember writing anything. It was hot. Too hot! And all I could think of was Gemma and Manny, Manny and Gemma.

*

It's after seven when Gemma leaves the house. Mom's asleep in front of the telly. Sweating, I go after her. She has on a short blue skirt and a tight-fitting black T-shirt. I think of the photos of Gemma and me when we were really close. Afterwards, when I've done whatever it is I end up doing, it'd be nice for us to look at those photos again: Gemma and me, me and Gemma.

I stop beside the gym and let her cross the field. It's funny how many of us hang around the school at night, like ghosts in search of our lost souls. I see Manny on the far side of the field. Despite the heat, the posey bastard is wearing his leather jacket. My mouth is dry and my head feels as if it's ready to burst. I think about hitting him. These days he's not much bigger than me and I have hate on my side. Maybe I could take him. But instead of trying I stay where I am – unseen – and watch as he takes Gemma by the hand and the two of them walk into the wood that backs onto the field.

Only then do I move: jogging, the baked ground jarring me, bright, gritty pain expanding to fill both my knees. Sweat dribbles into my eyes. I blink away the stinging. I'm in the woods now, following them down towards the golf course. The air's stale, the leaves are very green, but the undergrowth is rusty, tinder-dry.

Seen through the trees, the golf course is like a strange sea. Gemma and Manny aren't heading onto the course, though, they're moving parallel to it, high-stepping through the tangle. I know where they're heading. Stooping, I watch them. They stop when they reach the gardener's hut. They're a hundred yards away. It's getting dark quickly, like in a vampire movie. Gemma and Manny are surrendering their shapes.

When they go into the hut, I stand up. I move stealthily, my heart trying to hammer its way out of me. To the right of the hut is a seized up mower. I touch it, feeling the heat of the sun in the metal.

I move to stand outside the door, off its hinges, sagging open. Smells of creosote and piss wash over me. I breathe through my mouth so they won't hear me. The trees watch me, taunting, part of a grey patchwork linking earth to sky.

Gemma . . .

From my pocket I take a box of matches. My whole body's trembling – that or else the world's shaking, about to split apart and swallow us all. The tinder lights easily. Bright orange tongues lick the creosote greedily from the side of the hut. The sudden heat rushes at my face and I stagger backwards, tumble, fall, hitting the ground hard.

All the air has been sucked out of my lungs. My face is burning. The hut is burning. Gemma and Manny, I hope they're burning too. Things can't ever be the way they used to be between us. I hope they burn. I hope we all burn.

But we don't. Propping myself up on my elbows, I see Gemma and Manny run from the hut, the crackle of burning wood a counterpoint to their excited voices. They hurry away. By the light of the fire I see them make their way over to the golf course. I lie back down. Press my hands against my face. The skin feels tight, rubbery. The soles of my trainers start to smoulder, but I don't move them; I just close my eyes and wait to see what happens next.

Little Moscow

Mick Scully

Out. A week now. I've waited a full week before heading here, the Little Moscow. A basement bar on the edge of the Tyseley Industrial Estate. Not that there's much industry left, just a lot of broken-down factories nobody needs any more. Crumbleville.

The Little Moscow has always been a villains' bar, although in the sixties it doubled, briefly, as a trendy Mod bar. That's when I first descended its narrow flight of brick steps – in my Crombie and Ben Sherman shirts. I've always cared about my appearance. Even inside I take a pride in it. You can these days. Even the clink isn't the place it used to be.

Tonight I am here with a purpose different to those days. Then it was to be admired, to get a shag. And I usually did. I was a good-looking boy.

I've always been a criminal, and a good one, efficient. If you're around long enough you get a reputation, and a name. Mine is Office.

I've always been an independent character, usually worked alone. Small jobs, but plenty of them. Of course I'm talking about some time ago, when cash was king. People got paid weekly – cash, in fat little brown envelopes. I did wages jobs. Thursday nights, Friday mornings. They were my busy times. A cosh swung above the head of an accountant; a few threats. Easy. People didn't swear so much then either, so a few curses scared the shit – *Fill the fucking bag, you tosser. Or I'll spread your fucking brains all over the fucking walls.* I wonder how many times I've used that line. And I could always judge just how it needed to be said. Sometimes you lean in close to the face, so they can feel your breath, and hiss the words out; other times you scream them out like a fucking lunatic.

My old fella was a villain too, but not so successful. A team player he called himself. Meaning he had no ideas of his own, no initiative. And he always chose the wrong team. Even supported the Albion, and what the fuck have they ever won? Banged up most of his life. Died inside.

There's hardly anyone in the bar, but it's early yet. I look around. It's the same old place all right. A few tables and chairs. Photographs of Moscow pasted on chipboard, aka Athena, still hang from the walls. Faded now and tobacco-stained. The Kremlin. Some cathedral. Red Square.

I see Fat Alex is still here, behind the bar. He's taking bottles from a plastic crate to fill a low shelf. His big arse sticking up above the bar. It was his father who opened the Little Moscow in the fifties. A Pole who came over here in the War. There was a big Eastern European community in Brum at the time – Poles and Czechs mostly, a few Hungarians. Fuck knows why he called it Little Moscow, given what was happening in his country at the time. A joke? Maybe. A lot of gambling went on then. Alex's dad did a spell inside for it. I've been told that in those days you could hear three or four different languages being spoken in here.

Eventually, his task complete, Alex rises, wheezing, boots the empty crate under the bar, and turns towards me. 'Yes, mate?' Then his face does a squiggle as recognition comes.

'Office! Well fuck me. Good to see you, man.' His podgy fist grasps the beer pump, and he squints, taking me in. Then comes the usual crap. 'You're lookin good, kid. No doubt about it. Yes. Lookin very good. Nice suit. I eard you waz clear. Wondered if yow'd pop in. Yeah. It's good to see yow, mate.'

I bet it is. I let his awkward pause hang for a minute. Watch his eyes shifting uncomfortably. Then I help him out. 'You haven't lost any weight, I see. Ya fat bastard.' And I give him a bit of a smile.

Relieved, he laughs and slaps his bulging belly in confirmation. 'Shit. It's been a long time, Office.' I say nothing. 'How long is it?' Not the right question. Still, I'm here for a reason, so I answer the man.

'Sixteen years.'

'Fuck me rigid, Office. Sixteen years. Bloody ell. So. What yow drinkin?'

I scan the pumps. Same pumps. Different beer. Each shield bears the name of an unfamiliar brand. 'No Ansells any more, I see. Or Double D.'

'Fuck me. It as been sixteen years, asn't it? Ere.' He flicks the little knob of an electric pump. 'Try one of these fancy Belgian lagers. We're in the Common Market now, ya know.'

He places the foaming lager on the bar before me. 'On me. Free sample. Then he drops a double whiskey into a tumbler. 'Chase it down, Office. Welcome ome.' Yeah. I bet.

The trouble with returning to a place like this is the ghosts. Before I've had more than a gulp or two of lager, a shot of whiskey, they start to appear. Taking their places at the empty chairs. They hang around the old upright jukebox that's been shifted out now. They're leaning on the bar, heads close together, whispering. One ghost is missing, of course. And as I think of him my eyes flicker towards the door to the Gents. Still there. Where it was then. There's been no reconstruction in Little Moscow – of any sort.

Fat Alex is still jawing away, telling me things, as if he can fill me in on sixteen years in the time it takes to down a few drinks. Or maybe he's nervous. I'm not listening to him. Just nodding, making the right noises. Every now and then he mentions a name from the old days. I look around, and there they are, sitting at a table, lolling in a chair, walking across the dirty wooden floor, sharpening cues at the pool table in the big alcove.

Gradually a few bits of real flesh and blood start turning up. Nobody I know, of course. Youngsters, a lot of them. But all part of the Brotherhood. Or apprentices. Sitting together, gassing. One or two alone, standing. Moody. Watching. For someone, or something, to turn up. And as they arrive, gradually filling the place, they evict my ghosts.

Second pint. Third. And I start to get comfortable. Assam, a lad I knew inside, arrives and comes across, a piece of skirt hanging off his arm, and we exchange a few words. Buys me a pint. 'Are ya lookin for work? Might be able to fix ya up wiv somethin. Small it would be. But it's money.'

'You're all right, mate,' I reply. 'I'm OK for a bit. Thanks for the offer though.'

Assam pisses off with his woman and it's time to make my first move. I've waited till it's busy, but not packed. Now I catch Alex's eye with a serious look, raise my finger and curl it, beckoning. 'Over here, mate.' His eyes flicker to my glass but he sees it's still near full. He squints as he shuffles towards me. I lean forward across the bar, speak softly but firmly. 'I need to have a quiet word with you soon.'

A shifty look, which he drags into a smile. 'Imran, lad who helps out, e'll be in about nine. We'll talk then.'

A few minutes later I spot him on the mobile. He's turned

away from the bar, trying to make himself small. Some fucking chance.

I've rehearsed tonight. A thousand times at least. On the bunk, in the gym, on the bog. In the long sleepless nights – and I've had plenty of those over the years. And here I am. Walking the dream. Back in the Little Moscow. It's still here, and so am I.

Now there's a moment of panic. I pull hard on my fag. You stupid fucker, I'm telling myself. To believe in a promise made from the other side of a gun all those years ago. 'There's bugger all honour among thieves, son,' my old man used to tell me. 'Remember that.' Well, we'll see. I'm here, aren't I?

I'm careful about people. That's why I worked alone. I took only cash, so I was always my own man. But you get known. Like attracts like. I hung around this place like a flag – was on nodding terms with everyone. And when business was bad, or I needed to keep my head down, I did a bit of work for the Sanchez brothers – door work, spot of driving, sometimes a bit of back-up for a heavy job.

I'd been working for myself all that year, 1984. A good year. My pockets were full. It was a few days before Christmas. Pissing down outside. And cold. The usual Christmas crap pouring out of the jukebox, and hardly anyone in here. But there was this kid. He was in here when I arrived. Eyeing up everyone who came down the steps. Standing at the bar with a pint he wasn't enjoying much. Thin. Pimply. In an old-fashioned overcoat, sizes too big for him. I noticed he kept looking over. Apprentice I reckoned. Looking for a bit of work over the Christmas period. Now there's certain things you can work out straight away from a bloke's eyes – and his were strange. Watery. Too old for him. Greeny blue. The colour of the marbles I played with as a nipper. He was as nervous as fuck. Like a schoolboy outside the headmaster's study. Knows he's up for six of the best and just wants to get it over with. Doesn't care how bad it'll be. Just wants to get on with it.

The eyes slide towards me again. Lips tremble slightly. I nod. He nods back. What the fuck, I think, and push my glass a bit closer along the bar.

'Not seen you in here before,' I open.

'No,' he says. Sort of breathes it out. And his voice is funny. An accent. Foreign.

'You're not English.' A bit stupid really, but I'm not a natural conversationalist, don't find small talk easy. Better at listening.

'No.' He's not giving much away. Sensible.

'Where you from, then?'

'Poland.'

'Fuck. You're a long way from home.' He thinks this is funny and laughs.

There's a pause. I tap my finger to the stupid music. The kid can't take it. He moves closer. Shoves his watery eyes up at me, blurts out, 'Are you interested in buying something?' This is no apprentice. A complete bloody novice. Does a job and can't take the heat. 'Something valuable. Very rare. Expensive.' I feel a bit sorry for him – mistake number one. He's got no nerve. Blurting it out like that.

'I might be. What is it?'

'Jewellery.'

'Not really my bag, son.' I'm about to leave it there, but then – mistake number two – he's pissing himself with fright. 'I might be able to sort something out for you, though. I know a few people.' At this point I have him down as a novice climber. He's just shinned up his first drainpipe, nicked some rich tart's Christmas present, and wants to unload it quickly. I'd had a good year, plenty of cash; it might be worth a look. 'Have you got it with you?'

He straightens up. 'Follow me. In a minute.' And with that he turns and marches off, like a little soldier, towards the door marked 'Gentlemen' – always a bit of a joke in the Little Moscow.

I give it a couple of minutes, stub my fag and follow.

But he hasn't gone into the bog. There's a small lobby with a double fire-exit door leading out onto the towpath. Tonight there's a mangy Christmas tree blocking the exit. A few tired lengths of tinsel stretched across it. The kid's standing by the tree, pretending to admire it. He's got an envelope in his hand.

I stand beside him. Take out the fags, offer him one, but he shakes his head. 'I do smoke. But not now. Thank you.' He's calmer now he's out of the bar.

'Let's see the stuff then. How hot is it?'

He takes two photographs from the envelope. They're old pictures. Fawn with age. He hands one to me. It's a woman, about thirty, smiling into the camera. There's a cigarette on its way to her lips.

'Do you recognize this lady?' the kid asks. She's glamorous. Done up to the nines. I don't know who she is. Think maybe she's some film star from the thirties or forties.

'No. Can't say I do.'

He points to her hand. 'This is the ring I have to sell.' I see now there's a big sparkler on one of her fingers.

'It is a square-cut sapphire. Here in the centre. Large, yes? And these are rubies around it. With small diamonds, tiny ones, in between.' He's starting to sound like a salesman. 'It is a very beautiful ring.'

'Where is it?' I ask. 'Let's see the real thing.' But he just hands me the other picture. It confuses me for a second. All I take in is it's a picture of Hitler. In uniform. There are some other blokes with him. One is a fat, bald bloke. I ought to know his name. Then I see, in the middle, with old Adolf's arm around her, is the woman in the first photograph. Another fag on its way to her mouth. The ring singing out from her finger. You can see the flash of the stones in the light.

'What is this?'

'The lady. Her name is Eva Braun. You know of her? She was Hitler's mistress. He gave her the ring. He had it specially made. A Christmas present for her. It is a very expensive ring. Very beautiful. Very, very special. No?' He reaches for the photographs and replaces them in the envelope, which he places inside his coat. 'I have this ring. I wish to sell it. For twenty-five thousand pounds. So I can get to America.'

Fuck me, I think. You must be planning on going by Concorde if you need that sort of dough. 'That's a lot of money, kid. Well, let's see it, then.' He gives me a look as if I'm the novice.

'You do not carry such a thing. But I have it. I can quickly get it if you wish to purchase it.'

My brain's turning somersaults. 'Not me. This isn't my territory. Look, let's go back inside and talk about this.'

We carry our beers from the bar to a table in one of the small alcoves. He hasn't touched his, but I take a hefty swig from mine. This could be a big one, I'm telling myself. There's the chance for some real money here. A Big One. Mistake three.

The kid must trust me; he opens up. Apparently this bird, Eva Braun, was Hitler's favourite piece. They killed themselves together, which I sort of knew. The kid's grandfather was one of the soldiers who discovered the bodies. They'd been burnt. But the ring had survived the amateur cremation, and this kid's granddaddy had pocketed it. It'd been a sort of insurance for the family, and a huge secret.

When the kid decided to make a run for the West he stole

the ring from his father; it was his 'collateral'. He made me laugh as he said that word. So careful. With so much effort. A bright lad.

'I think I can help you out,' I tell him, 'but I need the photographs. Without them it's just a ring.'

'Yes. It is its antecedents which makes it so valuable.' Bloody hell. A bright kid, all right. He knows more words than I do. 'But it is a beautiful ring. Exquisite.'

'Yeah. Well, you wouldn't expect old Adolf to give his missis something from Ratners, would you?' He doesn't understand.

The next days were busy ones. While the city grew frantic with Christmas shopping I set about finding a buyer for the ring. It took some thinking about – this was big stuff. I decided to go straight to the top – Amsterdam Alf. Then I thought, no, the Sanchez brothers. Of course. They were pretty much running Birmingham at the time. Two big clubs in town, and a host of other business interests – property, porn, who knows what.

Ramon sat quietly behind his desk at the Candystrip, looking intently at the photographs laid out before him.

'You say you haven't actually seen the ring, Office? Touched it? Given it the once over?' His fierce little eyes burned at me. But Ramon didn't scare me. The brothers were businessmen. If they went for this they'd be serious. No messing. The brass was there. And they had the back-up if anything went wrong.

'No, Ramon, but my source is totally legit. Not local. European.' I thought he would like this. 'And you know me, Ramon, if the goods aren't up to scratch, then the deal is off. No problem.'

He thought for a moment. Sighed heavily. Then burped loudly. An unfortunate habit of his. 'Have you approached anyone else?'

'No. You were the first people I thought of.'

'So. No one else knows anything about it.'

'No one. Just you, me and the supplier.'

'Who is?'

'Oh, come on, Ramon. You know I can't tell you that. But you know me. I don't take risks. I wouldn't be anywhere near this if I wasn't sure it's absolutely kosher.'

He leaned back in his comfortable leather chair and spoke slowly in his soft Spanish accent. 'It certainly seems a very interesting investment. There's all sorts of . . . er, weirdos, who'll pay well over the odds, yes, very big sums, because of this ring's antecedents.'

Fuck me. That word again. I was beginning to think I ought to read more. Starting with a dictionary.

Ramon sighed, scratching his chins. Then he fixed the eyes again. 'You say the price is fifty grand?'

'Yep. That's it. On the nose.'

'Can't you bid it down?'

'Already have, Ramon. It started at nearly twice that.' The breath whistled out of him and I prepared myself for another burp. 'So it's come down a lot.' I paused. Let him think. 'The thing is, if we don't bite, it'll go abroad.'

'And yours?'

'I'm asking a couple of grand from you, and the same from the vendor.' Vendor. Not a word I use a lot, but I was feeling a bit touchy about my vocabulary. All these foreigners using words I didn't know.

'So. That will bring our investment to fifty-two thousand pounds.' He spoke the words with slow care, as if he needed to hear them to believe them. 'That's a lot of money, Office – that's a house or even two.'

Not where you live, I thought.

'Yeah, but as you said, Ramon, it's a hell of an investment. When will an opportunity like this come up again? The ring itself is top notch. Worth that money. Then there's the intercedence. It's money in the bank.'

His finger was tapping. Head bent, looking at the photos again. Then he carefully replaced them in the envelope.

'Give me a minute, Office.' He was off to see his brother. But I knew it was a done deal, and was cheering inside. If Ramon was happy, then brother Manolo wouldn't argue. Ramon was the gaffer.

All I had to do now was bid the kid down to twenty grand. Things looked as if they were turning out nicely, as my old man used to say. Poor sod.

I meet the kid on the towpath of the Tyseley Canal. Small patches of ice forming a seasonal patchwork across the filthy water. He's still wearing his old overcoat. A red scarf round his neck now. And bloody great workmen's boots. Not the trendiest youngster in the world.

'I wish you'd brought the ring. I've got to be sure the merchandise is up to scratch – for my clients.'

He doesn't flinch. Right little soldier. 'Your clients will not be disappointed. The merchandise is magnificent. I will produce the ring when you bring the cash.'

He's a puny little bastard. Shaking now. But he's no pushover. Skinny, but determined as fuck. Still, you don't climb out of a country unless you've got guts.

'The problem is, kid. Twenty grand is the total tops they'll go. I tried hard as I could for the full quarter. But twenty's all I can do.'

His breath is making small clouds of white smoke in the frozen air. A little dragon. He turns his wet eyes straight on me. 'Then I must thank you for your help. But there is no transaction.' Shit. What sort of school did he go to? I thought they were all piss poor in Poland.

'Come on, kid. Think about it. Fifteen thousand pounds will give you a great start in the States. Easy.'

'You said twenty.'

Time to toughen up. Let him know where he stands. 'I'm not doin this for nothin, y'know. I want somethin for myself.'

'You should add your commission to the purchase price. I told you I wanted twenty-five thousand pounds. Or a quarter as you say. That is the price. I will sell for nothing less.' And he means it. I can see that. 'I thank you for your efforts. I must leave now.' And he holds out his hand for me to shake. Tough little fucker. I like him. You have to admire guts.

'OK. Let me have another try. I'll see if I can push them up another couple of grand.'

'Another five.'

I laugh. 'All right. Another five. I'll see what I can do.'

Mistake number four. I've always claimed I'm not greedy. I've seen too many take the drop because they got too greedy. But somehow I manage to convince myself it's the kid who's the greedy one. He's the one pushing too far.

I'm still there, standing with frozen feet beside the canal, watching him climb the towpath steps towards the station when I decide. I'll go for the lot. Take the cash myself. Top the kid. I shiver a little, but it's a cold day. Brutal.

I've never even considered killing before. Rarely used any sort of violence. Don't have to if you scare them enough. But the decision's no surprise to me. I suppose I always knew I would. If it's worth it. And fifty grand is.

So, I arranged to meet Black Andy in Little Moscow. He'd been the Sanchez brothers' frontman for years. Sharp-suited lad. Always beautifully turned out.

'Have you actually seen this ring yet, Office?'

'Yeah.'

'And?'

'I'm no jeweller, Andy. But it looks fucking fabulous to me. Never seen anything like it.'

'Well. The brothers are very interested but only if it's the real thing.'

'There's no doubt about that.'

'I've been down the library today –'

'Bloody hell, And. Didn't know you could read.'

'– Looking at pictures of this Eva Braun tart. And I turned up two more showing this ring. Are you sure, absolutely sure' – and here he gave me one of his hard looks, meant to be sinister, but I've seen every look in the book – 'that it's the ring in the photographs?'

'Absolutely fucking certain.'

'You understand that if it turns out to be paste we get our money back, plus expenses, or . . .'

He didn't have to go on. Now it was my turn for the look. Cold as that fucking canal freezing out the back. 'Andy. How long have you known me? I've been around a long time. I do all right – and I know my place. I don't fuck with the Sanchez brothers. I want to keep my bollocks.

'I said I'm no jeweller, but I can tell paste from stones. I know quality. You've seen me walk away from a dozen chances. I wouldn't be here if I wasn't certain.'

He was convinced. I could tell. That's the beauty of a track record. He licked his lips. 'I'll get us another drink.'

The deal was done. The set-up was this. I'd meet Black Andy here on the night before New Year's Eve. It'd be quiet. Everyone saving their dosh for the festivities of the next night. Andy would pass me the notes and leave. But wait in the car outside. When I had the ring I'd take it out to him in the car. Everything was sorted.

My plan was: I'd do the kid. Hand the ring over as arranged. Keep my share of the money. Get out.

I thought the kid would be pleased. He probably was. But all he did was nod his head. He was seeing America, I suppose.

'Now look, kid. I'm sticking my neck out for you. If you

don't come up with the goods we're both dead. These are big timers we've got involved. There's none bigger in this city.'

'You do not need to worry. I will be there with the ring.' He gives me a look. 'The merchandise. Once I have counted the money it will be yours. Thank you for your work. I hope you have negotiated a good commission for yourself.'

Cheeky little ponce. With his big words. Suddenly I don't feel sorry for him any more.

Christmas Day, and I changed my plan. I'd picked up this bird in the Locarno, Christmas Eve, and was shagging until dinnertime. Then all of a sudden she noticed the clock. 'Bloody hell! Me mum'll kill me if I'm not there for the turkey.' With that she had her knickers on and was away. I rolled a Chrissy joint, a great fat bastard, and got greedy.

This was the Big One. Of course it was. Everyone talked about the Big One. The one that will change everything; the retirement job. I knew it was a myth. Just something to keep the blokes going. Always thought I was too realistic to swallow it myself.

Then by the time the ads for summer holidays started on the telly, about teatime, I was saying to myself: This is the Big One. It could be. It is. It's just tumbled into your lap, son. A gift from Santa. And I laughed. Go for it. Go for it all. You'd be a prat not to. It was then, watching the ads for holidays in Spain and Portugal which punctuated *The Great Escape*, that I decided. OK. I'll go for the whole fucking lot. All the money. The ring. And piss off for ever. I'd do the kid in the toilet. Out through the fire exit. Along the towpath. Have a motor by the bridge half a mile up the water. And away.

The festivities were over. There was that lull, dead time, before New Year's Eve. I decided to use a knife. Planned it meticulously. Wondered if the kid knew that word.

When the time came, there I was.

Standing here. Right here, where I can see the stairs. First down is Black Andy. Immaculate as ever. 'Have a good Christmas, Office?' he smirks.

'Quiet, And. How about you?'

'Quiet.'

We're both on shorts. Mine a whiskey mac to keep out the cold. Andy, a rum and black. A couple of drinks and a bit of football talk, when he says, 'Couldn't get your pressie round for the big day. But here it is.' And he pulls this thick package, all shiny and glittery with little snowmen on it, out of his overcoat pocket. 'Happy Christmas, Office. This is from the family.'

'Cheers, Andy. I've got yours, but I'll have to give it to you later.'

'I'm lookin forward to it.' He finishes his drink and pushes off. 'See you later, mate.'

The kid isn't late. I knew he wouldn't be. I see the boots first, trudging down the steps, then the overcoat, the red scarf. It's started snowing. A few flakes are melting on his hair and shoulders. He spots me straight away.

I buy him a beer. He seems as nervous as fuck, but I know him a bit better by now. 'Have you got it?'

'Of course.'

'We'll have a bit of a drink. Then, as before – the bog.'

'That was my idea too.' He takes the tiniest mouthful of beer. 'Did you enjoy Christmas?' he asks.

'Quiet. You?'

'It was quiet for me too. I am alone and without money. But it was the last Christmas that will be this way. Next year I will be in America.'

'Why d'you want to go to America so much?'

'It is a great land. Free. I am a musician. I will join a band and become a rock star.'

So that was it. The dream that had dragged him out of his land. Led him to do whatever he had to do to get the ring, to get here. Dreams. Dangerous things.

He takes a swig of his beer. A surprisingly long one. Empties half the glass.

'Thirsty?'

He smiles, which is something I haven't seen him do much before. He looks even younger. 'No. It is part to celebrate, and part to give me the courage of the Dutch. In a minute I will sell what has been in my family all my life. Our secret. Our security.' He notices my look. 'Do not be afraid. I will do it. But it will be my final betrayal. I drink to my treason. I hope one day I will be able to make amends.' He takes another swig, which empties the glass. He's still reading my look. 'Do not look so worried. I will give up the ring readily. It is the price. I will pay it.' He shuffles on his seat. 'I will go to piss now. Really. I need to piss.'

I nod. 'I'll give you a minute. Go into the lock-up when you've finished – but don't bolt the door. I'll be in soon.'

He turns and marches off across the bar. The little soldier. This is it. The beautiful adrenaline starts to flow, glow through me. He pushes open the door unsteadily.

Slowly I count to twelve, like the twelve days of Christmas. Then action. Swiftly to the door. In the lobby I kick the tatty Christmas tree away from the fire exit, my hand reaching into my jacket for the knife taped inside.

Knife in hand, I boot open the bog door. The kid is still pissing. One leap and I'm on him. Grab his head, yanking it into the crux of my shoulder, exposing the full throat, twisted back. His hands reach for mine and his cock springs upwards, piss shooting into my face. I tug his head further back, pulling him up on tiptoe. Lower my own head into his neck to avoid the splash and plunge the knife into the centre of the throat. The gush of blood splatters like rain against the ceiling. In a stroke I push the knife left towards the ear then drag it back right. Grab the hair back, and the throat opens up with a gurgle. I hear cords tearing apart. I let go. The kid flops down like a puppet. I skim him over. Go for the pockets. Fuck. Nothing. Check again. Fuck. Then I see it. A plaster at the base of his dripping cock, like a garden hose still seeping water. I rip it off. And there it is. Eva's sparkler. Slip it inside my jacket and I'm away.

I shoulder-charge the fire escape. The doors flap open easily and I'm out into the freezing darkness. The reflected lights of factories and high-rise flats twinkle dismally in the black canal. The cold air filling the lungs is a treat. Out. And now to the motor.

Near the bridge the shape of a bush at the side of the towpath suddenly expands into a suit. Just a suit. Then a mouth opens. Black Andy. Sneering. 'Silly boy, Office. Very silly boy.' I sense, more than see, another figure behind me. Then hear his breathing. I'm transfixed by the small glint of the gun in Andy's hand. Waist level. He hasn't even bothered to raise it.

So this is it, I think. The Big One. This is the end of the story. And I realize that always in a life such as mine there is the knowledge that this might be the way it ends.

'The ring!' Andy mutters. 'That's right.' A touch of Christmas glitter on the package catches the light reflected on the canal and sparkles briefly, before disappearing into Andy's coat. 'Now the money.' Then, 'Good boy,' as I hand it over. 'Now. Turn round.' Just like a film. I turn, thinking of the firm courage of the little soldier. Scared. Yeah. But they won't know it. No noise. No shaking or twitching. No begging. I am pleased with myself.

I don't recognize the other guy. See his gun. Fuck. Back? Front? Both together. That's simultaneous. Wonder if the kid knew that word.

Head. I feel the small nudge of the barrel touch my neck,

just below the skull. Then Andy leans close and whispers in my ear. 'Walk. We're going back.'

Inside the bog the kid lies red and mangled on the floor. 'Now. Don't be a stupid fucker twice, Office. This is your job. Not a word.'

'I'll get you for this, Andy. That's a promise.' I can see Fat Alex shuffling up behind him, keys jangling from his fist. And you, you bastard, I think. The door bangs shut, and I hear a key turn in the lock.

For half an hour I am alone with my handiwork. The kid's body was curled, knees up. The head, almost off, faces the door. Eyes open, but no longer watery. Hard and glazed like boiled sweets. A small stream of blood still trickles into the urinal. Splatters of blood across his face have hardened into rusty scabs. I smash the lights so I don't have to look at him. Sit in the lock-up, eating fags, listening to the hiss of the urinals. Knowing he is lying there. And smelling the stink. The astringent combination of piss and disinfectant. And, rising above it, clawing its way into my churning belly, the metallic odour of fresh blood.

Then the key turns again: this time it's the filth.

Life sentence, of course. Served sixteen. And now I'm back. Back to the scene.

I make my way to the bar. There's an Asian lad serving now. Scar down the side of his face. Order another pint. He knows who I am. 'It's on Alex,' he says tersely, as I reach for my pocket.

I'm bursting for a piss. This is the moment. I can't put it off. I go back in there, or I piss myself here in the bar. Just for a second, as I make my way, I see him, the nervous little fucker, standing hunched over his untouched beer at the bar. Just for a second. The blink of an eye.

It's the same stinking hole. Graffiti on the walls. That's new. Jesus! There's still some Blues fans left. Everything else is the same. The piss streams out of me. Relief. I'm back. Back in Little Moscow. Of course, I've returned here many times in the last sixteen years. I've been a good lad. Kept my nose clean. Gone to psychology sessions, talked to the God Squad, repented my crime. It's the only way to get parole. In my bunk at night I've relived it – time and again. I put my dick away. Turn and take a proper look. I stoop down. It was here. Touch the tiles. Trace my finger across them. This is where he lay. This is where his feet would've been when I pulled him up onto his toes.

I'm sorry, kid. Sorry it was you. Inside, sometimes, when I was watching telly and something in America came on, or a rock band full of young kids, I'd think of you. And I dreamed about you. We are here. We go into the lock-up. You open a wooden box. 'Here's the ring,' you say. 'Eva's ring.' And it's there all right. I can see it sparkling in the darkness. But as I reach for it, it's still on a charred finger. I feel the hard, burnt flesh and I recoil. You start to laugh, a real belly laugh. Throw back your head. And your throat opens up.

I trace the tiles again. This is the place you died. Where I killed you. Sorry, kid.

Close my eyes. See it again. How many times have I seen it? Felt my head push against his neck. The give of flesh beneath the blade. The tension in his bony body, then its collapse. Like when a woman yields in your arms.

And how many times have I wanted to do it again? Wanted to. Do it again. And again. Once is not enough.

I stand up. My chest is sore where the shooter chafed it as I stooped. It's time for my chat with that fat bastard Alex. Alex the Key.

The door swings open right in front of me. Black Andy. And behind him, just like before, Fat Alex.

'Hello, Office. We must stop meeting like this.'

Doctor's Orders

Judith Cutler

Meena Sangra twisted and tugged at the bright new gold ring. It was too tight to let her scratch the rash developing underneath. But there wasn't time to worry about that. She stooped for another attack on the piles of newspapers. The binder tape cut into yesterday's blisters.

There. The last pile in place, ready for the paperboy. Poor little thing: he didn't look strong enough to carry such a load. And he was so well-spoken: she could understand his accent, at least, and he always made sure his nouns agreed with his verbs. She could trust his personal pronouns, too. So many of the people here in Smethwick seemed to find them difficult. 'Us are off down the market,' for instance: what did they mean by that? Her father would never have permitted such sloppiness. He had learned English from a teacher straight from England: he had the purest vowels, the most clipped enunciation, of all their acquaintance. He regretted deeply that even the good girls' school his daughter had attended had English teachers who were not UK-born – time and again he would mock her accent when she drove with him on his rounds in the old Morris. Meena swallowed hard. Half of her was glad that he wasn't alive to see to what depths she had been brought; half resented his early death, which had reduced her to this.

Putting her hand to the small of her back, she straightened. Five past six. Vinod would be expecting his tea by now. And her mother-in-law must be bathed and dressed. Although the routine was less than a week old, it irked already.

Oh, my daughter, that you should have come to this, she heard her father lamenting.

She looked down at the ring. In England, Father had told her, the Christians used to marry 'for better, for worse, for richer, for poorer'. Neither her Hindu nor her civil marriage ceremony had used those precise words, but she understood them very clearly on this cold wet morning. The words 'worse' and 'poorer' had the heaviest weight.

The marriage broker had given her mother to understand that Vinod was a rich businessman. He'd shown her photographs of the home she was to expect, a spacious five-bedroomed house in the Birmingham suburb of Harborne. 'Very, very fine,' he'd insisted. 'A big wide road, lined with trees. The houses have such big gardens, front and back, that you cannot hear the big cars as they rush back and forth. And Mr Sangra has a fine car: look, there it is, in front of the garage. Neighbours? Oh, millionaires to a man. You have to be to live on Lordswood Road.'

Her dying mother was happy to take the broker at his word. And however independent Meena had wanted to be, life in India as a woman not quite young any more, with no family to support her, seemed less attractive than a traditional marriage. In her rush to escape the empty family home, Meena had even agreed to get together a dowry. The broker insisted that it was still the norm for decent Hindu women in England, whatever the law in India might be. What were a few hundred pounds, anyway? Even as she started to realize her capital, she heard her father say, as clearly as if he'd been at her shoulder, *Keep something in reserve, my child.* So she would not sell, but insisted on renting out the old family house. And before she handed the keys over, she took a spade and dug as deep as she could, so deep that no monsoon flood would wash away the earth, and no drought make cracks deep enough to show what she had buried. One day her new husband might be grateful for her forethought.

'Meena! Where are you? Come here at once!'

'Coming, Mother-in-law!' She ran upstairs to the best bedroom, recoiling at the smell of old woman and old woman's urine. Perhaps she would get used to it. Her father had got used to unpleasant smells. He'd conducted post-mortems on the long dead, so that one day he could become not just a family doctor but a famous pathologist. He'd come home stinking of the morgue: Meena could almost smell him now. But instead she gagged at the old woman and her chamber pot, and had to dress the former and empty the latter. *There, Father, you'd be pleased I got those right.*

The old woman was fat and arthritic. It didn't take her father to diagnose that. But he'd made himself unpopular among fat, arthritic old ladies by telling them that the best way to deal with their aches and pains was to get up and walk to market, as fast as they could. Lying in bed made them worse, he'd insisted. Mother-in-law had sniffed when Meena had relayed the advice, clear as if her father had spoken it from beyond the grave.

'Walk to market?' she'd repeated in disbelief. 'That's what you're here for: to run to the market.'

Or at least to the shops. Smethwick was well provided with shops selling familiar food: vegetables and spices lit up the eyes and nose with their freshness. She loved shopping. Even when the cold rain drenched down, she could bury her nose in a box full of methi and imagine herself at home. And there were shops selling cosmetics and saris to dazzle the eye and empty the purse. Not that her purse had much in it. It seemed it was the custom in Smethwick for men to dole out housekeeping money a coin or two at a time. She'd have to ask Vinod when she wanted more clothes. It seemed she even had to ask him when she wanted a simple walk along the High Street to Smethwick Library. For they were not living in a house on Lordswood Road, Harborne. Not yet. They were living at the back of their shop. And when she asked him when they were moving to the house in the glossy colour photographs, he hit her. Not very hard. There was no bruise to show on her cheek, but she needed mouthwash for the ulcers that came up. Ask Vinod for extra money? Thank goodness for her father's voice, telling her that ordinary salt dissolved in hot water was as good as anything she could buy from a pharmacist.

When she got used to English money, Vinod told her to make herself useful in the shop. She obeyed. Despite her efforts, it was clear he preferred to keep an eye on her. But one day Mother-in-law had an appointment with the doctor and needed Vinod to drive her. No, the car wasn't the gleaming Jaguar in the photo. To be fair, it wasn't an old Morris, either, but something in between. An Orion, that was it. Blue, with a scrape along one side.

'The girl comes with me!' Mother-in-law had insisted. 'Someone has to help me undress.'

Visibly Vinod agonized: Mother or making money? The latter won. *See, Father – I haven't forgotten.*

She still had difficulty distinguishing what the locals said. Everyone had the same whining gabble, whether it was the old white men coming in, whippets at heels, for a couple of ounces of rough tobacco, or the proud Sikh women with more bright Indian gold than she'd seen outside a jeweller's shop. It was one of the old men who asked her, 'Wor'appened to the other one, me love?'

'Other one?' she repeated.

'Ah. The other wench. Not so old as you, but not so pretty, neither. Worked here nigh on a year, dae her, Tom?' He addressed another old man, his upper lip stained by the snuff she now sold him. 'Ah. Then her went away.'

Meena smiled politely, but for the first time wished her husband were here beside her, if only to translate. 'Wench?' she ventured.

The first man slapped his thigh. 'Yow doe half talk funny. Like them folk at the BBC.'

'Wench,' his friend put in with a helpful smile. 'Someone like yourself as might be. And her was here for a bit, and then her went away. Go back to Pakistan, did she?'

Pakistan? What were they talking about? If only they would speak English! It was best to smile as she took their money and carefully counted the right change and say, 'I'm afraid I've no idea. You would have to ask my husband about this wench.'

The old men exchanged a glance. She'd no idea why, no clue what it meant. But the incident made her uneasy.

Mother-in-law was in a terrible mood when she came home. As Meena bent to ease off her sandals for her, a huge clout knocked her off balance. 'You and your exercise! So much for you and your exercise!'

Meena couldn't understand why she was being blamed. But she knew her ear was ringing, and that the wrist that she'd landed on was already swelling. A cold cloth, wrapped tight. That's best for a sprain, her father told her. So she gathered herself up and headed for the sink.

'Where do you think you're going? You pauper: a slut with a dowry your size, and you think you can go where you want? Come back here!' Mother-in-law's voice thundered round the small room.

'I've hurt my wrist, Mother-in-law.'

'Poor girl. Come here, let me see!' The old woman sounded contrite.

Meena approached, squatting, as before, at her feet. As she laid the damaged hand in the old woman's there was another vicious hammer-blow, this time to the other ear.

By now Meena was crying – shock, pain, anger. Vinod must hear of this. She stumbled into the shop. Vinod was stacking shelves. There was no one else to be seen. By now the pain in her wrist was so bad she knew she had broken a bone. She ought to find a doctor. She blurted it all out to Vinod, who carried on methodically placing one tin of cat food on another, just as if she didn't exist.

When the shelf was complete, he turned to her, and boxed both ears. 'You think my customers want to hear my wife snivelling and wailing like a mad woman? You think that's the way to make my customers happy so that they buy and we can have that house on Lordswood Road, Harborne? You think that? Let me tell you, wife, a woman who wants medical treatment will have to come up with more dowry. Let me assure you of that.'

'But there's the Health Service. It's all free!'

'Not dentists!' And he slapped her so hard across the mouth that she could swear her teeth moved in their sockets.

Thirty minutes? an hour? passed. She'd lost track of time. Huddled on the bed, she rocked herself backwards and forwards like a sick child. She didn't know which part of her body hurt the most. Sick, dizzy, and bleeding where he'd taken her by force, she wept for her father, and the books he'd read aloud to her when she had a fever he couldn't cure or a sorrow he couldn't soothe away. Cinderella, that was who she felt like. With her family already calling for their supper.

Grabbing a tea towel, she bound the throbbing, swollen wrist as tightly as she dared. Keeping it tucked as far from their eyes as she could, she picked over dhal and peeled garlic with as little movement as she could manage. She managed to press the chapattis into a semblance of a decent size and thickness. But when she came to lift the big heavy frying pan, she had to admit defeat. Tonight she would have to use one of the lightweight saucepans her mother-in-law despised. Once they had been non-stick, but Mother-in-law insisted on the vigorous use of scouring pads.

As she fried onions and added pinches of dhania and jeera, she tried to blot out what was happening. But it was all too clear. She'd read of countless women who had disappeared after marriages. Sometimes the pitiful remains of their poor charred bodies were found. Sometimes they were not. And it was clear that the police turned the blindest of eyes. Who'd ever heard of the husband or mother-in-law being brought to justice? Not in the whole of India, so far as she knew. Some women did contrive a risky escape: they told of beatings and cruelty like her own. Worse. It was the dowry their husbands wanted, the dowry and a domestic slave. And the police shook their heads in disbelief that their families should have so blatantly broken the law by handing over a dowry in the first place. If the Indian police were so unsympathetic, what could she hope for from these strange English people whose accents she could not penetrate and who didn't even know their personal pronouns?

No, it was to herself that she must look for salvation. Back home she had a house, after all, and the cache buried deep in the herb garden. But that was thousands of miles and an expensive air ticket away. Somehow, somehow, she must save odd pennies of change from her shopping, and hide them until she had enough. Months? Years? Who knew how long it would take?

Keep a low profile, daughter, her father said over her shoulder.

*

After three weeks, she had saved two pound coins and seventy-three pence. And gained a fresh black eye. The blue and purple marks on her wrist had subsided to greyish yellow smears. She was learning how to deal with the nightly rapes, using the breathing system her father had recommended for women in labour too poor for the painkillers they needed. She would smile and scrape before her mother-in-law, and flatter her husband. But she knew that she might as well have been nice to tigers. All the good meals and subservience in the world wouldn't stop them turning on her when the mood took them.

One Tuesday it did.

She was in the shop, stacking packets of cigarettes behind the counter. Vinod was dealing with Lottery tickets. Not daring to turn round, she recognized the voice of the man with the whippet. Quickly, silently, she passed Vinod the tobacco he'd want.

Vinod might not have registered her efficiency; the old man did.

'Ah, you'm got a good wench there, mate. I was asking her the other day, what happened to the other one? Where's she gone? Back to Pakistan?'

Vinod said dismissively, 'Oh, that young cousin of mine. She's gone back to India. To get married. Very hard-working girl.'

He was talking too fast. Meena knew there was something wrong.

'No better than this wench here. You know how to pick them, all right, Mr Patel. I'll say that for you.'

Vinod barely waited till the door had pinged shut before he gabbled, 'Ah! These stupid old men. Calling us all Pakistanis, and all Mr Patel.'

Appease, appease! Meena clicked her tongue in disapproval, as was expected, and continued with the cigarettes. She did not want to talk, after all. She wanted to think. So 'wench' meant 'woman'. And as far as she could recall, there'd been no mention in the broker's report about any dependent cousins working in the Sangra business empire. No respectable bachelor would have an unmarried female in his household, not without a wife to chaperone her. Even his mother would not do. Almost absent-mindedly, she scratched the rash on her ring finger.

She wasn't surprised when Vinod made a swift excuse and left the shop. He was going to speak to his mother. He was going to make sure they told the same story.

Meena took especial trouble with the meals that day: they could have no complaints there. She tried to ask Vinod sensible questions – even suggested, very tentatively, that they might free up floor space in the shop by storing stuff in the cellar.

'Damp,' he said, as quickly as he'd dismissed the old man.

Soon the tigers decided to strike. At least the old one did.

Meena was kneeling at her feet, cutting her toenails. The nails were thick, twisted into strange shapes. The scissors were clearly inadequate: they needed the sort of strong clippers her father had used on his mother's feet, so long ago she'd almost forgotten. Perhaps a momentary lapse in concentration was to blame. She had pulled on a nail and hurt the old woman. The yells brought Vinod dashing up. Before she knew it, she was on her knees, and Vinod was unbuckling his belt.

When she recovered consciousness she was in pitch darkness. For a moment she thought she'd died. For another, longer moment, she wished she had.

Use your wits, my child, her father told her. *Come on: think! Where are you?*

Rolling onto her knees, she made her fingers explore.

Small square tiles – the sort they had in the kitchen. If she crawled slowly forward, she might find – yes, a wall. Systematically working round, she found steps, and the rough wood of a door. No, not dead. Just locked in the cellar. She hauled herself up so that she could sit on the bottom step. Quickly she lay down again. It wasn't just the pain, though she was afraid of fainting again. It was the fear of Vinod finding her somewhere he hadn't thrown her.

Deep breaths. That was it. The sort she still had to practise at night. But something else seeped through the fog of her mind. A smell.

Of course there was a smell. Vinod had explained only a few hours ago that it was damp.

Her father might have been holding her hand: *My child, this is why we have to work quickly. That smell means someone is dead under there.*

There had been an earthquake – just a small one, not terrible enough to bring the world's press in – and she and her father had been among those struggling to claw out the living before they too started to give off that strange sweet smell. The same sweet smell she was breathing in now. That first time, with her father, she'd managed not to vomit. Now, holding her nose, breathing through her mouth, she might manage again. She knew it was vital – yes, Father, literally a matter of life and death – that she betray no hint to Vinod or his mother that she suspected something – someone – might be buried in the cellar.

Next time Vinod took Mother-in-law to the doctor, Meena bribed the paperboy to watch the shop and dashed down to the cellar, taking a lantern torch out of stock. Yes! The red quarry tiles were very slightly disarranged, over in the far corner. Half of her wanted to lift one to see if what she feared was correct. The other half feared dirt under the fingernails. She fled back upstairs.

As soon as the shop was empty, she prised some money from the Air Ambulance collecting box and replenished the till.

When a florid card invited them to a family wedding in Leicester, Meena wondered briefly if they would want her presentable enough to take with them, and that for a week she might be spared any beatings. For a day or so it seemed she might be right. But then the old woman's arthritis flared up: she would have to stay behind. And it didn't take Father's whisper in her ear to tell Meena that she would have to stay behind to look after her. Well, a night without Vinod's attentions would be a bonus, even if the old woman would be sulky and vicious-tempered at missing the celebrations.

Once the old woman was snoring, Meena crept down to the cellar. No, she was crazy. She couldn't believe it. Of course she could smell damp.

Damp, yes – and something else. You know what that something else is! Courage, my daughter: evidence – that's what the English police will want.

Meena nodded. Even the Indian police wouldn't argue with a body in a cellar.

Yes, there was a scrap of cotton: her predecessor had been reduced to the cheapest of saris. And a skein of long black hair. Poor woman. Meena didn't want to see any more.

Oh, you coward! You think the police will take the word of an Indian woman without a bone or two to show them?

The thought made her gag. She was concentrating so hard on not vomiting, she didn't hear the door creak open.

'You bitch! You interfering bitch! Well, there's no help for it now! You'll have to stay down here till Vinod comes back. He'll know what do!'

No. Meena wasn't going to stay in the cellar with only a half-exposed skull for company. She hurtled towards the old woman, who stepped back so quickly she lost her footing. There was a dreadful thud as her head hit the step. She slithered down, little by little. Meena was paralysed. She could hear the breath rattling in Mother-in-law's throat; she knew she was dying.

She ought to call an ambulance. The police. She knew she ought. And show them the hair and the sari. But what if they thought she'd killed the old woman? Vinod would certainly swear she had. Blindly, desperately, she pulled up more tiles, dashing into the kitchen for a knife to slice aside the damp earth. Scrabbling, dragging, at long last she got the old woman into the grave only just deep enough for her bulk. The earth she'd displaced? Thank God it was still night, and she could sprinkle it over the back yard, under the old TV and carpet Vinod had dumped there. As her hands and body toiled, her brain tried to work out what to do next.

If she robbed the till and fled, Vinod would set the police on her. There was no doubt about that. And she knew they'd soon find an errant woman. Interpol. The Indian police. She'd be hounded down and imprisoned for life.

Well, was that any worse than what she'd suffered recently?

Meena washed and dressed very carefully. There was no telltale earth under her fingernails. If she looked tired and pale when she opened the shop for the paperboy on Sunday morning, no one would be surprised. The customers were used to averting their eyes from her bruised arms and swollen face. In fact, the shop did its usual brisk business, the whippet man buying extra tobacco to celebrate his birthday. To his amazement, she pressed an extra packet on him.

When Vinod returned, still bleary though it was after midday, she was ready for him. Bringing tea as he took his place – still in his best clothes – at the till, she asked polite questions about the wedding, and replied indifferently to his questions about his mother. It was gone three when he decided he ought to see her.

Meena locked the shop and flicked over the Closed sign. The people of Smethwick would just have to wonder why they'd packed up so early.

Vinod was calling and calling, both for his mother and – now – for Meena. She went to the cellar head to wait for him. She had both the lantern torch and the heavy frying pan in her hands.

Keep your voice steady, daughter. Remember, you have to win this argument. Put down that pan. Right out of sight. Your only weapon must be your brain.

She returned the pan to the kitchen.

'So where the hell is she?' Vinod shook her.

'If you calm down I'll show you.' She stood back deferentially to let him go first: he'd see nothing sinister in that.

He stood on the step below her. Yes, with that pan she could have smashed his skull quite easily – are you sure you're right, Father? 'Your mother's down there.' She pointed with the beam of light from the torch. But she pointed to the corner where the young woman was buried. 'Oh, no. I've got it wrong. That's where the other body is, isn't it? No, I wouldn't advise touching me. Or you might well join them.' She pressed a finger into his back. Just as they did in films. Just as they did in films, he believed it was a knife. He raised his hands. 'Be quiet and listen. I have enough evidence to have you taken to prison.'

'But Mother – you've killed her!'

'In fact she had a heart attack or something. But it might take time for the pathologist to find that out. Stand still, I tell you.' She drove in her fingernail more firmly. 'I shall be leaving England as soon as I can get a flight. To pay for the flight I need money from you.'

He was ready to turn and bluster. She pressed harder.

'You don't deserve it, but I'm offering you a chance. What is a thousand pounds, five thousand pounds, to spare yourself prison? You'll buy two tickets, in fact, one for me, one for your mother. Different flights, I think. That should buy you a little time. The only time you'll ever hear from me is if I learn you've remarried. Yes, Vinod, you've got to stay here in Smethwick for the rest of your life. No more wives, no more dowries, no more dreams about Lordswood Road, Harborne.'

'But –'

'Is it a deal, Vinod? Because, frankly, if it isn't, I don't reckon much for your chances. Not if the police find you locked in here with the bodies of two dead women.' Another fingernail stab. 'Down the steps.'

It didn't take him long to agree. While he whimpered and snuffled in darkness, she used his credit card to book tickets. She raided the till for cash and slipped out to buy a new sari and travel bag.

She toyed with leaving him in darkness for ever, but it would look better if the street saw him waving her off in an A1 taxi. The club class flight was comfortable. The pounds sterling she flourished were quite enough to compensate the people who'd been renting her house. She dug at her leisure. In time, she acquired a new passport under a new name, and then a visa for the States.

She was waiting for the taxi to take her to the airport when she heard her father's voice again. *My child, this is your last chance. Write that letter to the English police now.*

'But what about our bargain? I promised I wouldn't split,' she replied.

And after all he did to you, my daughter, you think you're bound by a promise?

Obedient as always, she reached for pen and paper.

Means to an End

Claire Thomas

At first I was just so relieved to find somewhere to stay that I didn't consider the risks I might be taking; but now I was here I was having second thoughts.

I'd been walking for ages, so when I met this girl she was like my guardian angel. She seemed friendly enough, and keen to take me under her wing. Maybe she could see how vulnerable I was and took pity on me? Or maybe she just thought I looked desperate enough to believe that she wasn't the washed out drug addict and prostitute that she looked so much like? Either way, I was too tired and too cold to care.

'You can put your bag down there if you want, but make sure you don't leave any money in it!'

It seemed like a weird thing to say, but I did it anyway. I shoved my rucksack under the table, but took my purse out the side pocket first. Not that I had much money left; the train fare to Birmingham had just about cleaned me out. I was beginning to feel like coming here was a big mistake; this place was awful, and I couldn't breathe through my nose for fear of heaving. It stank of piss mixed with puke; God knows where it was coming from.

The girl was stood at the doorway staring at me. My expression must've been transparent, giving away my thoughts, because she shook her head and said, 'What the fuck are you doing here?'

How could I answer that? She was the first person to ask me, and even after racking my brains for three hours on the train I still hadn't come up with a cover story. I'd figured out what my name was going to be, but other than that . . .

'You runnin away from summat or what?' Her face was stern and questioning.

Think, think . . . Why am I here? 'Yeah, erm, I got in a bit of trouble . . .' My voice trailed off and before I could finish my sentence she turned and left the room, obviously satisfied that I was suitable: the inquisition was over.

My shoulders sagged and the butterflies in my stomach came back as I thought about where I was and what I'd done. How would I survive somewhere like this and be able to get on my with my life? One thing was for sure, I couldn't tell her the truth. She'd probably been doing this kind of thing for years and, compared to her life, my problems would seem so insignificant. She'd just tell me to smoke some heroin, chase the dragon, cook up – it makes everything better; that's what they say, isn't it?

Whatever it was, it was something I'd never experienced before.

My old life was over. I had to accept that, otherwise I wasn't going to last long. This damp, stinking bedsit was my new home and that skinny, pale prostitute downstairs was my new room-mate. I felt sick.

I left the room and walked down the narrow landing. It felt like the walls were closing in on me and I tried to make myself smaller so that nothing could touch me. The stench became even worse as I got closer to a door halfway down the landing, so strong my eyes smarted. The door, which was partly open, had a sign sellotaped to it: 'Keep Out!'

scrawled in childish writing. Intrigued, I reached out and pushed it, very gently . . .

A single bulb hung precariously from the ceiling. A thick, grey smog swirled and, as I inhaled, I felt it fill my chest and wrap around my lungs. Two people were lying on a mattress in the middle of the room. I could hear grunting as the one on top moved up and down. Through the fug I could make out a large, balding man, fully clothed, apart from his trousers round his knees. He was on top of a girl with long black hair. Her hands weren't wrapped around his body, as you might expect them to be if they were in the 'throes of passion'. In fact, all I could see of her was her head, which was turned to the side, towards me. Her expression was blank, lifeless. As he writhed around, my insides tightened and a deep sense of guilt and shame filled my stomach. I wanted to turn and leave, but I was rooted to the spot, completely frozen. Had she seen me? I couldn't be sure. It was obvious that he hadn't, he was too engrossed in satisfying his urges. But she was looking straight at me.

One final, exhausted grunt and then he collapsed onto her. I stood breathless in the hallway, and in a few moments an overweight, middle-aged man came down the stairs towards me. His face was flushed and he mopped the sweat from his forehead with a large handkerchief. He smiled nervously at me, even more uncomfortable about being here than I was. I lowered my gaze; I couldn't stand to look at him knowing that he must be thinking I was one of them, maybe his next choice. I felt dirty: this 'respectable' businessman, with his shabby navy suit and briefcase, was old enough to be my grandfather! He hurried past me and out of the front door.

Who was I trying to kid? I couldn't do this. I could never have someone like him on top of me, no matter how much

I needed the money; I'd rather die first. There had to be another way. I was about to go back upstairs to get my rucksack when the pale girl from earlier came out of a doorway to the side of me.

'Has he gone?' I nodded. 'Dirty old fucker! Has Becky come down yet?' I shook my head, presuming that Becky must be the dark-haired girl. 'I better check she's OK.'

She pushed past and for a second I saw concern in her eyes. I followed her upstairs, back to the room. I heard her gasp as she walked in. 'Jesus Christ, Becky! Why the fuck do you let him do it to you?'

As I entered the room, I stopped dead in my tracks. Becky, the girl who'd been lying underneath that fat man, was on her back, naked. I could see her clearly now, she was fragile like a bird. Her limbs were so thin and bony it looked as if her elbows and knees might break through the skin. She had the smooth face of a teenage girl and the body of a wasted forty-year-old. The other girl approached her and knelt on the mattress, scooping her up into her arms, trying to sit her upright, but Becky was floppy and kept sliding down.

'What did he make you do this time?' She was shouting 'Did you take anything?' She squeezed Becky's cheeks, trying to look in her mouth. 'Did you? Becky, did he make you take stuff?' I could hear panic in her voice and my heart beat faster and faster as I realized that something was really wrong.

Becky hadn't responded to us at all. She was lifeless, and her head rolled from side to side like a rag doll as the other girl began to shake her.

'Shit, shit! Go and get help!' This was directed at me, but I didn't know where to go or who to go to. So I knelt down next to the girl on the mattress and tried to help.

'Is she breathing?' I asked, surprised at how steady my voice sounded.

'I don't know, I can't tell!' She was frantic now, and I knew I had to take charge.

I took hold of Becky's wrists and tried to feel for a pulse, but there was a heartbeat pounding so loudly in my ears that I couldn't tell whether it was hers or mine.

'Lie her on her side, quickly, and tip her chin up to clear her airway.' The girl looked shocked at hearing my instructions but didn't question me; she just did what I said. I rested my hand against Becky's chest but still couldn't feel her breathing. 'I think she's dead!'

The other girl whimpered and began shaking Becky violently by her shoulders. Becky's dark hair was flying about wildly; her eyes were rolling in her head.

Then, suddenly, she let go of Becky and ran from the room. I was left alone.

Looking down at this broken body I saw a trickle of syrupy blood creeping from one of her nostrils. When I looked more closely, her lips were tinged blue and dark circles were forming around her neck. The mattress felt damp. Was it soaked with her blood, or had she been so terrified she'd pissed herself? It was so stained I couldn't tell. Her jeans were twisted around her left ankle and there was blood on her thighs. She was dead all right, probably had been for a while. Had the fat old man known that? Had he meant to kill her? Was that his sick urge? Or maybe he hadn't meant to strangle her, but had wanted the role-play to be so realistic that it had all gone horribly wrong? But then he'd done nothing to help her, nothing! Just left her lying there like a piece of meat, and now I was going to do the same.

I stood up, wiped my hands down the front of my top and left the room, quickly grabbing my rucksack from the other bedroom. I nearly fell down the stairs in my haste to get out of there. I didn't look back, not even to check if anyone saw me go. Head down, I walked up the dimly lit street, back to the train station, back to where I'd come from. I'd thought my problems were bad, but this, this was out of my league. Just one hour in a strange city had made me realize that it was too late for Becky and probably for the other girl too, but not too late for me.

Safe as Milk

Steve Bishop

What freaked me out when I came back from the hospital was how normal everything was. I thought that if I'd changed so much, then everything else must've done as well, but it hadn't. The same big suburban Moseley house shared between the five of us. They'd wedged a sheet of thick white polythene into the uPVC window frame so now it hung over the front door. There were crudely dribbled pictures and letters on it. A stick man waving and next to him a house and then a message. It said, 'Welcome Home Fatty.' There was my car, still sat in the drive, even the tyres hadn't gone flat. The honeysuckle still ran up the side gate and Steve's boxes of automotive junk still cluttered the garage doors. Andy saw me coming up the drive from the living room, came out and threw his arms around me.

He said, Welcome home, fella.

Then he patted me on the spare tyre that had grown around my middle while I was in there. – Looks like you're starting to live up to your name there, mate.

I laughed and said, Fuck off. It's the drugs they give you.

Then Steve and Bridget came out too and Steve said, Fucking hell, lardboy, what happened to you?

– It's the drugs, Andy told him.

– Living up to your name, then?

I told him we'd already got to there and he swung his arm and clicked his fingers to show his disappointment.

I don't know if they were all a little nervous of me or if it was just that I was on a comedown after finishing all my drugs courses, but everyone seemed like a caricature of themselves. It was like when I was thirteen and I realized what a string of clichés *The A Team* was. I'd done an acid trip at about four o'clock that afternoon so I could get to sleep later, but before I went out I had to sit with my family in a world that looked like it was made of really bad, but vividly coloured cardboard cutouts and pretend to eat a pile of bangers and mash. There was Hannibal and BA, shouting 'Let's get out of here!' and 'Your ass is mine, sucker!' and 'I pity the fool that tries to steal my van!' and all the rest of it. Then Bridget came and gave me a hug and the psychedelic sausage memory was gone.

– Welcome home, she said.

We went inside. My room. The Madonna and Child that my mum gave me on the bedside cabinet, the *Easy Rider* and *Hell's Angels on Wheels* posters and my karting trophies, more dust than usual, but all as I left it. I went in and looked around like it was someone else's room. The place belonged to some parallel universe version of me.

– So why haven't you got a bike if you're so into bikes, then?

I turned round. Behind me was one of the ugliest women I've ever seen. She was about four foot ten with no neck and a big wide head. Her skin was kind of grey and bobbly, like it was made of rubber and hadn't set properly.

– Dunno. Too dangerous I suppose.

– More like your mum told you not to.

– Nah.

– Gonna call me stumpy now? Most people do sooner or later.

– Why would I want to do that?

– Nothing. Never mind.

Andy appeared from his room and put his arm around this apparition. – You've already met Kate?

– Yeah, she thinks I'm too much of a coward to be a biker.

They both giggled and then went back into Andy's room across the hallway.

Downstairs, things were getting into a higher gear. There was already a fug of cooking food and heavily laden spliffs. Steve offered to cook for me. I sat at the breakfast bar watching him stir-fry vegetables, Dylan on the stereo, the late-evening sun's shadows through the steam, seemed like I was in exactly the same set of circumstances when I was a little kid, sometime in the late seventies.

– Met Andy's new chick, then?

– Yeah. What a weirdo.

– Like Miss Piggy took a few too many whacks from the ugly stick.

I threw my head back and laughed in a way I hadn't for more than a year probably.

The phone went. It was Jason and Carol. They wanted to know if we were going to the pub. I wasn't feeling up to it so Steve invited them round instead, and told them to bring an eighth and a crate of Stella as well. Tonight was the night. I was back with everyone, back into my life, making a new start. We had a stay-at-home party. By two a.m. there was just a lurch of pissed, stoned zombies sitting in the living room watching *Withnail and I*. Steve and Andy quoted from the film with the kind of accuracy that only comes from living like a student for way too long.

– We want the finest wines available to humanity, Steve bellowed across at Andy.

– We are multi-millionaires, Andy reciprocated.

It was like that all the way through. From 'His years at

Oxford, his sensitive crimes in a punt with a boy called Norman, whose books were stained with the butter-drips from crumpets,' right up to 'GET IN THE BACK OF THE VAN.'

– I always want to know what happens after the end of the film. This was Bridget missing the point.

– I'll tell you what happens, said Andy grimacing like Philip Marlowe as he pulled on a joint. – He wanders the earth as a lost soul, finally finding solace and redemption in inspiration, and, like, whatever bog sends

– Does he fuck

– Come on then, Stevie-boy, tell us what happens

– He descends into a spiral of alcoholism and despair, still mentally chasing rainbows and totally not getting anywhere

– That's what I said

– No, Andy, you went on some existentialist post-Freudian wank about

– It's from *A Clockwork Orange*

– I don't care if it's from bog's own ringpiece

– Who's bog? I wanted to know.

– Bog is something Andy's blown out of all proportion

– Bog is fate and serendipity combined. I think it's a true and pure romantic idyll

– It's in that bit where Little Alex clobbers the rest of them for rebelling against his authority

– Exactly, he takes his fate into his own hands

– Yeah and look where it got him

– That's just what bog sent him, bog is not a wrathful deity, like Blake's God the Father, bog is unseeing, unknowing. Bog has no agenda

– God, Andy, you're just making up excuses before you fuck something up because you know you're going to and if you come up with this crap first at least it won't have been your fault

– Fucking patronizing cunt!

I got ready to separate them but fortunately Andy was beer-drunk not whisky-drunk.

They argued like that for nearly an hour. The room became divided into post-Freudian romanticists (Andy) and pragmatists (everyone else) until everyone got too pissed and stoned to talk any more and that's when the JD and Coke came out. Steve took a swig then passed the bottle over to Bridget. As he did so he said, I went to market, and I got ripped to the tits on banana skins . . .

An old drinking game, a bastardized version of something that was dimly remembered from someone's adolescent summer camp in Maentwaerwrog that had become a thing to do when we got drunk together.

Bridget took a dainty sip and said, I went to market and I got ripped to the tits on banana skins and smoked your toenail clippings cos I thought they were crack . . .

She passed the bottle on to Jo, who took a man-sized slug and said, I went to market . . . did all that . . . an ah shagged your mum . . .

Andy seized the bottle and shouted at the ceiling, I shagged your mum, wiped my dick on the curtains and went back for more . . .

Then there was a bottle in my hand. I looked into it. The Virgin Mary stared up at me from the bottom of it. I went red.

– Come on, Fatty, your turn.

I took a deep breath, told myself that independence shows respect and said, Well I shagged your mum, came on her tits and told you it was mother's milk, and you believed me . . .

No one could top that. I was ashamed at their approval. I shuddered and felt cold – like someone had walked over my grave – and looked across the room. All I could pick out was Kate's face, staring at me, grinning like a gurning buffoon, like we were rock stars and she was our demented, obsessive fan. Then she noticed me looking and mistook it as a signal to come over and talk to me. She offered me a spliff and said, Me and Andy are going bowling tomorrow. D'you want to come?

– No thanks. She gave me the creeps. I wanted to get away, but everyone else was suddenly deep in conversation except Steve who was now comatose in the recovery position.

– I can see you don't trust me, she said, but that's cos I make you uncomfortable because you and your friends are so beautiful and I'm such a minger.

I pissed myself laughing but then I didn't know what to say. Later, I thought something like *Your candour is insulting* would've been a good line, but, you know, it was late and I was stoned so I let it go. She leaned in a little closer. She smelled heavily of booze and fags.

– Me and Andy, we've been playing a game.

– I've seen his collection of gas masks. Whatever it is, I don't want to know.

– It's nothing to do with sex.

– Oh yeah, I've used that one myself.

– No, really.

– OK, what is it?

She explained that Andy had devised it from his studies and it was part of his research toward his MA in psychotherapy. It started with free word association but quickly progressed into character descriptions of people you knew.

– OK then, let's give it a go. Here's one . . .

I did Andy, but she got who it was straight away.

– OK, try this one, I said. – It's someone I can always turn to with a problem, who always listens, never judges and always tries to put a positive slant on the situation whatever it is, and who's done loads of cool things.

– There's no one like that. It's impossible.

Suddenly my own piousness made me want to puke. Kate kept trying to guess who I was thinking of.

– It's someone close to you because you're totally not judging them.

I found myself looking around for people who it could be.

– You haven't got a girlfriend cos you told me that already.

Then a light went on inside her crusty noggin.

– I think Fatty's got a lovely big sister, she said.

– Actually, it's my dad. He's one of the Woodstock generation, a massive Dylan fan . . .

I was going to relate some new fiction about the summer retreats we'd had in the seventies to remote Wiltshire communes for 'spiritual realignment' but as soon as I said the word 'dad' her face clouded over and her plasticine brows knitted in a scowl. I could see a conversation about parental issues looming, so I made my excuses, said goodnight to everyone and crashed.

Next day the shadows were long by the time I got out of bed. I went into the kitchen to look for some Weetabix and there she was, frying bacon and eggs in Steve's white carpentry apron, looking like *The Evil Dead*'s answer to *Ready Steady Cook*.

– Andy'll be home soon, she said. – D'you want some as well?

I sat and waited for my plate of bacon and eggs. Somehow the conversation got round to girlfriends. Kate had a friend who she thought would be just right for me. I told her I wasn't interested in blind dates and she'd have to invite her to the house. Then Andy came in and she gave him a shifty look.

– What are you doing here?

– I've come to make it up to you. Here, I've cooked you some dinner.

Andy sat down opposite me without saying anything to her or looking at me. He seemed to be simmering with a silent rage. Kate behaved like a servant. She put his food on a plate and brought it to him. When she saw I'd finished, she took mine away and washed it up. I put the telly on to break the silence.

Andy said, Yes, telly, that's a good idea. I wonder if that *Desert Island* thingy's on. You know, what's it called? *King for a Day* or something.

Behind us, Kate dropped a plate. It didn't break, but she apologized, wiped it and put it back in the cupboard. Andy looked over at her, clenched a fist and sat tight. They must've had a domestic. It seemed such a contrast to how they'd been with each other last night. I'd never seen Andy like this. I wondered how long they'd been together.

Then he said, Some people are only fit to be eaten. Eaten. God, they don't deserve that. It's an honour to be eaten. Dogmeat is all they are.

Then he got up and went to his room.

After a few minutes, Kate showed me a photo of this girl. She was amazing. A blonde, but not in an obvious way. She was wearing a T-shirt and a sarong, drinking champagne on a beach with wooden sun shelters. Looked like Goa or somewhere.

I said, I don't normally do blind dates, but for her I'll make an exception.

I couldn't believe things were going to be that easy. I put it down to beginner's luck. It was going in at the deep end having a date so soon with such a gorgeous girl, but I thought, Fuck it, may as well do things in style. If it all goes wrong I've only wasted one evening. Still, I was nervous as hell when I picked her up. Her name was Mel, short for

Melissa. I decided to take her to a posh new international restaurant in Brindleyplace. She had very fair skin with a few light freckles that were all but covered with a layer of makeup thick enough to make her face seem like a flat surface, like an android. Like a blank space that the world had drawn its desires on. We walked up from the canal, past the Ikon into one of the squares. I told her about how I'd met Kate through a friend, and that I'd been working abroad for a few months. As the street opened out she pointed to a guy in the space underneath the arch in the Zen rock garden.

– Look over there. She gestured and spoke in a hushed tone. – I think that bloke's about to hit that girl.

I looked. The guy did look like a bit of a bruiser, leather jacket and glints off gold chains. I told Mel to wait while I walked along the opposite side of the square to the couple. As I came up level with them they started snogging. False alarm. I walked all the way back round the building and met her back at the entrance.

– No worries, I told her. – Just a badly timed PDA.

– PDA?

– Public display of affection. She thought this was funny. – They're big in Europe, I told her.

– Yeah, all those Italians. The men always grab your arse over there.

In Zinc, we got shown to a window seat, still chatting. She'd done some modelling a few years ago. All my first-night nerves were gone. I ordered some white wine and asked her how she knew Kate. They didn't seem like two people who'd have anything in common. This girl was so glam, Kate such a frump. I'd lucked out. The classic scenario: a gorgeous girl with the best mate who's a real munter.

– Kate tells me you're a biker. She moved the breadsticks as if to get a better view of me and smirked.

– No, not really. I'm just into the idea.

– Just a pretend biker? It's all right. I wouldn't go on one either.

I wanted to explain my thoughts about bikers representing personal freedom and being the last true outlaws and stuff, but realized I'd sound like Andy, all intense and analytical if I started off on that. It's weird. Important ideas are what I like to think about, but no one else is interested. Except Andy, and he's mad as a biscuit. The amount of girls I must've scared off by being like that in the past.

– So you're a model, then? I asked her.

– No, now I'm in PR.

– Handle anyone famous?

She thought this was funny too. – Yeah, one or two.

– Anyone I'd've heard of?

– Probably, yeah.

But now there was a string of zeds in her voice. I asked her about her ideal sort of job, if she went to the cinema, whether she thought flares would ever be anything more than student retro clothing. She came back to life and asked me what I did. The moment I'd been dreading.

– I design computer games.

I waited for her eyes to glaze, or a sudden change of subject if I was lucky.

– You're kidding! That's amazing! For a second the veneer of cool was gone. – What games have you done? *Driver*? *Colin McRea*? *Tony Hawke*? *Tekken*? I've got a PS2 but I'm getting bored of what's on there. I thought it was gonna change the way I look at games, but there's nothing really that you can't get on a PC these days.

– Yeah, true. I think things'll improve soon, but I'm more involved in strategy-based games at the moment.

– Oh, I love *Resident Evil* and *Tomb Raider* . . .

I assumed right from the start that she was taking the

piss. But her knowledge was too extensive, even for someone with an annoying little brother who never shut up. This was a girl who played games. We talked all the way through the starter and main. Even when her glass of wine went all over me we just laughed it off and kept right on talking, it was like when I met up with Andy and Steve down at the student union for the first time. We ordered another bottle of wine. Then she started telling me about her girlfriends. The one who had lied and slept her way to a top job in the City and was now cracking under the pressure, the one who lived in a community in India, another who was a primary school teacher. There was one who'd ended up living in a caravan after doing loads of smack.

– It's her own stupid fault, she said. – Girls are crap.

– What?

– Yeah, they believe what men tell them.

– Not you, though.

– Nah, I'm more like a boy. I do what I want.

– I met another woman like that recently.

I stood up to go to the toilet, but after nearly a year of not drinking I almost fell right on top of her. Staggering to my feet I told her I'd just be a second, then sat down again. The rest of the evening gets a bit blurred after that. I remember her asking me all these odd questions about Kate. What I thought of her background, how I knew her, what friends we had in common, didn't I think she had a weird personality. Stuff like that. She was making me drink loads of water until I could finally make it to the toilet.

When I came out, she was on the phone. Her face looked hard instead of sweet. As I got close I heard her say, What really happened to that bitch's face, Louie? I want to know – but the second she saw me she started smiling again and told me she'd just be a minute.

After that there must've been a taxi home and I must've

got into bed somehow. And that bucket must've appeared next to it somehow. There was a presence hovering above me as I finally lost consciousness, like when my mum would tuck me in at night. A woman's voice telling me, Sweet Dreams.

The week after my date with Mel, Kate was round our house constantly. She wanted to know all about the date. I told her very little. I don't know why. I suppose I thought Mel would tell Kate herself if she wanted her to know anything. I told her it went well, and that I might be seeing her again. Also, I thought if I was discreet it would both get rid of her and impress Mel. But Kate was undeterred. She was round every day, cooking for Andy and for me. She even offered to clean my room for me. And there *was* a lot of dust after being empty all those months, so on the Wednesday afternoon, I put all my valuable stuff and information in a locked filebox and set her off with the hoover. I have to admit she did a pretty good job. It took her ages. All the time she was in there she wouldn't let me look. She said it was going to be a surprise for me. I wondered what she was after at first, but then I started to see that she probably just wanted to be one of us. Her ironic comment about being a minger must've been how she actually felt. I thought I might as well let her do stuff if that's what she really wanted.

At the end of the week I had to go back into hospital. Nothing serious, just a small hernia. A one-day op. Kate said she'd look after me for a bit. She had a couple of days off, so it'd be like a working holiday, but she didn't mind. She wasn't doing all that much anyway. The op went OK and I went to spend the rest of the day crashed out on Kate's sofa with a hole in my side.

She woke me up around four with a cup of tea and asked

me what I wanted for dinner. She'd got some pies and Chinese chicken. I told her I wasn't bothered, which seemed to irk her, but it was just nice to go back to drug land for a bit, that serene neutrality that some tranquillizers and painkillers bring. My head felt like mashed potato, but I didn't care. It's in states like that that I've found what comes closest to happiness, where the world that thinks it's the real world doesn't invade your thoughts and you can switch off completely. The only thing that comes close is the games, but even then, there's background interference. Drugs are the only things that silence absolutely everything.

– Come on, eat up, it's good for you.

Kate was unrelenting in her care.

– I'm sorting out my stuff in my cupboard. It's sort of like my bottom drawer. You can help me if you like.

– I'm a bit spazzed really . . .

– Come on, it'll be good for you.

– I'm asleep . . .

– You should be up and about by now. Come on. I'm putting things in order. Look– She held up a weird ornamental animal. It looked like something from Indonesia or Thailand maybe. – What d'you think? Should I keep it?

– Do what you want with it . . .

– But what do you think?

– I dunno, do I? It's not mine, is it?

– It was my dad's –

– Yeah?

– So what should I do?

– I dunno, do what you want . . .

I started eating the pie she'd cooked for me, then jumped as she suddenly lunged towards me.

– I didn't say you could eat that.

– Well you cooked it for me. I laughed.

She started shaking then. I wondered if she was cold.

– This is a photo of my mum and this is something I had when I was a kid.

– Yeah?

– Yeah, so what d'you think I should do with them?

– Do what you want; they're your things. Can you pass us the ketchup?

– No, get it yourself.

– It hurts to move.

– Tough. You get it.

– Come on, it's only just there.

– I can't believe you're speaking like that to me!

– Now you're confusing me.

– You're not supposed to be like this.

I asked her how the hell I was supposed to be but she got all self-conscious. I tried to get her to tell me what she thought she was playing at but all I got was a stony silence. I reached over to the phone. Mel was out, so I left a message on her machine telling her where I was and to give me a call. We had a date in a couple of days, depending on how my recovery went.

– Hey, Fatty, d'you take acid trips?

– Used to, not any more.

– Come here, I want to give you something.

– What?

– I want to show you something. You'll really be into it if you've ever been into trips.

– It hurts to move.

– It's something really good, I promise you. It's like a real change.

I pulled myself to my feet, chucking a book on to the sofa to read afterwards.

– I'm in the bathroom, changing.

– I'll wait for you.

– OK, I'm changed now.

I took Andy's gas mask from the shelf above the telly and made my way through the kitchen to the back of the house. I thought I'd give her a scare. I pulled the thick black rubber on and put my head around the door to say, 'The force is strong with this one,' but before I could say anything, she threw something at me. A clear liquid flew at me from out of a glass jar. I drew back and it hit the wall opposite and started to sizzle. Acid. She'd tried to disfigure me with acid. I looked at her. She was naked, the colour of beetroot and shaking all over. Waves of hate were pouring off her like heat haze. There was some acid left in the jar.

– What do I do now?

I ignored her and thought about how best to secure the bathroom door from the outside.

– He made me like this, I might as well finish the job, I heard her say as I closed the door.

Then more sizzling and her screaming. I took an apron from the back of the kitchen door and tied it around the door handle and tied the other end to the boiler pipes opposite the bathroom door. Not brilliant, but some escape time.

I hobbled out to the front of the house. The front door was locked. I could hear the bathroom door shaking like something out of *The Exorcist*. The gash in my side was killing me. I could feel the two sides of the cut rubbing against each other as I walked. I moved back towards the living room. The bathroom door was rattling and over it were animal noises, growling, like hyenas feeding, tooth on bone. Was she gnawing at the door handle? I turned the drawers of the desk in the living room over, swept the shelves clear, found a bunch of keys and made a guess for the right one. Second time lucky. Turned the lock once and then again. As I got the front door open I heard the splintering of the bathroom door. I ducked out into the front garden and made for the street. A bleeding knot of fat and muscle came lurching after me. The front door swung wide again, then a dull crack as something heavy hit her on the head.

I looked round. Melissa was next to the front door with a tyre iron in her hand.

– Let's go, she said. I was never here. You did that, she said, gesturing to Kate. She dragged me into a car and drove me home. On the way she said, I don't know what the fuck you're mixed up in, but I think I know what that bitch had in store for you, and I know you don't deserve it.

I could only stare.

– Her old man was a seriously fucked up psychopath and the reason she looks the way she does is down to him. Did loads of weird experiments and stuff on her. And now she tries to take it out on pretty young men like you. That's what I heard anyway. When a minger like that shells out six hundred quid for a guy to spend an evening with me . . . well, let's just say alarm bells start ringing. So I found out what I could. I'm a professional, I'm not a fucking monster.

When she dropped me off at the house she said, This didn't happen. You got out alone, OK? I'm risking my life for you. You're very sweet, but don't call me again, OK? Then she drove off.

I went inside. Andy embraced me even more fiercely than the last time I got home.

– Thank God you're OK, he said. – I'm so sorry. His face was completely white.

– What the fuck's going on? I asked him.

– Let's just say, never bring your work home with you, and all that bog sends you is shit.

He'd tried to warn me that day in the kitchen, but she'd got too much on him. He was devastated when I told him what she'd been trying to do. He thought she was just after money.

I went inside. Again my room seemed like another dimension. It was as though someone else lived there and I was an impostor in my own life. I was a secret agent who'd been rehearsed with props similar, but not identical, to what was here and then briefed in how to play the part of me, but now the play was beginning for real. I looked at the Madonna and Child, then I remembered a dream from about a week ago. I was lying in my bed and Melissa was standing above me, holding one of Andy's gas masks and saying, It's fun to play jokes on people. When the time comes, you're going to surprise her with this mask, aren't you? Do it for me, there's a good boy.

And Andy's voice behind me said, Don't worry. You're safe now.

Vendetta

Zulfiqar Ali

They were back again.

Farid watched them from the window of the darkened bedroom. Two of them were smoking. Their cigarettes glowed red in the interior of the car.

Naz came up behind him and placed her hand on his shoulder. 'They'll see you,' she said.

'I'll go have a talk with them.'

'There'll be trouble.'

'It won't be of my making,' he said.

There were four of them. In their early- to mid-twenties. Pencil moustaches and what passed for beards these days. Crew-cut hair. Designer black tops and trousers. Gold chains. Gold rings. Vacant eyes.

Of the two in the backseat, one had his shirtsleeve rolled up. He was injecting himself in the left arm. The other watched him impatiently.

Farid tapped on the driver's side window with his knuckles. The tinted glass slid down in a whirr of electric motor. Heroin-infused smoke and the stench of cigarettes drifted out lazily.

'Time to move on,' Farid said.

'The fuck you said, motherfucker?'

Farid slammed his fist into the driver's face. Blood

spurted out the man's nose and torn lips. Before he could recover, Farid laced his fingers into his hair, twisted, pulled back hard and clamped the fingers of his right hand on the exposed neck. The man began choking. His limbs fluttered uncontrollably. Farid applied more pressure. The other three sat very still, like pond frogs mesmerized by a cobra.

'That's cool, bro,' the one in the front passenger seat said. In the light of his cigarette, Farid saw the white knife scar that snaked across the bridge of his nose and halfway down his left cheek.

Farid released the driver. 'This is not a good place to do your shit.'

'We're gone.'

The driver, gasping and massaging his neck, doubled up in a coughing fit. He was still coughing when the VW Golf VR6 shot off in a squeal of burning rubber. Farid watched its tail-lights head up the road and disappear round the bend.

When he got back from work the following evening, he saw with satisfaction that the parking spot outside his home was empty. Naz was at the workstation, preparing a final annual accounts report for a client. He went over to her and kissed her on the side of the neck. 'Want a drink?'

'Why not?'

In the adjoining kitchen, he half filled a small saucepan with cold water, added two teaspoons of green tea-leaves and a pinch of baking soda. He allowed the water to come to the boil slowly, until it was treacly brown. When he added milk, the brown transformed into a rich pink. A change that never failed to amaze him and which brought back childhood memories.

Using a strainer, he poured the tea into two large mugs, garnished it with flaked almonds and pistachios and sweetened it with honey.

Naz smiled in appreciation as she took the proffered mug from him.

'Where's Moon?' he asked.

'Gone to Ackers with Karl and some other friends. Shouldn't be too long.'

At two in the morning, Farid was shaken awake by cries from the back bedroom. He found Moon at the window, pointing outside. The shed was on fire. By the time he'd put on his dressing gown and rushed outside, the shed was completely engulfed in flames. Wood knots snapped viciously in the intense heat.

The fire engine arrived a few minutes later, but it was too late to save the shed. Only its gutted remains were left.

In the morning, Farid reported the arson to his insurance company. They faxed him the claim forms at home, which he completed and returned with estimates from a couple of reputable local companies. The following night passed without incident, as did the night after that. He'd stayed up both nights, knowing the men would be back.

It was just a matter of time.

'Every once in a while,' Naz said, 'you ought to listen. Might learn something.'

The third night, while lounging in his favourite easy chair, pulled up to the window of the front room, he fell asleep with the wheel brace across his lap. The sound of explosions woke him suddenly. Gunfire, he thought at first. He was back in Bosnia, in Mostar: the Croats and Muslims slaughtering each other in the grip of centuries-old enmity. By the time he'd jumped out of the chair and pulled away the netting, lights had come on in some of the houses across the street. As he peered out through his own sleep-fogged reflection, nothing appeared out of the ordinary. Then he saw the broken glass littering the pavement next to his flatbed truck.

Bill Monaghan, his next-door neighbour, was first on the scene, already out there when Farid got to his truck. He moved fast for an old man. All the truck's windows and both screens were smashed. The tyres appeared to be intact, but Farid examined them anyway.

'There was a bunch of them,' Bill said. 'With crowbars. Friends of yours?'

'Relatives,' Farid said.

Bill indicated the alleyway two houses down that led to the park. 'Went that way. Want me to call the police? Won't do your truck any good, though.'

'I've already called them,' Naz said, coming up behind Farid. Moon stood in the doorway. Farid made a mental note to have a talk with him later. The boy was confused and obviously frightened.

Twenty minutes later, the police showed up. Two cars. Four officers, one of them a woman. The helicopter got there a few minutes later, then the dog van too. A half-hour search of the park flushed no one out, dog and heat-seeking equipment notwithstanding. It was questions time, then. Lots of questions and Farid had no answers.

'Do you believe these were the same people who set your shed on fire?'

Farid looked at WPC Marion Parkes. Brunette. Late-thirties. Epicene eyes giving her an almost Oriental look. A little bit on the heavy side. Utility belt bulging around her waist as though with tumours. 'It's possible,' he said.

She handed him her card. 'If you think of anything, give us a call. The crime report form will be sent to you in a day or two. You'll need the incident number for your insurance company.'

The next morning, Farid contacted Mike, his crew foreman, told him he needed to take the day off. 'Something's come up,' he said. 'I'll call you later. Any problems, give me a ring.'

Naz had an office on the third floor of the Ryder Building in Great Charles Street, adjoining the Chest Clinic. Farid left his truck at a repairs garage in Severn Street. After arranging to pick it up later that afternoon, he walked up Suffolk Street, to Naz's office, for the keys to her Audi.

'I know you don't want to hear it,' she said, 'but be careful.'

He touched her fingers. 'Aren't I always?'

'No.'

Farid had a vague notion about where to begin his search. Snooker halls. All-night cafés. Known drug haunts: schools, parks, community and drop-in centres, employment agencies, sports and leisure centres. Nightclubs, too, but that was for later.

Not exactly specific, but it was a start.

By lunchtime, Farid had got nowhere. He needed to find someone who would be the first link in the chain that would eventually lead him to the men. But who? Someone young, of course, and an addict. Maybe a school kid. Moon? He was startled by the thought. He tried to shake it off, but couldn't. Maybe Moon, or one of his friends, knew who these men were? Seen them around, perhaps?

Maybe. If he didn't get anywhere, he'd have no choice, of course; but until then, he would stay away from Moon.

For almost half an hour he waited outside the employment agency at the corner of Regents Park Road and Coventry Road, peeked into the Neighbourhood Office right opposite, walked up and down the local shopping centre, even wandered over to Morrisons. There was no sign of the black VW Golf with the distinctive bodywork: fully kitted, flame marks on the sides, alloys, tinted windows. There couldn't be that many such vehicles on the road.

When Farid returned from Morrisons, Three Cues Snooker and American Pool was open. Bearded men in jeans and Taliban-type robes, feet in Doc Martens, loitered outside the hall in a loose group, chatting raucously and eyeing up the women shoppers, especially the young ones. Plenty of those. Even religious nuts need to unwind sometime, Farid thought, grinning.

From the pool hall, he drove down to Muntz Street, to the leisure and community centre. The complex included the secondary school, the library and the swimming pool. He roamed the car park, checked out the parked cars on the road. Still no sign of the Golf. From the library, he got a copy of the names of all the schools and colleges in the city. He was amazed at the length of the list.

The next stop on his itinerary was the Birmingham Sports Centre in Belgrave Middleway and the college next door. Then there was St Alban's School, back of Central Mosque. Matthew Boulton College on the Pershore Road. Bournville College on Bristol Road. He even cruised Millennium Point in Digbeth, and the universities, too: Birmingham and Aston, as well as the college of printing behind Aston.

From the bakery in Moseley, he picked up a slice of vegetarian pizza, a couple of cherry flapjacks, half a dozen small cartons of fruit juice and a large bottle of Evian. As he ate his lunch on the bench in St Mary's Row, he called Bob Meredith. Until their discharge a couple of years ago, he and Bob had served together in the Royal Armoured Corps, with the King's Royal Hussars. Bob now ran a franchise of imported American cars by Tyburn Island, across the road from the retail park. Farid explained what he wanted. Bob said he'd see what he could do.

At three, he dropped off the Audi keys with Naz, telling her he was still searching.

'I've been asking around myself,' Naz said. 'No one

seems to have heard of these people. But then my clients don't move in those social circles.'

'I'll find them,' Farid said.

'That's what I'm afraid of.'

'What's that supposed to mean?'

'Maybe you should just let this thing go,' Naz said.

'I can't.'

'There's too much at stake here.'

Naz spoke softly, patiently, as though explaining the obvious to a not-too-bright child. Until this moment, Farid hadn't realized just how much he'd come to resent this mannerism of hers.

'That's why I can't back off,' he said thickly. He was glad they were discussing this in her office. Through the glass partition, he could see Naz's PA hunched over the PC.

'You're taking this much too seriously. You're not fighting a war, Farid. These are just kids. You were a kid once yourself, not so long ago. Remember? You can't have forgotten that?'

She was smiling. The smile was an essential part of the same condescending repertoire she'd built up over the years.

'I have to go,' he said. They kissed briefly, their lips barely touching, and he left. He was suffocating.

The truck wasn't ready. It was pointless arguing; so rather than loitering at the garage, he decided to visit Andromeda, the speciality bookstore. Growing up in the seventies, he used to read a lot of science fiction and horror. But that was years ago. He'd moved on since then – not that he got much time for leisure reading these days, what with work and family commitments. When he reached the bookstore he found it all boarded up. Andromeda was no longer in business. Feeling strangely lost, he stood there for a few minutes, not sure what to do next, then carried on round the corner to Nostalgia & Comics in Queensway.

When he got back to the garage, the truck was ready and waiting for him. He settled the bill, shoved the receipt into his back pocket, and headed home.

Moon was in the kitchen, preparing a snack. 'Want anything to eat?'

Farid shook his head. 'I've already eaten.' He wondered vaguely when it was that Moon had last referred to him as *Dad* or *Father*. He found that he had no memory of the occasion.

Moon took his bowl of cornflakes and cold milk to the table in the dining area, sat down and started munching. Farid poured himself a glass of water and went to sit opposite his boy. 'How's school?'

Moon shrugged, working on a mouthful of cornflakes.

'And the Debating Society?'

'Same as always,' Moon said laconically. For someone who was president of the school's Debating Society, Moon didn't say much as a rule, unless he had to.

'Did you get the skates you wanted?'

'Last week. Karl got the same pair.' Moon's eyes lit up for a second. 'Karl had such a hard time getting his mum not to come with us.'

Farid grinned. 'You bothered by what's going on?'

Moon stopped munching. He looked up at Farid, but pointedly said nothing.

'I'll take care of it,' Farid said. 'You know that? Don't you?'

'I know.' Farid waited. 'They were at the school this afternoon.'

Farid felt as if a sliver of ice had been shoved into his stomach.

'I don't think they were there for me. They're always trying to get you to sample that shit. You know?'

'Drugs?'

'What d'you think I mean? Yeah. Drugs. Heroin. Crack. Ecstasy. Charlie. Weed. Shit. Take your pick. First, they let you have it, free. Go on, kid. Have a good time. Business investment, that's how they see it. Once you're hooked, you're fucked. Then you go to them. Works every time.'

Farid had never heard Moon speak this way before. He was unsure what shocked him the most: the boy's easy use of profanity or his knowledge of the local area's dark underbelly. 'They ever approach you?' Farid's heart was palpitating.

'Once. About a month ago. I told them. Not for me, thanks. Not interested. They're the ones got your truck, weren't they? And the shed?'

Farid saw no reason to lie, but he was thinking: *Your* truck? When had it become *his* truck?

'They're going to be back. Aren't they?'

Before he could frame a suitable response, his mobile rang. It was Ollie Lambert, not Bob Meredith as he'd been hoping.

'You know that snooker place in Walford Road? The one by the Hindu temple?'

'I know it.'

'That's where you'll find them. Laurie's girlfriend Joanna, her daughter Tess used to go out with this kid. Wait till you hear the name. Two-Tone.'

'*Two-Tone?* What kind of name's that?'

'Hey, he's one of your people, Farid,' Ollie said, laughing. 'You tell me.'

'You're confusing me with Moses, Ollie. I don't have any people. The only people I have are my wife and son.'

'Anyway,' Ollie said, still laughing. 'This Two-Tone's a real piece of work. Spent some time in prison. That's what gives him street cred. Car theft. Churning out ringers. GBH. Shit like that. Oh, and – get this – supplying controlled substances to a minor. That's what Joanna told Laurie. Swear to Christ. *Supplying controlled substances to a minor*. Tess says TT got the name because of his predilection for two-tone shoes and cars. Laurie says Joanna suspects the reason Tess left TT was because the guy wanted her to put out for his friends. Maybe go for the occasional gang bang. He's like Little Richard. A watcher. He's got a stable of girls working for him in Ladywood. You handle this any way you want, Farid, but I'd say stay away from this fuck. He sounds like a real sick bastard.'

At eleven that evening, Farid arrived at the Edwardian building that was now slumming it as a snooker hall. The black VW Golf VR6 was parked at an angle out front. Farid pulled his truck off-road directly behind it and cut the engine. The only way the Golf could get out now was if Farid moved his truck.

Inside the hall, smoke hung over the snooker and pool tables like a cloud of thick fog. The lowered fluorescent tubes over the tables made the smoke luminous, creating a very Victorian atmosphere. Knots of people – mostly men, though there were plenty of women too – were clustered about at tables, shooting with cues gripped like broadswords. Coloured and numbered balls rolled across the blue felt. Gales of laughter. The din of overlapping conversations like in a Robert Altman film. Drinks being consumed. Elevator music in the background.

Two-Tone was at a table at the far end of the hall. His three cronies with him. There were four girls with them, too: two whites, two Asians, all dressed like pros.

TT finished his shot, took a swig of Pilsner, pulled one of the Asian girls over, moulded his hand around her hip and bit her on the lower lip. When he raised his head, Farid was standing a foot away from him.

He was plainly startled. Then a wide grin split his face. In the piss-yellow light, his scar stood out in relief against his dark brown skin.

'I'm here to call a truce,' Farid said, taking the initiative.

'Truce? Truce?' TT turned to his friends to share the joke. They grinned obligingly. The girls giggled. The one TT had kissed played with the hair on his chest. 'Truce? What planet you come from? You think this some sort of fuckin turf war, man?'

'Call it what you want,' Farid said, not taking his eyes off TT's. This was strictly between the two of them, and he wanted TT to understand that. 'We're quits.'

'We're not quits, motherfucker,' TT said. He was no longer smiling. 'We're quits when I say so.'

'Yeah,' yelled the one Farid had punched in the mouth that evening – the driver of the Golf. He was standing on the far side of the table, and made no move to get closer. 'You tell him, TT. Tell the shit-eatin motherfucker. It's quits when we say so.'

'You got balls, man,' TT was saying. 'I'll give you that. Took real balls to come here. How d'you find me?'

'Wasn't hard,' Farid said.

'I'd like to know, anyway. If you can find me, so can others.'

'Drive a car like the one you do, might as well leave a business card.'

TT laughed out loud. 'Fuck me,' he said. 'Fuck me.'

'Just say the word, honey,' his woman purred close to his ear. 'Anytime, anywhere.' She was staring directly at Farid with her bloodshot eyes. Farid thought she was stoned.

'So you found me,' TT said. 'But let me ask you something. You think you're just gonna walk back out of here? In one piece?'

'We're obviously not communicating,' Farid said.

'Fuckin right, arsehole,' the driver screamed.

'Call it quits, TT,' Farid said, 'you don't lose face. You

win. That's got to count for something. I'm the one got my shed burnt and my truck smashed. You've made your point. Quit while you're ahead. How about it?'

TT appeared to be chewing it over, but only for a second. His grin was back in place. He shook his head. 'You don't understand,' he said, almost with sorrow, aiming the Yardie hand gesture at him: palm down, two fingers folded, the index and middle fingers pointing at him, the thumb bent trigger-fashion. 'You dissed me, man. No one disses TT. You dissed me in front of my boys. My posse. Can't let that go. I got my reputation to think of. You can't just forget shit like that.'

The flick knife was suddenly there in TT's hand. Farid had no idea how it got there. Light danced across the sharp, gleaming surface and he wondered idly when it was that young Asians had started aping black gestures and cultural references.

Farid never did find out how things would've developed. Two of TT's men pushed their girls aside and began sidling up behind him. It was obvious what they had in mind. Make a grab for him, pin his arms back, leave him open for TT to gut him.

Then the red rage took over.

Before TT could move, Farid's booted toe connected sharply with TT's groin, catching him completely by surprise. TT gasped as the breath was sucked out of his lungs. The knife dropped to the carpeted floor. Farid kicked it under the table. TT doubled over, gasping. Farid yanked the cue from his nerveless fingers and cracked it into his face so hard, it broke. TT collapsed. Farid kicked him where he lay, over and over: short, hard jabs designed to inflict maximum damage in the shortest possible time. TT was no longer moving. His girlfriend was screaming hysterically. Farid whacked her on the side of the head with the cue-half. She pitched forward, struck the table in front of her, then slid to the floor. After that, a lot of yelling and confusion. Punches were thrown. Cues were swung. A great deal of shouting and screaming as fists and booted feet connected with soft flesh. There was blood. Someone kept hollering for the police.

Farid found himself outside in the cold air. Other people were streaming out of the building. No one bothered him. He got into his truck and left.

When he got home, Naz was horrified at the sight of him. His shirt was torn and bloody; splashes of blood on the mustard-yellow fabric. His knuckles were skinned; his face bruised. But otherwise, he was unscathed.

'What are you bringing into our lives?' she said.

Mercifully, Moon was already upstairs in his bedroom. Farid hoped he was asleep.

Later, when Bob Meredith got back to him, Farid was relaxing in the bathtub, a face cloth folded over his eyes.

'The VR6 is registered to a man called Dilawer Khan. Lives in Moseley.' Meredith gave him the address: 253 Moorcroft Road. 'At least, that's what they've got at Swansea DVLC, according to my contact.'

'I know where Moorcroft Road is. I'm renovating a property near by. Thanks, Bob. Appreciate it.'

'No prob,' Bob said. 'Take it easy.'

'You too, Bob.'

Over the next few days – wherever he travelled, whether it was to work or out with his family – Farid began to suspect that he was being followed. It was more a gut feeling than anything else. All the same, he was spooked, knowing someone was keeping track of his movements. He didn't think it was TT himself. One of his gang members, probably, but certainly not TT. TT wasn't that stupid.

Farid found himself constantly checking the side and

rearview mirrors every time he was out on the road. Naz said he was getting paranoid. Things came to a head one evening when they were on their way to a Zakir Hussain concert at the NEC. They were driving past the airport when Farid stopped the family Subaru in the middle of the road and stormed out. But the young Asian man in the Rover behind him turned out to be an accounts executive, also headed to the concert. Farid was forced to apologize. It was all he could do to dissuade the man from calling the police.

Farid and Naz didn't go to the concert.

A week after the incident with the Asian driver, Farid was supervising the roofing of an extension in Chantry Road when he got the call he'd been expecting. It was from Naz. She was crying. When he got her to calm down, she told him their house had been broken into.

'Bill called me here at the office,' she said, in between sobs. 'He said they got in through the back.'

'How the hell does he know? Was he there? Did he see them?'

'Of course he saw them,' Naz snapped, the anger filtering through her initial shock. 'Why else would he say if he hadn't seen them? Are you satisfied now? You got what you wanted, all that macho bullshit. This is what you really wanted. Tell me it wasn't. Go on. Tell me. Lie to me. Lie to me some more.'

'You don't know what you're saying.'

'Don't I? Didn't I tell you? Didn't I warn you? Back off, Farid, I said. Stay away from them, I said. It'll lead to much greater trouble. Well, you've got your wish. Are you happy now? God damn you. God damn you and your pig-headedness.' She was crying again.

'You can't let yourself be pushed around, Naz,' he said stonily. 'You can't live like that.'

The high-pitched cackling sound that came floating over the line raised gooseflesh on his skin. 'Who appointed you the policeman? Tell me that. Who? Our house has been burgled. Do you know what that means? These people have come into our lives, violated our space. Our private space. I feel as if I've been raped.'

'Don't say that, Naz. Don't you ever say that.' He could feel the throbbing at his temples. 'I'll call you back from home,' he said.

'Don't bother. Your mess. You deal with it. I want no part of it.' Before he could respond, she'd slammed down the receiver.

The police car was waiting outside when Farid got home. There was no parking space near by, so he double-parked. Fuck it, he thought. Two uniforms got out. The WPC was the same one who'd answered the attack on his truck: Marion Parkes. The man with her was a bull-necked Irishman: PC Murphy.

'You're having a spot of bad luck, aren't you, sir?' Marion Parkes said conversationally.

'Shit happens,' Farid said, as he unlocked the front door. He did not care to make an issue of her humorous tone. He was painfully conscious of some of his neighbours watching from their gardens. Bill Monaghan tried to get his attention, but Farid waved him off. 'Later,' he said. The last thing he needed right now was Bill's banter.

'Is it all right if we come inside, sir?' PC Murphy asked.

'Give me a few minutes. This isn't easy.'

'Whenever you're ready, Mr Hashmi.'

Farid walked into the house. It was like a war zone. He wandered about in a daze; unable to recognize this place as the same home he had left that morning. He did his best to remain objective, but it was hard. The home he and Naz had tried to create for themselves and Moon was no more. Signs of ruin were everywhere, in every room. It was as though a devastating hurricane had ripped through the property. Slashed couches. Hacked furniture. Obscene graffiti spray-painted on the walls and the family portraits. Cleaning products poured on carpets and rugs. Even the Alma-Tadema print in their bedroom hadn't been spared. The small safe behind it was still there despite an attempt to dig it out of the wall. The plaster was chiselled all around it. Perhaps out of frustration, some kind of glue had been squeezed into the seam between the safe door and the frame. And the stench – the awful, gagging stench that hung over everything – a sickening melange made all the more potent by the mounds of human shit left on their beds.

Horrifying though it all was, it was the body of Moon's orange tomcat that wrenched most at Farid's heart. Furball was pinned to the living-room door with a two-pronged carving fork that had been driven through his neck. He had been disembowelled, too. Farid prayed that Furball had already been dead by then.

He let Parkes and Murphy into the house and followed them like a beseeching beggar as they went from room to room, examining everything with the detached air of officialdom. They took note of the faeces and the dead cat, the graffiti, the scattered photo albums, the torn curtains. Parkes made sympathetic noises, asked him if anything was missing. Farid suppressed the impulse to laugh out loud. *Anything missing? Yeah, my life. Everything I ever worked for, especially the memories*. Instead, he admitted that he had no idea at this stage. She nodded, then called Stechford, reported the incident and requested forensics' help.

Incredibly, within the hour, a male police photographer and a female technician with a large briefcase arrived. Photos were taken. The place was dusted for fingerprints. None were found. The tech then examined Furball.

Throughout, she kept speaking into the miniature CD recorder she carried with her. Farid assumed she was speaking in English, though the words sounded foreign.

'Is this going to take long? My son –' He found he could not complete the thought.

'Almost done.'

Farid went outside to stand at the gate. He was still there when Moon got back. The boy kept staring at the two police vehicles, then back at him. Karl, standing next to Moon, whispered something to him but Moon ignored him. 'Got burgled.'

'They take much?'

Farid wanted desperately to give the boy a hug but he knew it would be the wrong thing to do. Moon would think he was patronizing him, especially in view of the news he had to give him.

'Mum OK?'

'Furball's dead.'

The tears came without warning. Farid hugged him then, fiercely, without saying anything, just holding him. Moon suddenly screamed and pushed him away. 'You bastard. I hate you. This is all your fault. You killed Furball.'

Farid let go of the boy as though he were on fire.

'If you hadn't been such a hard-arse, none of this would've happened. So they were shooting up drugs. They weren't doing us any harm. But you couldn't leave them alone, could you? You had to push them. Now look where your pushing's got us. Just look at the fucking mess. Look at it.'

Moon hurled his school bag at him. Snivelling uncontrollably, he turned and dashed down the road, disappearing into the alleyway that led to the park. Karl sprinted after him. Farid bent down and picked up the bag. Some of the neighbours were grinning. Fucking *vultures*, he thought, and went back inside.

The forensics tech and the photographer left shortly after. Parkes and Murphy lingered. Farid decided to tell them what had been going on, how this nightmare had started. He deliberately left out the snooker hall incident. Why complicate matters?

Parkes looked at him. Farid knew she didn't believe that that was the whole story. 'I wish people wouldn't take things into their own hands,' she said. 'You should've allowed us to handle it.'

'I realize that now.'

'You'll need to come to the station. Make a formal complaint. We'll take it from there. We'll have TT picked up. If we can put him at the scene, it'll mean you testifying in court. You might want to think about that. People like TT have long memories.'

When they were gone, Farid flicked open his cellphone, hesitated, then closed it again. Naz would be waiting, he knew. He ought to be going after Moon, too. Bring him back. Talk to him. But that was just the problem. He could think of nothing to say, either to Naz or to Moon. Nothing made sense any more. It had all become so confusing and convoluted.

He put on the rubberized gardening gloves and set about clearing up as much of the mess as he could, wondering if there'd be anything salvageable amid the rubble. He felt strangely detached from everything.

A quarter of an hour later, when he dragged the soiled mattress off their bed, something on the floor caught his eye. Even as he reached through the pine slats of the divan, he recognized the six-by-four holiday snap. The Mediterranean coastline, sunlight glinting on the bluer than blue water. Him and Naz standing knee-deep in the foaming surf, his arm around her.

The frayed edges of the photograph didn't register with

him immediately, not until he realized that his other arm should've been around Moon's shoulders.

Moon was no longer there.

The message from TT couldn't have been more explicit if it'd been written in ten-foot-tall letters dripping with blood. As he stood there, rooted to the spot with shock, red darkness suddenly welled up deep inside him.

How he got outside and into his truck, he could never remember afterwards. All he could recall was setting off towards Moorcroft Road, driven by a single all-encompassing thought: *take out TT and his gang*. That, or be prepared to bury Naz and Moon.

He supposed he must've been aware of the irony, though: that whatever he did – whether he remained at home, waiting for the inevitable to happen, or took the fight to TT – either way he was going to lose the family he'd tried so hard to protect and to hold on to.

It still did not stop him.

The Way She Looks at Me

Pauline Gould

Being inside a shopping centre is like being in prison: no one really knows what's going on in the outside world, and vice versa. I like that.

I like the way natural light teeters to the brink of the Bristol Road entrance and cowers back before it hits the breakwater of trolleys and pushchairs in the taxi queue outside Peacocks. I like the way the artificial lighting in the shops rattles your senses, confuses your body clock and robs you of your sense of time. There's something safe about not knowing what time of day it is.

They come into the Grosvenor from the streets of Northfield to get out of the tropical temperature that's melting down Birmingham. Just the same as they did two weeks ago to get out of the rain, or will in two months' time to get out of the cold. Daft sods haven't worked out that it's only the sun they've escaped. The heat's less easily duped; basking in the ineffective air conditioning, and feeding off those sweltering bodies in this windowless thermos flask of a building. Only a gasp of something distantly related to fresh air shuffles in reluctantly through the stuttering automatic doors every now and again, when one of the assistants from the sportswear shop stretches out her arm to flick the ash from her cigarette onto the pavement.

Great leveller, heat. Everyone sweats. Emits their own personalized scent. Whether they're from Sutton or Stirchley. I've done all the centres. From the sublime to the less sublime. From City Plaza to the Kingfisher, Redditch. From Merry Hill to One Stop at Perry Barr. A day here, a day there. That way I don't become known. And believe me, some of them smell; I mean really stink, like skunks leaving a trail behind them. It makes you want to gag. Young blokes with their sweaty trainers and sweet and sour testosterone oozing from their pores. They'll grow out of it. And if they don't? They'll turn into old blokes doused in their own stench of grime and urine because it's not worth bothering any more. Then there are the women who sweep along in a cloud of perfume thinking it'll give them immunity from their own secretions. Makes no difference whether it's Gloria Vanderbilt or Yves St Laurent, they're all about as appealing as fly spray to me. You could follow them round and find them from their smell. But you'd have to be perverted to do that – or just plain unlucky.

Judy Summers' jumper, a dozen varying shades from sapphire to bruised blue, flashes across fifteen of the eighteen screens in the window of Crazy George's. An old woman, fresh from Three Cooks, stops right next to me and licks custard from a doughnut she grips, dildo-like.

'Cuppa tea'd be nice.'

Some of them think the security guard's sole purpose in life is to listen to their inarticulate dribblings. Big mistake encouraging them. You don't get respect by flattering any female over twelve and being every bloke's best mate. You want to keep them at a distance. Keep them in their place. Don't invite intimacy – unless it's for your own ends. It's in the stance, see? Straight back, square shoulders, head high. Slow, steady walk like a prowling tiger ready to pounce. Unapproachable. Always ready to make the kill.

I've got my own uniforms. Bottle-green and brown blazers and matching ties, white shirt and dark trousers. I'm always careful to wear different colours to the in-house security. Big mistake posing as one of their team players. That would only draw their attention. This way I look the part without breaking any rules. Can't help it if I look like a security guard, can I? And if Mr and Mrs Joe Public want to think I am, who am I to disillusion them? Looking like's not the same as impersonating.

I focus on the top row, third screen from the left. Judy Summers, beautiful in forget-me-not, bat-winged angora, curled up on the sofa reading *Cosmopolitan*, turns to the door, startled. Cue theme music and opening titles. The cult eighties soap, *Suburban City*.

The old woman taps my arm with her sticky paw. If she thinks she's going to engage me in a pointless conversation, she's mistaken. I don't do polite, and I don't do the 'Aren't old people wonderful' routine either. And besides, it's been a long day. 'I said a cuppa tea'd be nice.'

I laugh uproariously at this bit of improvised wit. Jeez, just look at her. Mouth moustached with sugar and phlegmy goo. Complexion like the Cuprinol man. Legacy of a sixty-a-day habit and an overdose of Max Factor panstick. All that crap about growing old gracefully. God, old women make me want to throw up.

'That's a good one,' I say, wiping the tears from my eyes. '*Cuppa tea*. Ha bloody ha. You should be on the stage.'

She looks more puzzled than scared. Must be losing my touch. Scuttles off like a lame woodlouse, bless her, towards the bloke in the sharp suit promoting a will-making service outside City Meat. He could be selling personalized keyrings or fitted kitchens for all the difference it makes to her. All she's after is an ear to bend. He falls for it. Thinks he's got a customer, poor sod. She thinks it's her birthday. Fucking stupid old cow.

I haven't really lost it – my touch. Still got it. Only I keep it hidden. Under wraps . . . just. You have to compromise or you're out of the game. *Go to jail. Move directly to jail. Do not pass Go. Do not collect £200*. But that's life. Only it wasn't life I got. You have to kill someone for that.

Back at *Suburban City*, things are about to happen. Icy slithers of panic shoot up my spine and back down again like those high-speed lifts in Bank House, and Flynn Jefferson strides in and pulls Judy into his arms.

Take your hands off her, you filthy bastard, she's mine.

He lifts a stray strand of hair from her face with his finger, tucking it behind her ear. The finger lingers, making small circles over her cheek and jawline. A muscle at the side of my face twitches.

It twitched like that for five months after that old bird died on me. Choked with remorse, my solicitor said; I'd only meant to startle her, not give her a heart attack. Guilt weighing on my soul, said the prison chaplain, for believing I was responsible for her death. It's all cobblers. Truth was I was mad with myself for not finishing her off properly. Bit like having a taste of the hors d'oeuvres in a top-class restaurant and then someone stealing the next four courses from under your nose just as you're about to pick up your knife and fork and get stuck in.

The fingertip traces round her mouth. Her lips part and he strokes inside where it's fleshy and moist.

'Marry me, Judy,' he's saying to her, his mouth on her neck. How do I know when I can't hear him? I just do. Every scene she's ever been in is stored in a filing cabinet in my head. Every word she's uttered, gesture she's made, outfit she's worn, are neatly and meticulously indexed and catalogued. Give me one reference and I can pull out all the other information, relevant and incidental, in a split second.

The camera zooms in on her face. I like the next bit. When she dumps him. She'll pretend to be sad, and look up at him with the corners of her mouth turned down. It's a killer. But what if she doesn't this time? What if someone's onto me and they've changed the plot?

'It won't work, Flynn.'

The tension that's built up inside, rendering me straitjacket rigid, disperses into relief. My body relaxes.

'What are you talking about?' he says. 'Judy, I love you. You know I've always loved you.'

She pulls his hands from her indigo-clad padded shoulders. 'But I . . .'

That's my girl. Make him sweat. Make him hurt. Tear him apart. Chew up the pieces. Spit out the bones.

'. . . I don't love you, Flynn.'

Destroy him.

'Is there . . . someone else?'

Poor sodding bastard – he's got no idea. My heart bleeds for the wanker.

She turns from him. Her eyes search out mine. When she looks at me it's like she's looking at the most important person, the only person in the universe. It's a great feeling.

'No, Flynn. There's no one else.'

Ah, but we know that's a lie. See, the eyes have it. Yes, they say. Fifteen times over. *Yes. Of course there's someone else*. And everyone knows the camera never lies.

I've loved Judy Summers for twenty-one years, from the first time she appeared in *Suburban City*. She was thirty-six then. Still is. Always will be. It took me eighteen years to catch up.

Then after six months they got rid of her, snatched her away from me, just like that. I took it hard. Really hard. Like they wanted me to. Oh yeah, I can guess what you're thinking: *Can't tell the difference between fiction and reality*. What do you know? Look, I'm not stupid: I know about the conspiracies. They knew what she meant to me and they got rid of her. Not convinced? Well, explain to me why else should she have to go when there were so many old women still around taking up valuable living space? Everywhere I went they were there, blocking the supermarket aisles with their tartan trolleys and hapless husbands. Blotting the landscape with their perms and showerproof macs. God, it made me angry.

I had this idea that getting rid of them would bring her back. But that was the lunatic in me talking. No one could bring her back. And knowing that made me more angry. I wanted to kill them. I nearly did.

They said I was despicable. The lowest of the low. Who'd want to frighten an old woman half to death for the sake of a few pounds? Exactly. I didn't want her money. But – and this is the clever bit – I let them believe it was. Handed me burglary with entry on a plate, and who was I to turn down a free meal? Sort of made it better in their eyes. Tell them the real reason and it would've been attempted murder, and I'd have been banged up in Broadmoor faster than you can say 'The Yorkshire Ripper'.

But while I was away it began to make sense. Most things happen for a reason. You get to see that. Judy had to go. Painful though I found it, she had to go. I realized that eventually. No two ways about it. Because she was thirty-six, and thirty-six is a good age: the best age. For a woman. A good number. Curved and balanced with no sharp edges. Neither under- nor over-ripe. Now look, if you don't believe me: Marilyn Monroe and Princess Diana. Two of the most perfect women of our time. How old were they when they died? Enough said. Judy Summers is in the best of company.

I've had Judy taped since 1990. She lies next to my bed, wrapped around the black spools of thirteen videos. I resented it when they first repeated *Suburban City*. Didn't want to share her with the rest of the world. Until I realized it was a sign: when they repeat it on telly, something's got to happen.

There hasn't been a summer as steamy as this since the last one. There's an old girl just asking for it at the 18 bus stop. Mouth opening and shutting like a demented trout, slopping her false teeth up and down and scaring the kids. Big fat kids eating chips out of cones. With big fat mums stuffing baguettes between fag puffs down their big fat throats.

Funny how the weather does things to your memory. That's where I went wrong before. Old women gave me grief, so I thought it was logical that if I wiped out old women, I'd get rid of the problem. But that's too focused. I'd be helping no one. Judy put me right.

'No,' Judy said. 'It's too late to get rid of the old women. We have to get them before they become old.'

Lateral thinking, you call it.

Judy Summers is going to die tonight. Her eyes will flicker open. *Do them a favour*, they'll say.

'Tell me what you want me to do, Judy.'

Go on; they're begging for it. Begging for you to do it to them. Go on: you owe them one. Think of someone else for a change.

I'll look at Judy and nod. I have to grant a dying woman her last wish. She'll gasp, and the monitor will beep in high-pitched straight-lined monotone, dead. Judy knows: *Perfect women die young. Young women die perfect.*

I don't mind any more that she's dead. Really, I don't. It means Flynn Jefferson can't touch her any more. It means she's closer to me. Each time she's died, she's been there just the same the next day. And I get her to myself again.

In a perfect world there will only be beautiful women,

and none of them older than thirty-six. Flaunting their brief but beautiful lives. Few, but well chosen. With me there to protect them and keep them safe. I have Judy's blessing: *Go get them, Carol . . . before it's too late.*

But there's no hurry. I haven't found the first one yet. Tomorrow I'll look for her. Tomorrow I'll find her. We have to watch her; get to know her. That won't be difficult: everyone trusts a security guard. Maybe follow her and find out where she lives. Get into her flat or house. Call her up and listen to her voice. Befriend her. Women are good at that. Make her scared. We do that best of all.

You want to know how to do it? This is what you do. It's easy, really. Just relax and enjoy. Put your fingers round her lovely throat and squeeze. Gently at first like you're coaxing expensive handcream out of a tube. Easy there. Yeah, I know it's easy to get carried away. But remember, control's the essence; think control. Don't want too much to come out in one go. That'd be a waste. That's it. There it comes. A carefully measured ribbon of carbon dioxide. Whoa! Careful. Remember, careful, because once it's out you can't put it back. Yeah, it'll run out in the end, but the trick is to draw it out slowly, make it last right to the last drop.

It'll be like she never went away; like someone pressed the pause button at her finest moment. There'll be photographs of her everywhere. She'll be remembered as she was – as beautiful and as perfect as she'll ever be. See what I'll have saved her from. She'll never be an old dried-up has-been. She'd thank me . . . really, she would.

Outside the Grosvenor, the old drunks with the cider bottles have taken up residence on the benches. One of them snarls and growls at no one and at everyone. Shielded from them all by an ancient coastal tide of splashed vomit stains that arcs the surrounding tarmac.

Cassiopeia's Nipple

John Mulcreevy

The story sat in a dense block under a big headline – bigger than the story about the council, which was bigger again than the story about job losses at Rover. Chico Casey's index finger flicked the pages of the *Evening Mail* with the speed of habit until page 31, where he stopped and snipped out the Chipper cartoon.

Well north of the city centre but just south of the Moscow winds that rushed Barr Beacon was Tame Valley, a tentacle of Birmingham's canal system that curled into Spaghetti Junction. Mostly ignored, the stretch cowered redundantly beneath the gloating motorway carrying bread, oil and salesmen. A cargo that once belonged to the water.

But today, as on past few days, Tame Valley found itself the talk of shops and houses as the hunt for Jack Small swayed from hope to resignation to conclusion. His gun had floated into a police diver's hand and, later, enquiring searchlights had witnessed a body gone white dragged from the water.

Until the adjective for Jack Small changed from 'missing' to 'murdered', no one had mentioned the Roman tits man; and until the chattering changed from speculation to suspicion, no one ever mentioned he had a proper name or an address or a life outside of being the Roman tits man.

Chipper was placed carefully into the photo album and the transparent film smoothed down to protect it. The album of strip cartoons was nearly full and looked as good as a *Peanuts* annual. Chico didn't know why the *Mail* didn't issue a proper *Chipper* annual every year. Chico thought he was a good funny dog, not as funny as Snoopy but better than Fred Basset. Before putting the mutilated paper into a carrier bag with other old copies and ready-meal packs for recycling, Chico paused over the big headline again. It hadn't occurred he could've been a Gregory, looking, as he did, much more a Ted or a Sid.

When they were still friends, and before they became old mates or kids he used to know, Chico and the others would knock about the canal. They got in off the Walsall Road. That was the best bit, by the thirteen locks where they could jump from one bank to the other over the black and white locks – looking at fluid reflections of themselves colouring the limpid water as they leapt. On weekends when there was lager to be drunk and chips to be eaten, they'd climb over Perry Barr Lock Bridge and head for No. 2 Reflux Valve to sit on the brick enclosure. It was on one of those nights Roman tits man had first spoken.

They'd seen him before; everyone who used the canal as a playground, cycle path or lovers' lane had seen him. He would emerge like an eerie Victorian apparition from hovering masks of mist, becoming delineated as a lump of typical late-middle-age in beige; with telescope hanging from shoulder instead of the usual stripy shopping bag.

'See it? Crackin tonight – the Plough and Little Bear.'

Chico and the others had been on their way back from climbing on top of containers in a yard when they'd seen him. He was standing on a plastic Co-op crate with his telescope pointed north.

'You don't often get a sight here, too much shit from the factories. Have a go.'

He handed the telescope to Mortiboys, who made a Lord Nelson joke and squinted through the lens.

'See those four stars and the two next to them: Little Bear.' Mortiboys nodded and raised an eyebrow at Chico. 'I know what you want to see,' said the amateur astronomer.

A tattered soft-cover book was squeezed out from inside his jacket and a centre spread of constellations like join-the-dots drawings pushed under the noses of Chico and the others. The astronomer tapped at a picture of an exotic-looking girl with long hair sitting on a chair.

'Move to the west. No, the other way and go up a bit. Got the five stars, yeah? The second one, that's Cassiopeia's nipple. Hur! Hur! Hur!'

Before that night he'd just been the bloke on the canal. After, he became known as the Roman tits man. Murph had coined the name: he said the girl with the long hair was from ancient Rome, recalling the phrase from *I, Claudius* on telly. The more people Chico and the others mentioned the episode to the more people recognized the description, and eventually the name began to circulate, even among the women at the garage shop.

He was spotted all over the canalways. Chico's workmate saw him under a bridge by Spaghetti; Mortiboys watched him being chased by kids on the stretch that meandered around the BT Tower in the city. Some said he lived rough in a yard hut, getting his breakfast from the grub van that serviced the industrial estate. They hadn't a clue really, they just thought someone like him who never spoke and always looked distressed when buying biscuits, mints and fruit from the supermarket would probably live in a yard hut. Chico and the others saw him often in the times before bum-fluff and the legal drinking age. In daylight hours he'd silently salute while scurrying past but at twilight, with telescope extended, he'd occasionally call out to let them know it was a good night for the stars.

'Are the nipples out tonight, eh, chap?'

'Oh arr, crackin. Hur! Hur! Hur!'

Chico was the only one of them who still walked the Tame Valley, mostly down the viaduct when his clutch wasn't working properly. He knew there would be a few tourists around now. They'd be peering into the Jacquard patterns of the water where, among the usual jetsam, the components of a murder mystery had been given up: eight-year-old Jack and his poundshop machine gun, a pair of scissors and a bleached edition of a children's astronomy guide. On the towpaths flowed a stream of flower bearers commemorating another soldier who hadn't come back from his war. And from above, the motorway gazed down as the arteries of old Birmingham pumped again, even though it had taken a death to bring the place to life. A policewoman questioned random parts of the macabre procession. Chico wasn't stopped; she was too busy consoling the elderly woman whose voice scraped agitatedly down the tin plate of clichés.

'You don't expect it on your doorstep. This used to be a nice area.'

Climbing out by the sports field, he stopped at one of the photocopied fly-posters pinned to a tree. They were obviously serious. A drawing pin pressed firmly in each corner, though the bottom left half of the paper had been ripped away, maybe by the wind or maybe by Gregory. He'd been a figure of amusement, a silly old sod. The Roman tits man was always good for a chuckle during small talk. *Why did he spend all his time walking up and down the canal? Maybe he was a North Sea fisherman who'd been blown astray and lost his trawler. That must be it. He's spent the last few decades wandering around looking for his boat. That'd account for the fishy smell he leaves behind after buying his mints.*

Chico hadn't seen him for a while. The last time was two months ago, while having a drink for Dunky's thirtieth. Roman tits man appeared from one side of the canal, heaved himself across the dual carriageway and vanished down the other side. He didn't have his telescope with him.

Chico remembered it because Anita was there that night and she'd been the one who pointed out Cassiopeia was actually Andromeda's mother from Greek mythology.

It didn't take long for whispers to become fly-posters. The day before the body was found he was a nameless, homeless enigma in beige. The day after he was Gregory Masters from one of the housing association flats by the athletics stadium. He had no job, no wife, no children, his place was filthy and, according to one of the checkout dawdlers at the supermarket, he'd always looked at kids in a funny way.

Chico stood in the queue, impatiently tapping a tin of mackerel as accusations took precedence over the gridlock of full trolleys.

'Luke and the man next door were going to go round but I told him leave it to the police.'

'I made an anonymous call.'

'I always thought he looked like one of them.'

'Is that a new coat, Maureen?'

It was ineffectual chatter, but a word to the wrong husband or son, a word to the wrong man with nothing to hunt and kill since technology had taken over . . . Chico thought it really was that fine a balance from walking the earth to lying under it.

In the car park outside, he stopped to snatch a fly-poster from under his windscreen wipers. Dunky's brother stopped by on his way into the shop. Chico pointed at the poster. 'Spelt paedophile wrong, ain't they?'

Dunky returned an English language GCSE grade 4 look. 'There's been nothing in the news about it being a . . . y'know, eh, Chico.'

'That's right. It's just a murder. They hadn't done anything to the kid, not like that.'

'They got it in for the tits man all right. See you about, Chico mate.'

Before he could open the car door he got stopped again, this time by the policewoman from the canal. Now she wasn't asking if anyone had seen anything in the canal that night, but asking about the fly-posters. Had he seen who'd been putting them under windscreen wipers? Chico shook his head apologetically, thought about making a gag about falling standards of literacy among local vigilantes but decided not to. She was a young copper and they were usually stern and humourless. He attempted to get into his car but wasn't quick enough to avoid another question.

'Do you use the canal much?

'Haven't been there for years, sorry.'

Kelly, waiting for his stepdaughter, gave a thumbs-up when on Saturday morning Chico mounted the kerb outside the primary school where the prayer service for Jack Small was being held.

'He was a little git; now he's a bloody angel. Load of bloody hypocrites.'

Chico agreed. Jack'd been one of those kids who'd kick and spit at things, usually things smaller than himself like girls from the year below, or dogs.

'Lynette came home crying once,' added Chico, looking at the newly planted saplings covered with wire mesh in the school garden. He reckoned they ought to do that with the kids. Protect them with mesh to stop them running wild or being vandalized. Then Jack would probably still be here today in person instead of in thought.

'Hope they get the bastard, though,' Kelly grunted.

The children and their mums, plus a few dads, poured out of the school. Chico dropped Kelly and his stepdaughter off and drove on, just him and Lynette. Over a burger and milkshake he began his weekly shift of parenting, which consisted almost exclusively of Donald Duck impressions and pulling funny faces at other customers behind their backs. Then an afternoon matinee, a go on the swings in the park and back to her mother's before dark. Lynette was quieter than normal, and before she left she asked why Jack had gone to heaven when she thought only old people were supposed to die. Realizing what was coming next, Chico promised her she wouldn't have to go to heaven until she was about a hundred years old. She seemed reassured and in return promised not to tell her mum about the funny faces and farting in the cinema. He sounded his horn as Lynette ran up the path to the open door where Sandra stood with arms folded. The last thing he heard as he wound up the window was Lynette shouting: 'I'm gonna live to be a hundred!' Chico felt relieved he was only a part-time dad. He thought nothing in life was worth doing full-time; nothing at all.

As he drove along the Walsall Road, the fly-posting continued. Despite appeals from the church and police, neither God nor law could prevent trees, bus shelters and windscreens conducting their clandestine case for the prosecution. According to Anita, who lived close to Roman tits man, the neighbours reckoned the coppers hadn't even been round to speak to him. They must've been holding a 24-hour watch on his ground-floor flat to know that. There must've been rows of houses on stakeout; a twitching of one set of net curtains followed by another throughout the day as one watch replaced another. All of them eagerly waiting for the screaming sirens and screeching brakes that would announce the arrival of panda cars bursting with constables. Anita Noone was probably Chico's favourite woman. She had the looks and knew more about stuff, which was a novelty to him. He would've liked to but preferred her as a fantasy, once or twice a week before he fell into sleep. He knew she wasn't the part-time type.

The stuff Anita knew; she'd told him that Cassiopeia was the wife of Cepheus, King of Ethiopia. She'd boasted arrogantly of her beauty, stirring anger with Poseidon who unleashed a sea monster upon her daughter Andromeda. Anita had finished by stating Gregory Masters hadn't done anything wrong, not that there was any evidence of, but was being punished just like Andromeda. Chico had added that maybe the god of the sea had returned and was operating in the Tame Valley canal.

Chico crunched into third and pulled out in front of a bus. He was in two minds whether to put his foot down and have his bhoona back at the flat or stop by the canal and eat it there. It was a warm, red-sky evening and the tourists wouldn't be around, they'd be back at home watching atrocities then variety shows on the box. A combination of roadworks and traffic from the Villa made up his mind.

It was a good walk to No. 2 Reflux Valve, but he felt a strange compulsion to go all the way there to sit on the brick like he'd done years ago. The bhoona wasn't great and he chucked half of it; he'd been off his food for a while. He stood up and studied the night rising over the sports field with its lopsided goalposts. There wasn't a thing up above – no Little Bear or Plough, no Greek queen on a chair, and no Roman tits man. Never again would the skies look down to see him staring back at them, or, for that matter, see Jack Small declaring war on ducks and lock gates.

Did Roman tits man and little Jack Small ever meet there on the towpaths: the labyrinths magnetizing those who didn't want to be among the people and pavements, didn't want to be held by their orders and orthodoxy? Would the tits man have handed his telescope to Jack and pointed out which stars corresponded to the swords of Athenian kings? Would Jack have been mesmerized by the magic of soldiers in the sky, or would he have treated his tutor as he treated little girls and tied up dogs – leaving Roman tits man scrambling on the bank as his telescope floated out of arm's reach?

It was a short drive home behind the tin boxes on wheels containing Chico's community, nearly all of them more recognizable by their number plates than their faces. And in his mirror he saw the remnants of flowers and fly-posters decaying on trees. He'd lived there for too long. The others had all gone: Mortiboys and Kelly were in another district, Ambrose in another city, Murph in another world – since going mad.

Counting the vacant pages, Chico calculated that in a fortnight the Chipper annual for Lynette's birthday would be finished. The big front-page headline was sticking up out of the carrier bag crammed full of papers and cardboard. He imagined burnt furniture and spitting electrics and a body gone black dragged from the fire. He decided to cut it out and went into the kitchen to get his new pair of scissors.

Pest Control

Kay Fletcher

Why had the old lady held on to the house so vehemently, when he'd been willing to arrange for her to go into a perfectly decent nursing home? Her daughter had been the same. Fifteen years he was married to that shrew while the other one sat on his shoulder like some succubus, nagging, always taking her daughter's part. Even about the mice.

'Caroline would never let anyone harm a fly while she was under this roof,' his mother-in-law had said shortly after his wife died.

Ian had called Quix-O-Kill about the rodent problem, but his mother-in-law made him cancel the appointment. Just like her mother, Caroline had been a respecter of life, preferring most species to her own. Where had that got her? Did she respect the bunch of misfired cells that swamped her body and eventually destroyed it? They showed as little consideration for her life as he would for these rodents now. He'd call Quix-O-Kill again, now that neither his wife nor his mother-in-law was here to tell him otherwise.

As for that inanimate object upstairs, of course it would have to be moved. He'd every intention of telling the authorities. He'd tried ringing them the day his mother-in-law departed, but there was something wrong with the line, all he got was crackle and a long hiss, as if the phone – like his mother-in-law – had breathed its last.

Ian had gone to live in the handsome Edwardian townhouse near Dudley as a newlywed. His wife's mother had made it very clear whose house this was; and although Ian had tried to wean Caroline away from her influence, eventually she'd become an echo of the old woman. This was, after all, the house where Caroline had grown up and her mother had grown old; where, before his mother-in-law hit the menopause, for one week in every month they'd turn grumpy and roaring like a two-headed lion. The house would simmer with the metallic reek of menstruation while Ian's ego shrank to a timid resentful thing that cowered behind the skirting board with the mice.

Much later, when his mother-in-law's friends came to visit, the recently widowed Ian would be all polite smiles. He'd play waiter and amiable doorman to the spiritualist through whom she'd begun having conversations with Caroline, and to frail Miss Stitch with her sparrow legs, Sally Army uniform and shabby Bible, which she waved at him like incense, as if dispelling his smell from the room.

Towards the end, if his mother-in-law went out at all it was to séances or to church – which amounted to much the same thing in Ian's opinion. It was while she was away at one of these places that he'd bundled all his late wife's belongings together: the portraits of dewy-eyed children, the soapstone crosses and the Capo di Monte Virgin Mary, and took the lot to the Cancer Research shop. Don't look so grateful, he thought, as he hauled each bag onto the counter, you haven't seen what's in them yet.

When Caroline's mother saw the blank spaces on the walls and the items missing from around the house, the violence of her rage brought on a stroke. Her friends visited dutifully, and Ian accepted their premature condolences.

'Caroline's watching over you both, rest assured,' the spiritualist said, and Miss Stitch sang hymns over the paralysed woman as she twitched and muttered in her sleep.

The hospital staff said he'd find it difficult to cope at home, but Ian relished having his mother-in-law captive there. He took delight in describing to her how he planned to convert the house into flats and make enough money to live a life of relative leisure. She cursed him with her eyes, and rocked and boiled like a kettle. She stayed that way for days, refusing to eat, clamping her mouth shut against the dripping spoonfuls of soup he attempted to feed her.

The day Ian eased his mother-in-law into eternity, a hissing blanket of rain kept him indoors. As the storm raged, he dug out her savings book. He knew the old woman had no intention of leaving him a penny; she'd made no secret of the fact that she'd bequeathed all her money to the World Wildlife Fund.

There were innumerable examples of her handwriting lying about the house: the accounts she'd kept so meticulously, the psalms she'd liked to copy out of her Bible when various aches and pains tested her faith. Ian practised forging her signature while the rain splashed down the sooty chimney and forced a puddle under the front door.

Occasionally the pressure of falling rain harassed the house into a groan, or noisily relaxed the ageing brickwork; otherwise the silence was disturbed only by the scratching of those few indestructible mice.

Ian marvelled at the tenacity of these creatures. How could something so insignificant prove so difficult to destroy? Had their tiny organs become immune to the poison he put down? They certainly seemed intelligent enough to learn from the demise of their companions. There'd been no sign of the mice for days; the pieces of cheese with which he'd attempted to entice them into traps had shrunk to mouldy pebbles. And yet their musty smell was everywhere; the growing itch of their presence was becoming intolerable. Unable to bear it any longer, Ian decided to get some air. From his tiny front garden he could see Dudley Castle: a granite-coloured silhouette through a petrol-blue haze. It was a mile or so away, and yet he felt he could reach out and pluck the ruin from its densely wooded crest.

Belladonna Avenue was a quiet, elderly place; he rarely saw any of the neighbours coming or going. In the few times he'd been out since his mother-in-law's death he hadn't bumped into a soul. It would be easy enough to say she'd gone away, that it had become too difficult to look after the old lady unaided, so he'd placed her in a good nursing home. Then he could quietly disappear, and no one would be any the wiser.

A short walk from Belladonna Avenue was Dudley town itself. During the day the town centre swarmed with elderly men and women. The walking dead, as Ian thought of them. After nine thirty, they crowded onto the buses with their free passes. Soon, with their drab raincoats and threadbare shopping bags, they possessed the outdoor market and the shopping precinct. What use are these people to the economy? Ian thought. They spend next to nothing and they're always at the doctor's or queuing at the chemist or the post office for their free handouts.

'You'll be old one of these days,' Caroline used to say.

Ian had hated her for reminding him of this fact, and he resented her still for having escaped that horrible fate herself. At least she'd never grow *old*.

An incessant rattling drew Ian out of his thoughts. He was surprised to find himself near the Churchill precinct, opposite the tail-end of the outdoor market. Miss Stitch occupied her usual spot, shaking a collection tin. She stood on that draughty corner for hours at a time telling people how glorious heaven was, how eager she was to meet her Lord. He was certain she'd seen him, but she didn't smile or raise her copy of *The War Cry* in greeting, the way she would have done if his mother-in-law had still been alive. It was at that moment that Ian realized Miss Stitch *knew* everything.

He rushed through the precinct into the department store his mother-in-law used to call her second home, up the escalator, past the china figurines in their revolving glass cases. He happened to glance at one of the mirrors on display near by, and what he saw appalled him.

No wonder Miss Stitch had looked at him so oddly in the precinct just now. She must have seen what those mirrors so deftly reflected. His guilt. And worse – just under his left eye, he saw it quite distinctly – a splatter of blood. In the Gents, Ian leaned against the porcelain washbasin. Of course there wasn't any blood. He'd suffocated his mother-in-law while she slept, with a pillow from her own bed.

He turned off the cold tap and dabbed his chilled wrists with toilet roll. Only one person knew his secret. Only one person could spoil it for him now.

Ian was astonished by the speed at which his thoughts arranged themselves into a plan. Back at Belladonna Avenue, he took a sheet of his mother-in-law's best Basildon Bond and wrote:

> Dear Miss Stitch,
> Going through my mother-in-law's effects at this sad time, I have discovered that she wished to make a small donation to the Salvation Army. I would be most grateful if you could come to the house, at your convenience, so that we can discuss this further.
> Yours sincerely, Ian

Exalted by his own cleverness, Ian called Quix-O-Kill and explained that he wanted the whole house scouring from top to bottom: 'This rodent problem's getting way beyond a joke.'

'We're very busy at the moment, sir,' the calm and sensible woman on the other end of the line told him, 'but we'll rush someone out to you as soon as one of our operatives becomes available.'

Ian decided not to leave the house until both the rodents and Miss Stitch had been dealt with. He was sure the old woman would come as soon as she'd read his letter, eager to get her hands on his mother-in-law's money. The old hypocrite.

Next morning, however, Ian discovered his cupboards were bare, except for a few tins of rice pudding and cream of tomato soup. There was no way he could touch those, so he nipped out early, planning to get to Spar and back in double-quick time.

He hurried along to the shops, buzzing with excitement and anticipation. The feeling didn't abate, not even when – coming out of Spar with his bag of supplies – he saw Miss Stitch walking very determinedly along the other side of the road.

Ian's exuberance rose. What better opportunity to rid himself of Miss Stitch than right now? It wasn't unknown for an old body to be found among the bushes in the park, which was quiet on weekdays now that the Council no longer employed a warden.

It was easy to shadow Miss Stitch. She was bound to be preoccupied with her new inheritance, and all those good deeds it would make possible. As she approached the park gates, Ian prepared to cross the road and usher her inside. 'A short cut,' he'd say, and the old dear wouldn't realize until it was too late.

He made his dash, and was about to tap Miss Stitch on the shoulder when something caught his arm, yanking it backwards so that his carrier bag was tossed up into the air, raining cartons of milk, tins of baked beans and London Grill down all around him. Something struck his head, and the world greyed out. When he came round, he was lying in the road and Miss Stitch was bent over him.

'Oh dear, oh dear, oh dear . . .'

A can of macaroni cheese came to rest, almost guiltily, against his cheek. Beyond it loomed a large black doughnut.

'He just walked out . . .'

A man stood beside Miss Stitch, his white overall looked medical. Perhaps someone had already called an ambulance?

'Oh dear . . . first the wife, then the mother . . . oh dear, dear, dear . . .' Miss Stitch went on.

The two of them were at a funny angle and, though he tried, Ian couldn't alter the position of his neck, which felt oddly tingly. The world floated in and out of focus. In a clear moment Ian realized that the black doughnut was a tyre belonging to a large white van. The door was open and words were printed on its side.

'He shouldn't close his eyes, should he?' the man was saying.

Ian was intrigued by the words on that van. He struggled to read them, but his head was splitting. And what was that awful noise? Some cat being strangled? Ian winced.

'*Abide with me, fast falls the eventide. The darkness deepens, Lord, with me abide . . .*'

While the old woman sang, the man hopped from side to side behind her, gibbering into a mobile phone the size of a matchbox.

'Keep still, won't you?' Ian muttered. 'I'm trying to read what it says . . .'

Miss Stitch's voice faded to a scratchy hiss. She dropped her chin against her chest while behind her the man expended peak-rate silence into his mobile.

Ian was laughing. He could read it now, what it said on the side of the van. QUIX-O-KILL.

This Night Last Woman

Joel Lane

There's a pub in Acocks Green I used to go to regularly. For two reasons. Firstly, there's a lot of middle-aged single women drink there. Secondly, they have a karaoke night on Saturdays, with a late bar after. I think I'd seen her there a few times before we actually met. I'm not sure. Memories don't stay the same. That's why people need music, to help them remember. And help them feel. If you know what I mean.

It was in October last year. Not long after the attack on New York. Army shops all over the country had sold out of gas masks. People were scared. Nobody knew what was going to happen. Fortunately, it wasn't the kind of pub where wannabe squaddies went to shout and smash glasses. By Acocks Green standards, it was quite a mixed crowd. That night, a young black guy sang 'Everything I Own' and reduced the whole pub to silence, then a storm of applause. An Irish girl sang 'Zombie', a sadder and much better version than the original.

As usual I was standing near the front, close enough to the bar that I could get a refill every two or three songs. They had an all-night cheap doubles offer. I always like to finish the drink before the ice has melted. To the right of the stage, a group of brightly dressed youngsters were dancing and chatting. Behind me the older crowd, mostly women, were sitting around tables that were already covered with empty glasses. The standard AG types could be seen: young men with heads like light bulbs, women with short jackets and hair tied back hard. Two black security lads were standing just inside the door, keeping an eye out for trouble. Once when I came past this place, everyone was standing outside while five police cars lined up along the road. But that wasn't going to happen tonight.

The white-haired guy running the karaoke machine tried to alternate men and women. With the men, there's a certain kind of song you always get. Three generations of self-pity: Roy Orbison, Neil Diamond, Robbie Williams. The same lonely song, whatever the voice that carries it. The women are more resilient somehow. But as with the booze, it's the cumulative effect that gets to you.

A little fat guy in front of me kept punching the air on the choruses. If he'd had a lighter, he'd have waved it. People were calling for the black lad who'd sung 'Everything I Own', but he'd left to start his night shift. The karaoke ended with this girl singing 'Fields of Athenry', which I hadn't heard in years. There was something about the idea of a prison ship that made me start crying. I can't explain it.

As the last chords faded, there was a crackle of applause like the static on a poorly tuned radio. I turned back to the bar to get another cheap double vodka. Something tugged at the corner of my eye. A pale face wrapped in shadows. I glanced at her, then looked away. A woman with black hair and a coat the colour of autumn leaves. Her eyes were shining, wet. Someone pushed past me to get to the bar. I felt a kind of vertigo, like there was a darkness around my head.

In front of me, two blokes were talking. *I could change,* one of them said. *There was this night last woman. Made me feel like a different man. The way she was. All gets bright when you're with someone.* I wasn't sure which of them was saying that. Or was it just a voice in my head? I decided to get that drink, but somehow turned back to the dark-haired woman. She was looking straight at me. Her black mascara had run at the corners. We stared at each other for a few seconds.

I'm always nervous about talking to women in pubs. If she brushed me off, I'd have a burning wire in my stomach the rest of the night. But there was something about her, a loneliness in her eyes that held me. It felt like we'd already shared something. I crossed over to where she was standing and waited, looking past her at a couple kissing in the half-light. She didn't move away. I looked at her, smiled. Looked at her mouth. She smiled back.

'So you like karaoke too,' I said.

'Yeah. You can't beat those old songs.' She had a Black Country accent. I'd have guessed her age as early thirties. 'Did you hear that black kid earlier? The Ken Boothe song?'

'Yeah, he was brilliant.' I noticed she wasn't holding a glass. 'Want a drink?'

'Vodka and lime. Cheers.'

The disco was starting as I waited at the bar. Madonna, then Gabrielle. We found a couple of seats at the back of the pub, where it was a bit quieter. Her name was Carly. I only caught about half of what she was saying; enough to gather that she lived in Greet and managed a camera shop. She wasn't glamorous, but there was a fragility under the tiredness that appealed to me. And she smoked, which I've always found attractive. As we talked, I could feel her breathing smoke onto my face.

'Do you live on your own?' she asked. Her leg was pressed against mine under the table. But when I asked her for a dance, she said no.

Near midnight they rang for last orders. As I stumbled to

the bar in the half-light, a Judy Boucher song was playing. Couples swayed together, their faces motionless. Earlier, some of the women had been dancing alone; but now they were either paired up with men or sitting. One of them, hopelessly drunk, threw an arm round me at the bar and ruffled my hair. I shrugged her off and lifted the two drinks by way of explanation.

The lights were so low by then that all I could see of Carly was a ghost of her face, like a paper mask that her cigarette might set on fire. We were talking about our favourite records – a private exchange I won't share with you. It felt like she was a friend as well as someone I might end up fucking. She was a bit on edge, a bit reluctant to open up, but then so was I.

It was a surprisingly warm night for October. She wanted to get a taxi, but I said my flat was only a block away. I needed the walk to clear my head. It's a quiet road full of houses with driveways and security lights. A world away from the Fox Hollies estate on the other side of the pub. Every time a car drove past, she kissed me to hide her face. I wondered if she was married. Was that one of the things she'd said and I hadn't caught?

'The flat's in a bit of a state,' I mumbled as we reached the block. There was new graffiti on the locked garage doors, but I couldn't read it.

'Don't worry. Whatever it's like, I've seen worse.' Still, I noticed she was tense as I guided her through the heaps of books and records, and cleared a space on the battered sofa. 'Do you often bring women back here?'

'It's been a while,' I said.

'I was being sarcastic. Don't worry about it.' She sat down without taking her coat off.

'Would you like some coffee?'

Carly looked past me at a bookcase full of flying saucer and conspiracy books. 'Got any booze?'

'What would you like?' As far as I could remember, I had everything. A bit short on mixers, though.

'Vodka'd be nice.' She smiled. Although her face looked tired, her body was like a coiled spring. Maybe another drink would relax her. I needed coffee if we were going to do anything.

But I couldn't pour her a vodka and not have some. The bottle was in the freezer. It stuck to my fingers. I found a couple of shot glasses and washed them carefully.

When I came back into the living room, she'd taken off her coat and shoes. We drank and cuddled for a while, sharing vodka and smoke between our mouths. In spite of the drink, I was getting excited. The loneliness in her called to the loneliness in me. It didn't matter that we were hardly talking.

'Can I have a look at your records?' she said. Most of them were in boxes along the right-hand wall. She knelt there, drink in one hand, flicking through the dusty LPs. I noticed she was shivering.

'Are you cold?' I said. 'I can light the gas fire . . .'

'No, it's OK.' She stood up and came back to the couch, then reached down and touched my face. 'Let's go to bed,' she said quietly. 'I just have to . . . where's the bathroom?'

'Through there, second left.' She'd have to pass by the kitchen, but that couldn't be helped. She took her handbag with her. I went through to the bedroom and straightened the duvet, tidied some clothes away in the basket. It should have felt tacky, but it didn't. One-night stands don't have to be cold. It's a chance to be in love for a little while, then let it go. Before the wind blows through the cracks.

When Carly emerged from the bathroom, her eyes were glittering again. 'Are you OK?' I said.

'Yeah. Too much to drink. Could I have a glass of water?'

It took me a while to find another tumbler and wash it. While I was there I poured myself another vodka – a small one, in a shot glass, for later. A nightcap always gives me a sense of security. I took them through into the bedroom. Carly was lying on the duvet, still dressed. She took the glass of water and drank half of it. Her face was a mask. It felt like I'd known her all my life.

We undressed each other slowly. Cars passed by the window, each one lighting up the blind for a few seconds. Her body was taut and muscular. Maybe she went to a gym. She let me turn her on the bed and kiss my way down her spine. Which was when I noticed the scars. They were almost too fine to see, but my lips felt them. Like a white tattoo over her back and legs. A fishing-net, for her to flop and writhe in. I wondered how it would feel to walk around in a skin like that. Gently, I turned her round to face me.

The sex took a long time. Part-way through, we got under the duvet, where it was warmer. She didn't climax. Women usually don't. When I was spent, she let go of me and lit up a cigarette. I reached for my vodka glass, but my hand shook and I knocked her tumbler off the cabinet. If it'd been empty, it wouldn't have broken.

Carly reached down and started gathering the pieces of glass. 'Leave it,' I said. 'I'll tidy it later.'

'How much later?' She lay back on the pillow, breathing smoke. A light gleamed in her left hand: a fragment of glass. 'Give me your hand,' she said.

She held my arm in the air. Slowly, she drew the sharp edge of the glass along it, from the elbow to the wrist. For a few seconds, there was nothing there but a white groove. Then it filled with blood. She drew her tongue along the cut. I couldn't feel much. She looked away. Her face was closed in on itself. I lifted the vodka glass with my other hand and drained it.

Then, before I knew it, she was getting dressed. I said nothing. It was cold in the room. I put a tissue on my arm; it stuck there. 'I'd better get home,' she said.

'Would you like me to call a cab?'

'Cheers.'

I got dressed, made the call, then took her out into the courtyard. She was still tense, but fighting off sleep. A cat ran in front of us into some bushes, chasing something we hadn't seen. I scribbled down my phone number and passed it to her. Overhead, a few stars were visible through a gauze of cloud. When the cab arrived, she brushed her lips against mine and muttered, 'See ya.'

She didn't phone. I went back to that pub on the next karaoke night, but she wasn't there and I got so drunk I had to leave before I blacked out. I went to the karaoke nights at the Greet Inn and the Village in Moseley, but there was no sign of her. They were shit anyway. Then one evening in November, I was in Alldays buying a pint of milk when I saw her face on the front of the *Evening Mail*.

At first, I thought it was my mind playing tricks. You do that when you miss someone, see them everywhere. Especially as her name was given as Nicola. But unless she had a twin sister, it had to be her. There were more pictures inside. Apparently some guy had picked her up and she'd attacked him with a knife in his flat. He'd fought her off with a telephone, of all things. They'd both ended up in hospital: her with a broken face, him with a badly slashed hand.

But the real story came two days later. It was all over the national papers. She told the police she'd killed three men, only one of whom had already been found. The other two were where she'd said they were: in their city centre flats, stabbed. They'd been there for weeks. The *Mail* said she went for older men without family or friends, because their contacts were harder to trace. The police appealed for anyone who'd encountered her to come forward. I kept my mouth shut.

She was in a local prison by the end of the year. In Frankley, on the edge of the Clent Hills. I sent her a card at Christmas, and wrote to the prison requesting permission to visit. The hope of seeing her kept me going through to the New Year. I knew she felt as lonely as I did. That was why she hadn't killed me. There was something real between us. She'd been hiding my face, not hers. Yet she'd let me live.

In late January, I got a letter in a long Prison Service envelope. It was from her. Her handwriting was angular and ragged. She said I could come and see her that Sunday at four. It was signed Carly. That proved she remembered me. She understood what I'd been through. My anima, my secret soul.

The day I went out to the prison was cold and bright. The Clent Hills were crusted with dead bracken. I'd had nothing to drink all day, so I was feeling a bit shaky and sick. It was partly tension. How could I be sure? Pain is a one-way street. I stared at the dark ground and shivered. Her image in my mind kept breaking up into flecks, like a newspaper photograph.

The visiting room was a series of glass panels with chairs on either side. You talked through holes in the window. Her face wasn't quite the same. The broken bones hadn't set right. She didn't smile. Confinement hadn't brought her peace. 'How are you keeping?' she asked.

I shrugged. 'Same as ever. How's life here?'

'Not so bad. When you've lived in Tyseley, it all becomes relative.'

'Do they let you listen to music in here?'

'Somehow, I can't be bothered.' Her dark eyes watched me steadily. 'Don't take this the wrong way. But you'll probably never see me outside again.' I nodded. 'So why have you come?'

'I need to know something.' My throat was dry. It felt

like the walls around us had disappeared. 'I don't care about what you've done. I need to know . . . why you didn't kill me.'

There was silence. Twice she began to speak and stopped herself. Then she said quietly, 'Because it wasn't worth it. You're already dying.'

'You don't know that.' I felt the blood rush to my face. 'You don't know. I could break some woman's heart –' She looked away and laughed. I couldn't hear her laughter through the glass. But I could feel it.

As I left the prison, it was getting dark. The city's lights glowed in the distance, spread below me like a coral reef. From far away, I could hear the voice of a young black man singing 'Everything I Own'. I waited for the Midland Red bus to Edgbaston. But a local bus came first, and I got on it. I wanted to find a pub where men were playing darts. Where I could brag about my conquests. Have a man-to-man talk about the things that matter. Or just drink.

The Inland Waterways Association

Nicholas Royle

If Birmingham was the Venice of the Midlands, in Sir Reginald Hill's appropriated phrase, what did that make Venice? The Birmingham of the Veneto? From where I was sitting, sipping a glass of prosecco at a café terrace overlooking the Grand Canal, I couldn't see it catching on. The bright sunlight and fresh breeze turned the broad expanse of water into an inverted version of the Artex ceiling in my Yardley flat, white and choppy. I tried to picture the Grand Union Canal at the end of my road, midway between Acocks Green station and the Swan Centre in Yardley, and found that I could do so all too easily. Tench-green, oxygen-starved and barely two rod-lengths across, it would have a job making it on to the World Heritage list. To be fair, though, I'd seen canals in Venice that were not dissimilar. Only the setting was markedly different.

This was my last night in La Serenissima – the most serene republic – my last night of a week-long visit that I had nearly cancelled. Only two things had stopped me: firstly, the fact that the travel company offered no refund in case of cancellation and, secondly, Martin Weiss.

I left the café terrace and headed back towards the hotel to shower and change before dinner.

Martin Weiss was a friend from schooldays. In fact, although he and I had been at school together in Acocks Green, we hadn't been particularly close. But then we found ourselves attending the same college at London University. Anything to get out of Birmingham, had been pretty much my approach to further education, whereas Martin, if our conversations in the union bar were anything to go by, missed the Midlands and looked forward to going back as soon as he'd completed his degree, if not sooner. It seemed to me the particular area of London in which we'd chosen to study, the East End, was not much different from Birmingham anyway. Urban deprivation, a divided community, the subtle yet constant threat of violence: Martin should have felt at home.

For the first few months, Martin and I saw little of the neighbourhood, in any case, since we spent most of our free time in the union building. I would be reading, either set texts or potboilers, but I made little progress owing to Martin's constant interruptions as he showed off his talent for solving the *Daily Telegraph* crossword. Martin didn't read the *Telegraph* (I don't think he read a paper at all; he got it for the crossword), but that didn't stop the Labour Club types who controlled the union glaring at him disapprovingly. He made no effort to justify his choice to them.

'The *Guardian* crossword's too fucking hard,' he confided. 'Now, what about three down? "Bubblegum, chewed, loses fellow but gains one in country." Seven letters.'

'I struggle with the quick crossword,' I said.

'It's easy. Look.' He pointed with his pen. '"Bubblegum, chewed", i.e. anagram of bubblegum, but minus a word meaning "fellow". That's "bub". Then you add "i" – that's "one" – and the answer is the name of a country. Belgium. See? Piece of piss.'

'You're not just a pretty face, are you?' I said, smiling at him.

There was no warmth in his hazel eyes as he replied sharply, 'Fuck off back to GaySoc.'

The college had a good reputation for science-based courses, but I was doing English, while Martin was doing – or, to edge closer to the truth, not doing – history of art. He didn't last long. A term and a half into the second year, Martin vanished for two weeks, then reappeared, not as a remorseful student begging the vice-dean to let him stay, but as the featured artist of a one-man show at a scabrous basement gallery in Bethnal Green. His blurry photographs of East End murder sites, under the title 'Echoes of the Past', showed that he had, after all, found something to hold his interest in Whitechapel: the district's lasting association with the crimes of Jack the Ripper.

The show was both an inauspicious debut into the art world and his 'Goodbye, I'm off' note to the corridors of academia. He wasn't seen on the Mile End Road again, although the college paper was the only journal to include a review of 'Echoes of the Past'. A rather overlong, not entirely uncritical but largely positive write-up, it marked my own first appearance in the world that would later claim me for one of its own, newspaper journalism. In particular I praised the cryptic captions Martin had given his photographs: each, like a crossword clue, had to be worked out, making you think about the pictures.

When I eventually left college with my predictably average degree, it was back to Birmingham that I went, working for a spell as a sub-editor on the *Post*, then as a reporter on the *Evening Mail*. Gradually, telescoping a series of various staff positions, freelance gigs and 'rest periods', we return to the present day, which sees me employed as a crime reporter on a launch project for a rival publisher to the bunch that owns the *Post* and the *Mail*. A new daily paper for the West Midlands, it's likely to ditch into Edgbaston Reservoir within a year of launching, if we even get that far; but it seemed like a golden opportunity in the final dismaying weeks of 2001, when I was staring out the window cursing the name of Patricia Cornwell.

If it hadn't been for Cornwell, I would have been getting on with my book. For about eighteen months, I had been writing this book, on spec, entitled *The Art of Murder*, and had just reached the chapter about the Victorian painter Walter Sickert, in which I would explore the conspiracy theories that placed him at the centre of the Jack the Ripper case. Whether you buy the Sickert-as-Ripper theory or not (and I didn't), the work of the founder of the Camden Town Group is full of interest for those drawn to the representation of murder in visual art, with paintings such as *The Camden Town Murder* and *L'Affaire de Camden Town* indicating his own close interest in the subject. The chapter on Sickert was always going to be the beating heart of the book, but then Patricia Cornwell tore it out with her widely reported act of monumental stupidity. By buying up thirty-two of Sickert's paintings and having one ripped asunder in the hope of finding evidence to back up her 'one hundred per cent certain' view that Sickert and the Ripper were the same man, she had rather taken the wind out of my sails.

I remember emailing Martin Weiss on the day the story broke. I asked him if he'd seen it. He emailed me back and said he had, but added, 'So what?'

'Well, it's obviously a publicity stunt,' I emailed back. 'Guess what her next book's going to be all about?'

The phone rang. It was Martin.

'Listen,' he said, without preamble. 'She won't be the first person to argue in print that Sickert was the Ripper. Nor will she be the last.'

'Well, I might as well cancel my trip to Venice,' I

grumbled. Sickert had lived in the Italian city, producing numerous pictures of its people and places.

'Bollocks,' snapped Martin. 'Fuck Patricia Cornwell. She doesn't own Sickert or Jack the Ripper or the right to conjecture over any links between them. Of course you should still go.'

As I showered in the hotel, I thought of Martin back in Birmingham. We hadn't seen that much of each other since college, despite my occasional promptings that we should get together. I missed his company, but he had his own circle of artist friends, or so I presumed. It was Martin, though, who put me on to Sickert, sending me a series of postcards of his work: *Ennui*, *Sunday Afternoon*, *Mornington Crescent Nude*. He had emailed me a web address, which turned out to be a Masonic site with an endless screed devoted to the Sickert/Ripper theory, and the seed for my book idea was sown.

I tried to maintain contact with Martin, sending him a long, chatty email when I started researching the book and asking him what he was working on, but he didn't reply. Months later, I received another Sickert card in the post: *La Hollandaise*, another downbeat nude, a prostitute perhaps, on the back of which Martin had scrawled a note to say he was working on a big project that required all his energy. It would be the making of him, he wrote. I took the hint and got on with my research into Sickert, and the material for the other chapters, on my own.

For all its licentious reputation over the years, even earning the soubriquet Sea-Sodom from Lord Byron himself, Venice these days is rather tame and a man may have to travel away from the centre of things to satisfy his carnal desires, especially if those desires are of a homosexual nature. I selected a restaurant in between San Marco and the Rialto bridge, so that I could cruise Il Muro in search of a potential livener. The guidebook said there might not be that much action out of season, but it was even quieter than I'd feared, and I ended up eating on an empty stomach.

From the restaurant it was a short walk back to the Rialto, and thence to the hotel, but there was always a chance I might get lucky.

I didn't. I got unlucky.

As I approached the rio di San Salvador by the calle dell'Ovo, I noticed a large crowd gathering on the bridge. With my reporter's instinct, I eased through the crowd to the front. As long as you're polite and don't push too hard, no one really minds, especially in a country like Italy, where queuing is hardly a way of life. When I reached the parapet, I saw the humped shape in the water, the dark hair floating like seaweed. A police launch was just arriving and so I witnessed the body being pulled out of the water. She looked about twenty-five, still clothed, and couldn't have been in the water more than a day, although her face was a waxy grey under the harsh spotlight. Her eyes, thankfully, were closed. Mine were not, and even when I did close them later that night in the hope of finding some relief in sleep, I couldn't banish the image of her grey face, water trickling off the end of her nose back into the canal, drop by sickening drop.

There were even more upsetting images of the dead girl in the papers when I got home. They showed a pretty, lively 23-year-old management trainee called Hannah Power, from Balham in south London, who had gone to Venice with a group of girlfriends and never come back. Initial reports indicated a high level of alcohol in the bloodstream, so it was assumed she had simply strayed, slightly drunk, too close to the edge of a canal. According to her friends, she had left the bar they'd been in just to get some fresh air. When she did not reappear and then later failed to show up at their hotel, the girls raised the alarm, but by then it was too late.

Fortunately, I didn't have much chance to dwell on my memory of that last night in Venice. At work on the Monday morning, we were summoned to a meeting in McCave's office – James McCave was the editor – and told to prepare a dummy issue of the paper to an unpopularly tight deadline. The launch date had been brought forward by three weeks. We weren't told why.

With three days to go to the deadline, a new story broke. I was the crime reporter and this story wasn't a crime story, at least not yet; but the news guys couldn't keep up with the stories they were already chasing, so I volunteered, as my desk was pretty clear. I don't really know why I volunteered. Well, I do, but I don't, if you see what I mean. I'll tell you what I mean. The story was that of a Birmingham girl who had fallen into a canal in Amsterdam and drowned.

I should have realized when volunteering for the story that it would mean interviewing the grieving parents, but for some reason that didn't occur to me, not until the news editor gave me that specific instruction as he handed me a Post-It bearing the dead girl's name, Sally Mylrea, her parents' names, Bob and Christine, and their address on the Old Birmingham Road beyond the Lickey Hills. I was to get a cab, the news editor said, adding that I should make sure I got a fucking receipt.

'You want me to go now?'

The news editor, a hardbitten, hot-metal throwback called Paul Connelly, happened to be not very tall and suffered from Small Man Syndrome. Actually, it was the rest of us who suffered as he strutted about the office cursing and scolding whoever was daft enough to get in his way. 'No, I want you to go next fucking week,' he retorted. 'Of course I want you to go fucking now.'

As I walked out of the office, the last thing I felt like doing was finding a cab to take me to see Bob and Christine Mylrea. I wasn't a parent, so I could only imagine what they might be feeling. It was a bright January morning, almost lunchtime. Our office was located between Brindleyplace and the Vyse Street cemetery, which meant that most lunchtimes I would end up sitting in one or the other eating my sandwich in silent contemplation. That day in particular I could really have done with some time to sit and think. I find it impossible to relax stuck in the back of a taxi.

On any other day, on any other mission, it would have been good to get out of the city. The long straight run down the Bristol Road past Longbridge, the hills ahead full of the vague promise of wind in the hair, a spring in the step. But today I was rooted to the back seat of a Cavalier, dreading the moment when it would pull up by the side of the road and the driver would turn round to demand his fare.

The dreaded moment arrived. The Mylreas lived within yards of the Gracelands garage; its zoot-suited mannequin loiterers out front and lifesize Elvis on the roof seemed, for once, like a bad joke in poor taste. I paid the man and stepped out of the car, only remembering as he U-turned in the garage forecourt and headed back up the hill that I had forgotten to ask for a fucking receipt.

As I arrived, a photographer was leaving. Bob and Christine were standing at the front door holding a framed graduation picture of their daughter. Dazed, they invited me in and the three of us sat in an isoceles triangle formation in the front room; Bob and Christine, red-eyed, taking up their expected positions next to each other on the low-backed, high-cushioned sofa, while I perched on the edge of an armchair opposite them, notepad on my knee. As soon as I offered my condolences, the tears began welling up in Christine Mylrea's eyes. She lowered her face and her husband did the talking in a cracked voice, but I couldn't look away from the grieving mother, her tears dripping off the end of her nose, reminding me of the water that trickled off Hannah Power's nose as she was hoisted out of the rio di San Salvador.

Sally Mylrea's death didn't strike me as anything more sinister than a macabre coincidence – there had been no evidence that she was pushed or that she might have jumped, and trace elements of cannabis and alcohol in her blood were hardly surprising, given where she'd gone on holiday – until a month later.

Our dummy issue had been well received and we were starting to gear up for the actual launch. My piece on the Mylreas, onto the end of which I had tacked a brief, factual mention of Hannah Power's death in Venice, earned me a nod of acknowledgement from James McCave (and a disguised snort of derision from Paul Connelly). In a brief lull before the intense pressure of the next few weeks, I took a couple of days off, intending to decorate the grottiest parts of my flat. I lived in a modern conversion above a tools reclamation workshop (and if you know what one of those is, you're one step ahead of me) at the bottom end of one of the short ladder of streets that runs between the Yardley Road and the canal. The view from the back of the flat (my living room/study) was of Yardley Cemetery, while from the front (my bedroom, where decoration was most urgently needed) the vista was dominated by the green ribbon of the canal.

I wandered down the road to get a paper. As I was walking back, my eye fell on a story on page four: 'Canal death treated as suspicious,' ran the headline. 'The body of Marijke Sels, 25, was recovered from the Regent's Canal in London's Camden Town yesterday. Ms Sels, a student from

Amsterdam enrolled at London University, is believed to have drowned, but police are treating as suspicious certain marks found on her body, which could possibly have resulted from a struggle. Police are appealing for witnesses.'

Decorating forgotten, leave cancelled, I was at my desk inside half an hour.

Paul Connelly spotted me. 'What the fuck are you doing here?' he enquired.

I showed him the story.

'Don't waste your time,' he muttered.

'They must be related,' I persisted. 'The three deaths: Hannah Power, Sally Mylrea, Marijke Sels. It's too much of a coincidence. There must be a common thread.'

'Of course there's a fucking common thread. They're all dead. Now stop wasting your time. Since you're here, you might as well do something useful. Sub that.'

He dropped a galley on my desk and stalked off. I wasn't a sub, but nor did I fancy a four-hour wait in A&E with a broken nose, so I had a look at what he'd left me. It was copy for a canal walk, the first of a weekly column 'by our environmental correspondent Julie Meech'. This had run in the dummy, so shouldn't have needed subbing; but again it didn't seem my place to point this out, so I read it, marked up a few little things and scrawled Connelly's initials in the top right-hand corner before sticking it in the internal mail.

I spent the rest of the day digging up everything I could find on the three dead girls. Apart from the fact that they were all around the same age, nothing seemed to link them. I lay in bed that night unable to sleep as I turned the girls' names over and over in my head and watched their grainy newspaper faces swim past me into the murky depths. A phrase from Julie Meech's canal walk kept coming back to me: the Inland Waterways Association. Writer and still-water enthusiast Robert Aickman had co-founded (with

LTC Rolt) the Inland Waterways Association in 1946, Meech had written, to promote the restoration of his beloved canals and encourage more people to use them.

I got out of bed and walked to the window. I'd taken the curtains down in preparation for the now-abandoned decorating. The link between the three girls was staring me in the face. The canal. There was no other common thread. Whether they fell or were pushed, the three had died in canals. Different canals. One in Venice, one in Amsterdam and one in London. Gazing out into the darkness, I was struck by another thought, which hit me like a hammer in the back of the head.

There was no reason to assume that the killing of the Dutch girl was the end of it.

In fact, I realized as I hurried to work the following morning, there was one very good reason why it wasn't the end of it.

If the news editor had been anyone other than Paul Connelly, I would have gone straight to him – or her – with my theory. You could argue I should have gone straight to the police. But I waited, and while I waited I did some research. Using the phone book, the *A–Z* and the Internet, I scoured Birmingham for Italian communities or associations. I discovered that part of Digbeth had become a thriving Italian quarter following an influx of migrant workers from southern Italy more than a century ago. Whether their legacy amounted to more than a couple of Italian restaurants in the area was unclear, but even if it did, what good would that do me? What did I think I was going to do? Distribute flyers? Stand outside with a sandwich board? No. What was the point of working for the press if you didn't use it as it was meant to be used?

Assuming the intervals between the other deaths had set a pattern, I had at least a week before the final piece of the puzzle was slotted into place.

I wrote my article, describing the pattern I believed had been set and issuing the warning I thought necessary. I emailed it directly to McCave. Half an hour later the phone rang. I was to see the editor in his office.

'What's this?' he asked, waving a printout of my story.

'I'm completely serious about it,' I said.

'So I see. Why didn't you follow procedure and send it to the news editor?'

I looked at McCave as if seeing him for the first time. Broad-shouldered, straight-backed, he looked at home in his tailored suit. There was a tiny shaving cut just below his left ear.

'He seems to have a bit of a downer on me,' I said.

'He's got a downer on everybody, but he's good at his job. Pull a stunt like this again and you'll be looking for a new one. Is that clear?'

'Yes.'

'Close the door on your way out.'

Close the door on your way out. So people actually said that.

My piece appeared in the launch issue. I had no illusions about why McCave had ordered Connelly to run it: it was bound to generate publicity and McCave was gambling that it'd work for us rather than against us. Connelly had barely looked at me over the last four days, which I found more alarming than his usual confrontational methods of intimidation.

The reception was mixed. Briefly, I'd stated the facts. Hannah Power, from London, had been found dead in the rio di San Salvador in Venice. Sally Mylrea, from Birmingham, had drowned in the Keizergracht in Amsterdam. Marijke Sels, from Amsterdam, had been pulled out of the Regent's Canal in London. While the possibility remained that one or two or even all three of the deaths were accidental, if you considered the details, the coincidence seemed too unlikely; and once you factored in the evidence of assault in the Marijke Sels case, it became almost impossible not to conclude that all three girls had been murdered, presumably by the same person, who we should be expecting to strike once again. The missing piece in the jigsaw puzzle he (again, a presumption) was assembling would be the drowning of a Venetian girl in a canal in Birmingham.

The police didn't waste any time in calling to say they were dispatching two detectives to interview me at the office. The Heart of England tourist board were not best pleased, faxing the ad sales director to complain that this had set them back years. And readers – in their dozens – emailed, telephoned and even turned up in person at the Frederick Street offices to report suspicious sightings of strange men by canals throughout the Birmingham area.

I'd half expected to hear from Martin Weiss, so when I didn't I emailed him and later called; but if he was there, he didn't pick up.

I did, however, get a card the following morning. It was another of Martin's trademark Sickert postcards, *Nude on a Bed*, which showed a woman sitting on the edge of an iron bed with her hands clasped behind her head. On the back, Martin had written: 'Nice tits. I hope your bosses appreciated your "news story" as much as I did.' Unable to work out if he was taunting me – the pointed reference to the model's breasts seemed uncharacteristically vulgar – I slipped the postcard into my inside pocket and it went home with me at the end of a long day of police interviews and difficult phone calls, as many from cranks as from anxious Italian parents. What could I tell any of them that I hadn't put in my piece? Everything I knew for sure was there, and most of what I suspected. Should I have told them of my vague suspicions regarding an old friend? Such thoughts would have seemed monstrously fanciful with no real evidence to back them up.

The evidence arrived the next day in the shape of another postcard. Again it was a girl on a bed, lying back, one leg on the floor, the other hanging in the air. As with one or two of the Camden Town paintings, it was impossible to say if she was asleep or dead. The title was the one I should have been expecting if I'd done my research thoroughly: *Fille Vénitienne Allongée*.

On the back, in Martin's handwriting: 'Four down. Birmingham noir (10)'.

I took it straight to the photocopier, then to Connelly.

'Fuck's that?' he asked.

'Look,' I said, turning it over. '*Fille Vénitienne Allongée*. Venetian girl lying down. It's a direct reference to my piece.'

'I can see that,' he said icily. 'What about the fucking crossword clue?'

'Bournville?' I suggested hesitantly.

When I got to the stretch of the Worcester and Birmingham canal that passes through Bournville, alongside the railway line that runs right past the Cadbury factory, it was like a film set. Police cars, ambulances, reporters, TV crews, lights, lines and lines of police tape strung up like bunting between the trees, and crowds of onlookers.

I bitterly regretted that I was too late, but I was glad of one small thing: that I was too late to see the girl's limp body emerging from the dark water in the arms of a police diver. I saw the pictures later, but they didn't have the same power that seeing her in the flesh would have had.

I often go back there. Some kids have built a rickety stepladder up the side of a tree, leading to a couple of strategically placed sheets of hardboard where you can sit quite comfortably. It doesn't look new and has probably been there for years. It's as good a place as any to sit and brood. I tried to work out how far in advance Martin had planned everything. Did he only get the idea once I became interested in Sickert and decided to go to Venice, or had he been planning it from the moment when he first introduced me to the painter's work?

I don't know, but I remember his telling me he was working on a big project. So this was it. Right from the beginning, since his photographs in the Bethnal Green gallery, he'd been drawn to the overlap between violent crime and visual art. His series of murders, perfectly constructed, deftly executed, had been signed just like a painting. The police investigation proved that he'd flown to Venice while I was there and that he'd returned to Birmingham via Amsterdam. Apart from that, they were no nearer catching him than I had ever been, in any sense of the word.

The canal at Bournville is quite beautiful, especially at dusk. Sometimes I sit there for hours, until the sky turns purple over the chocolate factory, and I wonder about Martin, still out there somewhere. Is that it? Has he finished? Or will there be more? I realize that asking *Why me?* implies a solipsistic attitude when the tragedies affected so many lives, but I can't help wondering if the responsibility for the murders should really be all Martin's. Clearly, he used me because he knew I would be interested. He engineered things in such a way that I was bound to be interested. He wanted the world to hear about his work, just as it gets to hear about the work of any great artist, and I could be relied on to make sure of that. But was I not also being punished, or at the very least put in my place?

Passing Over

Elizabeth Mulrey

The bed was on the right of the room, up against the wall. The door into the bedroom was just past the foot of the bed and was always ajar. I was too scared of the dark to sleep in an enclosed room. Light from the landing would reassuringly seep through the half-open door. Muffled sounds came from downstairs where Mum, Dad and perhaps Sarah and John were still up.

I always faced this way, looking at the door. Never towards the window, in case the curtains moved in some way. A person crouching behind the window ready to pounce was always a possibility. Some malevolent being waiting for an off-guard moment to come and attack me. So, to stop myself staring at the curtains all night, I'd face the wall and the reassuring light.

Anthony came into the room. I saw him coming, of course, through the crack at the back of the door. Why was he awake, he's younger than me, has been in bed longer? Then Sarah came in just behind him. Why was she here? She's older than me and usually stays up watching telly. They looked odd. Anthony didn't say anything. Sarah said, 'Are you awake? We've got something to tell you.'

I didn't say anything. A feeling came over me. I didn't care about the curtains now. Now that fear was suddenly childish – something new, a grown-up fear had taken its place.

John had died. He was only seven. He'd been strange all his short life. He had an other-worldliness about him. It was as if he belonged somewhere else, somewhere inside his head. He never seemed completely at ease or completely connected. Barely on this side of the divide that separates this world from another. He saw things that upset him. He didn't understand them any more than we did. Dad put it down to a 'playful imagination', which always made it sound admirable, a quality that set him apart and could perhaps be useful later in life. I always felt that by comparison we must have dull and boring imaginations that didn't know how or, even worse, couldn't be bothered to play.

But even then I think I knew that Dad was trying to gloss over something a bit worrying. Was it really imaginative to be scared most of the time? Once, about six weeks before his death, John had come into my room in the middle of the night. He said he'd seen something. He wasn't all that coherent but referred to some battle that was going on in the garden between two opposing armies. He said it was the anniversary of a famous battle and ghosts were re-enacting it in our garden. There were men in floppy hats with sticks and they were on a hill, or on the edge of a hill, or something like that. He was definitely scared and so was I. I looked but of course nothing was there. He got into bed with me and we both slept.

He had died in his sleep. There was an inquiry. No obvious cause of death was found. I've thought since then that the expression 'passed over' applied more to John's death than anyone else's.

We moved, of course, but I'd liked living in the house afterwards and being able to remember John. I could pretend to play with him as if he was still there. Before, we used to sit on the floor and make up stories. He always had the best storylines. Mum sometimes listened in without us knowing and she was amazed at the stories he told. One day he'd be a famous author, she'd say, and he was to make sure he looked after his old mum and dad when that day happened. When Dad got home from work in the evenings she'd tell him about John's stories, laughing about how famous her son was going to be. OK, it did hurt a bit. I wanted to be famous too and look after Mum and Dad and Sarah and Anthony too, if it came to that. But I guess we all knew he had the gift.

We lived in Olton then. Dad's business was close by. We all went to St Andrew's School in Hobs Moat. Everyone was really nice to us afterwards. The teachers were great. On the first day back after the funeral Mr Jones, the headmaster, called me, Sarah and Anthony into his office and told us that if we needed to talk to anyone or just felt upset we could come to him or to any of the other teachers. Anthony started crying and Mr Jones looked really awkward. We knew he'd be having another cigarette as soon as we had left. He had yellow fingers and always smoked in the playground at lunchtime or at playtime if he had to be the supervisor. That didn't happen very often though, with him being the headmaster.

But it was Mum who couldn't stay in the house. I don't think it was the house so much as the people at church. We were Catholics and went to the Franciscan Friary in our road. Hardly anyone else was Irish from around there and Mum and Dad always said they felt a bit out of place. Mum said that even though we'd been living in that house for five years, we still weren't accepted and were seen as foreigners. John's dying just made it worse.

*

Sometimes during the day cars slowed down as they passed the house and people lingered at the bottom of the front garden and looked in, but you didn't always see them so it wasn't so bad. Nothing like John's death had ever happened before in our area. I remember the headline in the *Solihull News*: '7-year-old boy found dead in his bed.' Somehow it didn't seem connected to us as a family. But when we were at church together you could sense people watching us. Mum and Dad liked to sit in a pew quite close to the altar. I guess it was not as far to go for communion. Sometimes the queues would extend out of the church at Christmas and Easter. I'd get quite embarrassed walking back down after receiving communion with everyone in the pews staring at you. I always tried to look religious, like I was totally aware of the significance of having the body of Christ on my tongue, and I'd try not to chew it.

After John died we'd sit there and feel the congregation watching. Especially when the sermon was being delivered because no one had anything to do at this point. Mum said she could feel their eyes boring into her back as they tried to glean some hint of what she imagined they thought had really happened that night.

Even before he died the worst bit about going to Mass was when it was over. Instead of getting straight in the car and going home for breakfast (bacon and eggs: the best part of the whole proceedings), Mum and Dad would wait outside the church and talk to people. Which is when Sarah, John, Anthony and I generally got mauled. People ruffling your hair and saying how nice you looked in your coat or dress. We always wanted to go to Mass in our ordinary clothes but Dad insisted we dressed smartly. Mum agreed with Dad, so we were stuffed into our best clothes.

Anyway, all that stopped after John died. Mum and Dad would still wait outside and at first people would come up and say nice things about John and how sorry they were for Mum and Dad. They didn't maul us either, which was good. But after a while we didn't wait any more. I think it was because Mum didn't want to talk like she used to. Sometimes we even went to Mass in our ordinary clothes. This was because Mum couldn't go to Mass some Sundays and Dad didn't seem to care as much about what we wore. Once, just before we moved, we went on our own. Dad stayed behind to look after Mum and said he'd go to six o'clock Mass. He didn't though, but we said nothing.

We moved to King's Heath about six months later. Mum, Dad and I still live there. When I had Jamie I moved out of their house and got a flat near by. Sarah and Anthony have both gone to London. I don't see them much now.

The best thing about moving to King's Heath was that there were a lot of Irish people there and no one knew about John. We felt more relaxed in lots of ways. We never really got back into the best clothes thing for Mass. Everyone seemed to be more casually dressed and even though Dad still put his suit on, we were allowed to go in our best ordinary clothes. Mum didn't go at all for ages. But eventually she started going back. We never sat as close to the altar as we had done at the Friary. We sat nearer the back of the church, which was better for us. There were always more kids sitting towards the back and you could get away with being a bit naughty without anyone noticing. Mum wasn't as strict as she had been about behaving in church and often seemed not to notice what we were doing at all. She cried sometimes, which always made us start behaving. At other times she had this far-away look in her eyes, which frightened us. She always reminded me of John then. That was the look he'd had a lot of the time.

John and I had always been close. This really worried me

afterwards. I was always thinking that I was going to die in my sleep, that it was my turn now. Every night I'd look at the curtains and long for the days when I was scared about someone being behind them. How stupid. I wished that that was all I had to worry about now. Mum and Dad tried to reassure me, but they had their own grief to deal with. Part of me wanted to be important enough to be claimed by what had claimed John. Even his death had been imaginative. I wanted to be interesting too.

Sometimes Mum would look at me in a strange way. And occasionally I thought she thought I'd killed him. Some occult deviousness that I'd conjured up had spirited him away. Maybe I was a witch and had put a spell on him. I found myself feeling guilty, like I was a murderer or liar. With a child's logic I tried to practise magic to see if I had an amazing natural ability at it, which would confirm my witch status. I needn't have worried. I had, in fact, an amazing unnatural ability in that direction.

That phase passed and life got back to a sort of norm. Dad was and still is a tower of strength. He was really good when I became pregnant with Jamie. Mum was never the same after John's death but got a lot better with time.

So, we were all doing fine until last year. History repeats itself. My Jamie died. He was seven. Passed away in the night. The inquiry's still going on. The file on John's death has been reopened. Jamie was like John; he had that same imagination. I always got the impression he might have known him, met him before, on that other side, where John had come from and had been recalled to. I don't feel sad. They are reunited. Playing in that other field.

I do wonder if I did it. If I killed them. I don't remember doing it. But I guess the police will find out.

Mum will be passing over soon. This has been too much for her. She won't be meeting them, though. She is destined for a different place. None of us will ever meet them again, dead or alive. They had their allotted time and have returned to their origins. At least they now have company. That always bothered me, John being on his own. It's all very well having a playful imagination but he enjoyed making up stories with someone else. Once he'd gone back I imagined he might be lonely and miss that. So when I had Jamie I guess the idea was already born. I've made it right now.

His Own Skeleton

Andrew Newsham

Light crept under the door and illuminated his desperation among the paperclips and Post-It notes. Martin's eyes slowly adjusted and he read the labels on the paper stacked next to him: *A4 White 200 Sheets*. Two hundred slices of tree, cut into blissful conformity and freed momentarily from the horror of existence.

He was hiding from the man with hands the size of takeaway forks and trying to remain calm. He breathed deeply and loosened his tie, his heart beginning at last to stop beating like every drum since Goliath. He was safe for the time being. Now all he had to do was think of a suitable excuse in case anyone found him. He could say he was conducting an inventory but as Valerie was in charge of the stationery, she might take it the wrong way, as some kind of underhand sleight, and that would be very bad indeed. She was a fierce woman who banged a drum for the Salvation Army in her spare time and contemplated the world with a look of barely contained rage.

He sank to the floor and began to rub his nose where his glasses had ploughed a furrow into his sweaty face. Clearly, he needed some other excuse, one that also took into account the closed door. Even if he were checking the stationery, why would he choose to do it in the dark?

Maybe I am *mad*? he thought anxiously. He had, after all, become fixated with a man's little hands to the point of nauseous distraction. He felt ill at the prospect of seeing them, of being in the same room with them, of having them suddenly appear on his shoulders, slowly massaging him as he sat as his desk . . .

'I'm not mad,' he reassured himself, 'it's just those hands . . . like translucent crab claws . . .'

He looked at his watch. It was too dark to see so he pressed one of the little buttons to light up the face. Little watch buttons, he thought, it was almost as if they were made for little hands. He cringed and bit his lip, his heartbeat suddenly rising once more in his ears like a rollercoaster.

'Calm, calm, calm,' he muttered until he relaxed. The watch said 2:36. It was still too early to go out.

The man was amiable enough. In fact, that was the problem. He was too amiable, too happy, too friendly; it was as if his ridiculous appendages were a source of constant joy. Ever since they'd met, the man had just made too much of an effort to be his friend. He pummelled him with invitations. He slapped him about the face with pathetic jokes Martin had to fend off with fake smiles. It was never ending – and always the hands, flapping towards him like moths.

He could say he was looking for some staples and the door had blown shut by mistake and he only hadn't opened it again because he'd just at that moment got a text message on his mobile which he didn't need light to read since the screen lit up itself and that was why he was in the stationery closet in the dark. Pathetic, he thought. He climbed to his feet and took two deep breaths.

'If anyone comes,' he said to himself, 'I will just tell them I'm not feeling well, a bit of a migraine, and I was just taking a moment to rest my eyes in the dark.' Yes, that would work; the best lies always hid themselves in the truth and obviously it was true that he was feeling ill. The symptoms and causes would have to be bluffed – no need to start ranting in a rabid delirium about the man's shrunken hands making you sick – but they couldn't hold it against him, rather they would respect his dedication.

He sat back down and looked at his watch, pressing the little button with his little finger. It blinked at him: 2:45. He'd have to wait longer, maybe even an hour longer. The man would leave eventually; he couldn't just wait around for the rest of the day, trying to touch him with those things . . .

It had all come about because of a misunderstanding when he'd come across the man struggling with a water bottle he was replacing on the cooler.

'Do you need a hand?' Martin had asked, being polite.

'No,' said the man dropping the bottle and wheeling on him with his little hands. 'I've got two, they just shrunk in the wash . . .'

At first he'd laughed, automatically, but as the man continued to recite a litany of bad jokes he found his eyes drawn to the hands as they gesticulated in the air in front of him like small pink butterflies. They were *really* small. Smaller even than baby's hands, the fingers were like matchsticks and yet, amazingly, they were perfectly formed. He could bend and use each finger. On his right hand he even had a ring, a minute band of gold, a fly's tiara. His arms were normal and thick at the top but they tapered down evenly like a well-conducted diminuendo to the minuscule tips of his nails. Suddenly he noticed the man had fallen silent. He looked up nervously.

'Is that a wedding ring?' he'd stammered, rather embarrassed. The smile dropped from the man's face.

'No, well yes,' he said, looking down at his hands. 'It

belonged to my mother. It was her wedding ring. I'm keeping it for the right girl.'

In the closet, Martin began to laugh. *I'm keeping it for the right girl*, he'd never heard anything so funny, it was ridiculous, *the right girl* . . . as if. The right girl with hands the size of takeaway forks more like and, well, we all know that they're not the marrying type. He began to roll about on the floor, seized in the grip of lunacy. Didn't all mothers warn their sons about girls with hands the size of cornflakes? Heartbreakers, every damn one of them . . .

A sound at the door brought him up short like the snap of a noose, the laughter dropping from his throat like a dead clam. It was a scratching sound: could it be the desperate clutching of two very small hands around a button-mushroom doorknob? He swung his feet up against the door and held his breath; tensing his leg muscles in the silence for an imminent push. After a few moments the scratching stopped. The man couldn't work the handle with his miniature fingers; even with normal hands it was a bit stiff. Martin thanked his luck and waited to hear footsteps walking away. Instead, there came a small knock from the little hands. He must've heard him laughing. The bastard. As he strained to hear the man leave, he thought he could hear the hands twitching on the other side of the door. 'Oh mercy, Mother of God,' he muttered. It was getting hot in the closet; not enough air.

He wondered how it could've come to this, how somewhere in that first meeting the normal space between people had been bridged. The man invited him everywhere now and it baffled him how they'd become such great mates; he couldn't even remember the guy's name, just his hands, and yet to listen to him they were bosom buddies, with a whole wealth of humorous history between them.

On just one occasion he'd taken pity on him and they'd

gone for a quick drink after work. For a couple of excruciating hours he'd listened to the man make light of his disability: 'I'm never short of bus fare – they fit down the back of settees,' and even, 'The babes love the hands.' He drank green cocktails and gripped the glass stem in his tight little fist. After a while Martin made his excuses and left the man to his green drinks and yet it seemed that from then on they were great mates.

It made no sense. Maybe they'd talked a bit – a heart-to-heart, he couldn't remember exactly – but he was sure it was no basis for such overbearing familiarity. It never ended: Would he like to go for a balti? Did he want tickets for the Villa? He'd actually asked him if he wanted to go bowling. Bowling, for Christ's sake. He imagined the guy struggling with the ball or maybe he went to an alley where everyone had little hands and everything was built in proportion . . . he stifled a snigger and fell into a shaking paralysis of *don't laugh* . . .

'Bowling is not so funny,' he said under his breath like a mantra. 'It is *not* funny.'

The little knock came again on the door. He looked at his watch. 3:10. He couldn't believe it, he should've gone by now; he should be off on his rounds delivering water to all the other thirsty offices in Birmingham. This was harassment. He half expected an axe to come chopping through the wood, a little axe, a tomahawk perhaps with a special handle that would fit over his hand and up to his elbow so he could muster the power to chop his way in. Martin held his breath and waited for a thud and the splintering of wood.

3:15. An age passed. He looked at his watch again: 3:17. The door didn't break open.

3:30. No sound.

Maybe he'd imagined the whole thing? The thought sent a shiver up his spine and for the first time he felt the dampness of his sweat-soaked shirt. Did this kind of skulking, paranoid behaviour carry the hallmark of a complete mental breakdown? How could he have possibly heard the little hands twitching through a wooden door? He climbed to his feet and dusted himself down. This was no way to behave, lurking in closets from men with little hands. His father had seen active service in the army for NATO. What would he think if he could see him now, crawling on his belly in a dead-end office job? He hadn't been a man to hide from people with little hands; he'd had some serious tattoos. He would've walked up to the man and said: '*Get out of my way, FREAK!*'

Martin took a deep breath and cautiously opened the door. To his relief there was just an empty corridor outside. Brian the sales clerk was the only one in the office when he crept back in and made his way back to his desk.

'There you are, Martin,' he said, looking up from his computer. 'Your friend's been looking everywhere for you.'

He sat down uncomfortably. 'My friend?' he said in a disinterested tone.

'You know, the water man, I've forgotten his name . . . you know, err, he wears glasses.'

Fucking glasses! Martin thought. It was typical of someone like Brian to oh-so-carefully ignore the hands. It was that kind of sickening politeness that had meant no one mentioned the death camps in Germany when the local SS officer passed the after-dinner port. The world was full of Brians, with their colourful jumpers and their simple, ignorant lives, stepping through the flames and coughing gently so as not to wake the children as the world burned.

'Do you mean the freak with the hands?' he asked.

Brian blushed and looked away. 'Yes,' he said quietly.

'Well, why didn't you say so, then?'

The room fell into uneasy silence.

After a while Martin stood and looked out the window

and down into the car park. He was amazed to see the white van of the Kitwell Water Company arriving back exactly as it had almost two hours before. Jumping back in surprise, he shot from the office and ran as fast as he could down the corridor and out of the fire escape. Giving his so-called friend enough time to enter the office by the main reception, Martin walked round into the car park and jogged breathlessly up to the van. The logo on the side depicted a fountain spouting crystal-blue water into a wine bottle, and beneath it the company's name and telephone number were painted on like water ripples. Ah Kitwell, he thought, that well-known oasis paradise. It seemed that no one these days could call a spade a spade or a freak a freak. What had they done, set up a standpipe in a shady corner of the estate? On the back bumper a sign posed the question: 'How Am I Driving?' Taking his mobile out of his pocket, Martin tapped in the number.

The phone rang three times before it was answered. 'Hello, how can I help you?' a man's voice asked.

'I want to complain about one of your drivers,' said Martin. 'It's an absolute disgrace, he shouldn't be allowed on the roads. I've just seen him nearly kill a mother and her child. I followed him for ten minutes. He really is the most reckless driver I've ever seen. He has no control over the vehicle at all . . .'

There was an eerie silence before the man on the other end of the line began to laugh. 'You nearly had me fooled for a minute there, old pal,' he said.

Martin froze and an image of the little hands cradling a phone flashed through his mind. He edged round to the front of the van and peered in through the windshield. The steering wheel was full size and not the freak's special one, which was the size of a bottle cap.

'I was just round your place. Do you fancy coming bowling this evening? I know you're a bit conscious about your feet but you need to get out, you can't keep hiding away all your life . . .'

'There's nothing wrong with my feet,' said Martin with a trembling lip.

'Yeah, that's the spirit! You know people like us should stick together. I'll pick you up about seven.'

Brindley's Place

Mike Chinn

I took what I thought was going to be my first and only drink of the night to a table near the windows, and sat down. It was raining outside – but then, it'd been raining for what felt like for ever. That's why Birmingham has more waterways than Venice: they aren't canals, just drainage channels. As the rain trickled down the glass or coagulated against a greasy smear, it shattered the lights from the Convention Centre across the canal into twisting sparkles, like Christmas decorations seen through a hangover.

I like the Once Over. It's one of the new rash of bars and restaurants that've grown up alongside the canal just off Broad Street. All varnished blond wood floors and banquettes; Chardonnay that costs more for a glass than a whole bottle from a decent supermarket. But the beer's OK.

The place wasn't very full for the time of night – perhaps the rain was keeping everyone in – so it wasn't hard to notice Kitty when he stamped in. He was shaking water from his untidy mass of curls; his face lit up in his perpetual kid's grin. His dirty brown suede coat was further blackened by rain.

Perfect – my night was complete.

He spotted me and came ambling across, his grin getting wider, if that was possible. His huge black eyes were flashing infectiously. It's hard not to smile after being around Kitty for a while. Even harder to believe he'd probably killed at least three men.

'All right, Dazzler?' he asked. His parents were both pure Jamaican – not that you'd know it from his flat accent. Brummie to the point of caricature. 'How's it goin?'

'Fine,' I lied. 'I was just having a drink before heading off home . . .'

'Don't go yet, man,' he said. He eyed my barely touched, gradually warming pint. 'What you drinking?'

'Caffreys. Thanks.' I didn't waste time wondering where Kitty's generosity came from. He didn't usually offer to get in a round – so I knew it meant he'd got money, from somewhere. And that might mean I could get some too.

He ambled in the general direction of the bar, shouting greetings at anyone who'd listen. The barman eyed him suspiciously, but didn't seem able to think of a good enough reason not to serve him. Kitty was definitely not who the owners were thinking of when they planned their marketing strategy.

He came back with two full pints. I'd already finished my first. No sense wasting time when the opportunity's there. Kitty placed both glasses on the table, dropping into a sofa facing me. He took a long, slow pull at his own pint, daring me to ask what he wanted.

Fuck you, I thought, and started on my own. Silently.

Kitty replaced his glass, grinning. He sucked the foam from across his lower lip noisily. 'Graham's – you know – got a job for you,' he said.

I kept swallowing Caffreys as though what he'd said didn't mean a thing. I knew the evening had been going too smoothly.

'So I guessed,' I lied again. I was getting used to it. Kitty doesn't always turn up just as Graham Brindley's mouthpiece. Sometimes he's acting for some other piece of shit.

'There's this minge, right,' Kitty went on. 'A girl. You know, dancer, like. Works at the Thousand & One. Graham wants you to escort her to his place for eight. Private fuckin do – you know . . .'

I had to hand it to Graham – he could be a real bastard when he put his mind to it. I bet he hadn't stopped laughing for hours when he thought of me for the job. I knew the Thousand & One – but I hadn't been near it for a couple of years.

'Her name's Jamelah – least that's what she calls herself. Some kind of fuckin wog name, like.' He took another drink, sucked off the foam. I wished he were on lager; no one should have to sit through that ritual every time Kitty buys them a pint. He dug his free hand into his coat pocket and it came out swollen – puffed up by a fat wad of dirty notes. 'This should pay for a cab – both up there and to Graham's place, like.' He passed the money over, not caring if anyone saw.

'You're really discreet, you know that, don't you?'

Kitty grinned wider, drank and sucked, drank and sucked. Quickly, his pint was all gone. 'I'll love you and leave you.' He stood up, tugging at his damp coat. 'Don't be a clever cunt and take too fuckin long over that drink, like? Graham's in a hurry, you know.' He turned and left, waving goodbye to a disinterested bar.

I pocketed the money, feeling that old familiar shakiness: the result of helpless fury. Graham didn't have to pay me – Christ knows – but it seemed to be all part of the same joke to him. Perhaps he wrote it off as expenses. I finished the Caffreys, though I couldn't taste it any longer, and left the Once Over.

The rain wasn't heavy, but now it just depressed me. I got

to Broad Street and found a cab easily enough. They were starting to queue up – ready for the feeding frenzy after ten o'clock when Broad Street fills up with kids leaving the pubs and wanting to get to the clubs. It made me smile, thinking that. When I was their age, we walked . . . not that there were too many clubs back then. Samantha's, the Cedar Club, Barbarella's – just seedy memories now. Then there was the Thousand & One.

The cab driver made no comment when I gave him my destination – though he seemed surprised when I asked him to wait once we got there. Probably thought I was going in for the fastest grope in history.

The Thousand & One Club is a couple of miles up the Hagley Road – almost in Bearwood. It stands out like an ageing bruise among the small hotels, B&Bs and tiny restaurants. They catered for the itinerant businessman in their own quiet way; the club in its own gaudy style. It's no cheaper than any of the lap-dancing joints springing up in the city centre – at least, not in any way that affected your wallet – but it saved a taxi or bus ride.

The rain had eased off a little, and I reached the bored-looking bouncer at the entrance without getting any wetter. He was Asian; a couple of sizes too small for his tuxedo. If any of the girls had started a fight, I doubt he'd have lasted long.

'Darren Toye,' I said without waiting. 'Mr Brindley wants me to . . .' I faltered, not sure how to phrase it.

'There's a package for you to deliver.' He wasn't quite leering – but whatever he was doing was a close relative. He ducked his head inside. 'She's waiting in the back.'

I passed through the entrance doors, not caring whether or not it was allowed. I'd earned the privilege.

Inside, everything seemed to glow blue. The lights off the stage fanned across a room filled with smoke: refracting and reflecting until the air itself was phosphorescent. I found myself gazing at my shoulders – expecting to see dandruff glowing spectrally against the dark material of my jacket.

The music was loud, and hard to recognize. Nothing but a deep, gut-filling vibration. A spectrum of whirling lights in the ceiling pulsed varying colours – never quite hitting the beat. It was disconcerting, like some kind of subtle sense deprivation torture.

Several girls were already well into their acts. They worked the room, stepping off the swelling that called itself a stage, grinding past a sea of cloned faces, all bright with sweat, until some punter waved a big enough note in their direction. All of the girls were young – barely out of their teens; but none of them looked younger than my mother. Most lap-dancing clubs employed girls who were happy to exploit us grubby males in the name of cash – they all had plans, and no contribution was going to be turned away. But Graham's girls had lost all their dreams – whatever escape they found came out of the end of a needle. So long as they had decent bodies with no obvious track-marks, Graham kept them on. And you could score quite a stash for the cash so eagerly shoved into thong-straps. Everybody's happy.

I made my way towards the curtain through which the girls emerged. A peroxided Valkyrie blocked my way, disliking me on general principle. I imagined the girls had less to fear when wriggling on some fat businessman's lap than if they let Brunhilde into the dressing room while they were alone in there.

'I'm Darren Toye,' I yelled above the what-passed-for music.

'I guessed,' she replied. Somehow, even though she seemed to be talking normally, her voice carried over the background din.

'Fame at last.' I tried to get past her, but a meaty arm blocked the way.

'Just watch it, pal,' she snarled. And it really was a snarl. 'I know all about you.'

'I doubt that,' I said, batting the hunk of beef to one side. I hate it when people make assumptions.

Backstage was as dark as the club was bright. Twenty-watt bulbs stuck naked out of crusty brick walls. I swear you could hear the rats running blindly into each other. The dressing room was just the end of a bitter corridor marked by an old curtain strung across it.

'Jamelah!' I called in place of a knock.

'Who wants to know?' A head poked through the curtain: orange-tanned, even blonder than Brunhilde, scarlet mouth gnawing a wad of chewing gum to death.

'Her prince is here,' I said. The head frowned, as if the owner had been asked to give the value of pi to a thousand decimal places.

'You what?'

'I'm here to take her to Graham's place,' I explained slowly. 'Graham Brindley.'

'Oh – right.' The head vanished. A moment later the curtain twitched aside and a cheap fur coat appeared. From inside, struggling out of the collar and below the hem, was a girl. Jamelah, I presumed.

She looked older than I'd expected. Knowing Graham's sense of humour, I was expecting a girl who could pass for someone in her mid-teens. What bits of her showed outside the coat were olive-skinned, and she had a long mass of hair so black it shimmered with blue highlights. Huge hooped earrings showed through the curtain of hair. Her face was heart-shaped, and her jet eyes had a hint of the Orient about them. Malaysian, I guessed, or Indonesian. A little more exotic than Graham's usual tastes, anyway. He had to be entertaining.

'Shall we go, then?' she said. The look she gave me was neutral – I couldn't tell if they'd warned her about me and she was being aloof, or she simply didn't know me from Adam. Whichever, it wasn't my business.

She headed for the front of the club without further prompting. Perhaps this wasn't exactly her first time. I followed in her wake, ignoring Brunhilde's glare as we passed, letting Jamelah's perfume of choice wash over me. It wasn't cheap, that much I could tell. It made me wonder just a little about her – Graham's girls never shopped at Rackhams' perfume counter, to put it bluntly. I wondered if the crummy fur coat wasn't simply a prop after all.

The cabby's eyes lit up when he saw her; he even got out and opened the door to let her in. Maybe he didn't want her to get her nice coat all wet. The look he gave me hinted at some kind of shared, men-only experience. I was ready to smack him one if he so much as winked – to hell with getting to Graham's on time. Either way, he could kiss a decent tip goodbye.

I gave him the address and he spun the cab around – turning 180 degrees across the Hagley Road, regardless of the traffic.

'So you're the Dazzler?'

I turned towards Jamelah, about to tell her just what I thought of people who use that nickname – especially ones that I've just met. The words never got said. She was looking at me appraisingly now. Her almond-shaped eyes seemed to be trying to smile, but the weight of it was too much for her lips. She'd allowed her coat to fall open, too – and what it revealed made me ache all over.

'I don't like being called that,' I said. I turned away, concentrating on the rain-streaked windows.

'Yeah – that's what Graham said. What he always calls you, though.'

'Graham's a prince, isn't he?'

I heard her shuffling in the seat. 'You don't look like what I was expecting.'

'Sorry – I left my dirty raincoat at home.'

'That's not what I meant.'

I managed to turn round and look at her. The fur coat was still gaping, showing acres of olive flesh, a diamond-pierced navel, and a lot more besides – but she wasn't being provocative. She didn't even realize. After however long she'd been at this game, she noticed her body – and how little covered it – about as much as I knew what colour socks I'd dragged on that morning. 'So what were you expecting?'

She shrugged and stared out of the cab window as intently as I had. 'Graham makes you sound like, you know, some kind of sad pervy wanker. The kind that's like, into Internet porn – you know.'

I knew all right. Two years ago that would've made me furious; now I can't even get mildly irritated. Things don't seem to matter like they used to.

Neither of us said anything else until we arrived at Graham's – not that the silence was anything like comfortable. What do you say to a young, really attractive girl who's sitting next to you wearing nothing but a few shoelaces? Nothing I could think of that didn't sound stupid, aggressively moronic – or just plain cheesy.

The cab pulled up outside Graham's place. Wharfside Court. It wasn't his main flop, of course – just somewhere in the city where he could impress his friends. Not too far from the NIA: perfect for watching Tim Henman disappoint his fans at the next Davis Cup. For all its upmarket pretensions, the apartment block still faced a partially demolished warehouse, a clutch of cranes standing guard over the carcass. The street was dark, with not nearly enough streetlamps. Or maybe it just seemed that way because of the rain.

The building was brick and stucco-faced, quite traditional in some ways, but with pieces of tubular steel propped against corners and under eaves, just so we knew the architect was one of the new boys. And a mock-Dutch look; all of which had something to do with sitting on the canal, I suppose. A low brick wall was topped by a high wrought-iron fence to keep out the commoners. Visitors announced themselves through speakers mounted next to the only gates, which led to a central courtyard and parking area. But tonight, a uniformed guard was on duty, wearing a yellow reflective waterproof that glowed brighter than any of the streetlights.

I leaned out of the cab window and told him whom we'd come to see. Judging by the speed at which we were admitted, he'd been expecting us. The cab pulled up outside one of the two main lobbies, and Jamelah and I got out. The grounds were decorated with ornamental shrubs, and the air was rich with the putrid smell of over-watered vegetation.

I paid the cabby, tipping him generously, after all. Hell, it wasn't my money. Jamelah and I stood outside the lobby doors for what felt like an age before someone thought of answering the buzzer. Jamelah kept hopping about on the ludicrously high-heeled shoes she was wearing; I didn't know if she was cold or just half-crippled.

'Yeah?' came a distorted voice through the grill just above the buzzer. 'What you want?'

'Darren Toye,' I said. 'I'm here with someone for Mr Brindley.' I could've said Graham – but I thought it might not have been good for my health. Graham didn't like familiarity – not to his face, anyway – and I haven't been keeping my Hospital Fund premiums up to date.

'Hang on a minute.' The voice was cut off with an electronic snap.

Jamelah and I hung on, me getting wetter, and her still

doing the forlorn hop, hop, hop from one stiletto to another.

'You'll end up breaking one of those,' I said.

'You what?' she began, but a light came on above us, and a door swung open. Another Asian guy stood in my way – this one looked a lot handier, and his tux fitted him a treat.

'You're late,' he said. I wondered if I'd dragged him away from something interesting.

'Take it out of my pay.' I glanced past him – towards the well-lit and presumably warmer inside. 'And you're not making us any earlier.'

'Girl first,' he grunted and stepped aside – just enough to rub up against Jamelah as she pushed her way past. I accidentally barged him with an elbow as I followed her in.

'Save it for the bog, spanky,' I muttered into his face. He breathed garlic over me, wrapped around a very Anglo-Saxon phrase.

Inside was not what I'd expected. I'd thought it'd be like a five-star hotel: entrance leading to a kind of foyer, then a corridor, stairs and lift, with apartment doors leading off. In fact, it was spartan; minimalist, even. The foyer was there all right, but I've seen bigger living rooms. If there were any stairs, I couldn't see them. All of which added up to a hell of a lot of unexceptional suburban style for what I guessed was a hell of a lot of money. Even when I could maybe have afforded it, I wouldn't.

Several heavy, dark and probably fireproof doors led off a short, narrow corridor. A hell of a lot of noise was percolating through one of them. Graham's friends.

The doorman stepped past us, once again taking the chance to rub up against Jamelah. He needed to get out and mix with people, I thought. Ordinary people. He swung open the noisy door – immediately, the din in the hallway grew three times worse.

He shouted something I couldn't hear, but it got

Graham's attention. He appeared suddenly – five foot nothing of fake bonhomie. Almost as wide as he was tall, Graham was dressed in what was probably an expensive suit – Prada, Armani, I couldn't tell the difference – but on him it looked cheap, damp and crumpled. He was sweating heavily, his lacquer-stiffened comb-over of thin grey hair dark with it. He patted the doorman on the arm, dismissing him, and turned a vast, insincere grin on Jamelah and me. 'Dazzler!' he laughed. I couldn't see the joke. 'My dear!' He kissed Jamelah paternally on the cheek. 'Glad you could make it.'

'Well, the mayor's washing his hair and the weather's crap,' I said. 'So I thought, what the hell?'

The smile cooled a few degrees. 'Funny, Dazzler – very fucking funny.'

Graham turned his back on me, throwing an arm around Jamelah's shoulders. Even she had a few inches on him – short-arsed little runt. He likes to think he looks the businessman – not the petty crook who started out with a drinking and illegal gambling club in Sparkhill – but he doesn't; not by a mile. He might own half the pubs in Birmingham – or at least the land they're sitting on – but he's still small-time. A narrow-minded little bully with a foul and limited vocabulary; no manners, no taste. His only yardstick is price. If something's expensive, it's good. There's nothing to redeem him as a human being.

No wonder he's a success.

I followed them in as Graham led Jamelah into the apartment. He whipped the damp fur off her shoulders and a cacophony of whistles, catcalls, approving cheers and suggestions as to what she could do for them broke out. With a somewhat less than fatherly pat on her exposed backside, he propelled her into the room full of noise, which was one of three that led off a broom cupboard the estate agent had no doubt called an entrance hall.

That's when he turned back to look at me. 'You too, Dazzler. I know you won't want to miss this.' There wasn't even the ghost of a smile on his oily face now. He didn't have the sense to know when he was supposed to be acting the pantomime villain.

He jerked his head towards the room, where lights had started to pulse – like in some cramped disco – and an almost sub-aural music was sending seismic waves along the floor. It was like the Thousand & One in miniature. The same blue luminescence, the same kind of clientele. The only difference was in the dancer's actions: a private party – anything goes.

I was halfway through the door – Graham's short, sharp fingers urging me along – when Jamelah pulled off the thin strips she'd been wearing. Swaying in the gaudy light, in nothing other than her earrings and ridiculous shoes, she did the bump and grind around the room. Few men in there were sitting, so even a pretence at lap-dancing was out. Instead they contented themselves with plenty of touching. They were willing to pay, all right – even in that light I could see plenty of fifty pound notes being offered for a few moments of Jamelah's attentions. But with no costume to take the cash, the punters vied with each other for somewhere increasingly inventive to slip their money.

And there wasn't a man in the room who didn't want her. Me included. I'm not dead yet – not quite anyway. Just like all Graham's friends, I couldn't take my eyes off her. Jamelah swayed and undulated to the beat, her body growing slick with heat. Her diamond navel-stud flashed back the lights brilliantly. She seemed to glow red against the room's ultraviolet background. Hands, tongues and lips reached out for her, but she always slipped away – just in time, receiving no more than a grope or track of saliva. She worked us, all of us, like the professional she was.

I don't know how long she was centre stage: an hour,

two – there was nothing to gauge the passing of time. The music never changed, and no one grew tired of chasing her taunting figure. Several times I caught her looking straight at me – but I had nothing to give her. Nothing she needed. I'm nobody's knight.

My only surprise was that she didn't get raped. I was expecting it – hell, I was waiting for it. The atmosphere was right; you could smell the testosterone. If ever there was a time for a gang bang, this was it. Maybe that's what she was looking at me for. Waiting for a sign. Wanting to know if I'd save her.

Or if I'd be joining the queue with everyone else.

After all, Graham had told her all about me, hadn't he? She knew what a pervy little wanker I was.

Finally, Graham called a halt. He bustled into the centre of the room, grabbed Jamelah by an elbow and hauled her out of the circle of men. The boos and groans of disappointment were loud against the background throb, but he fended everyone off with a wide jokey smile and a wave of a cigar only slightly smaller than himself. I wondered if he was going to get lynched. But somehow it all became part of the game: Graham got his sycophants lathered up – then cleaned them off with plenty of cold water.

Whatever he'd got on them all, and Graham has something on everyone he knows, it must've been good.

He pointed to one of the other doors. 'In there. I'll get you a cab.'

Jamelah opened the door and walked into a darkened room less than half the size of the one in which Graham was hosting his party. As I followed her in, I felt around for a light switch. I found one and flicked it. Nothing happened.

With suspicious familiarity, Jamelah went to the window and opened horizontal blinds. Almost directly opposite was one of the area's rare streetlights; its glare threw sodium tiger-stripes across the room and us. It was, I could now see, totally empty.

Jamelah stayed by the window, staring out. The pattern of the rain running down the window cast weird swirls across the strips of lit flesh. It made her look as though she was dripping after emerging from a bath, or streaming with more sweat than is healthy.

'How did you meet her?' she asked abruptly, eyes still blindly fixed on the street.

I didn't have to ask who she meant. From the moment we'd met, she'd probably been wondering. 'At the Thousand & One,' I said – slowly, reluctantly. It's not something I like to talk about, especially to people I don't know.

She nodded. I think she'd already guessed. 'I never met her,' she said, almost to herself. 'But I know a few of the girls who did. They said she was pretty – far too pretty for one of his . . .' The last word was spoken with just enough force. She didn't want me to get the wrong impression.

'Don't do yourself down,' I said.

She looked away from the window then. In the yellow light angling across her face I couldn't be sure, but I think she smiled. 'Did you love her?'

It was my turn to get all interested in the half-demolished warehouse outside the window. 'I doubt it.'

I heard her sigh. 'I think . . . I think she died. Last year. It's one of those things we don't talk about.'

I suppose I should've felt something: loss, grief, a sense of inevitability. But there was nothing. 'You know what killed her?'

'The usual . . .'

The usual. Heroin. She'd been using when I'd known her, of course; and never could get enough of a good thing. Neither of us had been under any illusions about where that was likely to end. It wasn't a relationship with much scope for illusion.

'Sally,' I murmured. She had a name – let's use it. Tears should've been running down my cheeks; there should've been some kind of ache, somewhere. Only Sally was beyond that kind of pain now.

'You were lucky, though,' Jamelah said. 'Graham hushed it up.'

I almost laughed. 'Yeah – I was lucky.'

I was lucky to meet a girl at the Thousand & One Club during a company boys' night out and fall in instant lust with her. I was even luckier to find out – after the affair had been going for three months – that Sally wasn't quite sixteen. And really fortunate that Graham Brindley knew all about it, and was happy to keep it quiet – for a price.

But then, he'd set the whole thing up – with Sally as the honey trap. I was just what he wanted: someone from the class he aspired to whom he could jerk around at will. Someone who could feed him the occasional piece of potential blackmail material. Someone who was happy to do the occasional favour, if it saved him a monthly payment. He loved it.

Not long after, my wife left – taking the kids with her. I'd said nothing and I trusted Graham enough to know he hadn't, the payments were all on time. She'd guessed I'd done something, despite my every protest. Women just know.

And, finally, I lost my job. Made redundant, along with 70 per cent of my colleagues. All part of the new MD's policy of moving Birmingham's most famous confectionery company down to London. Where he just happened to live. The golden handshake – though generous – lasted no time once Graham learned about it. But he was big enough to keep me around as an odd-job man, paying enough so I could keep myself in something like the old style.

Any luckier and I'd have topped myself.

The door swung open and the doorman appeared. He threw Jamelah's tiny costume and fur coat at her. 'Cab's here,' he muttered. Pausing just long enough to give me a look that clearly said, even in the poor light, *Why haven't you been giving her one?* he backed out.

Jamelah pulled on the coat, bunching it up tight under her throat. Of course, she was probably cold now; it should've occurred to me. 'You ready?' I asked, just to hear something other than the party in the next room – noisy as ever. She nodded.

I opened both doors – room and street – holding them as she passed through. The rain was a fine drizzle, but the street wasn't any brighter. Of Graham, there was no sign. I didn't expect one.

Jamelah was already sitting in the cab; the cabby was keeping the door open. She looked up at me. Even I could figure out what she was offering – what she was expecting.

I pulled out what was left of the wad of notes Kitty'd given me. Maybe it wasn't up to choking a horse, but it could probably give one a nasty case of heartburn. I peeled off a couple of fifties, then leaned inside and handed the rest to Jamelah. I could see what she thought. I shook my head, suddenly feeling old.

'Do me a favour?' I said. 'Don't do anything stupid.' With the money she'd taunted out of Graham's friends, it probably added up to quite a bundle.

Her almost-smile looked as tired as I felt. And, Christ, I wanted to kiss her.

I stood up, taking the door away from the cabby and slammed it shut, fast. I gave him a hundred quid. 'Wherever she wants to go, OK?'

He shoved the money away without even looking at it, but from the quick grin I guessed he'd figured about how much there was.

'Cheers, mate.' He disappeared inside his cab, revved the engine and pulled away. As they drove off, I thought I saw Jamelah watching me through the back window – but I was probably wrong.

I checked the time: too late for another drink, even if I'd had the money for it. Shame. I was in the mood to murder a pint.

Trashman

Paul Finch

I was late for duty that day. I'd been drinking heavily the night before, and had slept clean through my early morning alarm-call. I only arose when I did with a thick head, buzzing ears and a mouth full of fur. I'd forgotten all about the seven o'clock raid on Wayne Devlin's pad.

When I finally got there, scruffily suited and stinking of beer, the crummy Castle Vale maisonette was already cordoned off. Uniforms were bringing out evidence bags.

'Another top show, Jack!' said Detective Sergeant Lambton, as I sidled into the hallway.

I tried to apologize but Lambton wasn't interested. 'It's a good job we didn't need you. Devlin came without a fight, and we've got more than enough bodies to search his drum.' He shook his head in disappointment. 'I sometimes wonder if we need you at all, Jack.'

I pushed through into Devlin's lounge, where a few DCs were emptying out boxes of rubbish, looking under carpets, slashing sofa cushions. They'd made an incredible mess already, though it was hard to say what was new clutter and what was old. Like so many in the criminal subculture, Wayne Devlin didn't keep an especially tidy home.

Ribald cheers greeted me as I walked in. Then I saw

myself in the cracked mirror resting on the mantelpiece, and grimaced. My hair was a disgrace, my face pale and sallow. People used to say I was good-looking; not any more, I guess.

'Detox want a word,' someone jibed.

'Yeah . . . and the DCI,' someone else added. 'Then you've got to see a man about a P45.'

I took it in good heart. They annoyed me, though; these trim young detectives with their short slick hairstyles, designer suits and flash ties. I'd been in the job twice as long as some of these monkeys, and they still thought themselves my equal. That was probably my own fault, of course. I hadn't done much recently to enhance my reputation. I touched a throbbing temple. Quite the opposite, in fact.

'What've we found so far?' I asked.

'You don't mean you're interested, Jack?' somebody said. One or two of them thought themselves more than my equal.

'My case first,' I reminded them. 'My snout gave us the tip-off.'

Shoulders were shrugged. Sleek young cops turned round and got on with their work. And why not? I thought. I'd got the tip-off, but other, more ambitious people had done the spadework. I knew that bastard Lambton had only wanted me on the raid to make up the numbers, and I hadn't even managed that. Was I washed up already? At thirty-nine? I couldn't remember the last time I'd made a decent arrest. I couldn't remember much, these days.

'Plenty to tie Devlin in with the Bromwich burglaries,' one of the lads finally admitted. 'And a few others. Must've been at it twenty-four hours a day.'

I nodded, then stood there like a spare part for a couple of minutes before making a tour of the rest of the house. Even as lowlife hovels went, this place was a squalid nightmare: no paper on the walls, no carpets on the floors, filth everywhere, broken furniture, crusted crockery. It reeked of sweat and old urine and . . . something else too. Something oddly fragrant. I followed the scent into one of the upstairs rooms. Behind a mass of tossed bedding, I saw a gutted dresser. Clearly the lads had already been in there – the drawers were all over the floor, what had been in them either bagged and tagged, or left scattered.

There was one thing they'd somehow missed, though: a sealed envelope propped up on top of the dresser. It probably wouldn't have caught my eye if it hadn't been for the name written on it in a most elegant hand: *Trashman.*

I gazed at it for a moment before digging into my pocket for a crumpled evidence-sack, then picking the envelope up by its corner and slipping it in. I stared at it again through the clear plastic. It might mean nothing at all, but it was that name . . . *Trashman.*

It was curious the lads downstairs had missed it.

The so-called Trashman had struck now on a number of separate occasions: burst into seedy sex shops or smoky, booze-filled stay-behinds in the back rooms of disreputable pubs and card schools, then blown people away . . . mainly villains and toe-rags, scumbags with serious form, though innocent individuals – including women – who'd just happened to be working at the scene, had got popped as well. There'd been no attempt at robbery, no sign of sexual deviation, but ten lives had been snuffed out in as many months. And not just here in Birmingham. There'd been one incident in Coventry, and two in Wolverhampton. With the first one, we'd marked it down as a contract hit; then, when body bags two and three got brought in, as part of a gangland war or vendetta. No one in the underworld was talking; at least not yet, which meant there was stunningly little to go on. Scarcely anyone had seen the guy in action and lived; he hadn't left any trace-evidence . . . which marked him out as a pro, and that didn't boost the investigators' confidence much. The only real clues were the weapons he'd so far used: a Browning nine-millimetre and a Beretta, often employed in tandem on the same victim. Multiple gunshots to body and head seemed to be the favoured approach. Even then, neither firearm had proved traceable.

Pretty soon, whether the Chief Constable's PR people liked it or not, the news had filtered out to the public who, as always, revelled in it . . . especially as on this occasion, it didn't appear to be them on the receiving end. Whoever the perp was, the press labelled him Trashman, because the only purpose he seemed to have at present was taking out the trash.

I pocketed the envelope and went downstairs, where I rode a few more jokes at my own expense, then made my way back to Kingsbury Road nick and a carpeting from the DCI. I didn't mention the envelope. Not for the time being. It might be empty for all I knew. But then it might not.

'Marsden House,' the card read. 'Off the A46, part-way between Wolverton and Snitterfield. Thursday 19th, 7 p.m.' And that was all.

I looked at it perplexed, then sat back on the pub barstool. Was it an invitation? It was certainly quality – printed in silver on a piece of stiff black card. Vague, though. An invitation to what?

I took another bite of sandwich, another sip of beer. It was always possible that this was a genuine invitation to some bona fide get-together, but knowing Wayne Devlin I couldn't believe that. Course, that still didn't mean it had anything to do with the Trashman murders. But on the other hand?

I went over everything that was known about the West Midlands' latest psycho killer. There was even an article in that day's *Post*: a mock-up of how he was supposed to look, featuring a male model done out in combat fatigues and ski mask, hefting a revolver in either hand. I wasn't attached to the task force formed to deal with the Trashman – once a special team fuck-up, always a special team fuck-up; after the Serious Crime Squad fiasco I'd been lucky to find my way back to the carrot-crunchers on Division – but from what I already knew, the profilers had branded our perp an out-and-out whacko.

A power-motivated repeat murderer, I'd seen on one report. The gist of which was that though superficially he's doing this for revenge, or for financial gain because he's being paid as an assassin, neither of these is his prime objective. He sees himself as a predatory animal in a dangerous jungle, and enjoys the feeling of dominance his ruthlessness generates, not to mention the fear he spreads among his prey. The fact that his attacks are wild and savage, seemingly carried out with minimal planning, indicates a disorganized but opportunistic psychosis, which might be difficult to mask in normal life. But clearly he has masked it. This suggests more than mere personality disorder, but rather borderline, if not total, schizophrenia.

What was puzzling me was the association with Wayne Devlin. If there was one. Devlin was a career criminal, a burglar primarily, but he had no form for violence. What connection might he have with the Trashman? I couldn't fathom it. I put the card back in the envelope. One thing was for sure. I was in a good position to find out.

Thursday 19th. Whatever was going on at Marsden House was going on tonight. I didn't see any reason why I couldn't toddle along with the invite and tell them I was the Trashman. The Ways and Means Act allows you a range of options in order to get jobs done, but even that wouldn't cover something like this. But so what? If I took it to the gaffers, they'd only steal my thunder. Either that or laugh at me. This job was mine. I'd sniffed it out, I'd investigate it. That was the way we'd done it in the old days when I first started. No special squads taking over all the juicy jobs while you got left with the crap; no well-preened career men popping up here, there and everywhere, not actually doing any work but still getting through their promotion boards because they knew the buzzwords. I didn't have any O Levels, or a pair of lips that fitted neatly onto the chief-super's arse-cheeks . . . and I'd never regretted it either. That doesn't mean I didn't have ambition. A time was definitely coming when I planned to teach all those plastic people a lesson they'd never forget.

As I drove out from the pub car park, it crossed my mind that I should at least bring someone along just in case it turned nasty, but the truth was I didn't like or trust anyone well enough. And at the end of the day, it didn't matter. I still had my mobile, and the heavy truncheon I kept in my glovebox. I'd be OK.

The A46 runs down into Shakespeare country, through the rural heart of Warwickshire. It's normally busy, but at this time on a September evening there was little traffic about.

Dusk was settling when I found Marsden House. It was secluded, but not hidden. Tall wrought-iron gates opened onto a long gravel drive, which wound for several hundred yards through dense beech woods. Lights were visible at the far end and I drove steadily towards them. I was surprised that nobody was controlling the gate, but maybe whoever lived here had nothing to fear. In that case, I had nothing to be nervous about. I *was* nervous, though.

It was a palatial residence – a virtual mansion, white-walled and slate-roofed, with fake Greek pillars along the front and a row of poplars separating the parking area from an immense lawn. I pulled up warily. Several other vehicles were already there. One was a station wagon, caked with mud; another a scruffy rust-box of a van. The others were plain and nondescript saloons. Nothing looked as if it might belong to the master of this house.

I sat for a moment, watching. Curtains were drawn across all the windows. Nothing moved. I glanced at my watch. I was already four minutes late. Licking my fingers, I flattened my hair, then tightened the knot of my tie, stowed the truncheon under my jacket and put my mobile in my pocket. Taking the invitation from my pocket, I set out for the front door. It opened as I approached it. A tall, cadaverously thin man, dressed in an old-fashioned butler's outfit, was waiting there, holding a pen and clipboard. I walked up the steps towards him and held the card out. He took it, examined it intently, then looked at me with something like keen interest.

'Trashman,' I said. 'I am on your list, I assume?'

'Yeah, mate . . . you're on my list,' he replied in a strong cockney accent. Then he smiled. With his ashen skin and skeletal features, it was not a pleasant sight. Surely he was far too old to be in service? For some reason, he looked familiar, though I couldn't work out why.

With a tidy flourish, he ticked his list and stepped aside. I walked past, murmuring thanks. A grand hallway lay before me. Bland music was playing somewhere and I could hear the mumble of voices. I ventured forwards. Ahead, a sweeping stairway with ornate banisters rose into darkness, but to either side doorways led off into well-lit chambers where glasses clinked.

A young woman in a short waitress outfit passed through from one room to another. She was carrying a tray with empties on it. Glancing into the chamber she'd just left, I saw a sofa, easy chairs and one end of a huge fireplace. Handsome oils hung on the walls. Feeling easier, I ambled in.

There were three people inside. A man and a woman

stood talking in one corner; he had a powder-white face and wore a black suit, black shirt and black tie; she was broad and butch, wore country tweeds, jodhpurs and boots, and carried a riding crop. The third person was a youth in ragged denims, with hanks of oily hair dangling to either side of his face. He was sitting in a big armchair, avidly watching a porno flick on the TV screen in front of him. It wasn't your average porno flick, either. A muscular guy in a red leather rapist-mask was kneeling over the open mouth of some slapper in white frillies, forcefully pissing.

Just one of the many uplifting things I've seen in my twenty-three years of police work. I glanced from person to person. Then at the screen again. Things had now progressed to their natural conclusion, from liquids to solids. The greasy-haired lad was still gawping; the man in black and woman in tweeds were paying no attention to the on-screen activities.

I backed slowly out.

And a hand fell on my shoulder.

'Gosh the time . . . old boy?' asked a dapper bloke in a white silk scarf and white dinner jacket. He spoke with a ludicrous Bertie Wooster accent, and tottered drunkenly from side to side. 'Only just gosh here, y'see . . . rather late, I know. Still . . . besher late than never, eh?' He offered me his hand, which was clad in a white glove; the palm of it was stained a ruddy brown.

I made no effort to take it, but if the drunk was insulted he didn't show it. He grinned, then hiccupped. 'Can't tell you who I really am, old sshport, bu they call me Carnation.'

I noticed the shrivelled carnation in the man's buttonhole. A sudden association of ideas sent a chill through me. Then a gong sounded in the other room. I looked around. Through the open door, I could see more guests standing in groups.

'Our hossht, I think,' said Carnation, putting an unwelcome arm around my shoulders and steering me through. 'Then dinner, what? Hope ssho, a least!'

I was aware of the odd threesome from the pornography room coming in behind us; but the new crowd, if anything, were even weirder. A fat bald man, dressed in overalls, was standing by a cold buffet on a side table. He was picking at the food with grubby fingers and glancing suspiciously around. Again, I thought he looked familiar.

The same could be said of the hulking, bearded figure in rags who stood at the other side of the room, drinking wine from a bottle. He was surely a derelict, yet I felt certain I ought to know him. I glanced from guest to guest. There were thirteen in all. Some looked normal – quiet, suburban, ill at ease even. Others, like the bald man and the derelict, were furtive and fidgety, or strangely dressed.

'Welcome,' said a resonant voice.

Now another character appeared. He emerged from behind a pair of drapes and stood on a small podium of polished wood. To either side of him, brass censers gave off sweet fumes. I recognized the scent from the invitation card and wondered if it contained some sort of narcotic – all of a sudden, the atmosphere was heady.

'Welcome to you all,' the man said again, arms open.

He wore robes of black silk, but still looked very gaunt. If the butler was thin, then this bloke was a rake. His hair was colourless, lank and greased back, his face ash-grey and cut into angles by the sharp edges of his bones.

'It's a pleasure to be in such esteemed company,' the man said, with apparently sincere warmth. His eyes were his healthiest feature; they sparkled like broken glass as he surveyed us. 'You may wonder what you are doing here. I will answer that question shortly. But let me tell you again what a pleasure it is to meet you. I know you all well. I have studied some of you for years.'

For some reason I didn't doubt that this was the truth. Emaciated as he was, this guy radiated authority. His audience listened, absorbed.

'My real name is unimportant,' he went on. 'But you may call me Luther. As you will have noticed, I am wealthy. And so can you be . . . if you heed what I have to say.'

He cleared his throat. 'The organization I represent is very interested in the work you are doing here. I mention no names, but as a movement we were born in the United States several decades ago. And we prosper. We now cover Latin America, Canada and the former Soviet Union. We have firm footholds in western Europe, primarily Holland, Belgium and Germany. Now it is Great Britain's turn.' His pallid face twisted into a smile. For a moment, I half expected his skin to crack and split, and start flaking off. 'Instead of working for yourselves,' Luther added, 'we want you to work for us.'

Immediately I sensed a wave of unease. Guests exchanged glances, voices muttered dissent. Then I looked at the bearded tramp again and a really crazy thought struck me.

Luther, meanwhile, was holding up a hand for peace. 'Please do not feel threatened by this. We will not interfere in your personal routines. Far from it, in fact. We positively encourage you to continue with the successful modus operandi each one of you has developed.'

I was staring at the tramp, transfixed. Two students . . . beaten to death for their wallets, somewhere on the South Coast. Brighton perhaps. A short while later, there'd been two more, in London. The tramp on the photofit . . . the tramp with the black beard and huge shoulders . . .

I turned to study the man who'd called himself Carnation. And I thought about the mysterious 'Carnation Man' – an upper-class twit, distinctive for his evening dress and pink carnation – who'd lured six women out of nightclubs down in the Home Counties, then raped and garrotted them. Starting five years ago, and still nobody had been convicted.

I was stunned. Surely this couldn't be what I thought it was? I looked at more faces – the bald man, the riding-crop woman – and I thought about other unsolved murders, about wanted posters in police stations all over the country. Then I looked back at Luther.

'And we will pay you,' he was saying. 'Yes, for every piece of work we identify, our organization will pay you a substantial sum.'

'How mussh, old boy?' Carnation asked.

Luther wagged a finger. 'Suffice to say . . . continue at a steady rate, and you'll all be rich by the time you retire. Assuming you evade detection, of course, which is also important. That is something we can help with to a degree, though we cannot guarantee immunity, so please do not grow lax in your methods. We have no intention of going down with your ship, if that happens.' Fleetingly, Luther's eyes hardened. 'Any attempt to engineer that will incur a most serious reprisal. But why dwell on the negative?' he continued. 'Let us be positive . . .'

I started edging towards the door. Nobody seemed to be watching me. From what I'd seen, there was no security . . . apart from that butler, whom I now also recognized. He was Charles Meredith, a poisoner of three wives. He wouldn't be a problem, though; he'd only been out of Ashworth six months, after serving nearly forty years.

In the background, Luther's voice was rising. 'My associates and I have devoted our lives to this vocation. In the cause of those who deserve to be called human . . .'

I closed the door behind me, then moved across the hall to the far wall. I was frightened, yes, stunned and appalled, choked by the whole thing. But I was also in a frenzy of excitement. I couldn't overlook an opportunity such as this. I'd wanted some kind of break; and what other copper had ever been given a break like this? Who else in any walk of life had ever been offered such a chance? I stopped still, thinking hard, trying to work out what to do, what would be the safest and surest course of action. Then someone glided past me. Right past my shoulder. I froze.

But it was only the waitress.

I watched her as she moved from shelf to table, scooping up empties. She was a pert, pretty little thing. The short black uniform nicely set off her blond bobbed hair. And weren't those the lacy tops of stockings I could see under her skirt as she walked? Briefly, that distracted me. But not for long.

I glanced up at her face again. From this range, she wasn't as young as she'd first seemed, which was hardly a surprise . . . they rarely are in the meat trade, and that was doubtless where the maniac in charge of this house had found her. Her age didn't worry me, though; it was something else. Like the rest of them, I felt there was a familiarity about her, but not in the way there had been with the others. In her case, it was more 'real': more like I'd actually met her, rather than just heard descriptions or studied photofits.

As I pondered this, she moved through into the television room, quite oblivious to my presence. I thought about all the hookers I'd rousted over the years, but I didn't find her there. I ran a rule over the other ranks of filth and infamy, thinking particularly about their girlfriends, wives and sisters. Still, nothing came to light. Then it struck me that she might hail from the other side of the fence. Had she been a victim of crime? Or a witness to it?

A witness.

It clicked. She was Mary Lockwood, an ex-stripper and peep-show girl who'd supposedly, after giving a shed-load of evidence to the Trashman team, gone securely to ground.

Hers was a particularly chilling story. It seemed she'd been hard at work one night, bumping and grinding in the little plywood cubicle Bull Ring XXX Books & Videos allowed her, when the perp came barging into the shop, both guns blazing. This was the second or third time he'd struck, I can't remember for sure. Anyway, he put three slugs through the owner, who was behind the counter, and another five into the owner's business partner, who'd come charging out from the back room. There'd been no customers in at the time, luckily for them; but Birmingham city centre isn't exactly a quiet neighbourhood, even at half past midnight, so the killer made sure he got out quickly, for once not stopping to search the premises and guarantee he'd nailed all potential witnesses. That rare error of judgement on his part saved Mary Lockwood's life. But probably not her sanity. She'd been a drink-sozzled, chain-smoking wreck by the time the inquiry boys had grilled their information out of her. By then, she'd wanted to make tracks, to disappear, to become a nameless non-person reachable only by the most trusted senior police officers in the West Midlands.

Pretty ironic, then, that she'd ended up here.

Knowing I had no option, I glanced around quickly to check I was still alone, then nipped into the room behind her. She was clearing up fastidiously, not interested in the on-screen atrocities. The original duo had increased to an octet; carved wooden dildos were now on view. And thanks to the groans pumping from the tube and the crunching industrial rock accompanying them, Mary hadn't even heard me follow her in.

I stood there for a moment, unsure how best to approach her. Then a sudden noise from somewhere in that capacious house decided me. I fumbled under my jacket.

But unfortunately there was no gun there – I hadn't had my permit to carry a gun on duty renewed since the Serious Crime Squad controversy. It would have to be the truncheon. Which wasn't going to be easy. I drew it out, then looked back towards Mary. She'd finally realized I was there, and was now staring at me intently. Her eyes locked with mine, and she knew immediately what was going on.

Through no fault of their own, the moment ordinary citizens witness a major crime, they transmogrify into sheep. Whether they like it or not, they are from that point on nothing but prey, constantly in danger from the most vicious and bloodthirsty kind of wolf. Witnesses to serious crime even start to look like sheep. Their biochemistry alters so that at the least little thing they stop what they're doing and stand there trembling uselessly; they develop glazed, ovine eyes; their skin pales to grey.

It's astounding really. But, believe me, I know.

A lot of the guys involved in the Serious Crime Squad scandal didn't just lose their pensions or their jobs, they lost their liberty. Not me. I've always believed that what I have I hold.

So I killed her there and then. With a single blow, full on the cranium, the crack like willow on leather. She went down poll-axed: not a jerk, not a twitch. I stepped over her to check the job was a good one. It was. Blood seeped from her ears. The pupil of one eye had dilated; the other had shrunk to a pinhole. Her head had actually changed shape.

Satisfied, I turned to the doorway. The man called Luther was standing there, his deranged cohorts ranked behind him. He smiled warmly.

'And welcome to you especially,' he said. 'Welcome, Trashman.'

Lucy

Pauline E. Dungate

I watched the news today. No sound came to me through the toughened glass of the TV shop, but I knew what they were talking about. It grieved me, casting a shadow on my present happiness because I knew what that mother was going through. It had happened to me once. Losing a child can seem like the end of the world.

I don't have much – there's just me and the baby. I follow the news by picking up discarded papers from park benches, and scavenge around the markets for food. It's surprising what drops from the stalls during the day, but they say a vegetarian diet is good for you. I hope so. It's important I keep healthy, for her sake.

My first baby was taken away from me before she had a chance to live. The saddest thing was that I wasn't even able to hold her. It was because I didn't have a boyfriend then. At least, that's what my mother said. All babies must have fathers. But we're getting on all right without one at the moment. I don't really see what fathers are for – they can't feed the baby and I would have got on better without mine.

At the start I didn't know what was happening to me. The curse has always been irregular, so when it didn't come I shrugged. It would be back in a month or so and meantime there was no mess, no gripping bellyache and no furtive washing of underwear because I didn't want my mum to see the stains. It didn't even worry me when I got sick or didn't want to eat. But when she kicked, I knew there was a miracle inside me. And it was my secret. I began to dream of how it would be when she was in my arms.

Then my dad found out. It was one of those nights when Mum was took bad. I'd seen the signs of a spell coming on, she'd left the empty bottles behind the sofa for me to clear away. In better times, she managed to put them out for the dustman herself. She'd passed out downstairs so I'd gone up early. It was a hot night so I lay with just a sheet over me, thinking about the baby and stroking my belly. It was beginning to swell nicely but under my normal shapeless jumpers and T-shirts no one had noticed.

I heard Dad come in. He'd been at the Perry Barr stadium. He always goes there Thursday nights. He and Uncle George have got shares in a greyhound. It's called Plastic Paddy and it wins sometimes. He must've lost that night cos he was shouting at Mum. I knew she wouldn't answer. Once she's gone nothing can stir her till morning. So he gave it up as a bad job and came up after me. He's done it before, lots of times. I don't mind and usually he's quite gentle. This time, though, he must've noticed something because when he'd finished he put his hand on the baby. She kicked him.

He didn't say a word, just pulled his belt from its loops and hit me. The first blow landed across my belly. I curled up small to protect her. My back and shoulders were sore afterwards and I cried. Last time he belted me cos I'd taken a fiver from Mum's purse, but this time I couldn't understand what I'd done. I thought he would've been pleased.

No one spoke to me for five days, but I heard the whisperings.

'It's got to go,' Mum told me.

At first I didn't see what she meant. I carried on nibbling the piece of dry toast that was all I could manage for breakfast, and shrugged.

'We've made all the arrangements.'

'What arrangements?'

Dad came into the kitchen then. 'Are you ready?' he said. 'We mustn't be late.'

'For what?' I asked.

'I've made the appointment. Come on.'

He did give me a minute to collect my purse and change my shoes, but he was fretting all the while. He was even worse as we waited at the bus stop, keeping a hand on my elbow and peering anxiously round the shelter for the first sight of a bus turning the distant corner.

He took me to an ordinary terraced house in King's Heath. It had a neat pocket of front garden and a door painted in royal blue. The net curtains at the windows looked clean and bright. Definitely a much smarter house than the one we lived in.

'Why are we here?' I asked as Dad rang the bell.

'To get things sorted,' he said.

The lady who answered the door could've been any one of the older teachers from school. She was that kind. Neat like the house, her short hair permed and coloured. Dad ushered me inside and the lady led us up the stairs to what I suppose was the back bedroom. It had a reclining chair in it, like the ones at the dentist and a vanity unit in the corner. The lady gave me a cup of something to drink.

'What is it?' I asked.

'Just something to make you relax.'

'I don't want it. Why are we here, Dad?'

'Don't make a fuss, girl,' he said. 'Drink up.'

His voice had that edge to it that meant that if I didn't obey I'd feel his belt next. The liquid was sweet and bitter at the same time and there was brandy in it. I don't drink much, but I like a brandy when I can get someone to buy one for me. This mixture made me feel woozy. The lady guided me to the chair. Dad stood behind me, holding my shoulders. She hiked my skirt up round my waist and pulled down my knickers.

'What're you doing?' I asked. I could hear my words slurring and my limbs felt heavy.

She didn't answer me but said to Dad, 'It's rather big. You should have come sooner.'

Dad just growled, 'Get on with it.'

I was too lethargic to move. I don't really know what she did. I only felt the sharp pain and the cramps that went on and on. I tried to scream but couldn't. And when it was over, my baby was dead. I could forgive my dad a lot of things but not that. I bled for a week and when the ache in my empty womb had gone, I left. I had nowhere to go and I've never been back. They can't make me. Especially now I have this little darling. I feel so sorry for that mother who's had her baby stolen. I think, It could have been me.

When she first came, she cried a lot. So I wrapped her well and rocked her. I put her to my breast and she sucked so hard she made my nipples sore. Her little face would screw up in sleep; it's impossible not to love her. I don't understand how some people can be so cruel to babies. I won't risk them taking her away from me.

We live in a dilapidated house in Ladywood, one of a terrace that's been boarded up for months. I suppose they'll eventually knock them down, but for the moment they do as shelter for the likes of me. I keep clear of the end house, which is a hangout for junkies and glue-sniffers. Next door are a couple of winos, harmless to anyone but themselves. The old woman fell downstairs yesterday, and only the dozens of cardigans she wears saved her from injury.

I had to come here. I couldn't stay in the hostel. Not with a baby. They would've taken her away and I couldn't have that. And I didn't want to sleep on the streets. I did that when I first left home. It was the most miserable time I ever spent. The first night I slept under a bench in Cannon Hill Park. The smell of piss and dogshit made me feel ill and if I hadn't been so hungry I would've thrown up.

The second night I shivered in a shop doorway in the city centre. I'd tried the steps outside the NatWest Bank down Dale End first, but a smelly old tramp moved me on. It was his spot, he said. I was less tolerant then and focused my resentment on him. I waited until he was snoring, then crept up and kicked his head in. My Doc Martens crunched satisfyingly into his face. If my mum and dad had been there instead of him I would've enjoyed it even better. It was their fault I was cold and hungry with nowhere to go.

When you're desperate, you learn to survive. Too many people put their bags down while they're distracted by a shop assistant selling perfume. It's easy to snag something as you brush past, specially in a crowded store. Some actually leave their purses on top of their shopping. You'd think they'd know better. The trick, then, is not to leave the shop with the purse. Cash is virtually untraceable. And in the crowds of the Bull Ring it's even easier. In the jostle between the stalls, they don't notice as you lift the food they've just bought, and vanish. And I soon found the flops where the homeless doss. Old buildings mostly, derelict and dangerous, but offering more cover than a doorway or a bus shelter.

I lived like that for about three months before I got caught shoplifting in Marks & Spencer's food hall. They found me a social worker and a place in a hostel. The hostel was fine, the social worker was shitty. A wet blanket who insisted I called him Tony. He kept trying to get me to admit that my situation was caused by childhood trauma –

his words, not mine. I think he wanted me to say that my father had raped me and my mother was an alcoholic. True, but I wasn't going to tell him that. I feigned indifference to his questions. He did teach me, though, how to claim benefit. Not that that's much good to me at the moment. If I go to sign on they'll insist on knowing where I'm living and take my baby away. It's part of the terms of my probation that I live in the hostel, and I've broken that. I got twelve months, suspended, for the shoplifting, and a probation officer. She's supposed to meet me once a week but I reckon she's too busy with worse cases than me. The most I got was a message at the hostel, saying to ring her so she could say we'd had contact. I couldn't be bothered, so it'll be some time before she realizes I'm gone. The people who run the hostel haven't the time to care.

Once I knew I was going to have a baby, I saved as much from my benefit as I could and made a bit extra on the streets, begging and suchlike. I knew I'd need money for things like nappies, but I didn't like the idea of selling my body. I did it a few times when I was really desperate. A quick screw in a shop doorway isn't my idea of fun and I wouldn't want my baby to grow up thinking I was that kind of person.

As I stood watching the silent screens, I thought about what to call my baby. I hadn't given her a name yet. I liked Natasha. It's what I'd planned to call the one they took away. But seeing that poor mother, I wondered if Lucille would be better, after the missing baby. I turned away, tasting the name on my tongue, seeing how it would sound. Lucille. It didn't seem quite right, almost as if I were stealing someone else's joy. Lucy, perhaps. I must get back to her. I don't like leaving her alone, but there are times when I can't take her with me. She's a very good baby. She doesn't make much noise and she sleeps a lot.

*

Those two boys have spoilt everything. I just hope no one thinks to look in here, so we can go home as soon as it's dark.

Lucy is such a lovely baby. There's no way they can make me give her up now, though they'll try to take her away. They won't see how well I can care for her, only the damp, cold squat we live in and the fact that it has no water or electricity. They can't see that a mother's love is the most important thing a baby can have, and all my love is for Lucy.

I know babies cry a lot and Lucy did to begin with. She was always hungry; crying, feeding, sleeping – an endless cycle. She was only quiet when she was at my breast or sleeping. Often when I put her down she'd wake and call for my attention. It was almost as if she was afraid I'd abandon her. She couldn't know that I'd never do that. Those first few days, the only way I could sleep was to cuddle her. I'd hold her so her bare skin was warm against mine and wrap a blanket around both of us. It was a good thing I'd got in loads of food, because I couldn't risk going far from her.

After a while she settled. She'd sleep for longer periods and, between times, lie quietly. I'm sure she followed me with those big blue eyes of hers. She'd dream sometimes. I would hear her whimper in her sleep, the same way a dog does when it's dreaming of chasing rabbits. What do babies dream of? Once she settled I could leave her a while. I didn't like to but I couldn't take her with me. It's difficult to move quickly when you're carrying a bundle and I couldn't afford to get caught again. For her sake.

All went fine. Then I made a mistake. Two in fact. To begin with Lucy smelled wonderful – like milk and sunshine. But it's difficult to wash nappies with no running water. I do my best to keep her clean and sweet-smelling but after about three weeks I realized I had a problem. The flies noticed first. They'd run over her little face, quite unharmed. She'd blink them away or cry when they tickled too much, but she got used to them. I'd come back and find a dozen of the vile things settled on her cheeks. However much I shooed them off, they were on her again the moment I turned away.

When I came home and found a rat nibbling her toes I knew I had to do something. I decided to take her to the mother and baby room in the toilets by the station. I'd washed the nappies out there before and thought I could bathe her in one of the sinks. The first mistake was taking her out.

The second was stopping in the churchyard. Not the one round the cathedral in the city centre, but the one at the top of Warstone Lane, where the catacombs are. It's deserted most of the time except for the odd drunk or glue-sniffer, and it was a long walk from the squat to the station. Lucy was heavier than I realized. It was a hot day so I stopped to rest. I sat back against a headstone and unwrapped Lucy's shawl a little, thinking the fresh air and sunshine would be good for her. It was one of her sleeping times. She was quiet and the only real sounds were from the distant traffic. It's strange how entering a cemetery seems to muffle outside noise. Even the chirrup of sparrows was muted.

I must've dozed.

I remember jerking awake at the sound of giggles. There were two boys there, in T-shirts and torn jeans. One held a stick broken from a nearby tree. He was reaching out with it to prod Lucy, the end already hooked under her blanket. The other noticed me looking at them and nudged his friend. He grinned.

'What you got, lady?' he said, as if he couldn't see Lucy's beautiful sleeping face.

'Smells awful,' said his friend. 'Like a dead dog.'

The boy jerked the end of the stick, flicking the blanket from Lucy. A mass of disturbed flies exploded around us.

'Bastard!' I yelled and grabbed Lucy to me.

'Jesus Christ,' the boy said. 'It *is* a dead dog.'

The other child threw up, his vomit spattering my shoes and Lucy's blanket.

I scrambled to my feet and began to run, clutching Lucy to me. She belched but didn't otherwise protest.

There's a crumbling gatehouse at one end of the cemetery. It's surrounded by scaffolding and a battered fence. Hugging Lucy to my breast with one arm, I scrambled over the broken chain link, glancing back to see if I was being followed. I tripped on fallen masonry and heard the thud of Lucy's head hitting the ground. She didn't even whimper. I sprawled across her. I felt her little body deflate beneath mine like a broken balloon.

I got up carefully and carried her inside the building. I don't think anyone saw us come in, but we can't stay here for ever. Tomorrow is Monday and if they haven't found us by then, the workmen rebuilding this place will be back. In the meantime, I'll use what's left of the daylight shining through the window to try and put what remains of Lucy's decayed intestines back inside her sweet body.

Santa's Grotto

Don Nixon

'But why Birmingham?'

The social worker at the hostel was trying to appear interested, but it was the end of a long day and I was the last in her casebook. She managed a smile.

'I'd have thought you'd have stayed up in the north where you did your parole. After all, it's twenty years since you were in the Green.' She just about stifled a yawn.

I mumbled something about still having friends in the Midlands, but it didn't sound convincing even to me. What friends I'd had years ago were now dead or banged up, or had gone out of business in the eighties when new firms had flooded into the area with the expansion of gambling, the drug trade and the collapse of the Iron Curtain. The crime scene in Brum was in a different league to what it had been in my time. Now, rival gangs were fighting turf wars to protect their investments and there was no room for the small operator. Then, I could make an easy living freelancing and nobody ever carried a shooter. It's ironic. I'm fond of using this word. I picked it up from my tutors when I was doing the two Open University degrees that kept me sane in top security. It was ironic that I'd been sent down for a bungled armed robbery when I'd never packed a piece. No, I was here in Birmingham because I had unfinished business, but I could hardly tell the social worker that. And anyway I rather liked the place.

New Birmingham was not the boring provincial city I'd known. The centre was full of life and bustle, which I found exhilarating after so many years inside. They'd warned me in the rehab that I'd find the noise on the outside wearing, but I loved it. Even in October you could sit at a pavement café on New Street and watch the world go by, and I liked to have a coffee there most mornings before I sauntered up to the art gallery. Through my degree studies I'd developed a real interest in art, and I often spent an hour sitting in the Pre-Raphaelite gallery. After the tiny illustrations in the course books, the reality was stunning. I'm strictly traditional in my art. Pictures have got to tell a story, in spite of what my tutor used to say. It's my life that's an abstract – lots of lines going anywhere and nowhere.

Birmingham had certainly changed. Even the façade of Winson Green, my old Alma Mater, had had a facelift, though I guess inside there was still that sickly essence of piss and disinfectant, topped up with frustrated testosterone, that seeped through the wings of every prison I'd ever been in. I still sometimes wake up smelling it.

By December, I'd been in the hostel two months and my money was running out. I needed a job. I tried selling the *Big Issue* but couldn't take the punters' patronizing stares.

'You're setting your sights too high.' The social worker sniffed. 'Two degrees aren't going to count for much with an employer when set against a twenty-year stretch.'

Most of the ex-cons in the hostel were packing shelves or dabbling on the fringes of petty scams. The only one with any money was a young nonce who made a good living peddling his arse around the gay bars. He gave me a tenner occasionally to act as his minder, but I was getting too old to be a credible muscle.

I gave in grudgingly. 'You'll enjoy it, Roy,' the social worker promised. And though it pissed me off to admit it, I did.

And so I found myself, a week before Christmas, padded out in a red suit with white whiskers glued all over my face. I was coming back from a tea break when I saw him. Instinctively I stepped back, hiding behind Snow White's door so he couldn't see me. Then I shrugged and walked out on to Santa's throne, where I'd sit for the rest of the afternoon listening to the kids' requests. Under all that clobber I was hardly likely to be recognized, but seeing him again had resurrected all my old fears. I remembered how violent he could be. Once he'd nearly scalped a Digbeth fence who'd shortchanged us.

'Are you OK, Roy?'

The Guardian Elf came over and scanned me anxiously. Molly looked ridiculous in her pointed hat and green tights but the kids loved her. She was a good-natured old slapper from the hostel and had helped get me the job. I noticed my hands were shaking.

'Give me a minute, Molly,' I told her. 'Just got a bit too hot under the lights. Keep the kids waiting for the moment.'

She nodded and went back to the barrier of artificial snow and arranged the queue into a neat line. I liked Molly. She used to be on the game, but then the whole vice scene changed. Glitzy massage parlours and tarts doing business over the Internet drove out the girls and their small-time pimps who'd used to work the city centre pubs and the little hotels on the Hagley Road. Now Molly did some cleaning at the hostel for her keep. Some nights she'd come to my cubicle and we'd share a spliff, but that was as far as it went. She couldn't bear to be touched any more and I never even tried. After years inside, I didn't want to risk not getting wood, as the porno lads say. Didn't Freud say that vanity is the last thing to die?

George Lynch was standing at one of the toy counters, watching a small boy rifling through boxes of computer games. He'd aged well. The black hair probably owed something to the dye bottle, but it was still thick and swept into the old Elvis quiff. He had that light, even tan you don't get from sunbeds and, under his expensive jacket, his powerful torso and shoulders showed he worked out regularly. He was recognizable as the young hood who'd learned his trade in Derry, who'd been my partner and taught me all I knew about semtex. We'd been among the aristocrats of the business, two of the best petermen in the country. Inside, the screws had always given us respect and the tobacco barons carefully saw that we got our cut. But George had a clever, half-bent brief and after a neat piece of plea-bargaining he'd got a light sentence in a Category C while I copped for the lot and no remission.

For twenty years, banged up, I'd thought of George every night, and I'd sworn to get even with my grass of a partner.

The boy ran to George and his clear voice pierced through the muzak of Christmas bells and carols. 'Grandpa, there's Santa. I want to tell him about my presents.'

I looked at the child as George grinned down at him. I felt a stab of jealousy and of hatred. George the family man, the patriarch – all those things I could never be now. And all because that bastard used me to save his own skin.

Then his grandson was standing in front of me. He had George's eyes. What my mother would've called put in by a sooty finger. And, though he was only about six years old, he had his confidence. Most kids held back a little shyly when Molly brought them over to me, but this one had a swagger and a determined chin. He launched straight into a catalogue of the things he wanted for Christmas. Clearly money was no object as far as that family was concerned. I wondered if George was still in the business. He reeked of prosperity; he'd done well at my expense. The bastard looked over approvingly as the little monster racked up quite a bill.

The boy lowered his voice. 'And can you bring something for my grandpa?' he whispered.

'But I don't know where your grandpa lives. My reindeer won't be able to find him.' He leaned close to me. I could smell the gel on his spiky hair.

'I can tell you our address. Grandpa's come to stay with us.'

He told me and I wrote the details in my book of requests. George was doing well. The address was in the posh part of Edgbaston. Years ago he'd lived in a flat in Digbeth. I smiled down at the boy and patted his shoulder. 'You've remembered all that well. I bet you even know the telephone number too.'

He grinned. He was a cocky little runt. I found myself disliking the kid intensely.

'That's easy. And I know our email. Grandpa's teaching me how to use the computer. He says sometimes when there's someone on the telephone you can send an email instead.'

He recited it all proudly, the little show-off. Like George, he loved an audience. 'And I want him to have a good present. Don't bring any rubbish. He's always telling us to get the best. Second best is only for losers.'

It was one of George's old sayings. It was uncanny how he held his head at that superior angle so reminiscent of his grandfather. After delivering his orders, he nodded crisply at me and went back to George. My old partner gave the boy a hug and I watched them as they made their way up the stairs out of the basement of the store. I felt the tremor in my hands again and I dug my nails into the palms to stop the shaking. Still three hours to go before the end of my shift. I thought longingly of the stash of grass in my locker at the hostel. I badly needed a joint. I concentrated hard on how I was going to handle George, and gradually the trembling stopped.

That night at the hostel I could hardly touch my supper. I felt sick with excitement. Molly followed me out to the street.

'What's wrong, Roy?' Her wizened pixie face was twisted in concern.

'Just need a bit of fresh air. I think the fish was a bit off.'

I shrugged her away and, surprisingly, found a payphone down the street that hadn't been vandalized, though the graffiti inside the booth made the *Kama Sutra* look tame. I didn't dare use the hostel phone in case George was able to trace me. In the old days he'd had eyes and ears everywhere, which was why we'd lasted so long.

A woman's voice answered. George wasn't in but would be back later.

'Just tell him that an old friend happened to be in the area and would like a word. Say Roy King called.'

I went back to the hostel and rolled a joint, but then put it under my mattress. I needed to keep my head clear. George had always been able to manipulate me with words. This time it was going to be different.

When I rang later that night, he picked up the phone immediately. He must've been waiting by it.

'Yes, it really is Roy. This is the nightmare call you've been dreading all these years.' I kept my tone neutral, a shade amused. He came straight to the point.

'What do you want?'

In the background I could hear the drone of a television and a child chattering. 'You must be very proud of your grandson, George,' I said. 'He's the spit of you.'

He wasn't expecting that and I heard him draw his breath in hard. This was precisely the lever I'd planned to use after I'd seen them together.

'Leave the kid out of this,' he rasped.

'That's going to depend on you, George. I got to know a few paedophiles in prison. Some of them owe me.' I paused. 'He's a pretty little boy. They'd love to meet him.'

I was enjoying this moment of power. And it was true. The boy was attractive.

'What do you want?'

'How much do you think you owe me? Put a price on it.' My voice was nice and reasonable, as if we were bargaining easily over a car. George was silent. 'Well, let me make a start. How about two grand? Not much for twenty years.'

'OK. Where and how?'

I wasn't surprised at the speed of his acceptance. It was the threat to the kid. When we'd been planning jobs in the old days, George had always said that we must first discover the enemy's weakest point. I knew now that the kid was George's weakest point. I could play on that time and time again. That was why I'd pitched it as low as two grand. I could come back and gradually squeeze him as I upped the ante. This was going to be revenge eaten cold. Two thousand was just the beginning.

'Where and how?' he repeated.

The strain was there but he was doing his best to hide it. I spoke quickly. It was time to end the call while I still had the upper hand.

'You'll get an email with instructions tomorrow, George.'

Then I rang off.

I didn't sleep much that night. I half hoped Molly would come to my cubicle and hold me. But of course she didn't. I was alone.

*

In the morning I went to the cyber café in the shopping centre above New Street Station. I knew nobody could trace me from there. The email I wrote was short.

'Gift wrap the money in a box and leave it under the Christmas tree in the grotto in the basement of Rackhams. At three p.m. tomorrow.'

I remembered his weakest point and added,

'Bring your pretty grandson with you. My friends like to look at kids and looking is as far as it will go so long as you do as you're told.'

I sent it and stayed at the keyboard for a good five minutes until I could control the tremors that'd started again in my hands. I couldn't believe I'd dared to threaten George.

I walked back up New Street towards the art gallery and, sitting on one of the steps in Chamberlain Square, smoked the spliff I'd rolled the night before. My shift didn't start till midday, so I spent the time sitting in front of Millais' *Blind Girl*. I don't know why but it's my favourite piece of Victorian kitsch, with its little butterfly in the corner that stops it being too sentimental. When I was doing the OU art history course, my tutor said it showed I had a sensitive soul trying to get out from under my hardman image. But then he was a poof and I've noticed queers are attracted to this combination of tough and soft. Looking back, I owe a lot to that kindly old queen, and if I ever met him again I might let him give me the blowjob he was clearly gagging for. The Millais worked its usual magic and I was calm and collected by the time I stuck on Santa's whiskers back at Rackhams.

Three o'clock: my tea break, and George and the boy turned up on the dot. I hid behind Snow White's house to watch them. George was carrying a box covered in silver paper. He gave it to the boy, who ran over and placed it under the Christmas tree. Then they left, George's arm placed protectively around his grandson's shoulders. They never looked back. I wondered if George had planted any muscle in the crowd in the basement, but I'd allowed for that. I wouldn't collect the box until the store closed and the public was gone. Even so, I had to exercise superhuman self-control not to rush and pick it up. By the time I got to the last child, my concentration was shot and I forgot to thank him for the Christmas card he gave me.

Then, just before closing, the fire alarm went off. Instructions blared over the Tannoy and everyone filed out obediently. I was forced to leave with the rest. I looked back at the box gleaming under the Christmas tree. Molly was still there, darting around and putting her bits and pieces into a plastic bag.

'Come on,' shouted our supervisor, 'just leave everything.'

'It's a bomb hoax,' she whispered as we reached our designated positions outside. Police were all over the place. The explosion wasn't very loud, and I suppose by that time I was half expecting it. The silver box! George must still be in touch with the semtex boys in Prague. I moved nearer to the entrance. A few army lads were milling around. One came out in his bomb disposal rig and shouted to the others.

'Another bloody hoax. It wasn't a bomb, just a big firecracker. A big bang and lots of smoke. Bloody kids again.'

I staggered back, sick with relief. George hadn't found me. I realized I was still holding the last child's Christmas card. I opened it automatically. The message was short.

'Merry Christmas, Roy. If you're still alive to read this, make the most of it. It won't be for long.'

I shivered. George was playing with me. I was out of my depth. He'd always come out on top. In the phone call I'd told him I'd seen his grandson and he'd worked out where. He would've questioned the boy too. I'd pushed him too hard.

I glanced around. The police were shepherding curious onlookers behind a cordon. I searched their faces anxiously, but no George. Suddenly, a burly man slipped through the cordon and started to move in my direction. He had that blank expression I'd learned to recognize. He wore a sharp suit but looked like a thug. He must be working for George.

'Move along, Santa.'

A young constable put a kindly hand on my shoulder. I swung round and hit him as hard as I could. He went down and others grabbed my arms to restrain me. I shouted and yelled until I was hustled over to a police van. The nick was about the only place I was going to be safe.

'Leave him alone, you wankers. He's just an old man.'

Molly ran screaming up to the back of the van.

'Here, Roy, I picked this up for you from under the tree.' She cradled the silver box in her arms. 'It must be some present. It's heavy enough.'

'No,' I shouted.

Too late. She threw it over to me.

The young copper in front of me caught it and took the full force of the blast. I saw Molly disintegrate in a cascade of blood before I lost consciousness. They told me I was lucky to be pulled from the wreckage with just a broken femur. The steel grill on the police van saved me.

I was alive.

In the hospital I wondered how long for. The second day, while I was in the operating theatre getting my leg fixed, a huge bunch of white roses arrived. They were there on my bedside table when I came to. There was no card, but the sister said they'd been left by a charming man who had a little boy with him.

'Such gorgeous roses,' cooed the staff nurse. 'What caring friends you have, Mr King.'

How could she know? Back in the old days, white roses were George's calling card. He always sent them to funerals. No doubt there'd be a bunch on my coffin as it slid through the curtains at the crematorium.

For days I sat slumped by my bed. In plaster, there was no way I could get out and hide from George. It seemed hopeless. The young nonce from the hostel turned up and slipped me a wad of high-quality grass. When I was able to hobble to the sluice, there were enough containers around for me to fix up an effective bong, which meant I could get a hit twice a day. It helped dull the guilt I felt about Molly. I couldn't get her out of my head. I replayed the scene endlessly, that eager look on her face as she threw the box to me and that second of horror as she seemed to fly apart in a spreading red mist. She was the only person who'd ever listened to me since I got out, and she was dead because of my stupidity.

So, before leaving hospital, I broke the habit of a lifetime and told the police everything. Molly deserved that. An anonymous bloke from some government department appeared and didn't seem surprised when I went through the tale again. Apparently it was known that George had been keeping pretty dodgy company. Refugee running and illegal immigrants, but there was nothing concrete on him. My testimony was going to be enough to pull him in, but when they broke into his house in Edgbaston, the birds had flown. He must've had a tip-off. The house was rented and there was nothing of George's there, except for traces of semtex in an outhouse. He'd obviously not lost his touch or his supplier. My guess was that he'd left England, but I was sure that one day he'd be back. There are too many lucrative rackets going on in the Midlands and that's where all his contacts are. When the fuss has died down and is buried in yesterday's chip papers, he'll quietly reappear.

So I stayed in the city. I still go to the art gallery when I want to think about Molly. For me, she's the little butterfly at the edge of the picture. And I went back to selling the *Big Issue* in town. Nearly everybody at some time or another comes down the ramp from the station and walks along New Street. One day I'll spot George. And then I'll kill him.

The Mentality

John Dalton

OK, so it's the first law of life. Get the most for the least possible. I know there's no alternative. I do know it all comes down to the screw, that ultimate component of everything. Now, this is fine if you've got the mentality, an ingrained sense of how to get a good deal, but if you're a slack bastard like me – problems. There's one on my mobile right now, green light glowing in the glove compartment. That's Sidney Carslake, agency manager, trouble-shiter in chief. He's calculated how long it's taken me to get to Ladywood and do the business. Now he's ready to lay another load on me. No chance then for a trip down to the caff. No languid frothy coffee and a read of the faces in the street. Mentality. There's always some bugger, some mean-minded, nit-picking bloodsucker who's out to screw more for the least possible. I find it hard to cope. Me, the man who had his mom thirty hours in labour before crawling out the womb. Me? I've been struggling to catch up ever since.

Now don't get me wrong. Slack yes, but not lazy. I like the job. Honest toil is healthy. But there's got to be space, there's got to be an opening where you can still see who you are. So when I drive to Ladywood, maybe I look into windows or visit a street I've never been down before. And at the towerblock where I have to serve the writ, maybe I linger, look up and imagine weird goings-on. Then there's doing the business and trying to do it right. Making room for sympathy or just showing friendly curiosity at the client's plight. I can't just be a blunt messenger larding on the woe. The phone's at it again. There you have it. No space. The screw. The squeeze. Can't remember now what the woman I served on looked like; just remember she had a hole in her tights.

'Sidney.'

'Jace. What took you so long?'

'Sorry, boss, lost the thing, you know the state my car's in.'

'You should have it on you at all times.'

'I know, just keep forgetting.'

'Hope you didn't forget the writ for the Quinn woman?'

'Nah, all done and dusted.'

'Right. I want you back at the office straight away, got another job lined up for you.'

'Oh, well that's a surprise.'

'Cut out the crap, Jason, this is an OE case, right up your street.'

'Right . . . so what's it involve?'

'A bath with a large amount of blood in it.'

'Blimey . . .'

'Ten minutes – OK?'

I must say, really – 'blood in the bath' – I was well intrigued. I almost switched the ignition on straight away – but hell, ten minutes? I hate it, I can't cope. Pressure, deadlines, needles sticking into me. I reckon when I finally did slurp out of the womb, the midwife must've slapped me and said, 'What kept you, we've targets to meet!'

BM Investigations has the top floor of a yellow brick cube in the back streets of Nechells. Near enough to the city centre for the rich clients, far enough away for cheap rent. I hopped up the stairs three at a time, hoping to muster up a breathless state. Through his open office door, Sidney pointedly glanced at the clock. It's a battle of wills really, how much slack I can win before the bastard fires me. Still maintaining an impression of haste, I bustled in and slumped on the seat next to the bloodsucker's desk.

Sidney Carslake – balding head, bulbous nose, and cheeks slipping off his chin. Sid has a wrecked kind of face. He's aware of it too, and it's an image he tries to disguise by donning designer clothes (those ultimate *screw yous*). The effect is bizarre. Just like the trophies on his filing cabinet – clay pigeon shooting, ten-pin bowling, NAPI Bronze award – and the photo above, Sid clasping hands with one Sir Norman Fowler, their grins like death masks in a museum display. I awaited the man's words. OE – that's 'open ended', no time limit, and so plenty of potential to cream off the cash.

'Right, Jace, this is it. Tamara Astbury, thirty-six, a good-looking, busy sales rep for a specialist office stationery firm. She comes in this morning, po-faced and tearful, wearing a black trouser suit and I reckon not much else. You know the view, cleavage right to the V of the lapels. Anyway, she sits down and blurts, "My husband's dead." Well, you know me, tell me something new, but I manage to commiserate. "He committed suicide," she then says. "I found him after coming back from Bristol. There he was in the bath, unrecognizable, his wrists slashed and the contents of his veins in the bathwater." "Tough," I says, "that's really tough." "There was a bottle of sleeping pills on the rim too." "Jesus," I says, "looks like the guy didn't want to screw up."'

'So was there a note?'

'No, Jace. The police did an investigation and reckon the suicide is genuine. Doesn't sound as if they bust a gut though, and they couldn't come up with a convincing reason as to why the guy did it.'

'What does our Tamara think?'

'Well, Jason, this is it, she doesn't get it either. She can't think why and that's where we come in.'

'Can't she just ask around herself?'

'No time, too much work.'

'Come on, it's her husband.'

'Yes I know, but you know the working world, Jason, taking time off, it can put you in the firing line.'

Sidney smiled at me then, a very nasty smile, letting me know that his sights were on me. Bastard.

'Anyway, two days, I'm going to give you two days to come up with the report which tells the lady all she wants to know.'

'Do you, er, think that's enough?'

'Jason, that's generous.'

I took Tamara's address and phone number from Sidney and then stood up. Yeah, I was thinking, very generous, and he's going to charge for three days minimum.

There was no point in hanging around at the office, I'd only get another nasty smile if I did, so I hoofed it back down the stairs and got in the car. It's my office anyway. Tamara Astbury lives in Hall Green, so I got the old Fiat running and headed south. The first thing to work out was how to play the job. Go easy and make sure it lasts three days just for the hell of it, or get it done in one and skive off some free time. Too early perhaps to decide. The second job was to speak to Tamara myself. I looked around for a watering hole. Down a side street, Phil's Grill dangled out a gaudy sign. I took the bait. Wish I hadn't.

There wasn't anything nice you could say. Gloomy, unwashed windows. The smell of burnt fat and mould. Foam spewing out of seats and Formica tables scarred and pitted like the surface of the moon. Worst of all, the coffee had sterra in it. I slumped down at a table. An old guy was in my line of sight. Long wisps of white hair grew out of his ears, nose and shirt collar. 'They're all the bloody, all the bloody same,' he kept grumbling to himself as he clawed his crotch and shifted what seemed like a piss bag beneath his pants.

Great. I got out the mobile. This wasn't going to be easy. A mixed-race youth was watching me as he propped up the counter. Black eyes, a scar on his cheek. He was giving me the look, which said he was King Shit in Phil's Grill and he might want to prove it. Youth. I stared back. The message was: I was ready to kill and burn every bloody thing in this awful place. The kid backed off, just enough so as not to lose face. I'd live with that.

'Hello, is that Tamara Astbury?'

'Yes . . .'

'Hi, this is Jason Tardy, of BM Investigations. Mr Carslake has assigned me to your case.'

'Oh, right.'

'There's just a few questions I want to ask, to get started.'

'OK, but, well I'm on the M6 at the moment and there's a bloody great lorry right on my tail, oops, hold on a sec, I'm going to get into the slow lane.'

I could hear rumbling sounds, a klaxon burst and the rush of wind. I got a picture of it, was almost with the frantic flow, Tamara rushing to do a deal, distraught about her husband's death, misjudging a move maybe, not seeing a car come up behind fast –

'They're all the buggering same.' The old man brought me back to my own unpleasant reality.

'OK? This looks better. What do you want to know then, Jason?'

'I better make it quick, but I guess just the people I should talk to, you know, work, friends and stuff.'

'Gordon was an insurance assessor at County Life. He

was good at it, no complaints from him, though with me on the road, we didn't always get the chance to feedback. You could start there.'

'Right, and friends?'

'His main mate was Pete Moore, he works at County too. In fact, most of our friends are work-based.'

'Thanks, that should –'

'There were a couple of other things I wanted to mention.'

'OK . . .'

'Well, first, his laptop seems to have gone missing. Not at work or home. Don't know if that means much. And, well, this is more tricky, and it's probably just my imagination, but he did disappear at various times in the week and I could never get any clear idea from him as to where.'

'Huh-uh, and you kind of wondered whether he was . . .'

'You do wonder, we've been married seven years.'

'OK, I'll try and check. When are you due back?'

'God, good question, depends how things – hold on, I'm coming up to a tanker, better leave it, ring me later.'

The connection went dead. I was back to piss bags and sterra. Leaving the coffee untouched, I gave King Shit one final sneer and went. Sometimes you're better off avoiding the scenic route.

The Astburys live in a typical bayed semi, like millions of others in the sprawl. Spooky. Empty tree-lined streets and a silence that clings, makes you feel you're in violation by just being there. I did my best by checking out the neighbours. On the right, a woman with black dyed hair and a sad face was co-operative enough. Said she looked after the house when the couple were away, was utterly shocked when she heard about the suicide. Shocked maybe, but not surprised. The woman had a deadpan, bitter edge to her voice, as though disappointment was the norm for her. But she liked Gordon. Easy-going and considerate. Not the one who wore the trousers. A bit dopey. Like he'd sit in the garden, look at the sky and seem to be lost on another planet. They had a cat called 'Taxi'. This brought a smile to the dour woman's face. Calls in the night from next door. But nothing heard or seen on the night Gordon died. Nothing unusual. I had a vague feeling that maybe the lady hit the bottle when darkness fell. I moved on, but the other neighbour was a dead loss. A three-inch crack in the door and a brown face – 'No speak English' – and the three inches went with a solid clunk.

Four thirty. Not much time to check County Life. A hooter suddenly sounded in my head. Sorry, Gordon, when there's a chunk of time that isn't screwed down, you have to grab it. I got in the car and started for home. The Astburys are tomorrow. An intriguing tomorrow I reckon, since it's strange that no one thinks the guy was up for suicide. Nothing abnormal whatsoever bar a few unaccounted hours and a missing computer. The guy's got to have a secret, haven't we all?

It was getting near mad dash time, a peak moment for the mentality when you have to get free in the least time possible. I wavered. All that aggression, that stop/start, that second-stealing craziness in steel rivers of toxic fume and noise. Fuck the crawl, the squeeze and the petulance, I decided to take the back way home. Round the City Incinerator, skirting mosques, football grounds and gasometers, and into back streets heading home to a B35 box by the sludge-treatment works. Sid tried me once on the mobile, but I ignored it. I was forward-thinking to seeing Dita. Her turn to cook tonight. Kung Pao chicken. Lovely Dita. Born in Singapore, raised in Jakarta and now a nurse living with me in the sprawl. We'll have the whole evening together. Get a video perhaps. *Crouching Tiger, Hidden Dragon* is what I fancy. I'm quite getting into foreign films. Hollywood is so damn predictable. So fuck America, it's nice to see the rest of the world and its cultures. It's a bit of a drag, though, the subtitles, but I guess you have to make an effort to find out how other people live, or die.

A blue sky, sunshine morning. You could see it glint off the cars on the motorway. I wasn't feeling so good. Dita, the damn NHS is a bleeding treadmill and she was feeling stressed. She has a day off tomorrow and she wants me to skive. Practically the moment she said it and Sid was on line asking for a progress report. Me and Dita, we had a bit of a tiff and we said a few sour things. She mentioned the trouble I got into. That hurt but we managed to smooth it over. It settled my mind, though. I was going to get the Astbury job sorted today. Tomorrow, it was me and Dita up at the Water Park, squawking at ducks and getting naughty in the bushes. So I was back on the carbon monoxide run, late as usual, heading for County Life. Gordon slowly began to reappear in between thoughts of the film we saw. Jesus, wouldn't I just love to walk up walls and step across trees in a whispering forest.

County Life was big, a thrusting glass tower that made your neck ache just looking. There was an ochre stone forecourt with exotic-looking plants in tubs and a little shelter for fag-heads. A few workers were still hanging out there, grabbing their last fix before drudgery. I also saw this gorgeous black woman. She must've been six three and a multicoloured dress wrapped her up like she was the best present a man could have. I gave myself a mental thump. Inside the large reception hall, a bored guy behind the desk took the opportunity to exercise an arm. It flopped over to the phone and rang up Gordon's line manager. Then it was a name-tag and a silver lift up ten floors. The assessors' section was open-plan, around twenty desks knitted together with filing cabinets and screens. I got a fresh view of the sprawl as I trudged thick carpet to the gaffer's little den.

Mr Quick had black-rimmed glasses and sandy hairline that, unlike the tide, hadn't flowed back. He listened to my spiel and then went into his corporate charm bit.

'Yes, we were all very sad about Gordon. He was a very likeable guy and we can't understand what made him do it.'

Yeah, how many more times do I have to hear it?

According to Quick, Gordon was their best assessor. He could sniff out a scam in no time and his financial evaluations were almost like art – 'policies perfected through precise details'. Oh yeah. Gordon was promotion material, though he didn't seem to know it.

'No problems at all? No heavy office politics or tea break hanky-panky?'

'Nope, he was a very easy-going guy.'

'And no sign of his laptop yet?'

'He always takes it home.'

I guess I couldn't have expected anything else. These places, they cultivate consumer smooth and public smarm. They practically kill you with how nice they are. Mentality: in a big, thick velvet glove. Still, co-operativeness did get me a chance to talk to Pete Moore. We chatted by the lifts, propping up a window that gave a perilous view of dinky cars on Queensway.

'I'm still cut up rough, I tell you.'

He didn't look it.

'Gordon and I, we weren't massively close, just good work buddies really, but he was an OK guy, you know, good to be around.'

Pete Moore was six foot tall and chunky. He had close-cropped, jet-black hair and an amiable kind of face. The sort of guy you can't help but like and feel you can never really trust.

'I have to admit he was better at the job than me but, you know, give the guy his due, he didn't show off and was always helpful.'

'So what did you do out of office hours?'

'We'd meet maybe a couple of times a week. Thursday nights we always played badminton and then went down the pub. And then we'd often meet at weekends, go down the Villa, that sort of thing.'

'Of course, you don't know why he did it?'

'No, I'm still in shock.'

'Everything OK with his wife?'

'Yes, so he told me.'

'No money troubles, bullying bosses, lovers, gay encounters in loos, secret alcoholism, manic depressive tendencies . . .?'

'Look, he was just a regular bloke, but I didn't know him that well. I guess he must've had some dark secret, but he never told me and probably wouldn't have anyway.'

'Why?'

'We were workmates. You have to be a bit careful. You let something slip and it gets around – puts you at a disadvantage.'

'Well, that's really wonderful, Pete.'

I let the guy go then, back to being an office smoothie. I thumped the lift button and waited. Maybe our Gordon was just the secretive type and had a hang-up that no one ever knew of? I wasn't going to be writing much of a report. As the lift began to climb upwards, a young Asian woman came out of the office. She walked over. Suddenly I found myself looking into a pair of bright, brown eyes. I can be a total sucker for them.

'I overheard why you're here and I wondered, can we meet up later and talk?'

'You were friends with Gordon?'

'Sure, and I've got quite a lot I'd like to say.'

She turned her head then and looked back into the office. About twenty-five, I'd say, big eyes and hair that shone like black treacle.

'That sounds great.'

'How about we meet at the reservoir at seven, that's when I walk my dog?'

'Well, lunchtime would be much better.'

'Sorry, we don't get time for lunch round here.'

'Yeah? OK, so who will I be walking the pooch with?'

'My name's Sangheeta.'

We shook hands. She had an assertive grip. I could see she meant business.

'I have to go back now.'

The lift doors opened. Slightly shocked, I wondered whether the case was opening too. Was nice guy Gordon's secret about to be revealed? Nice guy. Isn't that in itself the kiss of death? Outside, the sun still shone but the forecourt was empty. No multicoloured Amazon for my eyes to feast on.

It was a bit of a bugger that I'd have to wait until seven. I had to stitch the case up today. Back at the car, I tried Tamara's number but her phone was off. Where else could I poke around? Right. So it was back south again to those tree-lined roads and the silence of suburbia. I guess I wanted to get a picture of the scene. Try and imagine maybe what went on when Gordon popped a pill and sat back in the bath to drain his life away.

I picked the front door lock and started to mooch around. The house was all very spare and modern, barely looked lived in and a world away from my junkyard of a pad. I headed up the stairs for the bathroom. A peek in the bedroom and it was the same minimalist scene, though there was a bookcase – science fiction stuff mainly. I felt a little shiver of dread when I opened the bathroom door, but it quickly passed. Whiteness. A gaping white bath, white tiles, shower curtain and loo. Even the blind over the open window was white, with just the cork-tiled floor adding colour. I couldn't imagine a suicide in there. It seemed so clinical and soulless. A very functional place to top yourself. As I struggled to make this fit with my image of Gordon, I heard the voices through the open window. I poked my head out. Next door's kitchen was down below and their window was open too. An Asian man and woman were rowing. It was the best English I'd heard all day.

When three inches came, so did my foot and helpful shoulder.

'I don't really want to intrude but, you know, the way you speak, you could be on telly.'

You've got an edge when you catch out a lie and it's just a case of making it pay. The woman at the door, thin face and defiant eyes, she had to listen as I told her why I was there. This brought her husband on the scene and then a Punjabi consultation ensued. The turbaned guy checked my credentials and then invited me into the front room. Mr Singh and Mrs Kaur, lion and princess. On the wall there was a golden temple with gold rippling in the lake beside it. They thought I was the police. They don't like the police. The police are intrusive, racist and treat them as terrorists. Sounded par for the course.

'We are just peace-loving doctors, but we do campaign for a Khalistan homeland. We don't promote violence, nothing like that, but still they come, the Special Branch, they come at dawn and turn our lives upside down.'

I was with them then, have had my own brushes with law, but Khalistan, it was a 'big' subject and I was conscious of time. I bluntly got them round to Gordon Astbury.

'Very nice, a very nice man.'

Here we go.

'Didn't see them much, but wasn't it awful what happened?'

And, of course, they had no idea why. I then found out they'd used the 'no speak English' routine on the police. It failed but they didn't co-operate anyway. So did they really see or hear anything that night?

'He had a caller, yes. I just caught a glimpse when I was closing the curtains. A man . . . white, dark hair and clothing, that was all. It seemed nothing unusual.'

Maybe, but it was new information, someone who saw him closer to the time of death. I was pondering this when something caught my eye outside. A flash of colour, like a sweet wrapper blowing in the wind. I went closer to the window. There she was on the other side of the street. She saw me too and started to move.

I've never been much good at tailing people. That slack and wandering eye of mine. Sid always gives such jobs to others. But this didn't seem too hard. The woman from outside County Life had a clapped-out Ford that was waging a one-car war against the ozone layer. I just followed smoke and wondered where the hell she fitted in. Was she the lover Tamara feared? Was this a heartbreaker I was following, an emotional H-bomb who'd tipped him over the edge? My phone flicked on. It was the vampire checking out his blood supplies. 'Sidney.'

'Jace. So how's it progressing then?'

'Hectic, this is one hell of a case you've got me on.'

'You mean you're down Murphy's Bar again, people watching?'

'No way. Three interviews so far, a new witness and I'm on a tail at the mo which could be promising.'

'Anything concrete you can report to the client?'

'Not as such, but I tell you, I reckon this could turn out a three-day job.'

'Really? We'll review exactly what you've got at the end

of the day.' Tight. How do people get that way? How can you live a life that's so bleeding tight?

I glowered at the mobile, was tempted to throw it away when I saw the cloud of smoke leave the main road. We were in Lee Bank. The rickety Ford pulled up in front of a modern terrace.

'Can't be coincidence, can it? You at County Life and Hall Green?'

I showed my card.

'I've been asked to look into the death of Gordon Astbury.'

'You better come in, then.' Her suspicious look changed to one of relief.

She had at least four inches on me and, what with the shapely coloured dress, I felt I'd be sitting at her feet before I was through. I sat down on the sofa while she made coffee. There was a clock on the wall in the shape of Africa. That'd be Tony G, the guy who made it.

'Lydia Holmes,' she said as she sat gracefully down on an armchair opposite me. 'I guess I have a story to tell.'

She had a nice lilting voice and a self-effacing manner. I hoped the story would be a long one.

'We met at the library on our ways from work. We both science fiction fan you see, which is small section, so we just kept bumping into each other. Then we talk bout our favourite author and him invite me for coffee.'

'A nice, easy-going guy, huh?'

'Yes, and him find out then I struggling single mum and him had proposition to make.'

'Oh, right . . .'

'That's what I thought, white guy, want him little bit of – you know – and in return, a contribution to the struggling parent.'

'The old sugar daddy bit, eh. Were you tempted?'

'No way. But that wasn't the proposition. What him

want was to hire my front room for some hour each week, some place him can go that no one know bout.'

'Just that?'

'Come, let me show you.'

As loyal as any pet, I followed Lydia into the front room. And there it was, on the coffee table, the laptop.

'This is what him want the space for.' Lydia went over and opened the lid. She switched it on. 'I'll show you the last thing that him wrote.'

> The studded wooden door creaked open. A carmine glow suddenly drenched our eyes; it covered our shirts and hands with a tinge of rose. Jubi touched my arm.
>
> 'Come, Wanderer, I will show you the source.'
>
> We stepped from the Citadel then and began to cross a square whose sandstone floor soaked up the sky and glowed like fire. Jubi's scaled sandals made strange slithering sounds as we headed for some steps and a long balustrade where weird fish sculptures were silhouetted against the red. We mounted the steps and there it was. Almost to the skyline, a huge lake stretched out before us, finger-shaped, a kilometre wide where great dams and city dwellings bordered it. The sky was now glowing so much that the lake itself seemed made of blood.
>
> 'West Lake, one of the four that power and feed our city.'
>
> Jubi begun to tell me how the hydro-generation system worked. I hardly listened. I was in awe of the water, of the boats that hauled in fish and of the sacred Kalunda birds that swooped from their roosts to join the harvest . . .

'Wow . . . I reckon I rate this guy.'

'Him been doing it for nine month. Mebbe twice a week

him come round, we have chat and then him disappear and do his thing, leave the rent when him go. I was so sad when I hear him was dead and I didn't know what to do. That's why you a see me. I knew him had Asian friend at work, so I wait round some time, ask people. But I couldn't find she. Then I think mebbe I should tell him wife but she hardly there or me chicken out if she is. I thought you was police.'

'Right . . . you think he committed suicide?'

'I don't know, I only know that this is just chapter ten.'

This was an unexpected turn. A complication. An extra angle turning up just when my day was running out. What made it worse was that I was starting to like the guy, a clever sod carving out his own niche against the mentality. I was getting kind of committed to seeing the whole thing through, however long it took. Lydia put the laptop on shutdown and sighed.

'I was going to make food, you want some?'

'Now you mention it, yeah, haven't eaten since breakfast.'

'Snappers all right?'

It wasn't far to the Rezza. After a nice meal and a chat with Lydia (we both like Philip K. Dick), I got there early and stood on the dam watching swifts swoop and anglers ponder the impenetrable. Was this the place of Gordon's story? No sunset skies this evening, but you could see how the imagination might fly. The view of the city – distant towers, gold Buddhist stupa and that soft expanse of water within a hard landscape. I then saw Sangheeta with lead and walking furball.

'Call that a dog?'

'Do you mind? This is Amber and she's a sweet little thing.'

'Well, I'm glad you want to talk to me. County Life, those places close ranks and spray deodorant in your face.'

'This is confidential, OK? No one must know or I get the chop.'

'I'd take great pleasure in keeping my gob shut.'

We began to walk, up to the Tower Ballroom and then on to the more wooded parts.

Sangheeta had worked with Gordon quite a bit. He was assigned to show her the ropes, and they'd had times out of the office where they'd do field checks. She liked him. But Sangheeta wasn't insular like Gordon. She was in on the gossip. She had her finger on the politics button. That's how she knew that Pete Moore was poison in Gordon's life.

'Pete and Gordon were in competition, you know, for when a supervisor's post comes free. Gordon, he didn't seem to bother. He was twice as good as Pete, but he was always helping him out. I told him he was mad, that he should let Pete swim for himself, but Gordon said they were mates.'

'Pete was using him?'

'Oh yeah, and it was dangerous, because there're always questions about Pete. Nothing definite, but you feel he cuts corners and you never know how far to trust him.'

'There's plenty of them about.'

'Yes, but this has a horrible side to it, something you really should know.'

'Yeah?'

'Pete and Gordon's wife.'

'You're kidding?'

'Common knowledge, everybody in the office knew.'

'Gordon?'

'I think he did. I've cried a few times since his suicide. It's so awful, so cruel and unfair. I've felt really bad about it but, work, I have to go in, slave away and act as though everything's normal.'

'Yeah . . . the pressure's always there all right. And the

shitfaces, the ones who buy into that, they're happy to carry on crapping over everyone else.'

'Pete Moore's got a clear run now.'

'Wait a minute –'

I stopped. Sangheeta did too, much to the annoyance of the furball who yapped and strained the lead. I looked at the water through the trees, darkness now falling, the water holding onto the day's brightness.

'The Wanderer and the Kalunda birds, I wouldn't let go of that.'

'What?'

'I need to find out where Pete Moore lives.'

Way past knocking-off time, but this was getting personal. Suicide or murder, it didn't matter, Gordon Astbury was owed one. Sangheeta hadn't known where Pete Moore lived but she had his phone number. I then rang Dita and asked her to check out the book for that area. He was in it. Dita had just finished her shift and had her feet up, blankly watching the box. I told her that this was my last call, that I'd be free tomorrow, that we were going to create fabulous new worlds right next to the sludge treatment works. It was dark now. Pete Moore lived in Quinton and I drove fast up the Hagley Road, pondering on how to nail him. With what? There was nothing but there was also plenty. Only one approach was possible. Out of the blue, off guard, and sling your biggest punch.

He opened the door looking nicely smug and a little stoned too, judging by his eyes. I thought of tight bastards, bloodsuckers, screw merchants and mincing machines. I made myself look as mean as the mentality truly was.

'You're in the deepest shit ever,' I said as I pushed past him and went for the low-lit lounge with its dope smells and sultry soul music.

'Hey, what the bloody hell –?'

He belatedly rushed after me, shocked and maybe too stoned to fully cope.

'You – you can't just –'

'Sit down and shut it, OK? Any pissing about and I'll sock you.'

Sock him? I could do it. When you serve writs like I do, the aggro can be viciously real. He did sit down. You could see his brain trying to click into gear. I followed, grabbing a high-back chair so I could stare down at him.

'Right, Pete, so you didn't tell me, or the police I guess, that you and Tamara are setting bedsheets on fire. You didn't say that you and Gordon were rivals for promotion. You didn't at all let it be known that you're a right little shit who has all the motive in the world to commit murder.'

'Come on, you – you've got a nerve. Bursting in here uninvited and then accusing me of something that didn't happen. Are you mad or something?'

'This is how it went, Pete. You know Tamara's in Bristol so you decide to pay our Gordon a call. Take a bottle with you, yeah, go through the old chummy work pal bit? And then, at a convenient point, you bung a couple of sleepers in Gordon's drink. You had all the opportunity in the world to get that sorted. The guy's not exactly sharp anyway. So he drops off and you run the bath. A bit of an effort getting him ready, yeah, but finally you plop him in the water and – slice.'

'This's total nonsense –'

'You were seen that night, clocked, mate,' I bluffed. 'You were there. So why the fuck didn't you tell anybody that?'

I reckon I'd got in that punch. It was always going to be hit or miss given what I had. Pete Moore sat back on the sofa, suddenly pale-faced. He frowned, chewed his lip, tapped his foot and looked everywhere but at me. He was silent for a long time.

It was then that I began to feel weary. Tired, grubby and drained. I'd had too much of trawling through the dirt of the sprawl. The case, it didn't seem to matter too much. It was way past clocking off time and I wanted to go home. I wanted to get foetal with Dita, crawl back to that warm, protected place and watch subtitled movies about poisonous witches and the honourable warriors who blow them away. Pete shifted in his seat. He then leaned forward, elbows on knees and his hands wrestling.

'I'm not admitting to anything, right? But first, Tamara, she doesn't know anything about this.'

'Why did she call us in? She might reckon we'd find out about you two.'

'Gordon knew, seemed to tolerate it. It's been going on over a year and she didn't believe it was a reason for . . .'

'She still cared for him.'

'Yeah, and she wouldn't divorce him.'

'I see . . .'

'Look.' Pete Moore stood up, the shock receding and the charm face cautiously feeling its way back. 'I want to show you something.'

He walked across the room and picked up a briefcase, then brought it over.

'Doing the job I do . . . situations develop, opportunities can be spotted. I did spot one, a totally phoney claim that I should've stopped but I didn't. I think Gordon knew that too. I did a deal, with a claimant, twenty per cent, and I'd like to think now that I did it for you.'

Pete opened the briefcase and there it was – the mentality, crisp and clear like sun on a dawn pillow. It was smiling, it was pouting, it even winked. Maybe ten thousand? The mobile went off then, vibrating, glowing in my pocket. That would be Sid, pissed off that I hadn't reported in. I looked back down at all that money.

Games Without Rules

Rubina Din

'Did you know that the canal behind the Ackers is haunted?' Imran asked ten minutes before kick-off.

'Is it?'

Sajid wriggled uncomfortably on the plush leather sofa, the smell of furniture polish catching his throat. He didn't like talking about that kind of thing. An electric shudder went through him as he suddenly remembered his experiences of Imran as a child. He shut his eyes as memories filled his head.

He could see clearly a boy of seven fixed to a wall by a group of bigger boys: about nine or ten years old, and led by Imran. The boy Adam had lost his shoe as he ran towards where his mum was parked. But when he stopped to pick the shoe up, he was swamped and dragged into a nearby hedge. Sajid watched, unable to take his eyes off the scene. He enjoyed the fear he saw in Adam's eyes. Imran picked up the shoe and the boys threw it to each other in a game of piggy in the middle. The other boys just laughed nervously at Adam's terror. 'Where's your money?' Imran demanded. Sajid could still hear Adam crying, 'Please give me my shoe, please . . . my mum'll kill me.' Imran made the boy turn out his trouser pockets, but he only had a few plastic toys he'd pinched from school. Sajid remembered the glow of power on Imran's face as he took a cigarette lighter from his pocket. He caressed it lovingly between his hands. The other boys watching in strange fascination as he lit it. The flame danced in Adam's fearful eyes. No one thought he'd do it, but he did. He put the lighter to the boy's sockless foot. And concentrated hard on his screaming face until he could smell the charring flesh. The others, unsure of his behaviour, laughed. 'Hold him still. Now, you little . . . If you don't get me some money tomorrow . . .' The words hung in the still air. He made him put the shoe back on. 'If your mum finds out about this you'll be dead meat. Understand?' The boy nodded and ran away as if from hell itself. Sajid shuddered when his eyes met Imran's while Adam escaped. Sajid watched his back every day after that. He knew he was lucky to have a brother in the gang.

Right now, back in the sitting room, he felt as if his fears were keeping him fixed to the seat, unable to move. He knew he mustn't let Imran see his fear. Imran enjoyed playing with people; it was as if he had an built-in ability to smell out fears and use them against his victims.

Another unwelcome memory flashed into Sajid's head. In his year at secondary school, Tariq had been constantly teased – bullied, really – by Imran and his gang. Sajid had once caught sight of the cuts and cigarette burns all over his arms. Then one day his mother found him hanging from the ceiling light. Tariq was lucky to be alive but he never came back to school. The family disappeared. Imran and his gang were never questioned.

Sajid stared through his thick round spectacles at the floor so Imran couldn't see his eyes. He watched the immaculate carpet as if it was showing the most exciting film of the year.

'Sajid,' Imran called and then waved his hand in front of Sajid's eyes. 'Hello . . . Earth calling number two. Earth calling. Are you there?'

Sajid refocused, looking at Imran as if didn't recognize him.

'You OK? You've gone as white as a sheet.' Imran said, amused.

Sajid, confused, closed his eyes to readjust to where he was. He finally opened his eyes to Imran standing in front of him, holding out a glass of water. The cold wet glass brought him back to reality.

'Sorry, mate. I seem to have lost it for a moment. What were you saying?'

Imran leaned forward and whispered in a low husky voice, 'Spirits.'

Sajid gulped down the water and dumped the glass on the table.

'Do you remember the time . . .' Imran was smiling like someone who'd just remembered a secret.

'Yeah. And I don't want to talk about it,' Sajid cut in, staring into the fire, wanting its life and warmth to wrap him up like a quilt on a cold night.

'I know, you never do, but it was so much fun. I watched it all from the bridge . . . you were hysterical.' He laughed as his mind flooded with the events of that night.

Sajid looked at Imran in shock. 'You were there! You watched! You evil . . .' Then, afraid of revisiting that night, Sajid chose not to pursue it.

The sound of bangles jangling came to the door. Imran smiled, he knew the discussion wasn't dead.

Imran's wife Aliya walked in with a tray full of piping hot masala tea, rich in milk and calories. It smelled of cardamom boiled in milk. Sajid's stomach clenched: he didn't like masala tea, but Imran always insisted that they should drink it together.

'I remember it as if it were yesterday . . .'

Sajid sighed, his teeth on edge.

'It was a Wednesday, wasn't it? . . . Put the bloody tea down, will you, woman?' he shouted, irritated at her hovering. A look of reminiscence crossed his face. 'Yes it was. The wind was howling and we all dared each other . . . How old were you?' he said. 'You were the youngest and skinniest.' He laughed, patting Sajid's slight paunch.

Sajid closed his eyes, reliving the whole event. Involuntarily he hunched up, his long thick legs tensed like an animal ready for its predator. He shivered.

It'd been really cold and his brother hadn't wanted to take him. They'd walked across the lawned area at the Ackers. Then wandered towards the canal. All of them telling stories of the terrible things that had happened there. The smell of rotting grass and the sewer-stench of the canal were making Sajid feel nauseous. He tagged along with the older boys. They stood beside the canal and took turns to have a drag on a joint. One of them was injecting himself.

'You can't give injections to yourself. Doctors have to do it . . . it's dangerous,' Sajid said with such innocence that the other boys laughed. He kept his mouth shut after that. He turned round to look at the dirty water in the half-lit canal. Rubbish floated in front of him. An icy wind blew straight into his face; he wiped his leaky nose with the back of his hand. When he turned back to where the boys were they'd gone. He called and called until his throat hurt. The trees around him looked as if they were coming to get him. Eerie sounds danced on the low wind and the stench of cigarettes filled his nostrils. He ran among the trees calling and shouting, but his voice, drowned out by the wind, just echoed back, his own enemy. He tripped over a black bag and fought with it as if it were alive. The bag tried to stab him with a jagged bottle. It attacked him until he fell into the stinking mud. The rain poured down, merciless. Noises all around seemed to be calling him. He could see the shadows of devils and monsters swimming in and out of his watery vision. And he fought every monster and devil that night.

The images were still vivid even after so many years. Now he had every home-security device money could buy. Every lock and bolt was secured without fail: he checked them all like a bank manager might check the vault. He took pills to keep his nerves from constant jangling. He knew Imran had set it all up that night, but they never talked about it.

A clattering sound pulled Sajid from the depths of his mind. He watched Imran walk over to Aliya and speak to her harshly. She'd bent down to clear the tea away when her ever-present scarf got caught under the table leg. It was on so tight that it nearly strangled her. Her breathing was jagged as she unclipped it, pulled it out from under the table and then off her head, relieved.

Sajid saw that the left side of her face was covered in what looked like screwed up clay. As if charred in a kiln. Though he knew Imran was watching him, he couldn't stop his revulsion coming to the surface.

Recovering quickly from the shock of Aliya's burnt face, Sajid got up from the sofa. He moved towards her. She didn't cough or splutter, but for a moment her eyes misted over with a thick film of water threatening to spill. A cruel smile crossed Imran's lips as he continued to gawk at his friend's discomfort. Sajid pushed the coffee table from between himself and Aliya. He spoke to her, full of sympathy. She just continued to stare at the floor. She was as damaged as he was. He could see it on her face and in those golden brown eyes. Morbid curiosity made him want to touch her; his fingers outstretched.

'You'd better not touch her, mate. You know the rules:

I'd have to kill you if you did.' Imran cackled, deadly serious.

Sajid looked at his friend, trying to make sense of what he was saying. His hand retreated. Aliya scuttled away.

'Come on, man, stop looking like a wet fish. Have your tea and let's watch the game . . . and turn off the lights.' He tutted loudly. 'You, my friend, are going to find yourself the victim of your own soft heart. If I've told you once I've told you a million times, that soft heart of yours will get you into terrible trouble.'

Then Imran was totally engrossed in the match. The cheers of the crowd stuck in Sajid's throat like fishbones; all he could see was Aliya's face. Questions whirled around in his head and he couldn't stop the words pouring from his mouth. Imran was sitting on the edge of his seat, willing the ball to disappear up the other end of the pitch.

'So what happened?'

'Shit, man, shit. You cursed the ball, didn't you? You thick or something? Can't you see, they scored? They bloody scored . . .'

'I wasn't talking about that, I was –'

Imran's silhouette turned to face Sajid, the light from the TV danced on his handsome profile. 'I know what you were talking about. I've always been at least three steps ahead of you.'

Sajid didn't dare ask any more. The thick layer of burnt skin on her face had worried him. Imran's strange behaviour was frightening him more than usual. His mind full of puzzles, he got up and mumbled his goodbyes. He realized he didn't know his friend at all – he'd thought he'd changed. Imran stood up and turned on the lights. The sudden glare burst into Sajid's pupils, making him squint as he looked up at his tall, lean friend. Imran put his arm around his shoulder.

'I know what you're thinking and believe me you're

wrong. Go home and get some sleep. Don't worry . . . it's over and done with.'

On the way home from the terraced street where they'd both lived as kids, the rain pelted down hard on the windscreen. Sajid arrived outside his house on Billesley Lane. He had no recollection of how he'd driven from A to B. The only thing he could focus on was the eerie look in her eyes.

How long had he known her? She'd been married to Imran for just three weeks, and Sajid had been there every day for the last week. Fumbling with the key, rain trickling down his face, Sajid tried to open the door to his detached bungalow. The rain made it difficult to get the key to fit. He looked up to see that the canopy above him had an enormous hole in it.

'Shit,' he muttered. He pushed and shoved the door that always seemed to stick deliberately when he was desperate to get in. Finally it gave way.

The kitchen door was open. Sajid was sure he'd locked it, he always locked it. Tonight had made everything more difficult. All he wanted was the comfort of his home and the routines he was used to. He walked into the room, half expecting to find someone there, his senses on high alert. He stormed the silent kitchen only to find the unsteady pile of pans by the sink collapsed. He looked around, frightened; then the fast beat of his heart began to slow as he saw nothing unusual. Panning the room again, he rubbed his forehead and laughed at his own stupidity, his voice sounding like a thick echo.

Sajid turned on the TV, volume loud. He needed company and this would have to do. Towel-drying his unruly hair, he sat down in front of the TV. The newsreader's voice droned on. A dead guy found in his own house, a baby abused by her step-parents. He flung the remote control at the screen.

'Where the hell is all the good news?' he asked. Exhausted, he dozed on the sofa. Imran's talk of spirits had triggered a recurring chain of events in his mind. He tried to turn the pictures off but with no success. He was all alone. The darkness ate at him. He screamed until his throat was hoarse but no one came. He cried and cried, not daring to move from the spot. Hours passed and the darkness froze his mind.

From somewhere, the sharp smell of cigarettes linked him back to that day. He felt an icy breeze touch his back. After the fight with the bin bag he'd calmed down and convinced himself that everything was just a trick. Then a cold hand. A force pushing him. Cutting though the air in slow motion, he tried to see who it was. There was nothing there. He hit the water hard, a sharp sting burning into his body. Gulping, he went under. Kicking and fighting, he came to the surface. Spitting out dirty water, he made for the bank.

His mind raced. As he came closer to the bank he reached out and caught hold of a mound. The smell of cigarettes grew sharper, the memory became real. It felt like wool. He tried to pull himself out, using the mound to help him. It began to slide and, afraid that he'd fall in again, he pulled really hard. His grip slipped and when he grabbed again he caught a hand. Suddenly he was holding an arm. He opened his eyes to look clearly. It was a man. The mound fell on top of him. He screamed and sank into the depths of the canal, the rain drumming its surface.

The telephone was ringing. He shouted out in shock. Then, realizing where he was, he picked up the phone. The TV was still on. The news had died and some trivial chatter filled the air. The clock on the wall told him it was half past midnight. The voice on the phone caught him by surprise.

Sajid sat up. 'Aliya, is that you?' he asked, unsure, his voice thick and gruff.

It was. An alert Sajid listened to her distress. She cried, 'Please, Sajid, you must help me. I shouldn't have taken the scarf off in front of you. I'm so scared . . . he's hit me again. I need help . . . please come quick!'

Each word opened up a wound of anger in him. He wouldn't allow someone else to suffer as he had.

The journey back to Imran's street seemed a long one. Sajid talked to himself. A habit he'd acquired a long time ago to keep sane. 'She can't stay with the bastard, he's mental, he needs help.' He felt responsible for how she'd been treated. 'I should've known something was wrong. What an idiot I've been,' he muttered.

The lights of the car flooded the dark terrace as he did a three-point turn to make sure the car faced in the right direction to get home. Quite why he'd done that, he couldn't say. He got out the car and allowed his leaden legs to carry him towards the house. The front step was covered in mushy leaves that squelched underfoot. Sajid rang the bell, waited with his heart in his mouth. The door didn't open. He tried again, the shrill noise rang out, but still the door didn't open. Thoughts raced through his mind. Imran wouldn't have been so stupid as to kill her, would he? The question remained. A car started up a few yards away from the house. Imran's car. Where the hell was he going at this time of night?

Sajid turned back to the house, his hand slipped off the bell. He realized the door was unlocked. He pushed it open to silence. The wooden floors seemed to hold a terrible secret; shadows from the streetlight outside danced heavily across the hallway. Sajid walked into the house, his mind telling him: 'Don't touch any weapons, they'll incriminate you . . . it'd be just your luck to . . .' He looked in the living room. The TV was on. He carried on through the house, his heart pounding loudly in his ears. His blood was pumping too much oxygen, too fast, too soon. Sajid was ready; his nerves were raw with tension.

The house was curiously normal. Each time he came to a room he sprung on the lights, his eyes poised to see a body and a bloody floor. But it was all fantasy, there was nothing there. He needed to find out what was going on soon or he'd lose his mind. He thought he saw the curtains in the house opposite twitch. Maybe it was just his imagination playing tricks on him.

'I'll kill you when I get hold of you, you bastard!' he shouted, echoes ringing through the house.

There was no one there at all.

Sajid decided that he'd had enough mystery for one night. He couldn't bring himself to turn off all the lights, but he checked everything was in order as he left the house. As the door closed behind him, his mobile rang. He jumped. '*Calm, Sajid, calm*,' he muttered, then answered. It was Aliya.

'Sajid, please come quick I need your help . . . I don't know what's the matter with him but he –' A piercing scream shot through the phone.

'I'll call the police. Where are you, can't I help you?' Sajid shouted.

'I'm . . . I'm at the place he was talking to you about,' she whispered, as breathless and scared as if married to the devil himself.

Sajid asked again where she was. No reply. The phone was alive, but all he could hear at the other end were distant screams. Without a second thought, he leapt into his car. Lights on full beam, he screeched down the road. *Where? Where?* The answer was there in his mind. His hands turned the steering wheel in a familiar direction.

The car raced towards the Ackers Trust Park.

Sajid drove carefully as he came closer. The rain had

eased a little. Trying to take the edge off his fear, his mind fixated on Aliya. He could imagine making love to her. In a strange way he found the burn on her face attractive. Did that make him depraved? he wondered.

Sajid looked at his watch to slow time down. Feelings he'd buried kept coming to the surface; haunting memories flooded his head. As he started to brake, he saw a figure running away. She was so slight. Sajid shouted to her as he stopped the car. The tangled seat belt initially refused to let him out, but then tipped him onto the floor.

Sajid chased her. She seemed so helpless and confused. Sajid vowed to marry her as soon as she was free of her husband. A man like Imran didn't deserve a woman like her. His shouts carried over the wind, drowned by the rain, stripped the breath from Sajid's face. But Aliya stopped and turned. Sajid looked at her, water running fast down her frightened face. He moved towards her. As he opened out his arms to comfort her, she stumbled over something. Sajid saw a muddy figure rise from the ground. Not believing what he was seeing, he wiped the rain off his glasses. They fell off. Powerless, sightless, he panicked.

Tales of the haunted canal and dead bodies came back to life. Sajid looked at the creature on the ground. He was a child and this creature was going to attack him. All the memories he'd buried came screaming into view. All he knew was that he had to save himself from this evil monster. The monster, covered in muddy leaves and rain, stood up to its full height. It smelled of the smoke of hundreds of cigarettes. Sajid coughed. It made a gruff noise and threw itself at him. Sajid leapt onto the creature. He found himself beating it up. Liquid was pouring from its muddy surface. He couldn't stop: he was going to conquer it for ever. The cigarette smell overtook his actions. He wouldn't allow this monster to live inside him again. He would cut it out and throw it away.

While he fought this demon, someone – he didn't know who – handed him a knife. He lifted the knife above his head. This was his nightmare, he was going to kill it. It would never ever hurt him again. The knife came down again and again until the rain sapped his energy and rage. Coming to his senses, he looked at the pathetic creature in the muddy leaves. Aliya was standing near by, seemingly in a trance. Adrenaline made him light-headed. He couldn't see straight. Behind Aliya he thought he saw a flashing shadow, someone leaving. Utterly dazed, he straightened himself. His bloodied and dirty body ached. He'd finally beaten his demon. It would never return . . .

Aliya stood looking at the ground. A cold reality began to dawn on him. He looked down at the mud-covered, lifeless figure. He'd expected it to disappear like it would on TV. He bent down to touch it. He could feel the sticky ooze on his fingers, it was real. He had the same stuff all over his clothes. The blade glimmered in the mud-ridden grass, a river of black-red crying across the earth. Sajid stood still, shock seizing up his body.

He made himself bend down to see who or what was lying in the grass. It seemed to be one of those large hessian sacks used for storing cement. Gripped by fear, he pulled open the cord at the top of the sack. The twitching of death rocked the hessian violently. Sajid stepped back, afraid of what he would see. The world blurred. He sank to the ground as void enveloped him.

Thrashing from side to side, Sajid couldn't stop himself from shouting out, 'The devil is after me . . . I'm going to burn in the fires of hell.'

His eyes shot open. Aliya was standing in front of him. Her face was no longer covered and she was holding his hand tight. 'Get well soon . . . everything is going to be all right,' she cooed.

Sajid smiled. Surely it'd all been a terrible nightmare and he'd be able to put it behind him as soon as he was out of here? A nurse came and checked his pulse. She shuddered as she took his temperature. A cold feeling of unease pulsated through his veins. Aliya held his hand more tightly. 'Feeling cold . . . here.' She placed another blanket over him and smiled.

A muscular Asian man, smelling like a smoking shop, walked up to the bed. Sajid realized that for the first time in ages he didn't react badly to the smell of cigarettes. The man placed his arm around Aliya's shoulders. Aliya smiled. Sajid felt uncomfortable watching them. This was not on, she was his friend's wife. He struggled to sit up.

'Aliya. I don't think Imran would approve, do you?'

Aliya smiled secretly. 'I don't know what you're talking about . . . this is my cousin Abid. He's here to help me get over my bereavement.'

The nightmare returned. 'What bereavement?'

'Don't tell me you don't remember . . . Imran is dead.' A smile tugged at her lips.

Sajid's heart stopped, his body jerked involuntarily. Cautiously he asked, 'When did this happen?' His heart was threatening to leap out of his rib cage.

'Two nights ago . . .'

Just then a policeman arrived. He acknowledged Aliya, who snuggled even closer to Abid. Then she rummaged through her handbag. She took out a photograph of the man who'd been killed. Sajid couldn't believe his eyes. He'd killed his friend. His spirit needed to escape from his body. How could he have done this?

The policeman asked questions but Sajid could only hear *Murderer! Murderer!* in his head. As he thought about what he'd done, his head became more and more twisted up. His breath became shallow. He had killed and that was unforgivable.

Aliya watched impassively as his emotions played out on his face.

Sajid leapt out of the bed like a wild cat, wounded and full of fury.

He saw the window. It was open. He had to set himself free. He pushed against it hard. People to the left and right were trying to stop him. But he had to do it. He didn't deserve to live. With all his strength, he shook off the men holding him and flew out the window. The great rush, the feeling of freedom went with him. A wild smile crossed his lips as he hit the pavement below. Faces from the window above looked down to the street. The thud, though expected, shook their bodies.

Aliya ran down the stairs, pushing past the crowd surrounding Sajid. She stood beside the broken man, watching his ragged breaths rack his body. She sat beside Sajid as his eyes locked onto hers.

Aliya couldn't help gloating a little. She spoke through clenched teeth, 'It *was* haunted after all, wasn't it?'

As the paramedics arrived, she stood up to leave. Sajid's hand touched her; she saw the look of pure hatred in his eyes. She moved away, afraid of death.

'They killed each other . . . I didn't do it . . . I didn't touch them . . . they were evil, they needed to die,' she chanted over and over again.

A few months later, the house empty and quiet, she was glad Abid wasn't around any more. He'd vanished, she didn't know where, but he'd gone. Abid was another one you couldn't trust, he knew too much. She sat in the dark rocking backwards and forwards, screams filling her head.

The Art of Leaving Completely

Simon Avery

Off the plane in the morning: Birmingham International. All the police have concealed machine-guns owing to a terrorist alert; she is shunted through. A heavy-set man with tattoos snaking up out of the collar of his shirt, and a shadow of hair across his skull, meets her. He asks for her passport and she retrieves it from her handbag. Pushes her hair back behind her ears. She is tired. Struggling with a suitcase that the man doesn't offer to take.

A small child is pointing through the windows at a plane slanting down out of the clouds: 'Look! *Look!* A plane! *A plane!*'

'I'm Sutcliffe,' the heavy-set man says finally. He fixes her with implacable eyes, then pockets the passport. This is the first door swinging shut behind her. She drags her case along the floor through the knots of people, out through the doors, past the taxi ranks, and across into the car park where Sutcliffe's shabby BMW is waiting. The sky is immaculately blue, but the air so cold that she can hardly stop her teeth from grinding together. She is trying to find something different here so she can feel she really is in a new country, but all airports are the same: huge and anonymous, even in Romania. Sutcliffe throws her case into the boot. Looks at her. She is trying to catch her breath. She can feel the sweat patch growing on her back. Can taste the meal that she had on the plane, in her throat. There is that first seed of trepidation; of fearing what she has got herself into.

'You're nineteen?' Sutcliffe asks, touching her cheek with the back of an index finger. 'Elena Targovista?'

She nods. 'Yes. Nineteen.' She pronounces her name properly. Emphasizes the corrections as if they're important.

She is in the massage parlour by late afternoon. Her first eight-hour shift. Prices drummed into her: £30 for a massage and hand job; £60 for a massage and full sex. Repeat this. This is the way it will be. A knife is waved in her face when she makes her first protestation. She lapses into angry Romanian until Sutcliffe makes a cut below her armpit. She cries quietly like a scolded child. She bleeds. Wipes it away with toilet roll.

By teatime she has been fucked by a fifty-year-old man with gonorrhoea and no protection. He smells of vegetables and he wipes his prick on a towel before he leaves. It is dark outside when she is fucked anally by a large youth with a crewcut and dark hollows for eyes. Afterwards she examines herself with her fingers and finds blood on them. Sutcliffe tells her to *stop fucking crying* before the next customer.

She attempts to escape the next day. Bolts into the street, still crying. Heart frozen in her chest. Fleeing blindly down the Lozells Road. She sees the sunlight turning the leaves on the trees transparent, and the dust on the shop windows. Sutcliffe breaks her ankles and the following day he carries her to a bed so she can continue to service the clientele from six in the evening until two in the morning. Her bones aren't set correctly. They hurt enough for her to pass out, in coitus. Sutcliffe forces painkillers down her throat. As if that isn't enough, she has discovered a discharge from her urethra, and there is a constant pain in her pelvic area. It takes two weeks until the pain of anal sex is not like broken glass being inserted and withdrawn.

She stares out of the window and sees no stars. Just the streetlights gone soft through the condensation. How did this happen, silly girl? she wonders. You have degrees; you speak three languages, she thinks.

By the sixth week she knows a third of her customers by name. She thinks of home when they fuck her.

Six months later

I have a black and white picture of Grace from twenty-five years ago, back when we weren't even married, long before Heather was even a twinkle in either of our eyes. She's on the bonnet of my old Anglia in a short dress and sunglasses, holding her sandals by the straps. Her head is thrown back in a fit of laughter. The Welsh coast curving away behind her. An impossibly perfect sky. Grace is happy. Vivacious.

When we were courting we used to drive up to the airport in Elmdon some evenings and park in a lay-by, watch the planes taking off and landing. You could drink in those days without being pulled over for it, so we'd take a bottle of plonk from the off-licence with us. We'd sit on the roof of the Anglia and cover our ears as the plane's engines roared above us. Late summer evenings. Perfect. I've only started to remember all of this now that we are no longer together.

Sometimes when I couldn't sleep, I went into Mickey's office, sat in his chair and stared at the safe. I'd had a key cut for it long before all of the shit happened. Mickey hardly ever showed his face at the garage any more, so I needed to have access to the petty cash in there. I already dealt with most of the paperwork, the bills, the banking;

worked alone three days out of five with just the radio and the yellowed Pirelli calendar girls for company.

And, of course, Mickey kept more than petty cash in the safe. He had 'other incomes'. At some point during the late eighties, he'd become someone else entirely. No longer the big glib Irishman from a poor estate in Offaly who'd been my best man, prone sometimes to bouts of depression and turmoil. He'd fallen in with what my old man would've called the wrong crowd; made some shady contacts somewhere along the line in the paddy gaffs and snooker halls he'd frequented in Digbeth, and then started to get his hands on stolen merchandise, got wind of all the fights and races that got thrown. Started gambling in the casinos on the Hagley Road, arranged himself some middlemen whom he supplied with high-grade Columbian cocaine, the odd key of heroin. Somewhere along the line he'd found his stride, a self-assurance that put me into the shade, and the garage became a front for him. His old life far behind him. He wanted to be Michael Caine. Became an illusionist: everyone was looking at what the hand in front was doing, not the one behind his back.

In the course of the previous six months, I'd been moved from the marital bed to the sofa in the front room; and then, without Grace or myself ever explicitly discussing it, to my moving out of the family home on the Soho Road entirely. There were no specifics, no conditions, no voices raised in anger. And no attempts made at reconciliation either. At some point we'd both lost the energy to *try*. The course had been run. But even then, I'd found myself only taking the barest minimum with me when I left; the essentials required to live by. I assumed that by taking more I'd be accepting defeat, that eventually all I'd have to return for was my daughter. So that every other Saturday, so we could piss away a weekend down the park or at McDonald's, until she grew old enough to be irritated by her old man and his failings. Once you begin to pick at a frayed thread, you find that everything unravels at a frightening speed.

I spent the first month racked with panic. Insomnia every night. I moved into Mickey's garage without informing him. At least I was never late for work. I'd stuffed two Tesco carriers with clothes, and a holdall with toiletries, razor blade, comb and a couple of Grace's paperbacks. Kept them in the boot of the car. Slept on the back seat, shivering my bollocks off as autumn turned colder and colder. I squeezed myself in front of the sink in the khazi every morning, straining over a little shaving mirror. Old *Sunday Mercury*s, going crisp behind the door. Spiders curled up in the corners. The smell of oil and damp clinging to me. When it pissed down, it leaked everywhere. When the trains thundered over the bridge above, the windows rattled in their frames.

In the afternoons I'd stand outside with a cup of coffee going cold in my hands, and watch the traffic slithering down Camp Hill, close my eyes and think of Grace, reading a magazine in our front room, with her bare legs up beneath her; Grace, three years ago, in a restaurant on Broad Street in a backless black dress, pulling her face at the wine; Grace, on the first night we'd spent in the house on Soho Road, lying back on the newly delivered bed, slowly opening her legs for me while I undressed. For a month I did this religiously. I felt helpless. I'd spent the month before lying on the sofa with my prick wilting in my fist, trying in vain to remember when we'd last fucked.

By the second month, I'd started driving down Soho Road and passing the house. Middle of the night. Mickey's Audi was sometimes parked up on the kerb outside. I slowed my motor down every time, but I never managed to stop.

Sometimes I'd unlock Mickey's safe and take the money out. Count it out on the desk. Try to find some clarity in what I was contemplating. Sometimes I'd look at the picture of Grace and feel nostalgic.

And sometimes not.

Eight p.m. I hovered outside for a time in the rain. Felt it crawling down my neck as I locked the car, stood on the pavement on the opposite side of the road. Listening to its empty sound on the last of the leaves on the trees down Lozells Road. The hiss of tyres slipping on wet tarmac. They were all losing traction somewhere.

Sutcliffe was outside the massage parlour, the light from the windows and streetlamps luminous on his shaven head. He was in a black high-collared shirt, so that the tattoos on his throat looked like brilliantly coloured champagne bubbles bursting from the knot of his tie. He was smoking roll-ups. Fielding calls on his impossibly small mobile. Flexing the muscles in his jaw, grinding his wisdom teeth down. When the rain gusted sideways, he retreated into the shelter of the doorway.

When I pulled my coat up over my head and ran across the road, Sutcliffe watched me from the corners of his dark, elusive eyes. I hesitated at the doorway, chanced a glance at him. But you couldn't know what he was thinking. He was made from stone. He stepped aside.

Elena saw me straight away; knew me well enough to forgo all the usual preamble; was comfortable enough to let me sit on the bed and slide off my boots while I watched her surreptitiously as she wiped between her legs with a towel. She held her hair back in a bunch above her head so that it didn't fall in front of her face. Something about that gesture made my heart quicken. She unfastened her suspenders with a knitted brow. The concentration on her face made her look like a child. Briefly I was seeing her in a school photo, gap-toothed and awkward with puppy fat. Finally she remembered herself and held my gaze until I had to look away, confused, befuddled. I was cold and aroused, while she was helpless and provocative. This slow familiarity had made us uncertain about how to act towards each other.

But there was this: Elena, nineteen years old, fooled like many before her into flying to England with the promise of well-paid work; the promise of her sister being saved from a life of poverty in Romania too. Elena the trafficked teenager. She pulled down my trousers and slipped my cock out of my underwear, into a sheath and into her mouth. She straddled my thighs while I stroked the purple bruises above the white fishnets on hers. Hair falling over her face, sticking to her lipstick. She touched my face, held it between her palms. Looked at me with a measure of fondness and sadness. She was perhaps only ever seeing herself at these times.

And then there was this: Elena in a grubby shithole of a room where the walls were bruised with damp, the windows plugged with rotten newspaper; the smell of cheap men's deodorant and semen like wet grass, embedded in the sheets. Massage oils on a tray on the table. My money beside the tray. She raised her hips and gripped my cock with stiff fingers. She felt as harsh as paper. Guided my cock inside her. Lowered her hips again and held me there; moved in careful, measured rhythms. Unhooked her bra, slid it away from her breasts and placed my palms around them. I looked away at the forty-watt bulb and then simply closed my eyes until I was finished.

Grace was late, but Heather hadn't made her way out of class anyway. I'd tried to spot her through the cheerfully decorated windows, but all I could see for my efforts were rows of desks and shadows. I hesitated in the fine rain until the streetlights started to flicker on around me. Shitty British afternoons. I pulled up the collar on my coat and went back to sit in the car. I put the heater on full blast to warm my frozen hands.

I didn't have any of this worked out in my head. I only saw events at a distance, felt myself running towards them: undignified, desperate. When I spotted Grace in the congregation of other mothers, the heat in the car suddenly felt smothering. Damp patches forming on my back, in my armpits. I felt like I had all those years ago, walking to the social club where I could watch Grace through the window, halfway through her ballet class. Twenty or thirty teenagers, up on their toes, new muscles straining on the parquet floor, their bodies growing more fluid with every passing week. I'd watch her, drunk with confusion and formless lust. Holding the image of her breasts in the tight grey leotard, her toes curling, soles covered in dust, sweat on her brow and top lip, so I could masturbate to it later, huddled over myself in the bathroom.

There was still enough of the young girl I'd harboured fantasies for in the mother of my daughter for my mind to erase itself as soon as I laid eyes on her. Absence had taken her a remove away from me. There was a little bit of grey in her red hair which, even now, she would part with both hands away from her eyes: soft sad eyes that seemed to only ever betray her better moments or the casual sensuality of her smile. Like Elena, everything was a transaction to her: everyone had something to take or give. Her eyes told you this if you saw them for long enough. I was well aware that I'd romanticized her day by day.

She hovered at the gates in a long black coat that I didn't recognize, and which made me think of Mickey. In seconds I was out of the car and moving towards her. At the last I felt as if I didn't really want her to see me. I dreaded the moment that her eyes would fall upon me and her expression would falter, and say everything.

And it did.

She closed her eyes briefly – *give me strength* – then returned to herself with a guarded anger that made me forget why I was even there. She stepped away from the throng and said with a note of exasperation in her voice, 'What do you *want*?'

I noticed then that there was a bandage covering her wrist and part of her right hand. 'What have you done to yourself?' I asked, reaching down, intending to lift it into the light for me to inspect.

She shook her head. A tiny motion. Then she lowered her face away from me. A couple of the other mothers were glancing over at us.

She gathered herself. 'Stop it, Frank. Look, why are you here?'

Something about the gesture, the tone of her voice, made me say quite involuntarily, 'I'm not a part of your life any more.' And then, 'Am I?'

There was a pause. I thought I heard her sigh through her nose. 'But I hope you'll always be a part of Heather's,' she said finally.

Something broke in me then. I felt a sudden vertigo, as if my head were falling to the pavement between us. Anger flared in me but I managed to contain it. The wind was scattering crisp yellow leaves around our feet. I glanced past the school gates as the bell rang. All the chairs were up on the desks in the classroom I'd peered into earlier. The silence between Grace and me was building. She watched as the kids came hurrying out of the school. I couldn't think of anything to say to close the wound. Suddenly it seemed very important to finish this before Heather spotted me.

I could see the lines on Grace's face gradually becoming more and more marked as her patience waned. 'What's this all in aid of, Frank? What do you expect me to *say*, for Christ's sake?'

I looked around at the parents' cars, hemmed into the surrounding kerbs; then I was back to the school windows, looking at the fog that was turning the streetlights into soft stars. Then back to the bandage on Grace's wrist. I felt bereft. I was being a child. 'I can't accept this,' I said.

'Well, you'll bloody well have to.' There was unbridled anger in Grace's voice now. 'I can't change how I feel. You'll survive, I daresay.'

I stepped forward, Grace's anger finally igniting mine. 'What is this, anyway? A fucking midlife crisis? I mean, Jesus.' Before I turned and made for the car, I said, 'I'll fucking kill that cunt, you know. I'll *fucking* kill him.'

That night I told Elena about the safe in Mickey's garage. Her face in the dim neon from the launderette sign on the wall outside was immobile. She sat on the edge of the bed, a cold palm on my shin, her head half-turned to stare at a place between me and the window. Shadows pooling in the naked hollows of her rib cage, her cheekbones, the ladder of her spine.

'Grace let me take Heather out one Sunday afternoon, a couple of weeks ago. We went to the park. Stood there in the cold while she threw bread at the ducks. Every time I looked at her, I could feel my chest tightening, my throat closing. She acted like nothing had changed. She didn't understand. She expected that I'd be coming home with her, not dropping her off and then wasting the rest of my Sunday in a pub in Digbeth.

'In the car, taking her back to her mother, I kept looking at her, strapped in her seat. She looked out of the window, the image of Grace, and I thought, I'm losing all of this, and Mickey's gaining it. It's being taken away from me without anyone asking.

'And now it feels like I should do the same,' I said.

Elena was quiet for a while. Then she started telling me

about her first few weeks here, this squalid little hole in Handsworth. She told me everything without moving, without bitterness: the plane from Romania, the airport, Sutcliffe, her first few shifts; the old man with gonorrhoea, the attempt at escape, how she walked with a limp because Sutcliffe had broken her ankles so viciously. After, she fished out a packet of Sovereign from her bag, lit one of them and pressed her face against the window. Exhaled.

'You should spend your Sundays with me,' she said lightly, and then added, 'Not *here*, though. Somewhere better. The two of us. I'd like that.' Then, after a moment, she stubbed out the cigarette and said, 'I think you should take everything he has. All of his money.'

She came back to the bed, sat directly in front of me and said, 'Fuck them all, Frank. And take me with you.'

After leaving Elena, I drove to the airport, stopping on the way at an off-licence to buy a bottle of Smirnoff, twenty Marlboro. I parked in a lay-by with my head back, seat reclined, hearing the roar of huge engines first, and then seeing the wing-lights, the tail-lights descending from the dark fog; a soft meniscus of light that made me think there were tears in my eyes.

Mickey was waiting for me when I got back to the garage. Long past midnight. I'd fumbled with the keys, half-cut, head down, swaying from side to side. When I opened the doors, he was just inside, sat on the bonnet of his Audi. He was holding a crowbar. Huge sad eyes, gone feral. Out of place in his Armani suit. He'd taken off the jacket, was rolling up his sleeves, loosening his tie. I laughed to myself. Looked around unsteadily for the vodka, but it was still in my car. A train roared overhead. Pigeons erupted out of the hollows above us. Grey feathers and shit dislodged around our heads. It started to rain. The fog was gone and the world had a cold, hungover clarity.

'I'll kill that cunt,' Mickey said. 'I'll fucking kill him.'

'Mickey . . .'

'It's better if you don't talk, Frank. Better all round.'

The train had gone but the rain on the bridge sounded just as loud. I could hear myself breathing heavily out of fear. Cold. Rain rolling down my neck.

'You and Grace,' Mickey was saying, rising from his car, 'that's all over now. She doesn't want to see you any more. Not around the school. Not driving by the house. Nothing.'

I hovered in the doorway. Eyes clinging to the sway of his hand around the crowbar. 'She's still my fucking wife, Mickey.'

'That doesn't mean *fuck all*,' he spat, and I could see that flare of rage in him that he'd nurtured; grown from a cutting others had given him, somewhere in the confusion of the eighties. It wasn't from seed.

There was no placating him, but I tried. 'Look, Mickey, if she doesn't want to see me then she doesn't want to see me. But Heather. She's my *kid*, for Christ's sake. You've got no right.'

Mickey stepped into the light, fluid and without hesitation. I was hoping he wouldn't try anything if I drew him out into the street. But I was mistaken.

'You're a useless cunt, Frank. Always have been. You don't deserve Grace and you certainly don't deserve Heather. You're a piece of shit. No prospects. No life. What have you ever had to offer anyone? And then you crawl back here to sleep. You *give in*. Straight away. No complaints. You make me fucking sick.'

There was nothing I could say. His anger was already in place, eager to be released. Too late, I watched as his hand described an arc; out of the gloom and into the light. It took seconds but it felt like hours. His teeth were bared. I raised my hands without conviction. When the crowbar connected with my temple, it felt like ice being forced down behind my eyes. Suddenly it was too light. I stumbled backwards. Mickey swung it again, faster now, with more abandon. I couldn't keep up. The second time, something shattered in my collarbone. I fell back against my car, grunting in pain. Through the sound of rain, like a waterfall in a cavern, I watched Mickey's mouth moving. The sheen of sweat on his forehead. The crowbar, flashing intermittently in the glow of the streetlamps. Desperate, I glanced to my left and right for a witness, an ally, but there was no traffic. It was too late. All the pissheads had already caught the last bus home or found themselves a lock-in on some back street.

I didn't see the next blow but I felt some of my ribs break, and my breathing went jagged. My vision was full of black smears whenever I moved my head. The bridge above us was shaking, rattling as another train went over. I felt rain on my face, but then realized it was blood.

Mickey dragged me up by my collar, pulled me back into the dark of the garage, closed the doors. Flung me across the floor. Both of us panting like the old farts that we were. He paced around me, back and forth, catching his breath. Like a prizefighter sizing up his next blow. When he levelled a boot into my gut, I vomited until my throat was raw. Then he knelt on the floor, got close to my face. Wild eyed. Hair and forearms shining with sweat. 'Listen now, you cunt. Leave *her* alone.'

And then, because he knew it would feel like the final nail: 'Leave *us* alone.'

He went into my pockets, but couldn't find my keys there. Didn't have the patience to search any harder. Instead he said, 'Don't come back here. You're not welcome. Do you understand? *All right*, Frank? *All right?*'

I nodded as well as I was able. Then Mickey dragged me back outside and left me on the pavement while he reversed his Audi out of the garage and locked up. I only wanted to sleep, to curl up in motor oil and puke, but my breathing felt like shattered glass dragging on my lungs. I lay beside my car, staring at the bridge, trying not to breathe. Mickey spat on me out the window of his Audi and drove away.

Elena's shift was almost over by the time I returned to Lozells Road. I'd forced myself to stay conscious. It took an age to get myself off the pavement and into my car. Whatever Mickey had broken in me was hurting with vicious abandon. White fireworks of pain and heat in my chest and sides; a black cloud lurking behind my eyes. I could no longer see out of my left eye by the time I was behind the wheel. I angled the rearview mirror away from me, so I couldn't see the damage. I put the heater on and sat there for a while with my forehead pressed against the steering wheel. Trying to regain composure. Then I fished out the bottle of Smirnoff. Polished it off there and then.

The keys were still in my hand. Absurdly, I must've imagined they would lend weight to a fist I'd never managed to throw at Mickey. I started the car up and aimed it at Handsworth. The drive was a blur. I couldn't remember navigating my way through the city centre: onto and off the Queensway, down Constitution Hill and then Great Hampton Street, until I was streaming across the Hockley Flyover in a haze that felt almost euphoric. There was very little traffic about. I kept my foot down and tried not to pass out. It was like swimming against the heaviest of tides.

I parked down a cul-de-sac off Lozells Road, acutely aware of Sutcliffe's whereabouts. It was nearly two o'clock. Elena would be leaving the massage parlour soon, making her way out to wait for the taxi that Sutcliffe called ahead for.

I felt a surge in my chest that I couldn't define when she stepped outside. I fooled myself that it was hope. She hesitated beside Sutcliffe, who was having an animated discussion with the occupants of a souped up Escort. 'You'll get the money,' I thought I heard, but then Elena was moving away, looking up and down the street. There was a latent tension in the scene that I didn't want to understand. I watched her instead, balanced on the kerb: those dark European eyes; that still, pensive face that tried to show nothing of herself. Her hair was tied up, wisps of it escaping until she tucked it behind her ears: a gesture I'd observed a hundred times or more with no less delight. As she stood there in shabby jogging pants and trainers, pulling her coat tightly around her slight frame, I felt like I was adolescent again, watching my future wife stretch and curl. I closed my eyes and could smell her skin; feel her pubic hair, spiky on my thigh; could feel her parting around my fingers, hot and wet. But I couldn't see her face. I didn't know who I was feeling beneath my hands.

In my reverie I nearly missed Elena getting into the cab that'd pulled up, just as the Escort roared away, all squealing tyres and furious quick gearshifts.

I gave it a moment, then pulled out and followed the cab. Sutcliffe didn't notice; he seemed shaken by the exchange he'd just had. He retreated to the doorway of the launderette, rubbing at the shadow of hair on his skull, searching for a number on his mobile.

The cab didn't have far to go. I took my cues from the tail-lights, keeping Elena's outline in the back as my guide when I started coughing up blood. I followed them to Handsworth Wood, where Sutcliffe rented a bedsit for her. Fallen leaves huddled in kerbs between car bumpers. High-rises in the distance in Hamstead; off-licences sealed up like fortresses on every other corner.

Elena had paid the cabby and was already at the door of

the shabby Victorian terrace, fumbling with her keys, when I pulled into the kerb. I tried to get out of the car but all the breath went out of me, and I toppled out into the shadow of a naked tree, hot and empty and beyond caring. She must've heard the door or me cry out. I saw her turn and clock me, come hurrying down the driveway after her shadow and onto her knees beside me. I heard her saying my name with such concern in her voice that it made want to weep. She tried to lift me but couldn't. I was a dead weight. Fucked up and drunk. When we finally had me on my feet, I curled an arm around her waist, pressed my bloody face into her neck until her hair clung to my lips, my cheek. 'I love you,' I said. She took me inside without another word.

There was a postcard from Elena's sister, propped up on the mantelpiece over the gas fire. When Elena lit the fire, I could smell dust burning. I stared at her sister's handwriting, leaving smears of bloody fingerprints. 'I can't read this,' I said helplessly as Elena went through the cupboard under the sink, searching for cream and bandages.

'That's because it's in Romanian, you fool,' she said flatly.

I attempted to take an inventory of the room, but there wasn't enough to see. I'd hoped for more of Elena, but there was just some dusty CDs piled by the bed, paperbacks going yellow on the window ledge, stockings drying on the radiators. It didn't seem enough. I asked her what the card said.

There was a pause. Then she said, 'Nothing. Just that she has a new job, moved out of the old house and got a flat in the capital. She's met someone who's actually good to her.' If she was bitter, then I couldn't hear it in her voice.

She sat beside me on the bed, dropping what she'd

unearthed between us. Tucked her hair back behind her ears, then acknowledged me staring at her. 'What?'

'Are you going back? To Romania?'

'Never. One day. I don't know.' And then, so full of regret that I had to reach out and touch her face, 'I just wish I could get away from here.'

'You can,' I said, my mouth engaging before my thoughts were properly in order.

'How's that then?' she asked as she unravelled a length of bandage, undid my shirt. The way she said it sounded endearingly English. She was trying, I assumed, not to seem too eager, too expectant.

'I take the money.' I said it for myself first, to hear the words, feel how they changed me. Again: 'I take Mickey's money and we go. We just fucking leave. Me and you.'

She busied herself for a while with the cuts on my face, avoiding my gaze. So I touched her again gently to prompt her. When she met my eyes, hers were hard and implacable. Not the eyes of a teenage girl. 'You would do this? You *mean* it?'

I felt my ribs with my fingers. Heard myself wheezing. 'Yes,' I said finally. 'Give me a day to sort everything out and to pack some things, and then we'll go.'

Elena shook her head.

'*What?*'

'Do it now,' she said. 'You have to do it now. Tomorrow you'll wake up and see sense. You'll look at a picture of your daughter and wonder how you can run away from her with a *prostitute*. Fathers are sentimental. If you're going to leave, you have to do it all tonight. Make a complete break.'

I didn't want to hear the truth: I didn't want to hear *Forget all your ties before they forget you first*. There was no joy in her words, despite the prospect of release. There was no immediate way to mend what was broken in her.

I fished out a cigarette and stared at my hands. Still shaking from the beating. The keys in my fist. The keys to Mickey's safe. These were the options. These were the facts. This was what I had to do. Otherwise my life would progress, sideways; never really forwards or even back: sideways. I wanted to look at the picture of Grace on the bonnet of the Anglia one last time. But I knew I wouldn't.

I let Elena wash my wounds, bandage me up, and then I returned to the car.

Halfway back to the garage, I realized that it wasn't enough to simply take Mickey's money. By the time I was parked (a street away, just to be careful) and slipping my old damp trainers on from the boot, I had it all formulated in my head. Once inside, I had to do everything in darkness, save for a little torch that Elena had found along with the bandages and ointments. I wasn't going to risk putting on the strip lights now.

It took some time. My ears were ringing and my left eye was completely closed. Elena had stemmed all the wounds and made me choke down aspirin but, despite them, everything I did made some part of me ache.

I'd told Elena to pack her bags and wait for me. An hour. No more. Once I had the money, I'd be back and then we'd leave Birmingham. No one would piece anything together until the next day. By that time there'd be more than a couple of hundred miles between us: us and Mickey, us and Sutcliffe, us and the past.

I had the keys in the safe when I heard voices.

I froze in the darkness. Switched off the torch. Couldn't move. The voices were close by. With the blood waterfall roaring in my ears, it was difficult to locate them, identify them. I heard their footsteps. A pair of shoes, a pair of steel toecaps. Swallowing down the fear, I crept back into the workshop, hovered in the office doorway. Through the windows all I could see was the darkness between streetlights, the huge iron underside of the bridge. I couldn't breathe for long moments. I felt horribly exposed, staring through the gloom at the doors, expecting to hear a key in the lock. I was paralysed again. It took several minutes for me to realize that I couldn't hear the voices any more. Just pissheads leaving a lock-in. When I exhaled I doubled over in pain. Coughed up some more blood. Returned to the safe wheezing.

I didn't count the money. I just emptied it into an old adidas holdall and then zipped it up. The last time I'd counted, there'd been at least ten grand in there. Ridiculous money. More than enough for us to get wherever we might be going and start something new, without having to look back. I closed the safe. Locked it. Stared at the bag in my hands. Closed my eyes. 'Come on,' I said.

But I couldn't leave it at that. I had to make a point. Draw a line in the sand and say, this is as far as it goes. This was the point where I realized that you had to put yourself at risk in order to really live.

So I made my point.

Even after I was back in the car, my back soaked in sweat, the holdall there on the passenger seat, I couldn't start the engine up, put it in gear and just go. Instead, I watched out of the rear window, transfixed at the flickering yellow-orange light, and the shadows as they leapt around beyond the garage windows. I watched as the smoke started to escape, soft belching plumes of grey rising up past the bridge, across the moon. It was going to get messy soon. There were still a couple of customers' cars inside: a Renault 19 and a lovely red Hyundai with a knackered gearbox. Petrol tanks. I'd finally turned my car around when the first of the sirens came calling through Digbeth. Just before they arrived, the glass blew out of the windows and I took off with my head down as blue lights began flickering up and down Camp Hill.

In the event, I didn't hear the petrol tanks go. I was already halfway back to Elena by the time that happened.

Four a.m. Only adrenaline and excruciating pain were keeping me conscious by the time I made it back to Handsworth Wood. I pulled up outside the house and sat there, my fingers tight around the wheel. Tried to level my breathing. There was a knot unravelling in my chest. We were on the way. Elena's light was on, but I couldn't see her silhouette in the window. I eased myself out of the car and stumbled up the driveway. Left the money on the passenger seat. This wouldn't take long. We'd put a few hours between us and Birmingham, then find a hotel somewhere down south. Maybe stop at the seaside for a spell.

When I knocked on the door, there was no answer. I knocked again, propping myself against the doorframe. *Come on*. Suddenly I felt like I was full of caffeine. Jittery. Paranoid.

Sutcliffe answered the door. Shattered half my jaw with the butt of his sawn-off shotgun, then dragged me inside.

I didn't go out completely. I heard Sutcliffe grunting with my dead weight, glimpsed his face, twisted in disgust at mine, already black and blue and bleeding. He dropped me on Elena's bed, and I heard the bedsprings complain. The aspirin foil was still there on the sheets, the bandage and scissors and ointments. Blood was trickling down the back of my throat. I swallowed it down and felt a spasm in my jaw. Like having teeth pulled without the anaesthetic.

Sutcliffe was pacing back and forth at the foot of the bed but I couldn't lift my head sufficiently to look him in the eye. All I could see was his sheer bulk, the immaculate shirt, the leather gloves, a glimpse of purple ink at his throat. If my body was incapacitated, my mind was racing. Where was Elena? Why had Sutcliffe been waiting? How did he know?

Sutcliffe swung the shotgun around. Pushed it under my wet chin until I grunted with pain. 'So did you get my money then, Frank? Planning to fuck off with one of my girls, were you?' He leaned over into my field of vision. 'Shouldn't take me for a cunt, Frank. You do not want to fuck with me.'

I tried to speak but my jaw felt as if it was wired shut. When I coughed, it felt like knives up and down the side of my face.

'It doesn't pay to have ambitions beyond your means, Frank,' Sutcliffe was saying as he looked carefully at something beyond the window. 'You're just not in that pedigree.' He glanced back at me. 'No more than a useful pair of hands. Manual labour. That's all you're good for, Frank. We both know that though, don't we?'

'Fuck off,' I managed, and Sutcliffe snorted back laughter. As he did I closed my hand over the scissors beside me. Pulled them across to my side, concealed them in my fist. My heart seemed to stop for a while. I felt greasy with sweat and blood.

'Money in that shitheap outside? That's mine now, Frank. You understand? I come waltzing in and fuck you over. It's that easy for people like me.'

People like me. I wondered if he'd ever been like Mickey. On the straight and narrow until someone or something had come and shoved him away from that path onto an entirely more dangerous and enthralling one. Where you lived from day to day. You ran, never walked. And when you left your old life, you left it behind completely.

I wondered where his locus had been. Mine had been in this room, an hour ago. But I hadn't been ready to run fast enough. I looked at Elena's CDs, at the yellowed paperbacks. The postcard on the mantelpiece. I couldn't stop shaking. I felt sad and afraid to be leaving.

As Sutcliffe returned to level the shotgun at me, my muscles tensed up involuntarily. This was the point of no return. If you looked back now, you would only see your old life falling away behind you like the earth crumbling into itself.

Sutcliffe had a wet shaky finger on the trigger. Teeth gritted. Jaw clenched. I saw the muscles in his arm tense, and then I swung the fist holding the scissors around and into his side. I didn't hear them break his flesh but I felt it give beneath the force of the blow, then felt the scissors penetrate something soft, vital. Sutcliffe exhaled and his mouth opened into a dark O, his face as if in the throes of orgasm. There was a moment of nothing and then I felt his blood spill out onto my hand, down over my stained shirt. He stumbled forward, then listed to one side of me, the shotgun falling from his grip.

My mind swarmed. I couldn't focus. Adrenaline was rushing to my head. Outside of myself I heard us both grunting like animals in their death throes. I shoved him away while he was off balance, and he fell heavily away from the bed, onto the shabby rug. His head collided with the fireplace. I hesitated. I knew what I had to do, before he got over the initial shock. But not with the shotgun. I stared at it briefly, lying on the bed. I couldn't use that. It was too loud.

Instead I raised the scissors, fell to my knees beside him, plunged them into his chest until I heard his breastbone splinter. And again. I was crazed with fury. My hands were so slick with blood that the scissors slid out of my grip. I grasped frantically for them, retrieved them, raised them again and then realized that Sutcliffe was already dead. I stared at him, my ears ringing. Closed a palm over my mouth. I had to raise myself up off the floor and stumble to the bathroom to be sick. The effort made everything that was broken in me flare up again like a Roman candle. These were, I believed, the birth pains of my new life.

After five minutes of kneeling over the toilet, I got to my feet and went to the window. Stared out at what Sutcliffe had been looking at, and felt curiously disappointed at what I saw. Looked back at the corpse on the floor. Then at the shotgun. I thought about him earlier on Lozells Road, arguing with the occupants of the Escort, and then things started to make some sense.

Across the street, Elena was waiting in Sutcliffe's car. When she turned and saw me crossing over, and the new blood on my hands and face, bright red in the streetlamp's glow, she seemed to crumple in her seat. Perhaps she'd got used to being wrong-footed at every turn. I knew I had.

But I heard her say, '*Jesus*,' and then she was out of the car and limping across the street, up the drive to the house. I watched her go. Just somebody's daughter in her trainers and cords and pigtails. She should never have been in this predicament. I stood in the middle of the road, looked up and down at the streetlights fading into the fog. Silent at this time of night. Perfectly still. When I tried to hurry after her, I discovered that I couldn't. So I hobbled.

By the time I'd made my way back up the staircase and into her room, she was sat on the bed beside Sutcliffe's body, the shotgun across her lap. At my arrival, she lifted it and levelled it at me. But it was a half-hearted gesture, and I think she realized that I'd removed all the shells.

'He only wanted the money. You know that, don't you?'

But she wouldn't look at me, nor at Sutcliffe's corpse any more. She laid the shotgun back on the bed, and put her hands delicately together between her knees.

'I suppose he had outstanding debts, didn't he? Drugs. Gambling. All the usual shit. He was probably skimming the profit margin from the parlour too. But he needed more than he could lay his hands on. Had people on his arse for it, like tonight. And so he was just waiting for a cunt like me to spill his guts to one of his girls.'

'I wanted to believe you, you know?' Elena said, lifting up her trainers as Sutcliffe's blood pooled at the base of the bed. 'That you'd take me with you.'

'But you thought it was safer on his side of the fence than on mine. He wouldn't have let you go. People like us are just part of the transaction, aren't we?'

Elena bit her lip. Stared at her feet again.

'You won anyway,' I said finally. 'You're free now, if you want to be. We both are.

'But clean this mess up first,' I said, and left.

I sat in my car for a while, staring at the adidas bag. When I looked up at Elena's window, I thought I could see her packing. It was five in the morning. Light in a couple of hours. A new day. A new life.

Part of me wanted to take her with me, but I knew she was only ever a substitute for Grace. I would be running at my prospective new life with all the shit and detritus and failure of my old life still tangled around my feet. So I drove away without a second look.

I changed my clothes and cleaned myself up in that lay-by in Elmdon, then I drove to Birmingham International. I thought about everyone for a while: Grace, Mickey, Elena, Sutcliffe, until there was only my daughter holding me back. So I picked a destination and then I lived from day to day. I ran, never walked. I left my old life behind completely. And after a while, everything stopped hurting.

Biographical Notes

Zulfiqar Ali studied creative writing and modern film studies at Birmingham University. He is currently editing his novel *Smoke: The Revenge of Johnny Orlando*. His stories have appeared in *Hardlines*, *Fingerprint* and *Fingerprint 2*. He reviews books for *The Heathan*, has worked for *Saltley News*, and is the editor of the book *Muslims in Kashmir*.

Simon Avery lives and works in Birmingham. His short story 'Leaving Seven Sisters', published in *Crimewave*, was nominated for the Crime Writers Association Short Story Award. It's due to be reprinted in *The World's Finest Crime and Mystery Vol.3*, and further stories will be published in *Crimewave 6* and *Beneath the Ground*. He writes a regular column for *Tripwire* and is currently at work on a novel.

Steve Bishop is the author of several published stories of noir and dirty realist fiction. He's worked as a creative writing tutor and as a general assistant at Screen West Midlands. Fronting the award-winning Fix Film Club in Birmingham, he has promoted experimental film events, and also worked for the Fierce Arts Festival. He is currently writing a novel, *The Birkenhead Book of the Dead*, and is the author of several screenplays.

Mike Chinn tells us: 'It started one Sunday afternoon: *The*

Maltese Falcon was showing on ITV. The first one's always free, and I was hooked. Two monkeys on my back, names of Hammett and Chandler. These days I score what I can round the literary ghettos of horror and fantasy; but my 1998 collection, *The Paladin Mandates*, came closest to scratching that old itch – combining hard-boiled detective story with Pulp-age spookiness. And I figure the third monkey in the shape of occasional comic scripting will be the one that finally gets me.'

Judith Cutler, a prize-winning short-story writer, is the author of two Birmingham-based series of crime novels. The first features Sophie Rivers, the second Detective Sergeant Kate Power. Author of some sixteen novels, Judith's latest titles are *Dying in Discord* (Headline, 2002); *Hidden Power* (Hodder and Stoughton, 2002); *Head over Heels* (Severn House Publishers, 2001).

John Dalton is 53 and has two children. He works in adult education as a basic skills tutor. His crime novel *The City Trap* was published by Tindal Street Press in 2002.

Wayne Dean-Richards has been an industrial cleaner, an actor, a caretaker, a boxer, a salesman, a fitness instructor, a painter & decorator, an editor, and a teacher. He's a polished performer of his own work – live, on video, and on radio. His stories are collected in *At the Edge*, and Spouting Forth Ink published his novel *Breakpoints* in 2002. Asked why he writes, he replied, 'The words I write keep me sane.'

Rubina Din is a literacy consultant with Birmingham Education Department. She was a finalist in Focus on Talent 2 (a competition run by Black Coral, with the BBC and Channel 4). Her story 'Battle of Wills' was published in *Whispers in the Walls* (Tindal Street Press, 2001). She likes writing psychological thrillers with a science fiction or supernatural element, and her ambition is to write for the big screen.

Pauline E. Dungate's science fiction, horror and fantasy short stories have been published in the USA and the UK. She also writes articles, reviews and poems. In her day job she works as a teacher at Birmingham's Nature Centre, and at night you might find her out hunting bats.

Paul Finch, a full-time writer, is a former cop and journalist. He now pens scripts for madcap TV animation shows and episodes for the *The Bill*. In his quest to emulate personal hero Andrew Vachss, Paul's had nearly 200 short stories published on both sides of the Atlantic. He's also sold the script for a full-blown horror movie to Talisman Films.

Kay Fletcher has lived in Tipton, in the Black Country, all her life, and has published poetry and fiction in small press publications including *Ghosts & Scholars*, *Enigmatic Tales*, *The Dream Zone*, *Planet Prozak*, *Psychotrope* and *Roadworks*. Her hypertext fiction appears on her website 'The Jenny Haniver'. She self-published her novel, *Searching for the Reincarnated*, on CD-ROM in October 2002.

Pauline Gould began writing short stories about six years ago. In 1998 she won the *Sunday Mercury* short crime story competition, and in 1999 was shortlisted for the Asham Award. 'The Way She Looks at Me' was indirectly inspired by the modern noir film, *Body Heat*. Pauline works as an administration assistant for a playwriting organization in Birmingham.

John Harvey is best-known for his sequence of ten Nottingham-based crime novels featuring police detective Charlie Resnick, the first of which, *Lonely Hearts*, was chosen by *The Times* as one of the '100 Best Crime Novels of the Century'. After spending nearly two decades in the Midlands, Harvey has returned to London, hence Jack Kiley, ex-copper, ex-soccer player, here plying his trade as a private detective in Birmingham.

Joel Lane's tales of darkness and suspense have appeared in various anthologies and magazines. He is the author of a collection of short stories, *The Earth Wire* (Egerton Press, 1994); a collection of poems, *The Edge of the Screen* (Arc, 1999); and two novels, *From Blue To Black* (Serpent's Tail, 2000) and *The Blue Mask* (Serpent's Tail, January 2003). He has edited *Beneath the Ground*, an anthology of supernatural tales (Alchemy Press, 2002).

Elizabeth Mulrey first started writing in 2001 – when she surprised herself with the macabre nature of the work she produced. In 2002 she had a poem published in *The Gift*, a book of new writing for the NHS, and 'Passing Over' is her first published short story. A radiographer, Elizabeth has worked in the NHS in Birmingham for the last 24 years.

John Mulcreevy's first published short story appeared in *Platform*, a 1970s school magazine. After school he spent time cutting things – steel sheets, grass lawns – and drawing things – cartoon strips, the dole. His second published short story appears here. John has spent all his life so far in north Birmingham and will probably continue to do so.

Andrew Newsham was born in Burnley in 1975. Having travelled the world, he now lives in Moseley where he writes and performs comedy. He recently won the *Esquire* prize for short fiction and is working hard on his first novel.

Don Nixon has worked as a tutor in prisons and started

writing about three years ago. He admires writers such as Ian Rankin and Michael Connelly – for how their novels deal with contemporary issues of urban life. His ambition is to write a full-length crime novel set in the West Midlands.

Nicholas Royle, born in Manchester in 1963, is the author of four novels including *Counterparts* and, most recently, *The Director's Cut*. His short stories have been widely published. His favourite writers include Steve Erickson, Derek Marlowe and the two Raymonds: Derek and Chandler. He lives in London, but visits Birmingham whenever he needs to remind himself what a decent balti tastes like.

Mick Scully is an acupuncturist working in Birmingham. He also lectures in oriental medicine and teaches English and media. Kafka and Dostoyevsky are the writers he most admires.

Rob Smith lives and works in Birmingham. He is interested in identity and the politics of aesthetics. He finds enlightenment in the shadows at the edges of life in the besieged Minority World.

Rachel Taylor was born in 1974 and lives in Birmingham. Having worked her way through various desk jobs, she is still trying to decide what she wants to do with her life. At the moment, the only certainty is that writing will be a part of it. 'Dyed Blonde' is her first published short story.

Claire Thomas is Birmingham born and bred. 'Means to an End' is her first published story. She's worked in a mortuary, trained as a nurse, and been a police officer – all before the age of thirty! Her fascination for the darker side of life began in her late teens with books by James Herbert and Richard Laymon.